SPECTRUM II

By the same editors

SPECTRUM

SPECTRUM II

A Science Fiction Anthology

edited by
KINGSLEY AMIS
and
ROBERT CONQUEST

HARCOURT, BRACE & WORLD, INC.
NEW YORK

"Sf's no good," they bellow till we're deaf.
"But this looks good."—"Well then, it's not sf."

CONTENTS

ACKNOWLEDGEMENTS

These stories are copyright by their authors and

Beyond Bedlam, which first appeared in *Galaxy*, 1951, by the
Galaxy Publishing Corporation.

Bridge, which first appeared in *Astounding Science Fiction*,
1952, by Street and Smith Publications Inc.

There is a Tide, which first appeared in *New Worlds Science
Fiction*, 1956, by Nova Publications Ltd.

Second Variety, which first appeared in *Space Science Fiction*,
1953, by Space Publications Inc.

The Feeling of Power, which first appeared in *If: Worlds of
Science Fiction*, 1958, by Quinn Publishing Co. Inc.

Sense from Thought Divide, which first appeared in *Astounding
Science Fiction*, 1955, by Street and Smith Publications Inc.

Resurrection, which first appeared in *Astounding Science
Fiction*, 1948, by Street and Smith Publications Inc.

Vintage Season, which first appeared in *Astounding Science
Fiction*, 1946, by Street and Smith Publications Inc.

INTRODUCTION

In INTRODUCING the first *Spectrum*, we addressed ourselves largely to such readers and critics as were not very familiar with science fiction—denouncing those among them who even so felt themselves empowered to issue judgements about it, and giving what we felt to be necessary clarifications to the more level-headed and open-minded. We were naturally encouraged and pleased by the variety of people who told us that *Spectrum I* was the particular instrument which dissolved their no doubt already crumbling prejudices, or got them over a difficulty always acute with any new art form—that described by a science fiction writer as "the bouillabaisse problem", i.e., persuading oneself to try it for the first time.

Whatever *Spectrum*'s contribution may have been, we have noticed a general breaking down of barriers over the past year or so. Readership of science fiction has grown, and even rather solemn publishers are tending to produce it without special pleas. Penguin Books, which held out for so long against all but the most Anglocentric of science fiction, have finally yielded to pressure. *Books and Bookmen* now has a regular science fiction column. Undergraduate literary magazines present serious critical discussions of the genre without apology. A massive new edition of Jules Verne has been appearing, including several previously untranslated works. Raymond Williams, stern critic of what he takes to be the vulgarities and vapidities of mass-culture, has (in *Britain in the Sixties: Communications*) perspicaciously remarked, " 'low' equals 'unfamiliar' is one of the perennial cultural traps", while calling for open-mindedness about science fiction.

Signs of the acceptance of science fiction into general litera-ture have, indeed, been building up for some time. The work of one of the best of our post-war novelists, Mr. William Golding, often borders on, and sometimes lies quite overtly within, what would ordinarily be described as science fiction. Collections of short stories can come out, such as Kurt Vonnegut's *Canary in a Cat House*, in which some of the contents are science fiction and some are not, without it being thought that there are two disparate readerships each of which will find itself equally disorientated. There are such phenomena as the extraordinary success in Scandinavia of Harry Martinson's space epic *Aniara*, published in 1956 and since performed as an opera, which is widely regarded as the greatest work in verse to appear there for many years. In the same way the Soviet poet Evtushenko in his newest long poem finds it natural to locate in a spaceship heading for Venus his dramatization of a personal rapprochement between Americans and Russians.

None of this yet amounts, of course, to official academic and "highbrow" approval. The present standing of science fiction recalls very strongly that of other twentieth-century art forms five, or ten, or twenty years ago: jazz, for example, and the cinema. It would no doubt have appeared shocking to the *Spectator* in 1910 if anyone had suggested that they would one day have a column on the vulgarities of the bioscope. Indeed, we can go further, and point to the low critical status of the novel itself in the eighteenth century, just before its greatest triumphs.

Science fiction, in fact, has had to grow up under its own power, developing its standards from within, from among its own writers, editors and readers. This may have slowed it down, for self-criticism does not flourish under conditions of intellectual isolation. And yet we cannot feel that what might be called the provincial status of science fiction has been altogether to its disadvantage. To put it no higher, people like ourselves have been enabled to put in a couple of decades of stimulating reading in a field where the writ of the more portentous type of literary critic does not run. In the last thirty or forty years there has been far too much self-consciousness about "significance", self-importance about "art", self-approval about "extending the bounds of moral awareness", with a corresponding lack of regard paid to older ideas of what fiction can and should provide: entertainment as well as edification, profusion and novelty of ideas as well as technical originality, speed and suspense and surprise in narrative as well as depth of psychological probing. These older ideas have, in our own day, found an important custodian in science fiction.

It is tempting to speculate what kind of treatment modern academic critics would mete out to a new Molière or Horace or Chaucer. That false perfectionism which dismisses from consideration anything short of a rigidly serious "masterpiece" would surely have rejected them. Cervantes and Rabelais would be written off as frivolous, Catullus and Ronsard as "limited". The mention of such names is a reminder that the traditional first aim of most sorts of writer has always been to please the reader, that even the most ambitious poetry, as Rossetti put it, must be "amusing". Science fiction writers cannot but share this aim, while "mainstream" fiction has, all too often, found its more intelligent writers becoming unreadable, and its more readable writers becoming unintelligent.

To end this part of the discussion on a more charitable note, critical thought in general is, we believe, becoming more empirical and liberal, and the dogmatic excesses of the generation or so just past are coming to be seen for the absurdity they are. Recognition of science fiction, in fact, can be taken as a sign not only of a maturing in the genre itself, but also of a general loosening of petty and doctrinaire attitudes in the mind of the literary critic—and the literary journalist too.

It would, of course, be sanguine to suppose that many old catch-phrases, reflecting deepset prejudices, will not linger on for long years yet. Among the oddest, still surviving in such cobwebbed purlieus as those of *The Illustrated London News*, is the sneer that science fiction is "escapist". One might imagine from this that the reader of an ordinary novel is not after all sitting in a chair letting the printed page affect his imagination, but performing some life-is-earnest practical activity. But leaving aside the obvious point that all literature is escape in the sense that one can only pursue it in intervals between one's immediate concerns, in what way is the inventive aspect of science fiction escapist?

Nobody would argue that fiction, to avoid the charge of escapism, must reflect the immediate problems of its readers in any literal way. We cannot see, therefore, why the doings of satellite crews or planetary administrators should be thought to encourage escapist leanings any more than the activities of mid-Victorian countryfolk or pre-Revolutionary Russians. Further—since "escapist" usually carries the implication "preferring cosy

fantasy to hard actuality"—there are many science fiction stories
that depict, with the most realistic intentions, a possible nuclear
war and its aftermath. Many others deal with the possible pre-
liminaries to such a war, exploring the complexity of risks
involved in the present situation. Others, again, forming at the
moment the most rapidly expanding type of story, attack such
problems as race and colonialism with a stringency not all that
common in novels of the main stream. In fact, we should stress
the deep perspectives, the sense of the human condition, to be
met with in the modern science fiction writers—often more
profound than in much professed social realism. They see, for
example (as in *Vintage Season*), that the sufferings of the past
can never be compensated for, and (as in *Beyond Bedlam*) that
a society which has solved all the problems besetting our own
may yet have its own tragic flaws. If this is escapist, what are
such writers and their readers escaping from?

It is also significant that to describe a human society better
than our own—a "eutopia"—is rather rare in science fiction:
Aldous Huxley's *Island* (reminding us once again of the science
fiction component in ordinary literary culture, though of course
in Mr. Huxley's case this is no new development) is in this
respect almost a freak. This remains true even when it is granted
that an abundance of shooting and sex could be held to con-
stitute an adequate eutopia for many—that sort of story is almost
as rare. In general, the implication that science fiction is largely
concerned with self-indulgent daydreams is simply false. On the
contrary, few kinds of writing attempt to explore more boldly
the disturbing areas of the human imagination or to deliver a
more urgent warning about the darker possibilities of human
ingenuity.

But the old-line opponents of science fiction are not the only
nuisances left over from the age of ignorance. There are also
critics, writers, and others who accept, and try to exploit, the
new forms without bothering to overcome inadequacy and
superficiality in their feeling for or knowledge of it. Science
fiction proper went through its phases of Super Science Marvel
and Horror a generation ago. The fact that similar attitudes are
now being reproduced by those inadequately aware of the genre
is significant. They substitute a childish crudity for the adult
development of the true sense of wonder. And, curiously enough,

they present in a gross and undigested fashion the very novelty and "science" which in science fiction proper is totally incorporated into the story in the most natural and unemphatic way.

Science fiction, as we have said, is a normal medium for anyone wishing to write imaginatively about the political or military problems with which the world is rather overwhelmingly faced. Much excellent writing has been done on these lines. It does, however, require a clear and sound knowledge of the relevant detail, just as much as that implied in the "realism" of a "realistic" novel. Many of those who feel that they have something urgent to say have launched into this milieu with insufficient preparation, or with an arrogant refusal to learn. And, public taste being still somewhat confused, these have sometimes had unwarranted, if ephemeral, success. Two examples of wrong ways of dealing with a nuclear war occur to us. First there was the late Nevil Shute's *On The Beach*—slapdash, to say the least, in its treatment of obvious physical facts. Worse still was the film *The Day The Earth Caught Fire* in which we were offered as a major menace of atomic weapons the unforeseen result of exploding a couple at the North and South Poles. But it is not the *unforeseen* results of nuclear warfare which should worry us, is it? If we are allowed to hypothesize unforeseen results, we can attach catastrophic importance on to anything from the output of nylon stockings to the saturation of the atmosphere with television broadcasts. This is the merest mumbo-jumbo, quite apart from the not unimportant point that the film's "unforeseen" effects are unforeseen because they contradict the laws of physics and mechanics.

This raises, of course, the question of the "science" in the word science fiction. It has often been pointed out that the word in many respects is an inadequate one and should be replaced by some expression like "possibility" fiction, or "context manipulation" fiction. But of course the term is now well established, and if the first half of it seems to give too much of a flavour of the exact sciences and of the technologies, one should at least note that the anthropological disciplines, such as they are, are equally involved in most science fiction. Nevertheless, even emphatically social and psychological science fiction is most conveniently set in the future, or on another planet, for reasons which are obvious enough. And if such a setting is needed, then it is essential for the writer to know enough about science and technology to make it plausible.

In one way, science fiction can never be quite the same again. During the past eighteen months men have gone into orbit round the earth. This illustrates a process which has been going on for some time. In the thirties and forties atomic power, space travel, the super-computer, and so on, were the biggest changes in the physical context of human life and thought which science fiction foresaw. They are now very much realities, and in particular it is clear that within a very few years the exploration of the solar system will have caught up with fiction. It is perfectly true that in all branches of knowledge there are endless possibilities. Nevertheless, this actual breaking out from the narrow confines of the atmosphere is a climactic dividing line for science fiction. It is true enough that the eutopias, or the alien species, can still be located in those endless stellar systems, even a start on the exploration of which will scarcely be made in the next few generations. But cosmic space is no longer a vague and distant idea for our culture as a whole. Atlantis has been replaced by an America, still largely unexplored no doubt, but open to the imagination, with its edges already penetrated by real people and the idea of its possibilities powerfully affecting the populations of our Old World.

In this collection, as in the last, we have limited ourselves in certain ways. We have again sought scope and variety rather than concentrating on formal excellence. We have not used stories by any of the writers who contributed to *Spectrum I*. And we have mainly avoided material which has had more than ephemeral circulation in this country. This has meant that the stories are largely (though not this time entirely) American. Modern science fiction is still predominantly an American art; but it is not so exclusively. (Nor is it the case that the American writers have made it a vehicle for anything resembling chauvinism: on the contrary, it might be complained that so much of the satire which forms such an important component of the genre is directed against the various unpleasant actualities and potentialities of American life, that too little has been left over for the—far nastier—totalitarianisms which we in Europe are more accustomed to.) And while the American magazines (and in particular the old *Astounding*) were creating the form, starting in the late thirties, a number of their leading contributors were in fact British—for example Eric Frank Russell, Arthur C. Clarke and A. Bertram Chandler. In any case, things have changed since then, and the British magazine *New Worlds* now deserves the same respect as *Analog, Galaxy* and *The Magazine of Fantasy and Science Fiction.*

Our thanks are again due to Mr. Leslie Flood and Mr. Bruce Montgomery for much generous help.

K.A.
R.C.

BEYOND BEDLAM

by *Wyman Guin*

THE OPENING afternoon class for Mary Walden's ego-shift was almost over, and Mary was practically certain the teacher would not call on her to recite her assignment, when Carl Blair got it into his mind to try to pass her a dirty note. Mary knew it would be a screamingly funny Ego-Shifting Room limerick and was about to reach for the note when Mrs. Harris's voice crackled through the room.

"Carl Blair! I believe you have an important message. Surely you will want the whole class to hear it. Come forward, please."

As he made his way before the class, the boy's blush-covered freckles reappeared against his growing pallor. Haltingly and in an agonized monotone, he recited from the note:

> *"There was a young hyper named Phil,*
> *Who kept a third head for a thrill.*
> *Said he, 'It's all right,*
> *I enjoy my plight.*
> *I shift my third out when it's chill.'"*

The class didn't dare laugh. Their eyes burned down at their laps in shame. Mary managed to throw Carl Blair a compassionate glance as he returned to his seat, but she instantly regretted ever having been kind to him.

"Mary Walden, you seemed uncommonly interested in reading something just now. Perhaps you wouldn't mind reading your assignment to the class."

There it was, and just when the class was almost over. Mary could have scratched Carl Blair. She clutched her paper grimly and strode to the front.

"Today's assignment in Pharmacy History is, 'Schizophrenia since the Ancient Pre-pharmacy days.'" Mary took enough breath to get into the first paragraph.

"Schizophrenia is where two or more personalities live in the same brain. The ancients of the 20th Century actually looked upon schizophrenia as a disease! Everyone felt it was very shameful to have a schizophrenic person in the family, and, since children lived right with the same parents who had borne them, it was very bad. If you were a schizophrenic child in the 20th Century, you would be locked up behind bars and people would call you——"

Mary blushed and stumbled over the daring word—"crazy". "The ancients locked up strong ego groups right along with weak ones. Today we would lock up those ancient people."

The class agreed silently.

"But there were more and more schizophrenics to lock up. By 1950 the prisons and hospitals were so full of schizophrenic people that the ancients did not have room left to lock up any more. They were beginning to see that soon everyone would be schizophrenic.

"Of course, in the 20th Century, the schizophrenic people were almost as helpless and 'crazy' as the ancient Modern men. Naturally they did not fight wars and lead the silly life of the Moderns, but without proper drugs they couldn't control their Ego-shiftability. The personalities in a brain would always be fighting each other. One personality would cut the body or hurt it or make it filthy, so that when the other personality took over the body, it would have to suffer. No, the schizophrenic people of the 20th Century were almost as 'crazy' as the ancient Moderns.

"But then the drugs were invented one by one and the schizo-phrenic people of the 20th Century were freed of their troubles. With the drugs the personalities of each body were able to live side by side in harmony at last. It turned out that many schizo-phrenic people, called overendowed personalities, simply had so many talents and viewpoints that it took two or more personalities to handle everything.

"The drugs worked so well that the ancients had to let millions of schizophrenic people out from behind the bars of 'crazy' houses. That was the Great Emancipation of the 1990s. From then on, schizophrenic people had trouble only when they criminally didn't take their drugs. Usually, there are two egos in a schizophrenic person—the hyperalter, or prime ego, and the hypoalter, the alternate ego. There often were more than two, but the Medicorps makes us take our drugs so that won't happen to us.

"At last someone realized that if everyone took the new drugs, the great wars would stop. At the World Congress of 1997, laws were passed to make everyone take the drugs. There were many fights over this because some people wanted to stay Modern and fight wars. The Medicorps was organized and told to kill anyone who wouldn't take their drugs as prescribed. Now the laws are enforced and everybody takes the drugs and the hyperalter and hypoalter are each allowed to have the body for an ego-shift of five days. . . ."

Mary Walden faltered. She looked up at the faces of her classmates, started to turn to Mrs. Harris and felt the sickness growing in her head. Six great waves of crescendo silence washed through her. The silence swept away everything but the terror, which stood in her frail body like a shrieking rock.

Mary heard Mrs. Harris hurry to the shining dispensary along one wall of the classroom and return to stand before her with a swab of antiseptic and a disposable syringe.

Mrs. Harris helped her to a chair. A few minutes after the expert injection, Mary's mind struggled back from its core of silence.

"Mary, dear, I'm sorry. I haven't been watching you closely enough."

"Oh, Mrs. Harris . . ." Mary's chin trembled. "I hope it never happens again."

"Now, child, we all have to go through these things when we're young. You're just a little slower than the others in acclimatizing to the drugs. You'll be fourteen soon and the medicop assures me you'll be over this sort of thing just as the others are."

Mrs. Harris dismissed the class and when they had all filed from the room, she turned to Mary.

"I think, dear, we should visit the clinic together, don't you?"

"Yes, Mrs. Harris." Mary was not frightened now. She was just ashamed to be such a difficult child and so slow to acclimatize to the drugs.

As she and the teacher walked down the long corridor to the clinic, Mary made up her mind to tell the medicop what she thought was wrong. It was not herself. It was her hypoalter, that nasty little Susan Shorrs. Sometimes, when Susan had the body, the things Susan was doing and thinking came to Mary like what the ancients had called *dreams*, and Mary had never liked this secondary ego whom she could never really know. Whatever was wrong, it was Susan's doing. The filthy creature never took care of her hair, it was always so messy when Susan shifted the body to her.

Mrs. Harris waited while Mary went into the clinic.

Mary was glad to find Captain Thiel, the nice medicop, on duty. But she was silent while the X-rays were being taken, and, of course, while he got the blood samples, she concentrated on being brave.

Later, while Captain Thiel looked in her eyes with the bright little light, Mary said calmly, "Do you know my hypoalter, Susan Shorrs?"

The medicop drew back and made some notes on a pad before answering. "Why, yes. She's in here quite often too."

"Does she look like me?"

"Not much. She's a very nice little girl . . ." He hesitated, visibly fumbling.

Mary blurted, "Tell me truly, what's she like?"

Captain Thiel gave her his nice smile. "Well, I'll tell you a secret if you keep it to yourself."

"Oh, I promise."

He leaned over and whispered in her ear and she liked the clean odour of him. "She's not nearly as pretty as you are."

Mary wanted very badly to put her arms around him and hug him. Instead, wondering if Mrs. Harris, waiting outside, had heard, she drew back self-consciously and said, "Susan is the cause of all this trouble, the nasty little thing."

"Oh now!" the medicop exclaimed. "I don't think so, Mary. She's in trouble, too, you know."

"She still eats sauerkraut." Mary was defiant.

"But what's wrong with that?"

"You told her not to last year because it makes me sick on my shift. But it agrees in buckets with a little pig like her."

The medicop took this seriously. He made a note on the pad. "Mary, you should have complained sooner."

"Do you think my father might not like me because Susan Shorrs is my hypoalter?" she asked abruptly.

"I hardly think so, Mary. After all, he doesn't even know her. He's never on her ego-shift."

"A little bit," Mary said, and was immediately frightened.

Captain Thiel glanced at her sharply. "What do you mean by that, child?"

"Oh, nothing," Mary said hastily. "I just thought maybe he was."

"Let me see your pharmacase," he said rather severely.

Mary slipped the pharmacase off the belt at her waist and handed it to him. Captain Thiel extracted the prescription card from the back and threw it away. He slipped a new card in the taping machine on his desk and punched out a new prescription, which he reinserted in the pharmacase. In the space on the front, he wrote directions for Mary to take the drugs numbered from left to right.

Mary watched his serious face and remembered that he had complimented her about being prettier than Susan. "Captain Thiel, is your hypoalter as handsome as you are?"

The young medicop emptied the remains of the old prescription from the pharmacase and took it to the dispensary in the corner, where he slid it into the filling slot. He seemed unmoved by her question and simply muttered, "Much handsomer."

The machine automatically filled the case from the punched card on its back and he returned it to Mary. "Are you taking your drugs exactly as prescribed? You know there are very strict laws about that, and as soon as you are fourteen, you will be held to them."

Mary nodded solemnly. Great strait-jackets, who didn't know there were laws about taking your drugs?

There was a long pause and Mary knew she was supposed to leave. She wanted, though, to stay with Captain Thiel and talk with him. She wondered how it would be if he were appointed her father.

Mary was not hurt that her shy compliment to him had gone unnoticed. She had only wanted something to talk about. Finally she said desperately, "Captain Thiel, how is it possible for a body to change as much from one ego-shift to another as it does between Susan and me?"

"There isn't all the change you imagine," he said. "Have you had your first physiology?"

"Yes. I was very good . . ." Mary saw from his smile that her inadvertent little conceit had trapped her.

"Then, Miss Mary Walden, how do *you* think it is possible?"

Why did teachers and medicops have to be this way? When all you wanted was to have them talk to you, they turned everything around and made you think.

She quoted unhappily from her schoolbook, "The main things in an ego-shift are the two vegetative nervous systems that translate the conditions of either personality to the blood and other organs right from the brain. The vegetative nervous systems change the rate at which the liver burns or stores sugar and the rate at which the kidneys excrete . . ."

Through the closed door to the other room, Mrs. Harris's voice raised at the visiophone said distinctly, *"But, Mr. Walden . . ."*

"Reabsorb," corrected Captain Thiel.

"What?" She didn't know what to listen to—the medicop or the distant voice of Mrs. Harris.

"It's better to think of the kidneys as reabsorbing salts and nutrients from the filtrated blood."

"Oh."

"But, Mr. Walden, we can overdo a good thing. The proper amount of neglect is definitely required for full development of some personality types and Mary certainly is one of those. . . ."

"What about the pituitary gland that's attached to the brain and controls all the other glands during the shift of egos?" pressed Captain Thiel distractingly.

"But, Mr. Walden, too much neglect at this critical point may cause another personality to split off and we can't have that. Adequate personalities are congenital. A new one now would only rob the present personalities. You are the appointed parent of this child and the Board of Education will enforce your compliance with our diagnosis. . . ."

Mary's mind leaped to a page in one of her childhood storybooks. It was an illustration of a little girl resting beneath a great tree that overhung a brook. There were friendly little wild animals about. Mary could see the page clearly and she thought about it very hard instead of crying.

"Aren't you interested any more, Mary?" Captain Thiel was looking at her strangely.

The agitation in her voice was a surprise. "I have to get home. I have a lot of things to do."

Outside, when Mrs. Harris seemed suddenly to realize that something was wrong, and delicately probed to find out whether her angry voice had been overheard, Mary said calmly and as if it didn't matter, "Was my father home when you called him before?"

"Why—yes, Mary. But you mustn't pay any attention to conversations like that, darling."

You can't force him to like me, she thought to herself, and she was angry with Mrs. Harris because now her father would only dislike her more.

Neither her father nor her mother was home when Mary walked into the evening-darkened apartment. It was the first day of the family shift, and on that day, for many periods now, they had not been home until late.

Mary walked through the empty rooms, turning on lights. She passed up the electrically heated dinner her father had set out for her. Presently she found herself at the storage-room door. She opened it slowly.

After hesitating a while she went in and began an exhausting search for the old storybook with the picture in it.

Finally she knew she could not find it. She stood in the middle of the junk-filled room and began to cry.

The day which ended for Mary Walden in lonely weeping should have been, for Conrad Manz, a pleasant rest day with an hour of rocket racing in the middle of it. Instead, he awakened with a shock to hear his wife actually *talking* while she was *asleep*.

He stood over her bed and made certain that she was asleep. It was as though her mind thought it was somewhere else, doing something else. Vaguely he remembered that the ancients did something called *dreaming* while they slept and the thought made him shiver.

Clara Manz was saying, "Oh, Bill, they'll catch us. We can't pretend any more unless we have drugs. Haven't we any drugs, Bill?"

Then she was silent and lay still. Her breathing was shallow and even in the dawn light her cheeks were deeply flushed against the blonde hair.

Having just awakened, Conrad was on a very low drug level and the incident was unpleasantly disturbing. He picked up his pharmacase from beside his bed and made his way to the bathroom. He took his hypothalamic block and the integration enzymes and returned to the bedroom. Clara was still sleeping.

She had been behaving oddly for some time, but there had never been anything as disturbing as this. He felt that he should call a medicop, but, of course, he didn't want to do anything that extreme. It was probably something with a simple explanation. Clara was a little scatterbrained at times. Maybe she had forgotten to take her sleeping compound and that was what caused *dreaming*. The very word made his powerful body chill. But if she was neglecting to take any of her drugs and he called in a medicop, it would be serious.

Conrad went into the library and found the *Family Pharmacy*. He switched on a light in the dawn-shrunken room and let his heavy frame into a chair. *A Guide to Better Understanding of Your Family Prescriptions. Official Edition, 2831.* The book was mostly Medicorps propaganda and almost never gave a practical suggestion. If something went wrong, you called a medicop.

Conrad hunted through the book for the section on sleeping compound. It was funny, too, about that name Bill. Conrad went over all the men of their acquaintance with whom Clara had occasional affairs or with whom she was friendly and he couldn't remember a single Bill. In fact, the only man with that name whom he could think of was his own hyperalter, Bill Walden. But that was naturally impossible.

Maybe dreaming was always about imaginary people.

SLEEPING COMPOUND: An official mixture of soporific and hypnotic alkaloids and synthetics. A critical drug; an essential feature in every prescription. Slight deviations in following prescription are unallowable because of the subtle manner in which behaviour may be altered over months or years. The first sleeping compound was announced by Thomas Marshall in 1986. The formula has been modified only twice since then.

There followed a tightly packed description of the chemistry and pharmacology of the various ingredients. Conrad skipped through this.

The importance of Sleeping Compound in the life of every individual and to society is best appreciated when we recall Marshall's words announcing its initial development:

"It is during so-called *normal* sleep that the vicious unconscious mind responsible for wars and other symptoms of unhappiness develops its resources and its hold on our conscious lives.

"In this *normal* sleep the critical faculties of the cortex are paralysed. Meanwhile, the infantile unconscious mind expands misinterpreted experience into the toxic patterns of neurosis and psychosis. The conscious mind takes over at morning, unaware that these infantile motivations have been cleverly woven into its very structure.

"Sleeping Compound will stop this. There is no unconscious activity after taking this harmless drug. We believe the Medicorps should at once initiate measures to acclimatize every child to its use. In these children, as the years go by, infantile patterns unable to work during sleep will fight a losing battle during waking hours with conscious patterns accumulating in the direction of adulthood."

That was all there was—mostly the Medicorps patting its own back for saving humanity. But if you were in trouble and called a medicop, you'd risk getting into real trouble.

Conrad became aware of Clara standing in the doorway. The flush of her disturbed emotions and the pallor of her fatigue mixed in ragged banners on her cheeks.

Conrad waved the *Family Pharmacy* with a foolish gesture of embarrassment.

"Young lady, have you been neglecting to take your sleeping compound?"

Clara turned utterly pale. "I—I don't understand."

"You were talking in your sleep."

"I—was?"

She came forward so unsteadily that he helped her to a seat. She stared at him. He asked jovially, "Who is this 'Bill' you were so desperately involved with? Have you been having an affair I don't know about? Aren't my friends good enough for you?"

The result of this banter was that she alarmingly began to cry, clutching her robe about her and dropping her blonde head on her knees and sobbing.

Children cried before they were acclimatized to the drugs, but Conrad Manz had never in his life seen an adult cry. Though he had taken his morning drugs and certain disrupting emotions were already impossible, nevertheless this sight was completely unnerving.

In gasps between her sobs, Clara was saying, "Oh, I can't go back to taking them! But I can't keep this up! I just can't!"

"Clara, darling, I don't know what to say or do. I think we ought to call the Medicorps."

Intensely frightened, she rose and clung to him, begging, "Oh, no, Conrad, that isn't necessary! It isn't necessary at all. I've only neglected to take my sleeping compound and it won't happen again. All I need is a sleeping compound. Please get my pharmacase for me and it will be all right."

She was so desperate to convince him that Conrad got the pharmacase and a glass of water for her only to appease the white face of fright.

Within a few minutes of taking the sleeping compound, she was calm. As he put her back to bed, she laughed with a lazy indolence.

"Oh, Conrad, you take it so seriously. I only needed a sleeping compound very badly and now I feel fine. I'll sleep all day. It's a rest day, isn't it? Now go race a rocket and stop worrying and thinking about calling the medicops."

But Conrad did not go rocket racing as he had planned. Clara had been asleep only a few minutes when there was a call on the visiophone; they wanted him at the office. The city of Santa Fe would be completely out of balance within twelve shifts if revised plans were not put into operation immediately. They were to start during the next five days while he would be out of shift. In order to carry on the first day of their next shift, he and the other three traffic managers he worked with would have to come down today and familiarize themselves with the new operations.

There was no getting out of it. His rest day was spoiled. Conrad resented it all the more because Santa Fe was clear out on the edge of their traffic district and could have been revised out of the Mexican offices just as well. But those boys down there rested all five days of their shift.

Conrad looked in on Clara before he left and found her asleep in the total suspension of proper drug level. The unpleasant memory of her behaviour made him squirm, but now that the episode was over, it no longer worried him. It was typical of him that, things having been set straight in the proper manner, he did not think of her again until late in the afternoon.

As early as 1950, the pioneer communications engineer Norbert Wiener had pointed out that there might be a close parallel between disassociation of personalities and the disruption of a communication system. Wiener referred back specifically to the first clear description, by Morton Prince, of multiple personalities existing together in the same human body. Prince had described only individual cases and his observations were not altogether acceptable in Wiener's time. Nevertheless, in the schizophrenic society of the 29th Century, a major managerial problem was that of balancing the communicating and non-communicating populations in a city.

As far as Conrad and the other traffic men present at the conference were concerned, Santa Fe was a resort and retirement area of 100,000 human bodies, alive and consuming more than they produced every day of the year. Whatever the representatives of the Medicorps and Communications Board worked out, it would mean only slight changes in the types of foodstuffs, entertainment and so forth moving into Santa Fe, and Conrad could have grasped the entire traffic change in ten minutes after the real problem had been settled. But, as usual, he and the other traffic men had to sit through two hours while small wheels from the Medicorps and Communications acted big about rebalancing a city.

For them, Conrad had to admit, Santa Fe was a great deal more complex than 100,000 consuming, moderately producing human bodies. It was 200,000 human personalities, two to each body. Conrad wondered sometimes what they would have done if the three and four personality cases so common back in the 20th and 21st Centuries had been allowed to reproduce. The 200,000 personalities in Santa Fe were difficult enough.

Like all cities, Santa Fe operated in five shifts, A, B, C, D, and E.

Just as it was supposed to be for Conrad in his city, today was rest day for the 20,000 hypoalters on D-shift in Santa Fe. Tonight at around 6.00 P.M. they would all go to shifting rooms and be replaced by their hyperalters, who had different tastes in food and pleasure and took different drugs.

Tomorrow would be rest day for the hypoalters on E-shift and in the evening they would turn things over to their hyper-alters.

The next day it would be rest for the A-shift hyperalters and three days after that the D-shift hyperalters, including Bill Walden, would rest till evening, when Conrad and the D-shift hypoalters everywhere would again have their five-day use of their bodies.

Right now the trouble with Santa Fe's retired population, which worked only for its own maintenance, was that too many elderly people on the D-shift and E-shift had been dying off. This point was brought out by a dapper young department head from Communications.

Conrad groaned when, as he knew would happen, a Medi-corps officer promptly set out on an exhaustive demonstration that Medicorps predictions of deaths for Santa Fe had indicated clearly that Communications should have been moving people from D-shift and E-shift into the area.

Actually, it appeared that someone from Communications had blundered and had overloaded the quota of people on A-shift and B-shift moving to Santa Fe. Thus on one rest day there weren't enough people working to keep things going, and later in the week there were so many available workers that they were clogging the city.

None of this was heated exchange or in any way emotional. It was just interminably, exhaustively logical and boring. Conrad fidgeted through two hours of it, seeing his chance for a rocket race dissolving. When at last the problem of balanced shift-populations for Santa Fe was worked out, it took him and the other traffic men only a few minutes to apply their tables and reschedule traffic to co-ordinate with the population changes.

Disgusted, Conrad walked over to the Tennis Club and had lunch.

There were still two hours of his rest day left when Conrad Manz realized that Bill Walden was again forcing an early shift. Conrad was in the middle of a volley-tennis game and he didn't like having the shift forced so soon. People generally shifted at their appointed regular hour every five days, and a hyperalter was not supposed to use his power to force shift. It was such an unthinkable thing nowadays that there was occasional talk of abolishing the terms hyperalter and hypoalter because they were somewhat disparaging to the hypoalter, and really designated only the antisocial power of the hyperalter to force the shift.

Bill Walden had been cheating two to four hours on Conrad every shift for several periods back. Conrad could have reported it to the Medicorps, but he himself was guilty of a constant misdemeanour about which Bill had not yet complained. Unlike the sedentary Walden, Conrad Manz enjoyed exercise. He overindulged in violent sports and put off sleep, letting Bill Walden make up the fatigue on his shift. That was undoubtedly why the poor old sucker had started cheating a few hours on Conrad's rest day.

Conrad laughed to himself, remembering the time Bill Walden had registered a long list of sports which he wished Conrad to be restrained from—rocket racing, deepsea exploration, jet-skiing. It had only given Conrad some ideas he hadn't had before. The Medicorps had refused to enforce the list on the basis that danger and violent exercise were a necessary outlet for Conrad's constitution. Then poor old Bill had written Conrad a note threatening to sue him for any injury resulting from such sports. As if he had a chance against the Medicorps ruling!

Conrad knew it was no use trying to finish the volley-tennis game. He lost interest and couldn't concentrate on what he was doing when Bill started forcing the shift. Conrad shot the ball back at his opponent in a blistering curve impossible to intercept.

"So long," he yelled at the man. "I've got some things to do before my shift ends."

He lounged into the locker rooms and showered, put his clothes and belongings, including his pharmacase, in a shipping carton, addressed them to his own home and dropped them in the mail chute.

He stepped with languid nakedness across the hall, pressed his identifying wristband to a lock-face and dialled his clothing sizes.

In this way he procured a neatly wrapped, clean shifting costume from the slot. He put it on without bothering to return to his shower room.

He shouted a loud good-bye to no one in particular among the several men and women in the baths and stepped out on to the street.

Conrad felt too good even to be sorry that his shift was over. After all, nothing happened except you came to, five days later, on your next shift. The important thing was the rest day. He had always said the last days of the shift should be a work day; then you would be glad it was over. He guessed the idea was to rest the body before another personality took over. Well, poor old Bill Walden never got a rested body. He probably slept off the first twelve hours.

Walking unhurriedly through the street crowds, Conrad entered a public shifting station and found an empty room. As he started to open the door, a girl came out of the adjoining booth and Conrad hastily averted his glance. She was still re-arranging her hair. There were so many rude people nowadays who didn't seem to care at all about the etiquette of shifting, women particularly. They were always redoing their hair or make-up where a person couldn't help seeing them.

Conrad pressed his identifying wristband to the lock and entered the booth he had picked. The act automatically sent the time and his shift number to Medicorps Headquarters.

Once inside the shifting room, Conrad went to the lavatory and turned on the tap of make-up solvent. In spite of losing two hours of his rest day, he decided to be decent to old Bill, though he was half tempted to leave his make-up on. It was a pretty foul joke, of course, especially on a humourless fellow like poor Walden.

Conrad creamed his face thoroughly and then washed in water and used the automatic dryer. He looked at his strong-lined features in the mirror. They displayed a less distinct expression of his own personality with the make-up gone.

He turned away from the mirror and it was only then that he remembered he hadn't spoken to his wife before shifting. Well, he couldn't decently call up and let her see him without make-up.

He stepped across to the visiophone and set the machine to deliver his spoken message in type: "Hello, Clara. Sorry I forgot to call you before. Bill Walden is forcing me to shift early again. I hope you're not still upset about that business this morning. Be a good girl and smile at me on the next shift. I love you. Conrad."

For a moment, when the shift came, the body of Conrad Manz stood moronically uninhabited. Then, rapidly, out of the gyri of its brain, the personality of Bill Walden emerged, replacing the slackly powerful attitude of Conrad by the slightly prim precise-ness of Bill's bearing.

The face, just now relaxed with readiness for action, was abruptly pulled into an intellectual mask of tension by habitual patterns of conflict in the muscles. There were also acute momen-tary signs of clash between the vegetative nervous activity charac-teristic of Bill Walden and the internal homeostasis Conrad Manz had left behind him. The face paled as hypersensitive vascular beds closed down under new vegetative volleys.

Bill Walden grasped sight and sound, and the sharp odour of make-up solvent stung his nostrils. He was conscious of only one clamouring, terrifying thought: *They will catch us. It cannot go on much longer without Helen guessing about Clara. She is already angry about Clara delaying the shift, and if she learns from Mary that I am cheating on Conrad's shift . . . Any time now, perhaps this time, when the shift is over, I will be looking into the face of a medicop who is pulling a needle from my arm, and then it'll all be over.*

So far, at least, there was no medicop. Still feeling unreal but anxious not to lose precious moments, Bill took an indivi-dualized kit from the wall dispenser and made himself up. He was sparing and subtle in his use of the make-up, unlike the horrible make-up jobs Conrad Manz occasionally left on. Bill rearranged his hair. Conrad always wore it too short for his taste, but you couldn't complain about everything.

Bill sat in a chair to await some of the slower aspects of the shift. He knew that an hour after he left the booth, his basal metabolic rate would be ten points higher. His blood sugar would go down steadily. In the next five days he would lose six to eight pounds, which Conrad would promptly regain.

Just as Bill was about to leave the booth, he remembered to pick up a news summary. He put his wristband to the switch on the telephoto and a freshly printed summary of the last five days in the world fell into the rack. His wristband, of course, called forth one edited for hyperalters on the D-shift.

It did not mention by name any hypoalter on the D-shift. Should one of them have done something that it was necessary for Bill or other D-shift hyperalters to know about, it would appear in news summaries called forth by their wristbands— but told in such fashion that the personality involved seemed namelessly incidental, while names and pictures of hyperalters and hypoalters on any of the other four shifts naturally were freely used. The purpose was to keep Conrad Manz and all other hypoalters on the D-shift, one tenth of the total population, non-existent as far as their hyperalters were concerned. This convention made it necessary for photoprint summaries to be on light-sensitive paper that blackened illegibly before six hours were up, so that a man might never stumble on news about his hypoalter.

Bill did not even glance at the news summary. He had picked it up only for appearances. The summaries were essential if you were going to start where you left off on your last shift and have any knowledge of the five intervening days. A man just didn't walk out of a shifting room without one. It was failure to do little things like that that would start them wondering about him.

Bill opened the door of the booth by applying his wristband to the lock and stepped out into the street.

Late afternoon crowds pressed about him. Across the boulevard, a helicopter landing swarmed with clouds of rising commuters. Bill had some trouble figuring out the part of the city Conrad had left him in and walked two blocks before he understood where he was. Then he got into an idle two-place cab, started the motor with his wristband and hurried the little three-wheeler recklessly through the traffic. Clara was probably already waiting and he first had to go home and get dressed.

The thought of Clara waiting for him in the park near her home was a sharp reminder of his strange situation. He was in a world that was literally not supposed to exist for him, for it was the world of his own hypoalter, Conrad Manz.

Undoubtedly, there were people in the traffic up ahead who knew both him and Conrad, people from the other shifts who never mentioned the one to the other except in those guarded, snickering little confidences they couldn't resist telling and you couldn't resist listening to. After all, the most important person in the world was your alter. If he got sick, injured or killed, so would you.

Thus, in moments of intimacy or joviality, an undercover exchange went on. . . . *I'll tell you about your hyperalter if you'll tell me about my hypoalter.* It was orthodox bad manners that left you with shame, and a fear that the other fellow would tell people you seemed to have a pathological interest in your alter and must need a change in your prescription.

But the most flagrant abuser of such morbid little exchanges would have been horrified to learn that right here, in the middle of the daylight traffic, was a man who was using his antisocial shifting power to meet in secret the wife of his own hypoalter!

Bill did not have to wonder what the Medicorps would think. Relations between hyperalters and hypoalters of opposite sex were punishable—drastically punishable.

When he arrived at the apartment, Bill remembered to order a dinner for his daughter Mary. His order, dialled from the day's menu, was delivered to the apartment pneumatically and he set it out over electric warmers. He wanted to write a note to the child, but he started two and threw both in the basket. He couldn't think of anything to say to her.

Staring at the lonely table he was leaving for Mary, Bill felt his guilt overwhelming him. He could stop the behaviour which led to the guilt by taking his drugs as prescribed. They would return him immediately to the sane and ordered conformity of the world. He would no longer have to carry the fear that the Medicorps would discover he was not taking his drugs. He would no longer neglect his appointed child. He would no longer endanger the very life of Conrad's wife Clara and, of course, his own.

When you took your drugs as prescribed, it was impossible to experience such ancient and primitive emotions as guilt. Even should you miscalculate and do something wrong, the drugs would not allow any such emotional reaction. To be free to experience his guilt over the lonely child who needed him was, for these reasons, a precious thing to Bill. In all the world, this night, he was undoubtedly the only man who could and did feel one of the ancient emotions. People felt shame, not guilt; conceit, not pride; pleasure, not desire. Now that he had stopped taking his drugs as prescribed, Bill realized that the drugs allowed only an impoverished segment of a vivid emotional spectrum.

But however exciting it was to live them, the ancient emotions did not seem to act as deterrents to bad behaviour. Bill's sense of guilt did not keep him from continuing to neglect Mary. His fear of being caught did not restrain him from breaking every rule of inter-alter law and loving Clara, his own hypoalter's wife.

Bill got dressed as rapidly as possible. He tossed the discarded shifting costume into the return chute. He retouched his make-up, trying to eliminate some of the heavy, inexpressive planes of muscularity which were more typical of Conrad than of himself.

The act reminded him of the shame which his wife Helen had felt when she learned, a few years ago, that her own hypoalter, Clara, and his hypoalter, Conrad, had obtained from the Medicorps a special release to marry. Such rare marriages in which the same bodies lived together on both halves of a shift were something to snicker about. They verged on the antisocial, but could be arranged if the batteries of Medicorps tests could be satisfied.

Perhaps it had been the very intensity of Helen's shame on learning of this marriage, the nauseous display of conformity so typical of his wife, that had first given Bill the idea of seeking out Clara, who had dared convention to make such a peculiar marriage. Over the years, Helen had continued blaming all their troubles on the fact that both egos of himself were living with, and intimate with, both egos of herself.

So Bill had started cutting down on his drugs, the curiosity having become an obsession. What was this other part of Helen like, this Clara who was unconventional enough to want to marry only Bill's own hypoalter, in spite of almost certain public shame?

He had first seen Clara's face when it formed on a visiophone, the first time he had forced Conrad to shift prematurely. It was softer than Helen's. The delicate contours were less purposefully set, gayer.

"Clara Manz?" Bill had sat there staring at the visiophone for several seconds, unable to continue. His great fear that she would immediately report him must have been naked on his face.

He had watched an impish suspicion grow in the tender curve of her lips and her oblique glance from the visiophone. She did not speak.

"Mrs. Manz," he finally said, "I would like to meet you in the park across from your home."

To this awkward opening he owed the first time he had heard Clara laugh. Her warm, clear laughter, teasing him, tumbled forth like a cloud of gay butterflies.

"Are you afraid to see me here at home because my husband might *walk in on us*?"

Bill had been put completely at ease by this bantering indication that Clara knew who he was and welcomed him as an intriguing diversion. Quite literally, the one person who could not *walk in on them*, as the ancients thought of it, was his own hypoalter, Conrad Manz.

Bill finished retouching his make-up and hurried to leave the apartment. But this time, as he passed the table where Mary's dinner was set out, he decided to write a few words to the child, no matter how empty they sounded to himself. The note he left explained that he had some early work to do at the microfilm library where he worked.

Just as Bill was leaving the apartment, the visiophone buzzed. In his hurry Bill flipped the switch before he thought. Too late, his hand froze and the implications of this call, an hour before anyone would normally be home, shot a shaft of terror through him.

But it was not the image of a medicop that formed on the

screen. The woman introduced herself as Mrs. Harris, one of Mary's teachers.

It was strange that she should have thought he might be home. The shift for children was half a day earlier than that for adults, so the parents could have half their rest day free. This afternoon would be for Mary the first classes of her shift, but the teacher must have guessed something was wrong with the shifting schedules in Mary's family. Or had the child told her?

Mrs. Harris explained rather dramatically that Mary was being neglected. What could he say to her? That he was a criminal breaking drug regulations in the most flagrant manner? That nothing, not even the child appointed to him, meant more to him than his wife's own hypoalter? Bill finally ended the hopeless and possibly dangerous conversation by turning off the receiver and leaving the apartment.

Bill realized that now, for both him and Clara, the greatest joy had been those first few times together. The enormous threat of a Medicorps retaliation took the pleasure from their contact and they came together desperately because, having tasted this fantastic nonconformity and the new undrugged intimacy, there was no other way for them. Even now as he drove through the traffic towards where she would be waiting, he was not so much concerned with meeting Clara in their fear-poisoned present as with the vivid, aching remembrance of what those meetings once had really been like.

He recalled an evening they had spent lying on the summer lawn of the park, looking out at the haze-dimmed stars. It had been shortly after Clara joined him in cutting down on the drugs, and the clear memory of their quiet laughter so captured his mind now that Bill almost tangled his car in the traffic.

In memory he kissed her again and, as it had then, the newly cut grass mixed with the exciting fragrance of her skin. After the kiss they continued a mock discussion of the ancient word "sin". Bill pretended to be trying to explain the meaning of the word to her, sometimes with definitions that kept them laughing and sometimes with demonstrational kisses that stopped their laughter.

He could remember Clara's face turned to him in the evening light with an outrageous parody of interest. He could hear himself saying, "You see, the ancients would say we are not *sinning* because they would disagree with the medicops that you and Helen are two completely different people, or that Conrad and I are not the same person."

Clara kissed him with an air of tentative experimentation. "Mmm, no. I can't say I care for that interpretation."

"You'd rather be sinning?"

"Definitely."

"Well, if the ancients did agree with the medicops that we are distinct from our alters, Helen and Conrad, then they would say we are sinning—but not for the same reasons the Medicorps would give."

"That," asserted Clara, "is where I get lost. If this sinning business is going to be worth anything at all, it has to be something you can identify."

Bill cut his car out of the main stream of traffic and towards the park, without interrupting his memory.

"Well, darling, I don't want to confuse you, but the medicops would say we are sinning only because you are my wife's hypo-alter, and I am your husband's hyperalter—in other words, for the very reason the ancients would say we are *not* sinning. Furthermore, if either of us were with anyone else, the medicops would think it was perfectly all right, and so would Conrad and Helen. Provided, of course, I took a hyperalter and you took a hypoalter only."

"Of course," Clara said, and Bill hurried over the gloomy fact.

"The ancients, on the other hand, would say we are sinning because we are making love to someone we are not married to."

"But what's the matter with that? Everybody does it."

"The ancient Moderns didn't. Or, that is, they often did, but . . ."

Clara brought her full lips hungrily to his. "Darling, I think the ancient Moderns had the right idea, though I don't see how they ever arrived at it."

Bill grinned. "It was just an invention of theirs, along with the wheel and atomic energy."

That evening was long gone by as Bill stopped the little taxi beside the park and left it there for the next user. He walked across the lawns towards the statue where he and Clara always met. The very thought of entering one's own hypoalter's house was so unnerving that Bill brought himself to do it only by first meeting Clara near the statue. As he walked between the trees, Bill could not again capture the spirit of that evening he had been remembering. The Medicorps was too close. It was impossible to laugh that away now.

Bill arrived at the statue, but Clara was not there. He waited impatiently while a livid sunset coagulated between the branches of the great trees. Clara should have been there first. It was easier for her, because she was leaving her shift, and without doing it prematurely.

The park was like a quiet backwater in the eddying rush of the evening city. Bill felt conspicuous and vulnerable in the gloaming light. Above all, he felt a new loneliness, and he knew that now Clara felt it, too. They needed each other as each had been, before fear had bleached their feeling to white bones of desperation.

They were not taking their drugs as prescribed, and for that they would be horribly punished. That was the only unforgivable *sin* in their world. By committing it, he and Clara had found out what life could be, in the same act that would surely take life from them. Their powerful emotions they had found in abundance simply by refusing to take the drugs, and by being together briefly each fifth day in a dangerous breach of all convention. The closer their discovery and the greater their terror, the more desperately they needed even their terror, and the more impossible became the delight of their first meetings.

Telegraphing bright beads of sound, a night bird skimmed the sunset lawns to the looming statue and skewed around its monolithic base. The bird's piping doubled and then choked off as it veered frantically from Bill. After a while, far off through the park, it released a fading protest of song.

Above Bill, the towering statue of the great Alfred Morris blackened against the sunset. The hollowed granite eyes bore down on him out of an undecipherable dark . . . the ancient, implacable face of the Medicorps. As if to pronounce a sentence on his present crimes by a magical disclosure of the weight of centuries, a pool of sulphurous light and leaf shadows danced on the painted plaque at the base of the statue:

On this spot in the Gregorian year 1996, Alfred Morris announced to an assembly of war survivors the hypothalamic block. His stirring words were, "The new drug selectively halts at the thalamic brain the upward flow of unconscious stimuli and the downward flow of unconscious motivations. It acts as a screen between the cerebrum and the psychosomatic discharge system. Using hypothalamic block, we will not act emotively, we will initiate acts only from the logical demands of situations."

This announcement and the subsequent wholehearted action of the war-weary people made the taking of hypothalamic block obligatory. This put an end to the powerful play of unconscious mind in the public and private affairs of the ancient world. It ended the great paranoid wars and saved mankind.

In the strange evening light, the letters seemed alive, a centuries-old condemnation of any who might try to go back to the ancient pre-pharmacy days. Of course, it was not really possible to go back. Without drugs, everybody and all society would fall apart.

The ancients had first learned to keep endocrine deviates such as the diabetic alive with drugs. Later they learned with other drugs to "cure" the far more prevalent disease, schizophrenia, that was jamming their hospitals. The big change came when the ancients used these same drugs on everyone to control the private and public irrationality of their time and stop the wars.

In this new, drugged world, the schizophrene thrived better than any, and the world became patterned on him. But, just as the diabetic was still diabetic, the schizophrene was still himself, plus the drugs. Meanwhile, everyone had forgotten what it was the drugs did to you—that the emotions experienced were blurred emotions, that insight was at an isolated level of rationality because the drugs kept true feelings from ever emerging.

How inconceivable it would be to Helen and the other people of this world to live on as little drug as possible . . . to experience the conflicting emotions, the interplay of passion and logic that almost tore you apart! Sober, the ancients called it, and they lived that way most of the time, with only the occasional crude and club-like effects of alcohol or narcotics to relieve their chronic anxiety.

By taking as little hypothalamic block as possible, he and Clara were able to desire their fantastic attachment, to delight in an absolutely illogical situation unheard of in their society. But the society would judge their refusal to take hypothalamic block in only one sense. The weight of this judgment stood before him in the smouldering words, *"It ended the great paranoid wars and saved mankind."*

When Clara did appear, she was searching myopically in the wrong vicinity of the statue. He did not call to her at once, letting the sight of her smooth out the tensions in him, convert all the conflicts into this one intense longing to be with her.

Her halting search for him was deeply touching, like that of a tragic little puppet in a darkening dumbshow. He saw suddenly how like puppets the two of them were. They were moved by the strengthening wires of a new life of feeling to batter clumsily at an implacable stage setting that would finally leave them as bits of wood and paper.

Then suddenly in his arms Clara was at the same time hungrily moving and tense with fear of discovery. Little sounds of love and fear choked each other in her throat. Her blonde head pressed tightly into his shoulder and she clung to him with desperation.

She said, "Conrad was disturbed by my tension this morning and made me take a sleeping compound. I've just awakened."

They walked to her home in silence and even in the darkened apartment they used only the primitive monosyllables of apprehensive need. Beyond these mere sounds of compassion, they had long ago said all that could be said.

Because Bill was the hyperalter, he had no fear that Conrad could force a shift on him. When later they lay in darkness, he allowed himself to drift into a brief slumber. Without the sleeping compound, distorted events came and went without reason. Dreaming, the ancients had called it. It was one of the most frightening things that had begun to happen when he first cut down on the drugs. Now, in the few seconds that he dozed, a thousand fragments of incidental knowledge, historical reading and emotional need melded and, in a strange contrast to their present tranquillity, he was dreaming a frightful moment in the 20th Century. *These are the great paranoid wars,* he thought. And it was so because he had thought it.

He searched frantically through the glove compartment of an ancient car. "Wait," he pleaded. "I tell you we have sulphonamide-14. We've been taking it regularly as directed. We took a double dose back in Paterson because there were soft-bombs all through that part of Jersey and we didn't know what would be declared Plague Area next."

Now Bill threw things out of his satchel on to the floor and seat of the car, fumbling deeper by the flashlight Clara held. His heart beat thickly with terror. Then he remembered his pharmacase. Oh, why hadn't they remembered sooner about their pharmacases. Bill tore at the belt about his waist.

The Medicorps captain stepped back from the door of their car. He jerked his head at the dark form of the corporal standing in the roadway. "Shoot them. Run the car off the embankment before you burn it."

Bill screamed metallically through the speaker of his radiation mask. "Wait. I've found it." He thrust the pharmacase out the door of the car. "This is a pharmacase," he explained. "We keep our drugs in one of these and it's belted to our waist so we are never without them."

The captain of the Medicorps came back. He inspected the pharmacase and the drugs and returned it. "From now on, keep your drugs handy. Take them without fail according to radio instructions. Do you understand?"

Clara's head pressed heavily against Bill's shoulder, and he could hear the tinny sound of her sobbing through the speaker of her mask.

The captain stepped into the road again. "We'll have to burn your car. You passed through a Plague Area and it can't be sterilized on this route. About a mile up this road you'll come to a sterilization unit. Stop and have your person and belongings rayed. After that, keep walking, but stick to the road. You'll be shot if you're caught off it."

The road was crowded with fleeing people. Their way was lighted by piles of cadavers writhing in gasoline flames. The Medicorps was everywhere. Those who stumbled, those who coughed, the delirious and their helping partners . . . these were taken to the side of the road, shot and burned. And there was bombing again to the south.

Bill stopped in the middle of the road and looked back. Clara clung to him.

"There is a plague here we haven't any drug for," he said, and realized he was crying. "We are all mad."

Clara was crying too. "Darling, what have you done? Where are the drugs?"

The water of the Hudson hung as it had in the late afternoon, ice crystals in the stratosphere. The high, high sheet flashed and glowed in the new bombing to the south, where multicoloured pillars of flame boiled into the sky. But the muffled crash of the distant bombing was suddenly the steady click of the urgent signal on a bedside visiophone, and Bill was abruptly awake.

Clara was throwing on her robe and moving towards the machine on terror-rigid limbs. With a scrambling motion, Bill got out of the possible view of the machine and crouched at the end of the room.

Distinctly, he could hear the machine say, "Clara Manz?"

"Yes," Clara's voice was a thin treble that could have been a shriek had it continued.

"This is Medicorps Headquarters. A routine check discloses you have delayed your shift two hours. To maintain the statistical record of deviations, please give us a full explanation."

"I . . . " Clara had to swallow before she could talk. "I must have taken too much sleeping compound."

"Mrs. Manz, our records indicate that you have been delaying your shift consistently for several periods now. We made a check of this as a routine follow up on any such deviation, but the discovery is quite serious." There was a harsh silence, a silence that demanded a logical answer. But how could there be a logical answer.

"My hyperalter hasn't complained and I—well, I have just let a bad habit develop. I'll see that it—doesn't happen again."

The machine voiced several platitudes about the responsibilities of one personality to another and the duty of all to society before Clara was able to shut it off.

Both of them sat as they were for a long, long time while the tide of terror subsided. When at last they looked at each other

across the dim and silent room, both of them knew there could
be at least one more time together before they were caught.

Five days later, on the last day of her shift, Mary Walden
wrote the address of her appointed father's hypoalter, Conrad
Manz, with an indelible pencil on the skin just below her armpit.

During the morning, her father and mother had spoiled the
family rest day by quarrelling. It was about Helen's hypoalter
delaying so many shifts. Bill did not think it very important,
but her mother was angry and threatened to complain to the
Medicorps.

The lunch was eaten in silence, except that at one point Bill
said, "It seems to me Conrad and Clara Manz are guilty of a
peculiar marriage, not us. Yet they seem perfectly happy with it
and you're the one who is made unhappy. The woman has
probably just developed a habit of taking too much sleeping
compound for her rest-day naps. Why don't you drop her a
note?"

Helen made only one remark. It was said through her teeth
and very softly. "Bill, I would just as soon the child did not
realize her relationship to this sordid situation."

Mary cringed over the way Helen disregarded her hearing,
the possibility that she might be capable of understanding, or
her feelings about being shut out of their mutual world.

After lunch Mary cleared the table, throwing the remains of
the meal and the plastiplates into the flash trash disposer. Her
father had retreated to the library room and Helen was getting
ready to attend a Citizens' Meeting. Mary heard her mother
enter the room to say good-bye while she was wiping the dining
table. She knew that Helen was standing, well-dressed and a
little impatient, just behind her, but she pretended she did
not know.

"Darling, I'm leaving now for the Citizens' Meeting."

"Oh . . . yes."

"Be a good girl and don't be late for your shift. You only
have an hour now." Helen's patrician face smiled.

"I won't be late."

"Don't pay any attention to the things Bill and I discussed this
morning, will you?"

"No."

And she was gone. She did not say good-bye to Bill.

Mary was very conscious of her father in the house. He continued to sit in the library. She walked by the door and she could see him sitting in a chair, staring at the floor. Mary stood in the sun room for a long while. If he had risen from his chair, if he had rustled a page, if he had sighed, she would have heard him.

It grew closer and closer to the time she would have to leave if Susan Shorrs was to catch the first school hours of her shift. Why did children have to shift half a day before adults?

Finally, Mary thought of something to say. She could let him know she was old enough to understand what the quarrel had been about if only it were explained to her.

Mary went into the library and hesitantly sat on the edge of a couch near him. He did not look at her and his face seemed grey in the midday light. Then she knew that he was lonely, too. But a great feeling of tenderness for him went through her.

"Sometimes I think you and Clara Manz must be the only people in the world," she said abruptly, "who aren't so silly about shifting right on the dot. Why, I don't *care* if Susan Shorrs *is* an hour late for classes!"

Those first moments when he seized her in his arms, it seemed her heart would shake loose. It was as though she had uttered some magic formula, one that had abruptly opened the doors to his love. It was only after he had explained to her why he was always late on the first day of the family shift that she knew something was wrong. He *did* tell her, over and over, that he knew she was unhappy and that it was his fault. But he was at the same time soothing her, petting her, as if *he was afraid of her*.

He talked on and on. Gradually, Mary understood in his trembling body, in his perspiring palms, in his pleading eyes, that he was afraid of dying, that he was afraid *she* would kill him with the merest thing she said, with her very presence.

This was not painful to Mary, because, suddenly, something came with ponderous enormity to stand before her: *I would just as soon the child did not realize her relationship to this sordid situation.*

Her relationship. It was some kind of relationship to Conrad and Clara Manz, because those were the people they had been talking about.

The moment her father left the apartment, she went to his desk and took out the file of family records. After she found the address of Conrad Manz, the idea occurred to her to write it on her body. Mary was certain that Susan Shorrs never bathed and she thought this a clever idea. Sometime on Susan's rest day, five days from now, she would try to force the shift and go to see Conrad and Clara Manz. Her plan was simple in execution, but totally vague as to goal.

Mary was already late when she hurried to the children's section of a public shifting station. A Children's Transfer Bus was waiting, and Mary registered on it for Susan Shorrs to be taken to school. After that she found a shifting room and opened it with her wristband. She changed into a shifting costume and sent her own clothes and belongings home.

Children her age did not wear make-up, but Mary always stood at the mirror during the shift. She always tried as hard as she could to see what Susan Shorrs looked like. She giggled over a verse that was scrawled beside the mirror . . .

> Rouge your hair and comb your face;
> Many a third head is lost in this place.

. . . and then the shift came, doubly frightening because of what she knew she was going to do.

Especially if you were a hyperalter like Mary, you were supposed to have some sense of the passage of time while you were out of shift. Of course, you did not know what was going on, but it was as though a more or less accurate chronometer kept running when you went out of shift. Apparently Mary's was highly inaccurate, because, to her horror, she found herself sitting bolt upright in one of Mrs. Harris's classes, not out on the playgrounds, where she had expected Susan Shorrs to be.

Mary was terrified, and the ugly school dress Susan had been wearing accented, by its strangeness, the seriousness of her premature shift. Children weren't supposed to show much difference from hyperalter to hypoalter, but when she raised her eyes, her fright grew. Children did change. She hardly recognized anyone in the room, though most of them must be the alters of her own classmates. Mrs. Harris was a B-shift and overlapped both Mary and Susan, but otherwise Mary recognized only Carl Blair's hypoalter because of his freckles.

Mary knew she had to get out of there or Mrs. Harris would eventually recognize her. If she left the room quietly, Mrs. Harris would not question her unless she recognized her. It was no use trying to guess how Susan would walk.

Mary stood and went towards the door, glad that it turned her back to Mrs. Harris. It seemed to her that she could feel the teacher's eyes stabbing through her back.

But she walked safely from the room. She dashed down the school corridor and out into the street. So great was her fear of what she was doing that her hypoalter's world actually seemed like a different one.

It was a long way for Mary to walk across town, and when she rang the bell, Conrad Manz was already home from work. He smiled at her and she loved him at once.

"Well, what do you want, young lady?" he asked.

Mary couldn't answer him. She just smiled back.

"What's your name, eh?"

Mary went right on smiling, but suddenly he blurred in front of her.

"Here, here! There's nothing to cry about. Come on in and let's see if we can help you. Clara! We have a visitor, a very sentimental visitor."

Mary let him put his big arm around her shoulder and draw her, crying, into the apartment. Then she saw Clara swimming before her, looking like her mother, but . . . no, not at all like her mother.

"Now, see here, chicken, what is it you've come for?" Conrad asked when her crying stopped.

Mary had to stare hard at the floor to be able to say it. "I want to live with you."

Clara was twisting and untwisting a handkerchief. "But, child, we have already had our first baby appointed to us. He'll be with us next shift, and after that I have to bear a baby for someone else to keep. We wouldn't be allowed to take care of you."

"I thought maybe I was your real child." Mary said it helplessly, knowing in advance what the answer would be.

"Darling," Clara soothed, "children don't live with their

natural parents. It's neither practical nor civilized. I have had a child conceived and born on my shift, and this baby is my exchange, so you see that you are much too old to be my conception. Whoever your natural parents may be, it is just something on record with the Medicorps Genetic Division and isn't important."

"But you're a special case," Mary pressed. "I thought because it was a special arrangement that you were my real parents." She looked up and she saw that Clara had turned white.

And now Conrad Manz was agitated, too. "What do you mean, we're a special case?" He was staring hard at her.

"Because . . ." And now for the first time Mary realized how special this case was, how sensitive they would be about it.

He grasped her by the shoulders and turned her so she faced his unblinking eyes. "I said, what do you mean, we're a special case? Clara, what in thirty heads does this kid mean?"

His grip hurt her and she began to cry again. She broke away. "You're the hypoalters of my appointed father and mother. I thought maybe when it was like that, I might be your real child . . . and you might want me. I don't want to be where I am. I want somebody . . ."

Clara was calm now, her sudden fear gone. "But, darling, if you're unhappy where you are, only the Medicorps can reappoint you. Besides, maybe your appointed parents are just having some personal problems right now. Maybe if you tried to understand them, you would see that they really love you."

Conrad's face showed that he did not understand. He spoke with a stiff, quiet voice and without taking his eyes from Mary. "What are you doing here? My own hyperalter's kid in my house, throwing it up to me that I'm married to his wife's hypoalter!"

They did not feel the earth move, as she fearfully did. They sat there, staring at her, as though they might sit forever while she backed away, out of the apartment, and ran into her collapsing world.

Conrad Manz's rest day fell the day after Bill Walden's kid showed up at his apartment. It was ten days since that strait jacket of a conference on Santa Fe had lost him a chance to blast off a rocket racer. This time, on the practical knowledge that emergency business conferences were seldom called after lunch, Conrad had placed his reservation for a racer in the afternoon. The visit from Mary Walden had upset him every time he thought of it. Since it was his rest day, he had no intention of thinking about it and Conrad's scrupulously drugged mind was capable of just that.

So now, in the lavish coolness of the lounge at the Rocket Club, Conrad sipped his drink contentedly and made no contribution to the gloomy conversation going on around him.

"Look at it this way," the melancholy face of Alberts, a pilot from England, morosely emphasized his tone. "It takes about 10,000 economic units to jack a forty-ton ship up to satellite level and snap it around the course six times. That's just practice for us. On the other hand, an intellectual fellow who spends his spare time at a microfilm library doesn't use up 1,000 units in a year. In fact, his spare-time activity may turn up as units gained. The Economic Board doesn't argue that all pastime should be gainful. They just say rocket racing wastes more economic units than most pilots make on their work days. I tell you the day is almost here when they ban the rockets."

"That's just it," another pilot put in. "There was a time when you could show that rocket races were necessary for better spaceship design. Design has gone way beyond that. From their point of view we just burn up units as fast as other people create them. And it's no use trying to argue for the television shows. The Board can prove people would rather see a jet-skiing meet at a cost of about one-hundredth that of a rocket race."

Conrad Manz grinned into his drink. He had been aware for several minutes that pert little Angela, Alberts' soft-eyed, husky-voiced wife, was trying to catch his eye. But stranded as she was in the buzzing traffic of rockets, she was trying to hail the wrong rescuer. He had about fifteen minutes till the ramp boys would have a ship ready for him. Much as he liked Angela, he wasn't going to miss that race.

Still, he let his grin broaden and, looking up at her, he lied maliciously by nodding. She interpreted this signal as he knew she would. Well, at least he would afford her a graceful exit from the boring conversation.

He got up and went over and took her hand. Her full lips parted a little and she kissed him on the mouth.

Conrad turned to Alberts and interrupted him. "Angela and I would like to spend a little time together. Do you mind?"

Alberts was annoyed at having his train of thought broken and rather snapped out the usual courtesy. "Of course not. I'm glad for both of you."

Conrad looked the group over with a bland stare. "Have you lads ever tried jet-skiing? There's more genuine excitement in ten minutes of it than an hour of rocket racing. Personally, I don't care if the Board does ban the rockets soon. I'll just hop out to the Rocky Mountains on rest days."

Conrad knew perfectly well that if he had made this assertion before asking Alberts for his wife, the man would have found some excuse to have her remain. All the faces present displayed the *aficionado*'s disdain for one who has just demonstrated he doesn't *belong*. What the strait-jacket did they think they were —some ancient order of noblemen?

Conrad took Angela's yielding arm and led her serenely away before Alberts could think of anything to detain her.

On the way out of the lounge, she stroked his arm with frank admiration. "I'm so glad you were agreeable. Honestly, Harold could talk rockets till I died."

Conrad bent and kissed her. "Angela, I'm sorry, but this isn't going to be what you think. I have a ship to take off in just a few minutes."

She flared and dug into his arm now. "Oh, Conrad Manz! You . . . you made me believe . . ."

He laughed and grabbed her wrists. "Now, now, I'm neglecting you to *fly* a rocket, not just to talk about them. I won't let you die."

At last she could not suppress her husky musical laugh. "I found that out the last time you and I were together. Clara and I had a drink the other day at the Citizens' Club. I don't often use dirty language, but I told Clara she must be keeping you in a *strait-jacket* at home."

Conrad frowned, wishing she hadn't brought up the subject. It worried him off and on that something was wrong with Clara, something even worse than that awful *dreaming* business ten days ago. For several shifts now she had been cold, nor was it just a temporary lack of interest in himself, for she was also cold to the men of their acquaintance of whom she was usually quite fond. As for himself, he had had to depend on casual contacts such as Angela. Not that they weren't pleasant, but a man and wife were supposed to maintain a healthy love life between themselves, and it usually meant trouble with the Medicorps when this broke down.

Angela glanced at him. "I didn't think Clara laughed well at my remark. Is something wrong between you?"

"Oh, no," he declared hastily. "Clara is sometimes that way . . . doesn't catch a joke right off."

A page boy approached them where they stood in the rotunda and advised Conrad that his ship was ready.

"Honestly, Angela, I'll make it up, I promise."

"I know you will, darling. And at least I'm grateful you saved me from all those rocket jets in there." Angela raised her lips for a kiss and afterwards, as she pushed him towards the door, her slightly vacant face smiled at him.

Out on the ramp, Conrad found another pilot ready to take off. They made two wagers—first to reach the racing course, and winner in a six-lap heat around the six-hundred-mile hexagonal course.

They fired together and Conrad blasted his ship up on a thunderous column of flame that squeezed him into his seat. He was good at this and he knew he would win the lift to the course. On the course, though, if his opponent was any good at all, Conrad would probably lose, because he enjoyed slamming the ship around the course in his wasteful, swashbuckling style much more than merely winning the heat.

Conrad kept his drive on till the last possible second and then shot out his nose jets. The ship shuddered up through another hundred miles and came to a lolling halt near the starting buoys. The other pilot gasped when Conrad shouted at him over the intership, "The winner by all thirty heads!"

It was generally assumed that a race up to the course consisted of cutting all jets when you had enough lift, and using the nose brakes only to correct any overshot. "What did you do, just keep your power on and flip the ship around?" The other racer coasted up to Conrad's level and steadied with a brief forward burst.

They got the automatic signal from the starting buoy and went for the first turn, nose and nose, about half a mile apart. Conrad lost 5,000 yards on the first turn by shoving his power too hard against the starboard steering jets.

It made a pretty picture when a racer hammered its way around a turn that way with a fan of outside jets holding it in place. The other fellow made his turns cleanly, using mostly the driving jets for steering. But that didn't look like much to those who happened to flip on their television while this little heat was in progress. On every turn, Conrad lost a little in space, but not in the eye of the automatic televisor on the buoy marking the turn. As usual, he cut closer to the buoys than regulations allowed, to give the folks a show.

Without the slightest regret, Conrad lost the heat by a full two sides of the hexagon. He congratulated his opponent and watched the fellow let his ship down carefully towards earth on its tail jets. For a while Conrad lolled his ship around near the starting buoy and its probably watching eye, flipping through a series of complicated manœuvres with the steering jets.

Conrad did not like the grim countenance of outer space. The lifeless, gem-like blaze of cloud upon cloud of stars in the perspectiveless black repelled him. He liked rocket racing only because of the neat timing necessary, and possibly because the knowledge that he indulged in it scared poor old Bill Walden half to death.

Today the bleak aspect of the Galaxy harried his mind back upon its own problems. A particularly nasty association of Clara with Bill Walden and his snivelling kid kept dogging Conrad's mind and, as soon as stunting had exhausted his excess of fuel, he turned the ship to earth and sent it in with a short, spectacular burst.

Now that he stopped to consider it, Clara's strange behaviour had begun at about the same time that Bill Walden started cheating on the shifts. That kid Mary must have known something was going on, or she would not have done such a disgusting thing as to come to their apartment.

Conrad had let the rocket fall nose-down, until now it was screaming into the upper ionosphere. With no time to spare, he swivelled the ship on its guiding jets and opened the drive blast at the uprushing earth. He had just completed this wrenching manœuvre when two appalling things happened together.

Conrad suddenly knew, whether as a momentary leak from Bill's mind to his, or as a rapid calculation of his own, that Bill Walden and Clara shared a secret. At the same moment, something tore through his mind like fingers of chill wind. With seven gravities mashing him into the bucket-seat, he grunted curses past thin-stretched lips.

"Great blue psychiatrists! What in thirty strait-jackets is that three-headed fool trying to do, kill us both?"

Conrad just managed to raise his leaden hand and set the plummeting racer for automatic pilot before Bill Walden forced him out of the shift. In his last moment of consciousness, and in the shock of his overwhelming shame, Conrad felt the bitter irony that he could not cut the power and kill Bill Walden.

When Bill Walden became conscious of the thunderous clamour of the braking ship and the awful weight of deceleration into which he had shifted, the core of him froze. He was so terrified that he could not have thought of reshifting even had there been time.

His head rolled on the pad in spite of its weight, and he saw the earth coming at him like a monstrous swatter aimed at a fly. Between his fright and the inhuman gravity, he lost consciousness without ever seeing on the control panel the red warning that saved him: *Automatic Pilot.*

The ship settled itself on the ramp in a mushroom of fire. Bill regained awareness several seconds later. He was too shaken to do anything but sit there for a long time.

When at last he felt capable of moving, he struggled with the door till he found how to open it, and climbed down to the still-hot ramp he had landed on. It was at least a mile to the Rocket Club across the barren flat of the field, and he set out on foot. Shortly, however, a truck came speeding across to him.

The driver leaned out. "Hey, Conrad, what's the matter? Why didn't you pull the ship over to the hangars?"

With Conrad's make-up on, Bill felt he could probably get by. "Controls aren't working," he offered noncommittally.

At the club, a place he had never been to before in his life, Bill found an unused helicopter and started it with his wristband. He flew the machine into town to the landing station nearest his home.

He was doomed, he knew. Conrad certainly would report him for this. He had not intended to force the shift so early or so violently. Perhaps he had not intended to force it at all this time. But there was something in him more powerful than himself . . . a need to break the shift and be with Clara that now acted almost independently of him and certainly without regard for his safety.

Bill flew his craft carefully through the city traffic, working his way between the widely spaced towers with the uncertain hand of one to whom machines are not an extension of the body. He put the helicopter down at the landing station with some difficulty.

Clara would not be expecting him so early. From his apartment, as soon as he had changed make-up, he visiophoned her. It was strange how long and how carefully they needed to look at each other and how few words they could say.

Afterwards, he seemed calmer and went about getting ready with more efficiency. But when he found himself addressing the package of Conrad's clothes to his home, he chuckled bitterly.

It was when he went back to drop the package in the mail chute that he noticed the storage-room door ajar. He disposed of the package and went over to the door. Then he stood still, listening. He had to stop his own breathing to hear clearly.

Bill tightened himself and opened the door. He flipped on the light and saw Mary. The child sat on the floor in the corner with her knees drawn up against her chest. Between the knees and the chest, the frail wrists were crossed, the hands closed limply like— like those of a fœtus. The forehead rested on the knees so that, should the closed eyes stray open, they would be looking at the placid hands.

The sickening sight of the child squeezed down on his heart till the colour drained from his face. He went forward and knelt before her. His dry throat hammered with the words, *what have I done to you*, but he could not speak. The question of how long she might have been here, he could not bear to think.

He put out his hand, but he did not touch her. A shudder of revulsion shook him and he scrambled to his feet. He hurried back into the apartment with only one thought. He must get

someone to help her. Only the Medicorps could take care of a
situation like this.

As he stood at the visiophone, he knew that this involuntary
act of panic had betrayed all that he had ever thought and done.
He had to call the Medicorps. He could not face the result of his
own behaviour without them. Like a ghostly after-image, he saw
Clara's face on the screen. She was lost, cut off, with only himself
to depend on.

A part of him, a place where there were no voices and a great
tragedy, had been abruptly shut off. He stood stupidly confused
and disturbed about something he couldn't recall. The emotion
in his body suddenly had no referent. He stood like a badly
frightened animal while his heart slowed and blood seeped
again into whitened parenchymas, while tides of epinephrine
burned lower.

Remembering he must hurry, Bill left the apartment. It was
an apartment with its storage-room door closed, an apartment
without a storage-room.

From the moment that he walked in and took Clara in his
arms, he was not worried about being caught. He felt only the
great need for her. There seemed only one difference from the
first time and it was a good difference, because now Clara was so
tense and apprehensive. He felt a new tenderness for her, as
one might feel for a child. It seemed to him that there was no
end to the well of gentleness and compassion that was suddenly
in him. He was mystified by the depth of this feeling. He kissed
her again and again and petted her as one might a disturbed
child.

Clara said, "Oh Bill, we're doing wrong! Mary was here
yesterday!"

Whoever she meant, it had no meaning for him. He said, "It's
all right. You mustn't worry."

"She needs you, Bill, and I take you away from her."

Whatever it was she was talking about was utterly unimportant beside the fact that she was not happy herself. He soothed
her. "Darling, you mustn't worry about it. Let's be happy the
way we used to be."

He led her to a couch and they sat together, her head resting
on his shoulder.

"Conrad is worried about me. He knows something is wrong.

Oh, Bill, if he knew, he'd demand the worst penalty for you."

Bill felt the stone of fear come back in his chest. He thought, too, of Helen, of how intense her shame would be. Medicorps action would be machine-like, logical as a set of equation; they were very likely to take more drastic steps where the complaints would be so strong and no request for leniency forthcoming. Conrad knew now, of course. Bill had felt his hate.

It was nearing the end. Death would come to Bill with electronic fingers. A ghostly probing in his mind and suddenly . . .

Clara's great unhappiness and the way she turned her head into his shoulder to cry forced him to calm the rising panic in himself, and again to caress the fear from her.

Even later, when they lay where the moonlight thrust into the room an impalpable shaft of alabaster, he loved her only as a succour. Carefully, slowly, smoothing out her mind, drawing it away from all the other things, drawing it down into this one thing. Gathering all her mind into her senses and holding it there. Then quickly taking it away from her in a moaning spasm so that now she was murmuring, murmuring, palely drifting. Sleeping like a loved child.

For a long, long time he watched the white moon cut its arc across their window. He listened with a deep pleasure to her evenly breathing sleep. But slowly he realized that her breath had changed, that the body so close to his was tensing. His heart gave a great bound and tiny moths of horror fluttered along his back. He raised himself and saw that the eyes were open in the silver light. Even through the make-up he saw that they were Helen's eyes.

He did the only thing left for him. He shifted. But in that terrible instant he understood something he had not anticipated. In Helen's eyes there was not only intense shame over shifting into her hypoalter's home; there was not only the disgust with himself for breaking communication codes. He saw that, as a woman of the 20th Century might have felt, Helen hated Clara as a sexual rival. She hated Clara doubly because he had turned not to some other woman, but to the other part of herself whom she could never know.

As he shifted, Bill knew that the next light he saw would be on the adamant face of the Medicorps.

Major Paul Grey, with two other Medicorps officers, entered the Walden apartment about two hours after Bill left it to meet Clara. Major Grey was angry with himself. Important information on a case of communication breaks and drug refusal could be learned by letting it run its course under observation. But he had not intended Conrad Manz's life to be endangered, and certainly he would not have taken the slightest chance on what they found in the Walden apartment if he had expected it this early.

Major Grey blamed himself for what had happened to Mary Walden. He should have had the machines watching Susan and Mary at the same time that they were relaying wristband data for Bill and Conrad and for Helen and Clara to his office.

He had not done this because it was Susan's shift and he had not expected Mary to break it. Now he knew that Helen and Bill Walden had been quarrelling over the fact that Clara was cheating on Helen's shifts, and their conversations had directed the unhappy child's attention to the Manz couple. She had broken shift to meet them . . . looking for a loving father, of course.

Still—things would not have turned out so badly if Captain Thiel, Mary's school officer, had not attributed Susan Shorrs' disappearance only to poor drug acclimatization. Captain Thiel had naturally known that Major Grey was in town to prosecute Bill Walden, because the major had called on him to discuss the case. Yet it had not occurred to him, until eighteen hours after Susan's disappearance, that Mary might have forced the shift for some reason associated with her aberrant father.

By the time the captain advised him, Major Grey already knew that Bill had forced the shift on Conrad under desperate circumstances and he had decided to close in. He fully expected to find the father and daughter at the apartment, and now . . . it sickened him to see the child's demented condition and realize that Bill had left her there.

Major Grey could see at a glance that Mary Walden would not be accessible for days even with the best treatment. He left it to the other two officers to hospitalize the child and set out for the Manz apartment.

He used his master wristband to open the door there, and found a woman standing in the middle of the room, wrapped in

a sheet. He knew that this must be Helen Walden. It was odd
how ill-fitting Clara Manz's softly sensual make-up seemed, even
to a stranger, on the more rigidly composed face before him. He
guessed that Helen would wear colour higher on her cheeks and
the mouth would be done in severe lines. Certainly the present
haughty face struggled with its incongruous make-up as well as
the indignity of her dress.

She pulled the sheet tighter about her and said icily, "I will
not wear that woman's clothes."

Major Grey introduced himself and asked, "Where is Bill
Walden?"

"He shifted! He left me with . . . Oh, I'm so ashamed!"

Major Grey shared her loathing. There was no way to escape
the conditioning of childhood—sex relations between hyperalter
and hypoalter were more than outlawed, they were in themselves disgusting. If they were allowed, they could destroy this
civilization. Those idealists—they were almost all hypoalters,
of course—who wanted the old terminology changed didn't take
that into account. Next thing they'd want children to live with
their actual parents!

Major Grey stepped into the bedroom. Through the bathroom door beyond, he could see Conrad Manz changing his
make-up.

Conrad turned and eyed him bluntly. "Would you mind staying out of here till I'm finished? I've had about all I can take."

Major Grey shut the door and returned to Helen Walden. He
took a hypothalamic block from his own pharmacase and
handed it to her. "Here, you're probably on very low drug levels.
You'd better take this." He poured her a glass of pop from a
decanter and, while they waited for Conrad, he dialled the
nearest shifting station on the visiophone and ordered up an
emergency shifting costume for her.

When at last they were both dressed, made up to their satisfaction and drugged to his satisfaction, he had them sit on a
couch together across from him. They sat at opposite ends of it,
stiff with resentment at each other's presence.

Major Grey said calmly, "You realize that this matter is
coming to a Medicorps trial. It will be serious."

Major Grey watched their faces. On hers he saw grim determination. On Conrad's face he saw the heavy movement of

alarm. The man loved his wife. That was going to help. "It is necessary in a case such as this for the Medicorps to weigh your decisions along with the scientific evidence we will accumulate. Unfortunately, the number of laymen directly involved in this case—and not on trial—is only two, due to your peculiar marriage. If the hypoalters, Clara and Conrad, were married to other partners, we might call on as many as six involved persons and obtain a more equitable lay judgment. As it stands, the entire responsibility rests on the two of you."

Helen Walden was primly confident. "I don't see how we can fail to treat the matter with perfect logic. After all, it is not *we* who neglect our drug levels . . . They *were* refusing to take their drugs, weren't they?" she asked, hoping for the worst and certain she was right.

"Yes, this is drug refusal." Major Grey paused while she relished the answer. "But I must correct you in one impression. Your proper drug levels do not assure that you will act logically in this matter. The drugged mind *is* logical. However, its fundamental datum is that the drugs and drugged minds must be protected before everything else." He watched Conrad's face while he added, "Because of this, it is possible for you to arrive logically at a conclusion that . . . death is the required solution." He paused, looking at their white lips. Then he said, "Actually, other, more suitable solutions may be possible."

"But they *were* refusing their drugs," she said. "You talk as if you are defending them. Aren't you a Medicorps prosecutor?"

"I do not prosecute *people* in the ancient 20th Century sense, Mrs. Walden. I prosecute the acts of drug refusal and communication breaks. There is quite a difference."

"Well!" she said almost explosively. "I always knew Bill would get into trouble sooner or later with his wild, antisocial ideas. I never *dreamed* the Medicorps would take *his* side."

Major Grey held his breath, almost certain now that she would walk into the trap. If she did, he could save Clara Manz before the trial.

"After all, they have broken every communication code. They have refused the drugs, a defiance aimed at our very lives. They——"

"Shut up!" It was the first time Conrad Manz had spoken since he sat down. "The Medicorps spent weeks gathering evidence and preparing their recommendations. You haven't seen any of that and you've already made up your mind. How logical is that? It sounds as if you *want* your husband dead. Maybe the poor devil had some reason, after all, for what he did." On the man's face there was the nearest approach to hate that the drugs would allow.

Major Grey let his breath out softly. They were split permanently. She would have to trade him a mild decision on Clara in order to save Bill. And even there, if the subsequent evidence gave any slight hope, Major Grey believed now that he could work on Conrad to hang the lay judgment and let the Medicorps' scientific recommendation go through unmodified.

He let them stew in their cross-purposed silence for a while and then nailed home a disconcerting fact.

"I think I should remind you that there are few advantages to having your alter extinguished in the *mnemonic eraser*. A man whose hyperalter has been extinguished must report on his regular shift days to a hospital and be placed for five days in suspended animation. This is not very healthy for the body, but necessary. Otherwise, everyone's natural distaste for his own alter and the understandable wish to spend twice as much time living would generate schemes to have one's alter sucked out by the eraser. That happened extensively back in the 21st Century before the five-day suspension was required. It was also used as a 'cure' for schizophrenia, but it was, of course, only the brutal murder of innocent personalities."

Major Grey smiled grimly to himself. "Now I will have to ask you both to accompany me to the hospital. I will want you, Mrs. Walden, to shift at once to Mrs. Manz. Mr. Manz, you will have to remain under the close observation of an officer until Bill Walden tries to shift back. We have to catch him with an injection to keep him in shift."

The young medicop put the syringe aside and laid his hand on Bill Walden's forehead. He pushed the hair back out of Bill's eyes.

"There, Mr. Walden, you don't have to struggle now."

Bill let his breath out in a long sigh. "You've caught me. I can't shift any more, can I?"

"That's right, Mr. Walden. Not unless we want you to." The

young man picked up his medical equipment and stepped aside.

Bill noticed then the Medicorps officer standing in the background. The man was watching as though he contemplated some melancholy distance. "I am Major Grey, Bill. I'm handling your case."

Bill did not answer. He lay staring at the hospital ceiling. Then he felt his mouth open in a slow grin.

"What's funny?" Major Grey asked mildly.

"Leaving my hypoalter with my wife," Bill answered candidly. It had already ceased to be funny to him, but he saw Major Grey smile in spite of himself.

"They were quite upset when I found them. It must have been some scramble before that." Major Grey came over and sat in the chair vacated by the young man who had just injected Bill. "You know, Bill, we will need a complete analysis of you. We want to do everything we can to save you, but it will require your co-operation."

Bill nodded, feeling his chest tighten. Here it came. Right to the end they would be tearing him apart to find out what made him work.

Major Grey must have sensed Bill's bitter will to resist. His resonant voice was soft, his face kindly. "We must have your sincere desire to help. We can't force you to do anything."

"Except die," Bill said.

"Maybe helping us get the information that might save your life at the trial isn't worth the trouble to you. But your aberration has seriously disturbed the lives of several people. Don't you think you owe it to them to help us to prevent this sort of thing in the future?" Major Grey ran his hand through his whitening hair. "I thought you would like to know Mary will come through all right. We will begin shortly to acclimatize her to her new appointed parents, who will be visiting her each day. That will accelerate her recovery a great deal. Of course, right now she is still inaccessible."

The brutally clear picture of Mary alone in the storage-room crashed back into Bill's mind. After a while, in such slow stages that the beginning was hardly noticeable, he began to cry. The young medicop injected him with a sleeping compound, but not before Bill knew he would do whatever the Medicorps wanted.

The next day was crowded with battery after battery of tests. The interviews were endless. He was subjected to a hundred artificial situations and every reaction from his blood sugar to the frequency ranges of his voice was measured. They gave him only small amounts of drugs in order to test his reaction to them.

Late in the evening, Major Grey came by and interrupted an officer who was taking an electro-encephalogram for the sixth time after injection of a drug.

"All right, Bill, you have really given us co-operation. But after you've had your dinner, I hope you won't mind if I come to your room and talk with you for a little while."

When Bill finished eating, he waited impatiently in his room for the Medicorps officer. Major Grey came soon after. He shook his head at the mute question Bill shot at him.

"No, Bill. We will not have the results of your tests evaluated until late tomorrow morning. I can't tell you a thing until the trial in any case."

"When will that be?"

"As soon as the evaluation of your tests is in." Major Grey ran his hand over his smooth chin and seemed to sigh. "Tell me, Bill, how do you feel about your case? How did you get into this situation and what do you think about it now?" The officer sat in the room's only chair and motioned Bill to the cot.

Bill was astonished at his sudden desire to talk about his problem. He had to laugh to cover it up. "I guess I feel as if I am being condemned for trying to stay sober." Bill used the ancient word with a mock tone of righteousness that he knew the major would understand.

Major Grey smiled. "How do you feel when you're sober?"

Bill searched his face. "The way the ancient Moderns did, I guess. I feel what happens to me the *way* it happens to me, not the artificial way the drugs let it happen. I think there is a way for us to live without the drugs and really enjoy life. Have you ever cut down on your drugs, Major?"

The officer shook his head.

Bill smiled at him dreamily. "You ought to try it. It's as though a new life has suddenly opened up. Everything looks different to you.

"Look, with an average life span of a hundred years, each of us only lives fifty years and our alter lives the other fifty. Yet even on half-time we experience only about half the living we'd do if we didn't take the drugs. We would be able to feel the loves and hatreds and desires of life. No matter how many mistakes we made, we would be able occasionally to live those intense moments that made the ancients great."

Major Grey said tonelessly, "The ancients were great at killing, cheating and debasing one another. And they were worse sober than *drunk*." This time he did not smile at the word.

Bill understood the implacable logic before him. The logic that had saved man from himself by smothering his spirit. The carefully achieved logic of the drugs that had seized upon the disassociated personality, and engineered it into a smoothly running machine, where there was no unhappiness because there was no great happiness, where there was no crime except failure to take the drugs or cross the alter sex line. Without drugs, he was capable of fury and he felt it now.

"You should see how foolish these communication codes look when you are undrugged. This stupid hide-and-seek of shifting! These two-headed monsters simpering about their artificial morals and their endless prescriptions! They belong in *crazy* houses! What use is there in such a world? If we are all this sick, we should die . . ."

Bill stopped and there was suddenly a ringing silence in the barren little room.

Finally Major Grey said, "I think you can see, Bill, that your desire to live without drugs is incompatible with this society. It would be impossible for us to maintain in you an artificial need for the drugs that would be healthy. Only if we can clearly demonstrate that this aberration is not an inherent part of your personality can we do something medically or psycho-surgically about it."

Bill did not at first see the implication in this. When he did, he thought of Clara rather than of himself, and his voice was shaken. "Is it a localized aberration in Clara?"

Major Grey looked at him levelly. "I have arranged for you to be with Clara Manz a little while in the morning." He stood up and said good night and was gone.

Slowly, as if it hurt him to move, Bill turned off the light and lay on the cot in the semi-dark. After a while he could feel his heart begin to take hold and he started feeling better. It was as though a man who had thought himself permanently expatriated had been told, "Tomorrow, you walk just over that hill and you will be home."

All through the night he lay awake, alternating between panic and desperate longing in a cycle with which finally he became familiar. At last, as a rusty light of dawn reddened his silent room, he fell into a troubled sleep.

He started awake in broad daylight. An orderly was at the door with his breakfast tray. He could not eat, of course. After the orderly left, he hastily changed to a new hospital uniform and washed himself. He redid his make-up with a trembling hand, straightened the bedclothes and then he sat on the edge of the cot.

No one came for him.

The young medicop who had given him the injection that caught him in shift finally entered, and was standing near him before Bill was aware of his presence.

"Good morning, Mr. Walden. How are you feeling?"

Bill's wildly oscillating tensions froze at the point where he could only move helplessly with events and suffer a constant, unchangeable longing.

It was as if in a dream that they moved in silence together down the long corridors of the hospital and took the lift to an upper floor. The medicop opened the door to a room and let Bill enter. Bill heard the door close behind him.

Clara did not turn from where she stood looking out the window. Bill did not care that the walls of the chill little room were almost certainly recording every sight and sound. All his hunger was focused on the back of the girl at the window. The room seemed to ring with his racing blood. But he was slowly aware that something was wrong, and when at last he called her name, his voice broke.

Still without turning, she said in a strained monotone, "I want you to understand that I have consented to this meeting only because Major Grey has assured me it was necessary."

It was a long time before he could speak. "Clara, I need you."

She spun on him. "Have you no shame? You are married to my hyperalter—don't you understand that?" Her face was suddenly wet with tears and the intensity of her shame flamed at him from her cheeks. "How can Conrad ever forgive me for being with his hyperalter and talking about him? Oh, how can I have been so *mad?*"

"They have done something to you," he said, shaking with tension.

Her chin raised at this. She was defiant, he saw, though not towards himself—he no longer existed for her—but towards that part of herself which once had needed him and now no longer existed. "They have cured me," she declared. "They have cured me of everything but my shame, and they will help me get rid of that as soon as you leave this room."

Bill stared at her before leaving. Out in the corridor, the young medicop did not look him in the face. They went back to Bill's room and the officer left without a word. Bill lay down on his cot.

Presently Major Grey entered the room. He came over to the cot. "I'm sorry it had to be this way, Bill."

Bill's words came tonelessly from his dry throat. "Was it necessary to be cruel?"

"It was necessary to test the result of her psycho-surgery. Also, it will help her over her shame. She might otherwise have retained a seed of fear that she still loved you."

Bill did not feel anything any more. Staring at the ceiling, he knew there was no place left for him in this world and no one in it who needed him. The only person who had really needed him had been Mary, and he could not bear to think of how he had treated her. Now the Medicorps was efficiently curing the child of the hurt he had done her. They had already erased from Clara any need for him she had ever felt.

This seemed funny and he began to laugh. "Everyone is being cured of me."

"Yes, Bill. That is necessary." When Bill went on laughing, Major Grey's voice turned quite sharp. "Come with me. It's time for your trial."

The enormous room in which they held the trial was utterly barren. At the great oaken table around which they all sat, there were three Medicorps officers in addition to Major Grey.

Helen did not speak to Bill when they brought him in. He was placed on the same side of the table with an officer between them. Two orderlies stood behind Bill's chair. Other than these people, there was no one in the room.

The great windows were high above the floor and displayed only the blissful sky. Now and then Bill saw a flock of pigeons waft aloft on silver-turning wings. Everyone at the table except himself had a copy of his case report and they discussed it with clipped sentences. Between the stone floor and the vaulted ceiling, a subtle echolalia babbled about Bill's problem behind their human talk.

The discussion of the report lulled when Major Grey rapped on the table. He glanced unsmiling from face to face, and his voice hurried the ritualized words: "This is a court of medicine, co-joining the results of medical science and considered lay judgment to arrive at a decision in the case of patient Bill Walden. The patient is hospitalized for a history of drug refusal and communication breaks. We have before us the medical case record of patient Walden. Has everyone present studied this record?"

All at the table nodded.

"Do all present feel competent to pass judgment in this case?"

Again there came the agreement.

Major Grey continued, "It is my duty to advise you, in the presence of the patient, of the profound difference between a trial for simple drug refusal and one in which that aberration is compounded with communication breaks.

"It is true that no other aberration is possible when the drugs are taken as prescribed. After all, the drugs *are* the basis for our schizophrenic society. Nevertheless, simple drug refusal often is a mere matter of physiology, which is easy enough to remedy.

"A far more profound threat to our society is the break in communication. This generally is more deeply motivated in the patient, and is often inaccessible to therapy. Such a patient is driven to emotive explorations which place the various ancient passions, and the infamous art of *historical gesture*, such as 'give me liberty or give me death', above the welfare of society."

Bill watched the birds flash down the sky, a handful of heavenly coin. Never had it seemed to him so good to look at the sky. *If they hospitalize me,* he thought, *I will be content forever to sit and look from windows.*

"Our schizophrenic society," Major Grey was saying, "holds together and runs smoothly because, in each individual, the personality conflicts have been compartmentalized between hyperalter and hypoalter. On the social level, conflicting personalities are kept on opposite shifts and never contact each other. Or they are kept on shifts where contact is possible no more than one or two days out of ten. Bill Walden's break of shift is the type of behaviour designed to reactivate these conflicts, and to generate the destructive passions on which an undrugged mind feeds. Already illness and disrupted lives have resulted."

Major Grey paused and looked directly at Bill. "Exhaustive tests have demonstrated that your entire personality is involved. I might also say that the aberration to live without the drugs and to break communication codes *is* your personality. All these Medicorps officers are agreed on that diagnosis. It remains now for us of the Medicorps to sit with the laymen intimately involved and decide on the action to be taken. The only possible alternatives after that diagnosis are permanent hospitalization or . . . total removal of the personality by mnemonic erasure."

Bill could not speak. He saw Major Grey nod to one of the orderlies and felt the man pushing up his sleeve and injecting his nerveless arm. They were forcing him to shift, he knew, so that Conrad Manz could sit in on the trial and participate.

Helplessly, he watched the great sky blacken and the room dim and disappear.

Major Grey did not avert his face, as did the others, while the shift was in progress. Helen Walden, he saw, was dramatizing her shame at being present during a shift, but the Medicorps officers simply stared at the table. Major Grey watched the face of Conrad Manz take form while the man who was going to be tried faded.

Bill Walden had been without make-up, and as soon as he was sure Manz could hear him, Major Grey apologized. "I hope you won't object to this brief interlude in public without make-up. You are present at the trial of Bill Walden."

Conrad Manz nodded and Major Grey waited another full minute for the shift to complete itself before he continued. "Mr. Manz, during the two days you waited in the hospital for us to catch Walden in shift, I discussed this case quite thoroughly with you, especially as it applied to the case of Clara Manz, on which we were already working.

"You will recall that in the case of your wife, the Medicorps diagnosis was one of a clearly localized aberration. It was quite simple to apply the mnemonic eraser to that small section without disturbing in any way her basic personality. Medicorps agreement was for this procedure and the case did not come to trial, but simply went to operation, because lay agreement was obtained. First yourself and eventually—" Major Grey paused and let the memory of Helen's stubborn insistence that Clara die stir in Conrad's mind—"Mrs. Walden agreed with the Medicorps."

Major Grey let the room wait in silence for awhile. "The case of Bill Walden is quite different. The aberration involves the whole personality, and the alternative actions to be taken are permanent hospitalization or total erasure. In this case, I believe that Medicorps opinion will be divided as to proper action and—" Major Grey paused again and looked levelly at Conrad Manz—"this may be true, also, of the lay opinion."

"How's that, Major?" demanded the highest ranking Medicorps officer present, a colonel named Hart, a tall, handsome man on whom the military air was a becoming skin. "What do you mean about Medicorps opinion being divided?"

Major Grey answered quietly, "I'm holding out for hospitalization."

Colonel Hart's face reddened. He thrust it forward and straightened his back. "That's preposterous! This is a clear-cut case of a dangerous threat to our society, and we, let me remind you, are *sworn* to protect that society."

Major Grey felt very tired. It was, after all, difficult to understand why he always fought so hard against erasure of these aberrant cases. But he began with quiet determination. "The threat to society is effectively removed by either of the alternatives, hospitalization or total erasure. I think you can all see from Bill Walden's medical record that his is a well-rounded personality with a remarkable mind. In the environment of the 20th Century, he would have been an outstanding citizen, and possibly, if there had been more like him, our present society would have been better for it.

"Our history has been one of weeding out all personalities that did not fit easily into our drugged society. Today there are so few left that I have handled only one hundred and thirty-six in my entire career. . . ."

Major Grey saw that Helen Walden was tensing in her chair. He realized suddenly that she sensed better than he the effect he was having on the other men.

"We should not forget that each time we erase one of these personalities," he pressed on relentlessly, "society loses irrevocably a certain capacity for change. If we eliminate all personalities who do not fit, we may find ourselves without any minds capable of meeting future change. Our direct ancestors were largely the inmates of mental hospitals . . . we are fortunate *they* were not erased. Conrad Manz," he asked abruptly, "what is your opinion on the case of Bill Walden?"

Helen Walden started, but Conrad Manz shrugged his muscular shoulders. "Oh, hospitalize the three-headed monster!"

Major Grey snapped his eyes directly past Colonel Hart and fastened them on the Medicorps captain. "Your opinion, Captain?"

But Helen Walden was too quick. Before he could rap the table for order, she had her thin words hanging in the echoing room. "Having been Mr. Walden's wife for fifteen years, my sentiments naturally incline me to ask for hospitalization. That is why I may safely say, if Major Grey will pardon me, that the logic of the drugs does not entirely fail us in this situation."

Helen waited while all present got the idea that Major Grey had accused them of being illogical. "Bill's aberration has led to our daughter's illness. And think how quickly it contaminated Clara Manz! I cannot ask that society any longer expose itself, even to the extent of keeping Bill in the isolation of the hospital, for my purely sentimental reasons.

"As for Major Grey's closing remarks, I cannot see how it is fair to bring my husband to trial as a threat to society, if some future change is expected, in which a man of his behaviour would benefit society. Surely such a change could only be one that would ruin our present world, or Bill would hardly fit it. I would not want to save Bill or anyone else for such a future."

She did not have to say anything further. Both of the other Medicorps officers were now fully roused to their duty. Colonel

Hart, of course, "humphed" at the opinions of a woman and cast his with Major Grey. But the fate of Bill Walden was sealed.

Major Grey sat, weary and uneasy, as the creeping little doubts began. In the end, he would be left with the one big stone-heavy doubt . . . could he have gone through with this if he had not been drugged, and how would the logic of the trial look without drugs?

He became aware of the restiveness in the room. They were waiting for him, now that the decision was irrevocable. Without the drugs, he reflected, they might be feeling—what was the ancient word, *guilt*? No, that was what the criminal felt. *Remorse*? That would be what they should be feeling. Major Grey wished Helen Walden could be forced to witness the erasure. People did not realize what it was like.

What was it Bill had said? "You should see how foolish these communication codes look when you are undrugged. This stupid hide-and-seek of shifting. . . ."

Well, wasn't that a charge to be *inspected* seriously, if you were taking it seriously enough to kill the man for it? As soon as this case was completed, he would have to return to his city and blot himself out so that his own hyperalter, Ralph Singer, a painter of bad pictures and a useless fool, could waste five more days. To that man he lost half his possible living days. What earthly good was Singer?

Major Grey roused himself and motioned the orderly to inject Conrad Manz, so that Bill Walden would be forced back into shift.

"As soon as I have advised the patient of our decision, you will all be dismissed. Naturally, I anticipated this decision and have arranged for immediate erasure. After the erasure, Mr. Manz, you will be instructed to appear regularly for suspended animation."

For some reason, the first thing Bill Walden did when he became conscious of his surroundings was to look out the great window for the flock of birds. But they were gone.

Bill looked at Major Grey and said, "What are you going to do?"

The officer ran his hand back through his whitening hair, but he looked at Bill without wavering. "You will be erased."

Bill began to shake his head. "There is something wrong," he said.

"Bill . . ." the major began.

"There is something wrong," Bill repeated hopelessly. "Why must we be split so there is always something missing in each of us? Why must we be stupefied with drugs that keep us from knowing what we should feel? I was trying to live a better life. I did not want to hurt anyone."

"But you *did* hurt others," Major Grey said bluntly. "You would do so again if allowed to function in your own way in this society. Yet it would be insufferable to you to be hospitalized. You would be shut off forever from searching for another Clara Manz. And—there is no one else for you, is there?"

Bill looked up, his eyes cringing as though they stared at death. "No one else?" he asked vacantly. "No one?"

The two orderlies lifted him up by his arms, almost carrying him into the operating room. His feet dragged helplessly. He made no resistance as they lifted him on to the operating table and strapped him down.

Beside him was the great panel of the mnemonic eraser with its thousand unblinking eyes. The helmet-like prober cabled to this calculator was fastened about his skull, and he could no longer see the professor who was lecturing in the amphitheatre above. But along his body he could see the group of medical students. They were looking at him with great interest, too young not to let the human drama interfere with their technical education.

The professor, however, droned in a purely objective voice. "The mnemonic eraser can selectively shunt from the brain any identifiable category of memory, and erase the synaptic patterns associated with its translation into action. Circulating memory is disregarded. The machine only locates and shunts out those energies present as permanent memory. These are there in part as permanently echoing frequencies in closed cytoplasmic systems. These systems are in contact with the rest of the nervous system only during the phenomenon of remembrance. Remembrance occurs when, at all the synapses in a given network 'y', the permanently echoing frequencies are duplicated as transient circulating frequencies.

"The objective in a total operation of the sort before us is to distinguish all the stored permanent frequencies, typical of the personality you wish to extinguish, from the frequencies typical of the other personality present in the brain."

Major Grey's face, very tired, but still wearing a mask of adamant reassurance, came into Bill's vision. "There will be a few moments of drug-induced terror, Bill. That is necessary for the operation. I hope knowing it beforehand will help you ride with it. It will not be for long." He squeezed Bill's shoulder and was gone.

"The trick was learned early in our history, when this type of total operation was more often necessary," the professor continued. "It is really quite simple to extinguish one personality while leaving the other undisturbed. The other personality in the case before us has been drug-immobilized to keep this one from shifting. At the last moment, this personality before us will be drug-stimulated to bring it to the highest possible pitch of total activity. This produces utterly disorganized activity, every involved neutron and synapse being activated simultaneously by the drug. It is then a simple matter for the mnemonic eraser to locate all permanently echoing frequencies involved in this personality and suck them into its receiver."

Bill was suddenly aware that a needle had been thrust into his arm. Then it was as though all the terror, panic and traumatic incidents of his whole life leaped into his mind. All the pleasant experiences and feelings he had ever known were there, too, but were transformed into terror.

A bell was ringing with regular strokes. Across the panel of the mnemonic eraser, the tiny counting lights were alive with movement.

There was in Bill a fright, a demand for survival so great that it could not be felt.

It was actually from an island of complete calm that part of him saw the medical students rising dismayed and white-faced from their seats. It was apart from himself that his body strained to lift some mountain and filled the operating amphitheatre with shrieking echoes. And all the time the thousand eyes of the mnemonic eraser flickered in swift patterns, a silent measure of the cells and circuits of his mind.

Abruptly the tiny red counting lights went off, a red beam glowed with a burr of warning. Someone said, "Now!" The mind of Bill Walden flashed along a wire as electrical energy, and, converted on the control panel into mechanical energy, it spun a small ratchet counter.

"Please sit down," the professor said to the shaken students. "The drug that has kept the other personality immobilized is being counteracted by this next injection. Now that the sickly personality has been dissipated, the healthy one can be brought back rapidly.

"As you are aware, the synapse operates on the binary 'yes-no' choice system of an electronic calculator. All synapses which were involved in the diseased personality have now been reduced to an atypical, uniform threshold. Thus they can be re-educated in new patterns by the healthy personality remaining. . . . There, you see the countenance of the healthy personality appearing."

It was Conrad Manz who looked up at them with a wry grin. He rotated his shoulders to loosen them. "How many of you pushed old Bill Walden around? He left me with some sore muscles. Well, I did that often enough to him. . . ."

Major Grey stood over him, face sick and white with the horror of what he had seen. "According to law, Mr. Manz, you and your wife are entitled to five rest days on your next shift. When they are over, you will, of course, report for suspended animation for what would have been your hyperalter's shift."

Conrad Manz's grin shrank and vanished. "*Would* have been? Bill is—gone?"

"Yes."

"I never thought I'd miss him." Conrad looked as sick as Major Grey felt. "It makes me feel—I don't know if I can explain it—sort of *amputated*. As though something's wrong with me because everybody else has an alter and I don't. Did the poor son of a strait-jacket suffer much?"

"I'm afraid he did."

Conrad Manz lay still for a moment with his eyes closed and his mouth thin with pity and remorse. "What will happen to Helen?"

"She'll be all right," Major Grey said. "There will be Bill's insurance, naturally, and she won't have much trouble finding another husband. That kind never seems to."

"Five rest days?" Conrad repeated. "Is that what you said?"

He sat up and swung his legs off the table, and he was grinning again. "I'll get in a whole shift of jet-skiing! No, wait—I've got a date with the wife of a friend of mine out at the rocket grounds. I'll take Clara out there; she'll like some of the men."

Major Grey nodded abstractedly. "Good idea." He shook hands with Conrad Manz, wished him fun on his rest shift, and left.

Taking a helicopter back to his city, Major Grey thought of his own hyperalter, Ralph Singer. He'd often wished that the silly fool could be erased. Now he wondered how it would be to have only one personality, and, wondering, realized that Conrad Manz had been right—it *would* be like amputation, the shameful distinction of living in a schizophrenic society with no alter.

No, Bill Walden had been wrong, completely wrong, both about drugs and being split into two personalities. What one made up in pleasure through not taking drugs was more than lost in the suffering of conflict, frustration and hostility. And having an alter—any kind, even one as useless as Singer—meant, actually, *not being alone.*

Major Grey parked the helicopter and found a shifting station. He took off his make-up, addressed and mailed his clothes, and waited for the shift to come.

It was a pretty wonderful society he lived in, he realized. He wouldn't trade it for the kind Bill Walden had wanted. Nobody in his right mind would.

BRIDGE

by James Blish

I

A SCREECHING tornado was rocking the Bridge when the alarm sounded; it was making the whole structure shudder and sway. This was normal and Robert Helmuth barely noticed it. There was always a tornado shaking the Bridge. The whole planet was enswathed in tornadoes, and worse.

The scanner on the foreman's board had given 114 as the sector of the trouble. That was at the northwestern end of the Bridge, where it broke off, leaving nothing but the raging clouds of ammonia crystals and methane, and a sheer drop thirty miles to the invisible surface. There were no ultraphone "eyes" at that end which gave a general view of the area—in so far as any general view was possible—because both ends of the Bridge were incomplete.

With a sigh Helmuth put the beetle into motion. The little car, as flat-bottomed and thin through as a bed-bug, got slowly under way on its ball-bearing races, guided and held firmly to the surface of the Bridge by ten close-set flanged rails. Even so, the hydrogen gales made a terrific siren-like shrieking between the edge of the vehicle and the deck, and the impact of the falling drops of ammonia upon the curved roof was as heavy and deafening as a rain of cannon balls. As a matter of fact, they weighed almost as much as cannon balls here, though they were not much bigger than ordinary raindrops. Every so often, too, there was a blast, accompanied by a dull orange glare, which made the car, the deck, and the Bridge itself buck savagely.

These blasts were below, however, on the surface. While they shook the structure of the Bridge heavily, they almost never interfered with its functioning, and could not, in the very nature of things, do Helmuth any harm.

Had any real damage ever been done, it would never have been repaired. There was no one on Jupiter to repair it.

The Bridge, actually, was building itself. Massive, alone, and lifeless, it grew in the black deeps of Jupiter.

The Bridge had been well-planned. From Helmuth's point of view almost nothing could be seen of it, for the beetle tracks ran down the centre of the deck, and in the darkness and perpetual storm even ultrawave-assisted vision could not penetrate more than a few hundred yards at the most. The width of the Bridge was eleven miles; its height, thirty miles; its length, deliberately unspecified in the plans, fifty-four miles at the moment—a squat, colossal structure, built with engineering principles, methods, materials and tools never touched before—

For the very good reason that they would have been impossible anywhere else. Most of the Bridge, for instance, was made of ice: a marvellous structural material under a pressure of a million atmospheres, at a temperature of $-94\,°C$. Under such conditions, the best structural steel is a friable, talc-like powder, and aluminium becomes a peculiar, transparent substance that splits at a tap.

Back home, Helmuth remembered, there had been talk of starting another Bridge on Saturn, and perhaps still later, on Uranus, too. But that had been politicians' talk. The Bridge was almost five thousand miles below the visible surface of Jupiter's atmosphere, and its mechanisms were just barely manageable. The bottom of Saturn's atmosphere had been sounded at sixteen thousand eight hundred and seventy-eight miles, and the temperature there was below $-150\,°C$. There even pressure-ice would be immovable, and could not be worked with anything except itself. And as for Uranus . . .

As far as Helmuth was concerned, Jupiter was quite bad enough.

The beetle crept within sight of the end of the Bridge and stopped automatically. Helmuth set the vehicle's eyes for highest penetration, and examined the nearby beams.

The great bars were as close-set as screening. They had to be, in order to support even their own weight, let alone the weight of the components of the Bridge. The whole web-work was flexing and fluctuating to the harpist-fingered gale, but it had been designed to do that. Helmuth could never help being alarmed by the movement, but habit assured him that he had nothing to fear from it.

He took the automatics out of the circuit and inched the beetle forward manually. This was only Sector 113, and the Bridge's own Wheatstone-bridge scanning system—there was no electronic device anywhere on the Bridge, since it was impossible to maintain a vacuum on Jupiter—said that the trouble was in Sector 114. The boundary of Sector 114 was still fully fifty feet away.

It was a bad sign. Helmuth scratched nervously in his red beard. Evidently there was really cause for alarm—real alarm, not just the deep, grinding depression which he always felt while working on the Bridge. Any damage serious enough to halt the beetle a full sector short of the trouble area was bound to be major.

It might even turn out to be the disaster which he had felt lurking ahead of him ever since he had been made foreman of the Bridge—that disaster which the Bridge itself could not repair, sending man reeling home from Jupiter in defeat.

The secondaries cut in and the beetle stopped again. Grimly, Helmuth opened the switch and sent the beetle creeping across the invisible danger line. Almost at once, the car tilted just perceptibly to the left, and the screaming of the winds between its edges and the deck shot up the scale, sirening in and out of the soundless-dogwhistle range with an eeriness that set Helmuth's teeth on edge. The beetle itself fluttered and chattered like an alarm-clock hammer between the surface of the deck and the flanges of the tracks.

Ahead there was still nothing to be seen but the horizontal driving of the clouds and the hail, roaring along the length of the Bridge, out of the blackness into the beetle's fanlights, and onward into blackness again towards the horizon no eye would ever see.

Thirty miles below, the fusillade of hydrogen explosions continued. Evidently something really wild was going on on the surface. Helmuth could not remember having heard so much activity in years.

There was a flat, especially heavy crash, and a long line of fuming orange fire came pouring down the seething atmosphere into the depths, feathering horizontally like the mane of a Lipizzan horse, directly in front of Helmuth. Instinctively, he winced and drew back from the board, although that stream of flame actually was only a little less cold than the rest of the streaming gases, far too cold to injure the Bridge.

In the momentary glare, however, he saw something—an upward twisting of shadows, patterned but obviously unfinished, fluttering in silhouette against the hydrogen cataract's lurid light.

The end of the Bridge.

Wrecked.

Helmuth grunted involuntarily and backed the beetle away. The flare dimmed; the light poured down the sky and fell away into the raging sea below. The scanner clucked with satisfaction as the beetle recrossed the line into Zone 113.

He turned the body of the vehicle 180°, presenting its back to the dying torrent. There was nothing further that he could do at the moment on the Bridge. He scanned his control board— a ghost image of which was cast across the scene on the Bridge —for the blue button marked *Garage*, punched it savagely, and tore off his helmet.

Obediently, the Bridge vanished.

II

Dillon was looking at him.

"Well?" the civil engineer said. "What's the matter, Bob? Is it bad——?"

Helmuth did not reply for a moment. The abrupt transition from the storm-ravaged deck of the Bridge to the quiet, placid air of the control shack on Jupiter V was always a shock. He had never been able to anticipate it, let alone become accustomed to it; it was worse each time, not better.

He put the helmet down carefully in front of him and got up, moving carefully upon shaky legs; feeling implicit in his own body the enormous pressures and weights his guiding intelligence had just quitted. The fact that the gravity on the foreman's deck was as weak as that of most of the habitable asteroids only made the contrast greater, and his need for caution in walking more extreme.

He went to the big porthole and looked out. The unworn, tumbled, monotonous surface of airless Jupiter V looked almost homey after the perpetual holocaust of Jupiter itself. But there was an overpowering reminder of that holocaust—for through the thick quartz the face of the giant planet stared at him, across only one hundred and twelve thousand and six hundred miles: a sphere-section occupying almost all of the sky except the near horizon. It was crawling with colour, striped and blotched with the eternal, frigid, poisonous storming of its atmosphere, spotted with the deep planet-sized shadows of farther moons.

Somewhere down there, six thousand miles below the clouds that boiled in his face, was the Bridge. The Bridge was thirty miles high and eleven miles wide and fifty-four miles long— but it was only a sliver, an intricate and fragile arrangement of ice-crystals beneath the bulging, racing tornadoes.

On Earth, even in the West, the Bridge would have been the mightiest engineering achievement of all history, could the Earth have borne its weight at all. But on Jupiter, the Bridge was as precarious and perishable as a snowflake.

"Bob?" Dillon's voice asked. "You seem more upset than usual. Is it serious?" Helmuth turned. His superior's worn young face, lantern-jawed and crowned by black hair already beginning to grey at the temples, was alight both with love for the Bridge and the consuming ardour of the responsibility he had to bear. As always, it touched Helmuth, and reminded him that the implacable universe had, after all, provided one warm corner in which human beings might huddle together.

"Serious enough," he said, forming the words with difficulty against the frozen inarticulateness Jupiter forced upon him. "But not fatal, as far as I could see. There's a lot of hydrogen vulcanism on the surface, especially at the northwest end, and it looks like there must have been a big blast under the cliffs. I saw what looked like the last of a series of fireballs."

Dillon's face relaxed while Helmuth was talking, slowly, line by engraved line. "Oh. Just a flying chunk, then."

"I'm almost sure that's what it was. The cross-draughts are heavy now. The Spot and the STD are due to pass each other some time next week, aren't they? I haven't checked, but I can feel the difference in the storms."

"So the chunk got picked up and thrown through the end of the Bridge. A big piece?"

Helmuth shrugged. "That end is all twisted away to the left, and the deck is burst to flinders. The scaffolding is all gone, too, of course. A pretty big piece, all right, Charity—two miles through at a minimum."

Dillon sighed. He, too, went to the window, and looked out. Helmuth did not need to be a mind reader to know what he was looking at. Out there, across the stony waste of Jupiter V plus one hundred and twelve thousand and six hundred miles of space, the South Tropical Disturbance was streaming towards the great Red Spot, and would soon overtake it. When the whirling funnel of the STD—more than big enough to suck three Earths into deep-freeze—passed the planetary island of sodium-tainted ice which was the Red Spot, the Spot would follow it for a few thousand miles, at the same time rising closer to the surface of the atmosphere.

Then the Spot would sink again, drifting back towards the incredible jet of stress-fluid which kept it in being—a jet fed by no one knew what forces at Jupiter's hot, rocky, twenty-two-thousand-mile core, under sixteen thousand miles of eternal ice. During the entire passage, the storms all over Jupiter became especially violent; and the Bridge had been forced to locate in anything but the calmest spot on the planet, thanks to the uneven distribution of the few permanent land-masses.

Helmuth watched Dillon with a certain compassion, tempered with mild envy. Charity Dillon's unfortunate given name betrayed him as the son of a hangover, the only male child of a Witness family which dated back to the great Witness Revival of 2003. He was one of the hundreds of government-drafted experts who had planned the Bridge, and he was as obsessed by the Bridge as Helmuth was—but for different reasons.

Helmuth moved back to the port, dropping his hand gently upon Dillon's shoulder. Together they looked at the screaming straw yellows, brick reds, pinks, oranges, browns, even blues and greens that Jupiter threw across the ruined stone of its innermost satellite. On Jupiter V, even the shadows had colour.

Dillon did not move. He said at last: "Are you pleased, Bob?"

"Pleased?" Helmuth said in astonishment. "No. It scares me white; you know that. I'm just glad that the whole Bridge didn't go."

"You're quite sure?" Dillon said quietly.

Helmuth took his hand from Dillon's shoulder and returned to his seat at the central desk. "You've no right to needle me for something I can't help," he said, his voice even lower than Dillon's. "I work on Jupiter four hours a day—not actually, because we can't keep a man alive for more than a split second down there—but my eyes and my ears and my mind are there, on the Bridge, four hours a day. Jupiter is not a nice place. I don't like it. I won't pretend I do.

"Spending four hours a day in an environment like that over a period of years—well, the human mind instinctively tries to adapt, even to the unthinkable. Sometimes I wonder how I'll behave when I'm put back in Chicago again. Sometimes I can't remember anything about Chicago except vague generalities, sometimes I can't even believe there is such a place as Earth— how could there be, when the rest of the universe is like Jupiter, or worse?"

"I know," Dillon said. "I've tried several times to show you that isn't a very reasonable frame of mind."

"I know it isn't. But I can't help how I feel. No, I don't think the Bridge will last. It can't last; it's all wrong. But I don't *want* to see it go. I've just got sense enough to know that one of these days Jupiter is going to sweep it away."

He wiped an open palm across the control boards, snapping all the toggles "Off" with a sound like the fall of a double-handful of marbles on a pane of glass. "Like that, Charity! And I work four hours a day, every day, on the Bridge. One of these days, Jupiter is going to destroy the Bridge. It'll go flying away in little flinders into the storms. My mind will be there, super-vising some puny job, and my mind will go flying away along with my mechanical eyes and ears—still trying to adapt to the unthinkable, tumbling away into the winds and the flames and the rains and the darkness and the pressure and the cold."

"Bob, you're deliberately running away with yourself. Cut it out. Cut it out, I say!"

Helmuth shrugged, putting a trembling hand on the edge of the board to steady himself. "All right. I'm all right, Charity.

I'm here, aren't I? Right here on Jupiter V, in no danger, in no danger at all. The Bridge is one hundred and twelve thousand and six hundred miles away from here. But when the day comes that the Bridge is swept away——

"Charity, sometimes I imagine you ferrying my body back to the cosy nook it came from, while my soul goes tumbling and tumbling through millions of cubic miles of poison. All right, Charity, I'll be good. I won't think about it out loud; but you can't expect me to forget it. It's on my mind; I can't help it, and you should know that."

"I do," Dillon said, with a kind of eagerness. "I do, Bob. I'm only trying to help, to make you see the problem as it is. The Bridge isn't really that awful, it isn't worth a single nightmare."

"Oh, it isn't the Bridge that makes me yell out when I'm sleeping," Helmuth said, smiling bitterly. "I'm not that ridden by it yet. It's while I'm awake that I'm afraid the Bridge will be swept away. What I sleep with is a fear of myself."

"That's a sane fear. You're as sane as any of us," Dillon insisted, fiercely solemn. "Look, Bob. The Bridge isn't a monster. It's a way we've developed for studying the behaviour of materials under specific conditions of temperament, pressure, and gravity. Jupiter isn't Hell, either; it's a set of conditions. The Bridge is the laboratory we set up to work with those conditions."

"It isn't going anywhere. It's a bridge to no place."

"There aren't many *places* on Jupiter," Dillon said, missing Helmuth's meaning entirely. "We put the Bridge on an island in the local sea because we needed solid ice we could sink the caissons in. Otherwise, it wouldn't have mattered where we put it. We could have floated it on the sea itself, if we hadn't wanted to fix it in order to measure storm velocities and such things."

"I know that," Helmuth said.

"But, Bob, you don't show any signs of understanding it. Why, for instance, should the Bridge *go* any place? It isn't even, properly speaking, a bridge at all. We only call it that because we used some bridge engineering principles in building it. Actually, it's much more like a travelling crane—an extremely heavy-duty overhead rail line. It isn't going anywhere because it hasn't any place interesting to go, that's all. We're extending it to cover as much territory as possible, and to increase its stability, not to span the distance between places. There's no point to reproaching it because it doesn't span a real gap— between, say, Dover and Calais. It's a bridge to knowledge, and that's far more important. Why can't you see that?"

"I can see that; that's what I was talking about," Helmuth said, trying to control his impatience. "I have as much common sense as the average child. What I was trying to point out is that meeting colossalness with colossalness—out here—is a mug's game. It's a game Jupiter will always win, without the slightest effort. What if the engineers who built the Dover–Calais bridge had been limited to broomstraws for their structural members? They could have got the bridge up somehow, sure, and made it strong enough to carry light traffic on a fair day. But what would you have had left of it after the first winter storm came down the Channel from the North Sea? The whole approach is idiotic!"

"All right," Dillon said reasonably. "You have a point. Now you're being reasonable. What better approach have you to suggest? Should we abandon Jupiter entirely because it's too big for us?"

"No," Helmuth said. "Or maybe, yes. I don't know. I don't have any easy answer. I just know that this one is no answer at all—it's just a cumbersome evasion."

Dillon smiled. "You're depressed, and no wonder. Sleep it off, Bob, if you can—you might even come up with that answer. In the meantime—well, when you stop to think about it, the surface of Jupiter isn't any more hostile, inherently, than the surface of Jupiter V, except in degree. If you stepped out of this building naked, you'd die just as fast as you would on Jupiter. Try to look at it that way."

Helmuth, looking forward into another night of dreams, said: "That's the way I look at it now."

III

There were three yellow "Critical" signals lit on the long gang board when Helmuth passed through the gang deck on the way back to duty. All of them, as usual, were concentrated on Panel 9, where Eva Chavez worked.

Eva, despite her Latin name—such once-valid tickets no longer meant anything among Earth's uniformly mixed-race population—was a big girl, vaguely blonde, who cherished a passion for the Bridge. Unfortunately, she was apt to become enthralled by the sheer Cosmicness of it all, precisely at the moments when cold analysis and split-second decisions were most crucial.

Helmuth reached over her shoulder, cut her out of the circuit except as an observer, and donned the co-operator's helmet. The incomplete new shoals caisson sprang into being around him. Breakers of boiling hydrogen seethed seven hundred feet up along its slanted sides—breakers that never subsided, but simply were torn away into flying spray.

There was a spot of dull orange near the top of the north face of the caisson, crawling slowly towards the pediment of the nearest truss. Catalysis——

Or cancer, as Helmuth could not help but think of it. On this bitter, violent monster of a planet, even the tiny specks of calcium carbide were deadly. At these wind velocities, such specks imbedded themselves in everything; and at fifteen million pounds per square inch, pressure ice catalyzed by sodium took up ammonia and carbon dioxide, building protein-like compounds in a rapid, deadly chain of decay:

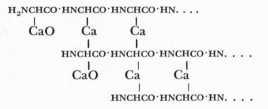

For a second, Helmuth watched it grow. It was, after all, one of the incredible possibilities the Bridge had been built to study. On Earth, such a compound, had it occurred at all, might have grown porous, bony, and quite strong. Here, under nearly eight times the gravity, the molecules were forced to assemble in strict aliphatic order, but in cross section their arrangement was hexagonal, as if the stuff would become an aromatic compound if it only could. Even here it was moderately strong in cross section—but along the long axis it smeared like graphite, the calcium atoms readily surrendering their valence hold on one carbon atom to grab hopefully for the next one in line——

No stuff to hold up the piers of humanity's greatest engineering project. Perhaps it was suitable for the ribs of some Jovian jellyfish, but in a Bridge-caisson, it was cancer.

There was a scraper mechanism working on the edge of the lesion, flaking away the shearing aminos and laying down new ice. In the meantime, the decay of the caisson-face was working deeper. The scraper could not possibly get at the core of the trouble—which was not the calcium carbide dust, with which the atmosphere was charged beyond redemption, but was instead one imbedded sodium speck which was taking no part in the reaction—fast enough to extirpate it. It could barely keep pace with the surface spread of the disease.

And laying new ice over the surface of the wound was worthless. At this rate, the whole caisson would slough away and melt like butter, within an hour, under the weight of the Bridge above it.

Helmuth sent the futile scraper aloft. Drill for it? No—too deep already, and location unknown.

Quickly he called two borers up from the shoals below, where constant blasting was taking the foundation of the caisson deeper and deeper into Jupiter's dubious "soil". He drove both blind, fire-snouted machines down into the lesion.

The bottom of that sore turned out to be forty-five metres within the immense block. Helmuth pushed the red button all the same.

The borers blew up, with a heavy, quite invisible blast, as they had been designed to do. A pit appeared on the face of the caisson.

The nearest truss bent upward in the wind. It fluttered for a moment, trying to resist. It bent farther.

Deprived of its major attachment, it tore free suddenly, and went whirling away into the blackness. A sudden flash of lightning picked it out for a moment, and Helmuth saw it dwindling like a bat with torn wings being borne away by a cyclone.

The scraper scuttled down into the pit and began to fill it with ice from the bottom. Helmuth ordered down a new truss and a squad of scaffolders. Damage of this order took time to repair. He watched the tornado tearing ragged chunks from the edges of the pit until he was sure that the catalysis had stopped.

Then, suddenly, prematurely, dismally tired, he took off the helmet.

He was astounded by the white fury that masked Eva's big-boned, mildly pretty face.

"You'll blow the Bridge up yet, won't you?" she said, evenly, without preamble. "Any pretext will do!"

Baffled, Helmuth turned his head helplessly away; but that was no better. The suffused face of Jupiter peered swollenly through the picture-port, just as it did on the foreman's desk.

He and Eva and Charity and the gang and the whole of satellite V were falling forward towards Jupiter; their uneventful cooped-up lives on Jupiter V were utterly unreal compared to the four hours of each changeless day spent on Jupiter's ever-changing surface. Every new day brought their minds, like ships out of control, closer and closer to that gaudy inferno.

There was no other way for a man—or a woman—on Jupiter V to look at the giant planet. It was simple experience, shared by all of them, that planets do not occupy four-fifths of the whole sky, unless the observer is himself up there in that planet's sky, falling, falling faster and faster——

"I have no intention," he said tiredly, "of blowing up the Bridge. I wish you could get it through your head that I want the Bridge to stay up—even though I'm not starry-eyed to the point of incompetence about the project. Did you think that rotten spot was going to go away by itself when you'd painted it over? Didn't you know that——"

Several helmeted, masked heads nearby turned blindly towards the sound of his voice. Helmuth shut up. Any distracting conversation or activity was taboo, down here in the gang room. He motioned Eva back to duty.

The girl donned her helmet obediently enough, but it was plain from the way her normally full lips were thinned that she thought Helmuth had ended the argument only in order to have the last word.

Helmuth strode to the thick pillar which ran down the central axis of the shack, and mounted the spiralling cleats towards his own foreman's cubicle. Already he felt in anticipation the weight of the helmet upon his own head.

Charity Dillon, however, was already wearing the helmet; he was sitting in Helmuth's chair.

Charity was characteristically oblivious of Helmuth's entrance. The Bridge operator must learn to ignore, to be utterly unconscious of anything happening around his body except the inhuman sounds of signals; must learn to heed only those senses which report something going on thousands of miles away.

Helmuth knew better than to interrupt him. Instead, he watched Dillon's white, blade-like fingers roving with blind sureness over the controls.

Dillon, evidently, was making a complete tour of the Bridge —not only from end to end, but up and down, too. The tally board showed that he had already activated nearly two-thirds of the ultraphone eyes. That meant that he had been up all night at the job; had begun it immediately after last talking to Helmuth.

Why?

With a thrill of unfocused apprehension, Helmuth looked at the foreman's jack, which allowed the operator here in the cubicle to communicate with the gang when necessary, and which kept him aware of anything said or done at gang boards.

It was plugged in.

Dillon sighed suddenly, took the helmet off, and turned.

"Hello, Bob," he said. "Funny about this job. You can't see, you can't hear, but when somebody's watching you, you feel a sort of pressure on the back of your neck. ESP, maybe. Ever felt it?"

"Pretty often, lately. Why the grand tour, Charity?"

"There's to be an inspection," Dillon said. His eyes met Helmuth's. They were frank and transparent. "A mob of Western officials, coming to see that their eight billion dollars isn't being wasted. Naturally, I'm a little anxious to see that they find everything in order."

"I see," Helmuth said. "First time in five years, isn't it?"

"Just about. What was that dust-up down below just now? Somebody—you, I'm sure, from the drastic handiwork involved —bailed Eva out of a mess, and then I heard her talk about your wanting to blow up the Bridge. I checked the area when I heard the fracas start, and it did seem as if she had let things go rather far, but—— What was it all about?"

Dillon ordinarily hadn't the guile for cat-and-mouse games, and he had never looked less guileful now. Helmuth said carefully, "Eva was upset, I suppose. On the subject of Jupiter we're all of us cracked by now, in our different ways. The way she was dealing with the catalysis didn't look to me to be suitable—a difference of opinion, resolved in my favour because I had the authority, Eva didn't. That's all."

"Kind of an expensive difference, Bob. I'm not niggling by nature, you know that. But an incident like that while the commission is here——"

"The point is," Helmuth said, "are we to spend an extra ten thousand, or whatever it costs to replace a truss and reinforce a caisson, or are we to lose the whole caisson—and as much as a third of the whole Bridge along with it?"

"Yes, you're right there, of course. That could be explained, even to a pack of senators. But—it would be difficult to have to explain it very often. Well, the board's yours, Bob. You could continue my spot-check, if you've time."

Dillon got up. Then he added suddenly, as if it were forced out of him:

"Bob, I'm trying to understand your state of mind. From what Eva said, I gather that you've made it fairly public. I . . . I don't think it's a good idea to infect your fellow workers with your own pessimism. It leads to sloppy work. I know that regardless of your own feelings you won't countenance sloppy work, but one foreman can do only so much. And you're making extra work for yourself—not for me, but for yourself—by being openly gloomy about the Bridge.

"You're the best man on the Bridge, Bob, for all your grousing about the job, and your assorted misgivings. I'd hate to see you replaced."

"A threat, Charity?" Helmuth said softly.

"*No.* I wouldn't replace you unless you actually went nuts, and I firmly believe that your fears in that respect are groundless. It's a commonplace that only sane men suspect their own sanity, isn't it?"

"It's a common misconception. Most psychopathic obsessions begin with a mild worry."

Dillon made as if to brush that subject away. "Anyhow, I'm

not threatening; I'd fight to keep you here. But my say-so only covers Jupiter V; there are people higher up on Ganymede, and people higher yet back in Washington—and in this inspecting commission.

"Why don't you try to look on the bright side for a change? Obviously the Bridge isn't ever going to inspire you. But you might at least try thinking about all those dollars piling up in your account every hour you're on this job, and about the bridges and ships and who knows what-all that you'll be building, at any fee you ask, when you get back down to Earth. All under the magic words, 'One of the men who built the Bridge on Jupiter!' "

Charity was bright red with embarrassment and enthusiasm. Helmuth smiled.

"I'll try to bear it in mind, Charity," he said. "When is this gaggle of senators due to arrive?"

"They're on Ganymede now, taking a breather. They came directly from Washington without any routing. I suppose they'll make a stop at Callisto before they come here. They've something new on their ship, I'm told, that lets them flit about more freely than the usual uphill transport can."

An icy lizard suddenly was nesting in Helmuth's stomach, coiling and coiling but never settling itself. The room blurred. The persistent nightmare was suddenly almost upon him— already.

"Something . . . new?" he echoed, his voice as flat and non-committal as he could make it. "Do you know what it is?"

"Well, yes. But I think I'd better keep quiet about it until——"

"Charity, nobody on this deserted rock-heap could possibly be a Soviet spy. The whole habit of 'security' is idiotic out here. Tell me now and save me the trouble of dealing with senators; or tell me at least that you know I know. *They have antigravity!* Isn't that it?"

One word from Dillon, and the nightmare would be real.

"Yes," Dillon said. "How did you know? Of course, it couldn't be a complete gravity screen by any means. But it seems to be a good long step towards it. We've waited a long time to see that dream come true—— But you're the last man in the world to take pride in the achievement, so there's no sense exulting about

it to you. I'll let you know when I get a definite arrival date. In
the meantime, will you think about what I said before?"

"Yes, I will." Helmuth took the seat before the board.

"Good. With you, I have to be grateful for small victories.
Good trick, Bob."

"Good trick, Charity."

IV

Instead of sleeping—for now he knew that he was really
afraid—he sat up in the reading chair in his cabin. The illu-
minated microfilm pages of a book flipped by across the surface
of the wall opposite him, timed precisely to the reading rate
most comfortable for him, and he had several weeks' worry-
conserved alcohol and smoke rations for ready consumption.

But Helmuth let his mix go flat, and did not notice the book,
which had turned itself on, at the page where he had abandoned
it last, when he had fitted himself into the chair. Instead, he
listened to the radio.

There was always a great deal of ham radio activity in the
Jovian system. The conditions were good for it, since there was
plenty of power available, few impeding atmosphere layers, and
those thin, no Heaviside layers, and few official and no com-
mercial channels with which the hams could interfere.

And there were plenty of people scattered about the satellites
who needed the sound of a voice.

". . . anybody know whether the senators are coming here?
Doc Barth put in a report a while back on a fossil plant he
found here, at least he thinks it was a plant. Maybe they'd like
a look at it."

"They're supposed to hit the Bridge team next." A strong
voice, and the impression of a strong transmitter wavering in
and out; that would be Sweeney, on Ganymede. "Sorry to throw
the wet blanket, boys, but I don't think the senators are interested in our rock-balls for their own lumpy selves. We could
only hold them here three days."

Helmuth thought greyly: *Then they've already left Callisto.*

"Is that you, Sweeney? Where's the Bridge tonight?"

"Dillon's on duty," a very distant transmitter said. "Try to
raise Helmuth, Sweeney."

"Helmuth, Helmuth, you gloomy beetle-gooser! Come in, Helmuth!"

"Sure, Bob, come in and dampen us."

Sluggishly, Helmuth reached out to take the mike, where it lay clipped to one arm of the chair. But the door to his room opened before he had completed the gesture.

Eva came in.

She said, "Bob, I want to tell you something."

"His voice is changing!" the voice of the Callisto operator said. "Ask him what he's drinking, Sweeney!"

Helmuth cut the radio out. The girl was freshly dressed—in so far as anybody dressed in anything on Jupiter V—and Helmuth wondered why she was prowling the decks at this hour, half-way between her sleep period and her trick. Her hair was hazy against the light from the corridor, and she looked less mannish than usual. She reminded him a little of the way she had looked when they first met.

"All right," he said. "I owe you a mix, I guess. Citric, sugar and the other stuff is in the locker . . . you know where it is. Shot-cans are there, too."

The girl shut the door and sat down on the bunk, with a free litheness that was almost grace, but with a determination which Helmuth knew meant that she had just decided to do something silly for all the right reasons.

"I don't need a drink," she said. "As a matter of fact, lately I've been turning my lux-R's back to the common pool. I suppose you did that for me—by showing me what a mind looked like that is hiding from itself."

"Eva, stop sounding like a tract. Obviously, you've advanced to a higher, more Jovian plane of existence, but won't you still need your metabolism? Or have you decided that vitamins are all-in-the-mind?"

"Now you're being superior. Anyhow, alcohol isn't a vitamin. And I didn't come to talk about that. I came to tell you something I think you ought to know."

"Which is?"

She said, "Bob, I mean to have a child here."

A bark of laughter, part sheer hysteria and part exasperation, jack-knifed Helmuth into a sitting position. A red arrow bloomed on the far wall, obediently marking the paragraph which, supposedly, he had reached in his reading, and the page vanished.

"*Women!*" he said, when he could get his breath back. "Really, Evita, you make me feel much better. No environment can change a human being much, after all."

"Why should it?" she said suspiciously. "I don't see the joke. Shouldn't a woman want to have a child?"

"Of course she should," he said, settling back. The flipping pages began again. "It's quite ordinary. All women want to have children. All women dream of the day they can turn a child out to play in an airless rock-garden, to pluck fossils and get quaintly star-burned. How cosy to tuck the little blue body back into its corner that night, promptly at the sound of the trick-change bell! Why, it's as natural as Jupiter-light—as Earthian as vacuum-frozen apple pie."

He turned his head casually away. "As for me, though, Eva, I'd much prefer that you take your ghostly little pretext out of here."

Eva surged to her feet in one furious motion. Her fingers grasped him by the beard and jerked his head painfully around again.

"You reedy male platitude!" she said, in a low grinding voice. "How you could see almost the whole point and make so little of it—*Women*, is it? So you think I came creeping in here, full of humbleness, to settle our technical differences."

He closed his hand on her wrist and twisted it away. "What else?" he demanded, trying to imagine how it would feel to stay reasonable for five minutes at a time with these Bridge-robots. "None of us need bother with games and excuses. We're here, we're isolated, we were all chosen because, among other things, we were judged incapable of forming permanent emotional attachments, and capable of such alliances as we found attractive without going unbalanced when the attraction diminished and the alliance came unstuck. None of us have to pretend that our living arrangements would keep us out of jail in Boston, or that they have to involve any Earth-normal excuses."

She said nothing. After a while he asked, gently, "Isn't that so?"

"Of course it's so. Also it has nothing to do with the matter."

"It doesn't? How stupid do you think I am? *I* don't care whether or not you've decided to have a child here, if you really mean what you say."

She was trembling with rage. "You really don't, too. The decision means nothing to you."

"Well, if I liked children, I'd be sorry for the child. But as it happens, I can't stand children. In short, Eva, as far as I'm concerned you can have as many as you want, and to me you'll *still* be the worst operator on the Bridge."

"I'll bear that in mind," she said. At this moment she seemed to have been cut from pressure-ice. "I'll leave you something to charge your mind with, too, Robert Helmuth. I'll leave you sprawled here under your precious book . . . what is Madame Bovary to you, anyhow, you unadventurous turtle? . . . to think about a man who believes that children must always be born into warm cradles—a man who thinks that men have to huddle on warm worlds, or they won't survive. A man with no ears, no eyes, scarcely any head. A man in terror, a man crying Mamma! *Mamma!* all the stellar days and nights long!"

"Parlour diagnosis!"

"Parlour labelling! Good trick, Bob. Draw your warm woolly blanket in tight about your brains, or some little sneeze of sense might creep in, and impair your—efficiency!"

The door closed sharply after her.

A million pounds of fatigue crashed down without warning on Helmuth's brain, and he fell back into the reading chair with a gasp. The roots of his beard ached, and Jupiters bloomed and wavered away before his closed eyes.

He struggled once, and fell asleep.

Instantly he was in the grip of the dream.

It started, as always, with commonplaces, almost realistic enough to be a documentary film-strip—except for the appalling sense of pressure, and the distorted emotional significance with which the least word, the smallest movement was invested.

It was the sinking of the first caisson of the Bridge. The actual event had been bad enough. The job demanded enough exactness of placement to require that manned ships enter Jupiter's atmosphere itself: a squadron of twenty of the most powerful ships ever built, with the five-million-ton asteroid, trimmed and shaped in space, slung beneath them in an immense cat's cradle.

Four times that squadron had disappeared beneath the clouds; four times the tense voices of pilots and engineers had muttered in Helmuth's ears; four times there were shouts and futile orders and the snapping of cables and someone screaming endlessly against the eternal howl of the Jovian sky.

It had cost, altogether, nine ships and two hundred and thirty-one men, to get one of five laboriously shaped asteroids planted in the shifting slush that was Jupiter's surface. Helmuth had helped to supervise all five operations, counting the successful one, from his desk on Jupiter V; but in the dream he was not in the control shack, but instead on shipboard, in one of the ships that was never to come back——

Then, without transition, but without any sense of discontinuity either, he was on the Bridge itself. Not *in absentia,* as the remote guiding intelligence of a beetle, but in person, in an ovular, tank-like suit the details of which would never come clear. The high brass had discovered antigravity, and had asked for volunteers to man the Bridge. Helmuth had volunteered.

Looking back on it in the dream, he did not understand why he had volunteered. It had simply seemed expected of him, and he had not been able to help it, even though he had known what it would be like. He belonged on the Bridge, though he hated it— he had been doomed to go there, from the first.

And there was . . . something wrong . . . with the antigravity. The high brass had asked for its volunteers before the scientific work had been completed. The present antigravity fields were weak, and there was some basic flaw in the theory. Generators broke down after only short periods of use, burned out, unpredictably, sometimes only moments after testing up without a flaw—like vacuum tubes in waking life.

That was what Helmuth's set was about to do. He crouched inside his personal womb, above the boiling sea, the clouds raging about him, lit by a plume of hydrogen flame, and waited to feel his weight suddenly become eight times greater than normal. He knew what would happen to him then.

It happened.

Helmuth greeted morning on Jupiter V with his customary scream.

V

The ship that landed as he was going on duty did nothing to lighten the load on his heart. In shape it was not distinguishable from any of the long-range cruisers which ran the legs of the Moon–Mars–Belt–Ganymede trip. But it grounded its huge bulk with less visible expenditures of power than one of the little intersatellary boats.

That landing told Helmuth that his dream was well on its way to coming true. If the high brass had had a real antigravity, there would have been no reason why the main jets should have been necessary at all. Obviously, what had been discovered was some sort of partial screen, which allowed a ship to operate with far less jet action than was normal, but which still left it subject to a sizeable fraction of the universal stress of space.

Nothing less than a complete and completely controllable antigravity would do on Jupiter.

He worked mechanically, noting that Charity was not in evidence. Probably he was conferring with the senators, receiving what would be for him the glad news.

Helmuth realized suddenly that there was nothing left for him to do now but to cut and run.

There could certainly be no reason why he should have to re-enact the entire dream, helplessly, event for event, like an actor committed to a play. He was awake now, in full control of his own senses, and still at least partially sane. The man in the dream had volunteered—but that man would not be Robert Helmuth. Not any longer.

While the senators were here, he would turn in his resignation. Direct, over Charity's head.

"Wake up, Helmuth," a voice from the gang deck snapped suddenly. "If it hadn't been for me, you'd have run yourself off the end of the Bridge. You had all the automatic stops on that beetle cut out."

Helmuth reached guiltily and more than a little too late for the controls. Eva had already run his beetle back beyond the danger line.

"Sorry," he mumbled. "Thanks, Eva."

"Don't thank me. If you'd actually been in it, I'd have let it go. Less reading and more sleep is what I recommend for you, Helmuth."

"Keep your recommendations to yourself," he snapped.

The incident started a new and even more disturbing chain of thought. If he were to resign now, it would be nearly a year before he could get back to Chicago. Antigravity or no antigravity, the senators' ship would have no room for unexpected passengers. Shipping a man back home had to be arranged far in advance. Space had to be provided, and a cargo equivalent of the weight and space requirements he would take up on the return trip had to be deadheaded out to Jupiter.

A year of living in the station on Jupiter V without any function—as a man whose drain on the station's supplies no longer could be justified in terms of what he did. A year of living under the eyes of Eva Chavez and Charity Dillon and the other men and women who still remained Bridge operators, men and women who would not hesitate to let him know what they thought of his quitting.

A year of living as a bystander in the feverish excitement of direct, personal exploration of Jupiter. A year of watching and hearing the inevitable deaths—while he alone stood aloof, privileged and useless. A year during which Robert Helmuth would become the most hated living entity in the Jovian system.

And, when he got back to Chicago and went looking for a job—for his resignation from the Bridge gang would automatically take him out of government service—he would be asked why he left the Bridge at the moment when work on the Bridge was just reaching its culmination.

He began to understand why the man in the dream had volunteered.

When the trick-change bell rang, he was still determined to resign, but he had already concluded bitterly that there were, after all, other kinds of hells besides the one on Jupiter.

He was returning the board to neutral as Charity came up the cleats. Charity's eyes were snapping like a skyful of comets. Helmuth had known that they would be.

"Senator Wagoner wants to speak to you, if you're not too tired, Bob," he said. "Go ahead; I'll finish up there."

"He does?" Helmuth frowned. The dream surged back upon him. *No.* They would not rush him any faster than he wanted to go. "What about, Charity? Am I suspected of unWestern activities? I suppose you've told them how I feel."

"I have," Dillon said, unruffled. "But we're agreed that you may not feel the same after you've talked to Wagoner. He's in the ship, of course. I've put out a suit for you at the lock."

Charity put the helmet over his head, effectively cutting himself off from further conversation, or from any further consciousness of Helmuth at all.

Helmuth stood looking at him a moment. Then, with a convulsive shrug, he went down the cleats.

Three minutes later, he was plodding in a spacesuit across the surface of Jupiter V, with the vivid bulk of Jupiter splashing his shoulders with colour.

A courteous Marine let him through the ship's air lock and deftly peeled him out of the suit. Despite a grim determination to be uninterested in the new antigravity and any possible consequence of it, he looked curiously about as he was conducted up towards the bow.

But the ship was like the ones that had brought him from Chicago to Jupiter V—it was like any spaceship: there was nothing in it to see but corridor walls and stairwells, until you arrived at the cabin where you were needed.

Senator Wagoner was a surprise. He was a young man, no more than sixty-five at most, not at all portly, and he had the keenest pair of blue eyes that Helmuth had ever seen. He received Helmuth alone, in his own cabin—a comfortable cabin as spaceship accommodations go, but neither roomy nor luxurious. He was hard to match up with the stories Helmuth had been hearing about the current Senate, which had been involved in scandal after scandal of more than Roman proportions.

Helmuth looked around. "I thought there were several of you," he said.

"There are, but I didn't want to give you the idea that you were facing a panel," Wagoner said, smiling. "I've been forced to sit in on most of these endless loyalty investigations back home, but I can't see any point in exporting such religious ceremonies to deep space. Do sit down, Mr. Helmuth. There are drinks coming. We have a lot to talk about."

Stiffly, Helmuth sat down.

"Dillon tells me," Wagoner said, leaning back comfortably in his own chair, "that your usefulness to the Bridge is about at an end. In a way, I'm sorry to hear that, for you've been one of the best men we've had on any of our planetary projects. But, in another way, I'm glad. It makes you available for something much bigger, where we need you much more."

"What do you mean by that?"

"I'll explain in a moment. First, I'd like to talk a little about the Bridge. Please don't feel that I'm quizzing you, by the way. You're at perfect liberty to say that any given question is none of my business, and I'll take no offence and hold no grudge. Also, 'I hereby disavow the authenticity of any tape or other tapping of which this statement may be a part.' In short, our conversation is unofficial, highly so."

"Thank you."

"It's to my interest; I'm hoping that you'll talk freely to me. Of course my disavowal means nothing, since such formal statements can always be excised from a tape; but later on I'm going to tell you some things you're not supposed to know, and you'll be able to judge by what I say then that anything you say to me is privileged. Okay?"

A steward came in silently with the drinks, and left again. Helmuth tasted his. As far as he could tell, it was exactly like many he had mixed for himself back in the control shack, from standard space rations. The only difference was that it was cold, which Helmuth found startling, but not unpleasant after the first sip. He tried to relax. "I'll do my best," he said.

"Good enough. Now: Dillon says that you regard the Bridge as a monster. I've examined your dossier pretty closely, and I think perhaps Dillon hasn't quite the gist of your meaning. I'd like to hear it straight from you."

"I don't think the Bridge is a monster," Helmuth said slowly. "You see, Charity is on the defensive. He takes the Bridge to be conclusive evidence that no possible set of adverse conditions ever will stop man for long, and there I'm in agreement with him. But he also thinks of it as Progress, personified. He can't admit—you asked me to speak my mind, senator—that the West is a decadent and dying culture. All the other evidence that's available shows that it is. Charity likes to think of the Bridge as giving the lie to that evidence."

"The West hasn't many more years," Wagoner agreed, astonishingly. "Still and all, the West has been responsible for some really towering achievements in its time. Perhaps the Bridge could be considered as the last and the mightiest of them all."

"Not by me," Helmuth said. "The building of gigantic projects for ritual purposes—doing a thing for the sake of doing it —is the last act of an already dead culture. Look at the pyramids in Egypt for an example. Or an even more idiotic and more enormous example, bigger than anything human beings have accomplished yet, the laying out of the 'Diagram of Power' over the whole face of Mars. If the Martians had put all that energy into survival instead, they'd probably be alive yet."

"Agreed," Wagoner said.

"All right. Then maybe you'll also agree that the essence of a vital culture is its ability to defend itself. The West has beaten off the Soviets for a century now—but as far as I can see, the Bridge is the West's 'Diagram of Power', its pyramids, or what have you. All the money and the resources that went into the Bridge are going to be badly needed, *and won't be there*, when the next Soviet attack comes."

"Which will be very shortly, I'm told," Wagoner said, with complete calm. "Furthermore, it will be successful, and in part it will be successful for the very reasons you've outlined. For a man who's been cut off from the Earth for years, Helmuth, you seem to know more about what's going on down there than most of the general populace does."

"Nothing promotes an interest in Earth like being off it," Helmuth said. "And there's plenty of time to read out here." Either the drink was stronger than he had expected, or the senator's calm concurrence in the collapse of Helmuth's entire world had given him another shove towards nothingness; his head was spinning.

Wagoner saw it. He leaned forward suddenly, catching Helmuth flat-footed. "*However*," he said, "it's difficult for me to agree that the Bridge serves, or ever did serve, a ritual purpose. The Bridge served a huge practical purpose which is now fulfilled—the Bridge, as such, is now a defunct project."

"Defunct?" Helmuth repeated faintly.

"Quite. Of course we'll continue to operate it for a while, simply because you can't stop a process of that size on a dime, and that's just as well for people like Dillon who are emotionally tied up in it. You're the one person with any authority in the whole station who has already lost enough interest in the Bridge to make it safe for me to tell you that it's being abandoned."

"But why?"

"Because," Wagoner went on quietly, "the Bridge has now given us confirmation of a theory of stupendous importance—so important, in my opinion, that the imminent fall of the West seems like a puny event in comparison. A confirmation, incidentally, which contains in it the seeds of ultimate destruction for the Soviets, whatever they may win for themselves in the next fifty years or so."

"I suppose," Helmuth said, puzzled, "that you mean antigravity?"

For the first time, it was Wagoner's turn to be taken aback. "Man," he said at last, "do you know *everything* I want to tell you? I hope not, or my conclusions will be mighty suspicious. Surely Charity didn't tell you we had antigravity; I strictly enjoined him not to mention it."

"No, the subject's been on my mind," Helmuth said. "But I certainly don't see why it should be so world-shaking, any more than I see how the Bridge helped to bring it about. I thought it had been developed independently, for the further exploitation of the Bridge, and would step up Bridge operation, not discontinue it."

"Not at all. Of course, the Bridge has given us information in thousands of different categories, much of it very valuable indeed. But the one job that *only* the Bridge could do was that of confirming, or throwing out, the Blackett-Dirac equations."

"Which are——?"

"A relationship between magnetism and the spinning of a massive body—that much is the Dirac part of it. The Blackett Equation seemed to show that the same formula also applied to gravity. If the figures we collected on the magnetic field strength of Jupiter forced us to retire the Dirac equations, then none of the rest of the information we've gotten from the Bridge would have been worth the money we spent to get it. On the other hand, Jupiter was the only body in the solar system available to us which was big enough in all relevant respects to make it possible for us to test those equations at all. They involve quantities of enormous orders of magnitudes.

"And the figures show that Dirac was right. *They also show that Blackett was right.* Both magnetism *and* gravity are phenomena of rotation.

"I won't bother to trace the succeeding steps, because I think you can work them out for yourself. It's enough to say that there's a drive-generator on board this ship which is the complete and final justification of all the hell you people on the Bridge gang have been put through. The gadget has a long technical name, but the technies who tend it have already nicknamed it the spindizzy, because of what it does to the magnetic moment of any atom—*any* atom—within its field.

"While it's in operation, it absolutely refuses to notice any atom outside its own influence. Furthermore, it will notice no other strain or influence which holds good beyond the borders of that field. It's so snooty that it has to be stopped down to almost nothing when it's brought close to a planet, or it won't let you land. But in deep space . . . well, it's impervious to meteors and such trash, of course; it's impervious to gravity; and—it hasn't the faintest interest in any legislation about top speed limits."

"You're kidding," Helmuth said.

"Am I, now? This ship came to Ganymede directly from Earth. It did it in a little under two hours, counting manœuvring time."

Helmuth took a defiant pull at his drink. "This thing really has no top speed at all?" he said. "How can you be sure of that?"

"Well, we can't," Wagoner admitted. "After all, one of the unfortunate things about general mathematical formulas is that they don't contain cut-off points to warn you of areas where they don't apply. Even quantum mechanics is somewhat subject to that criticism. However, we expect to know pretty soon just how fast the spindizzy can drive an object, if there is any limit. We expect you to tell us."

"I?"

"Yes, Helmuth, you. The coming débâcle on Earth makes it absolutely imperative for us—the West—to get interstellar expeditions started at once. Richardson Observatory, on the Moon, has two likely-looking systems picked out already—one at Wolf 359, another at 61 Cygni—and there are sure to be hundreds of others where Earth-like planets are highly probable. We want to scatter adventurous people, people with a thoroughly indoctrinated love of being free, all over this part of the galaxy, if it can be done.

"Once they're out there, they'll be free to flourish, with no interference from Earth. The Soviets haven't the spindizzy yet, and even after they steal it from us, they won't dare allow it to be used. It's too good and too final an escape route.

"What we want you to do . . . now I'm getting to the point, you see . . . is to direct this exodus. You've the intelligence and the cast of mind for it. Your analysis of the situation on Earth confirms that, if any more confirmation were needed. And—there's no future for you on Earth now."

"You'll have to excuse me," Helmuth said, firmly. "I'm in no condition to be reasonable now; it's been more than I could digest in a few moments. And the decision doesn't entirely rest with me, either. If I could give you an answer in . . . let me see . . . about three hours. Will that be soon enough?"

"That'll be fine," the senator said.

"And so, that's the story," Helmuth said.

Eva remained silent in her chair for a long time.

"One thing I don't understand," she said at last. "Why did you come to me? I'd have thought that you'd find the whole thing terrifying."

"Oh, it's terrifying, all right," Helmuth said, with quiet exultation. "But terror and fright are two different things, as I've just discovered. We were both wrong, Evita. I was wrong in thinking that the Bridge was a dead end. You were wrong in thinking of it as an end in itself."

"I don't understand you."

"All right, let's put it this way: The work the Bridge was doing was worth-while, as I know now—so I was wrong in being frightened of it, in calling it a bridge to nowhere.

"But you no more saw where it was going than I, and you made the Bridge the be-all and end-all of your existence.

"Now, there's a place to go to; in fact there are places—

hundreds of places. They'll be Earth-like places. Since the Soviets are about to win Earth, those places will be more Earth-like than Earth itself, for the next century or so at least!"

She said, "Why are you telling me this? Just to make peace between us?"

"I'm going to take on this job, Evita, if you'll go along?"

She turned swiftly, rising out of the chair with a marvellous fluidity of motion. At the same instant, all the alarm bells in the station went off at once, filling every metal cranny with a jangle of pure horror.

"*Posts!*" the speaker above Eva's bed roared, in a distorted, gigantic version of Charity Dillon's voice. "*Peak storm overload! The STD is now passing the Spot. Wind velocity has already topped all previous records, and part of the land mass has begun to settle. This is an A-1 overload emergency.*"

Behind Charity's bellow, the winds of Jupiter made a spectrum of continuous, insane shrieking. The Bridge was responding with monstrous groans of agony. There was another sound, too, an almost musical cacophony of sharp, percussive tones, such as a dinosaur might make pushing its way through a forest of huge steel tuning-forks. Helmuth had never heard that sound before, but he knew what it was.

The deck of the Bridge was splitting up the middle.

After a moment more, the uproar dimmed, and the speaker said, in Charity's normal voice, "Eva, you too, please. Acknowledge, please. This is it—unless everybody comes on duty at once, the Bridge may go down within the next hour."

"Let it," Eva responded quietly.

There was a brief, startled silence, and then a ghost of a human sound. The voice was Senator Wagoner's, and the sound just might have been a chuckle.

Charity's circuit clicked out.

The mighty death of the Bridge continued to resound in the little room.

After a while, the man and the woman went to the window, and looked past the discarded bulk of Jupiter at the near horizon, where there had always been visible a few stars.

THERE IS A TIDE

by Brian W. Aldiss

How soothing to the heart it was to be home. I began that evening with nothing but peace in me: and the evening itself jellied down over Africa with a mild mother's touch: so that even now I must refuse myself the luxury of claiming any premonition of the disaster for which the scene was already set.

My half-brother, K-Jubal (we had the same father), was in a talkative mood. As we sat at the table on the veranda of his house, his was the major part of the conversation: and this was unusual, for I am a poet, and poets are generally articulate enough.

". . . because the new dam is now complete," he was saying, "and I shall take my days more easily. I am going to write my life story, Rog. G-Williams on the *World Weekly* has been pressing me for it for some time; it'll be serialized, and then turned into audibook form. I should make a lot of money, eh?"

He smiled as he asked this; in my company he always enjoyed playing the heavy materialist. Generally I encouraged him; this time I said: "Jubal, no man in Congo States, no man in the world possibly, has done more for people than you. I am the idle singer of an idle day, but you—why, your good works lie about you."

I swept my hand out over the still bright land.

Mokulgu is a rising town on the western fringes of Lake Tanganyika's northern end. Before Jubal and his engineers came here, it was a sleepy market town, and its natives lived in the indolent fashion of their countless forefathers. In ten years, that ancient pattern was awry; in fifteen, shattered completely. If you lived in Mokulgu now, you slept in a bed in a towering nest of flats, you ate food unfouled by flies, and you moved to the sound of whistles and machinery. You had at your black fingertips, in fact, the benefits of what we persist in calling

"Western civilization". If you were more hygienic and healthy—so ran the theory—you were happier.

But I begin to sound sceptical. That is my error. I happen to have little love for my fellow men; the thought of the Massacre is always with me, even after all this time. I could not deny that the trend of things at Mokulgu and elsewhere, the constant urbanization, was almost unavoidable. But as a man of sensibility, I regretted that human advance should always be over the corpse of Nature.

From where we sat over our southern wines, both lake and town were partially visible, the forests in the immediate area having been demolished long ago. The town was already blazing with light, the lake looked already dark, a thing preparing for night. And to our left, standing out with a clarity which suggested yet more rain to come, stretched the rolling jungles of the Congo tributaries.

For at least three hundred miles in that direction, man had not invaded: there lived the pygmies, flourishing without despoiling. That area, the Congo Source land, would be the next to go; Jubal, indeed, was the spearhead of the attack. But for my generation at least that vast tract of primitive beauty would stand, and I was selfishly glad of it. I always gained more pleasure from trees than population increase statistics.

Jubal caught something of the expression on my face.

"The power we are releasing here will last for ever," he said. "It's already changing—improving—the entire economy of the area. At last, at long last, Africa is realizing her potentialities."

His voice held almost a tremor, and I thought that this passion for Progress was the secret of his strength.

"You cling too much to the past, Rog," he added.

"Why all this digging and tunnelling and wrenching up of riverbeds?" I asked. "Would not atomics have been a cheaper and easier answer?"

"No," he said decisively. "This system puts to use idle water; once in operation, everything is entirely self-servicing. Besides, uranium is none too plentiful, water is. Venus has no radioactive materials, I believe?"

This sounded to me like an invitation to change the subject. I accepted it.

"They've found none yet," I assented. "But I can speak with

no authority. I went purely as a tourist—and a glorious trip it
was."

"It must be wonderful to be so many million miles nearer the
sun," he said. It was the sort of plain remark I had often heard
him make. On others' lips it might have sounded platitudinous;
in his quiet tones I caught a note of sublimity.

"I shall never get to Venus," he said. "There's too much work
to be done here. You must have seen some marvels there,
Rog!"

"Yes . . . Yet nothing so strange as an elephant."

"And they'll have a breathable atmosphere in a decade, I
hear?"

"So they say. They are certainly doing wonders . . . You know,
Jubal, I shall have to go back then. You see, there's a feeling,
er—something, a sort of expectancy. No, not quite that; it's hard
to explain——" I don't converse well. I ramble and mumble
when I have something real to say. I could say it to a woman, or
I could write it on paper; but Jubal is a man of action, and when
I did say it, I deliberately omitted emotional overtones and lost
interest in what I said. "It's like courting a woman in armour
with the visor closed, on Venus now. You can see it, but you
can't touch or smell or breathe it. Always an airtight dome or a
space suit between you and actuality. But in ten years' time,
you'll be able to run your bare fingers through the sand, feel
the breezes on your cheek . . . Well, you know what I mean,
er—sort of feel her undressed."

He was thinking—I saw it in his eyes—"Rog's going to go all
poetic on me." He said: "And you approve of that—the change-
over of atmospheres?"

"Yes."

"Yet you don't approve of what we're doing here, which is
just the same sort of thing?"

He had a point. "You're upsetting a delicate balance here," I
said gingerly. "A thousand ecological factors are swept by the
board just so that you can grind these waters through your tur-
bines. And the same thing's happened at Owen Falls over on
Lake Victoria . . . But on Venus there's no such balance. It's
just a clean page waiting for man to write what he will on it.
Under that CO_2 blanket, there's been no spark of life: the
mountains are bare of moss, the valleys lie innocent of grass; in

the geological strata, no fossils sleep; no amœbæ move in the sea. But what you're doing here . . ."

"People!" he exclaimed. "I've got people to consider. Babies need to be born, mouths must be fed. A man must live. Your sort of feelings are all very well—they make good poems—but I consider the people. I love the people. For them I work . . ."

He waved his hands, overcome by his own grandiose visions. If the passion for Progress was his strength, the fallacy inherent in the idea was his secret weakness. I began to grow warm.

"You get good conditions for these people, they procreate forthwith. Next generation, another benefactor will have to step forward and get good conditions for the children. That's Progress, eh?" I asked maliciously.

"I see you so rarely, Rog; don't let's quarrel," he said meekly. "I just do what I can. I'm only an engineer."

That was how he always won an altercation. Before meekness I have no defence. But hostility ran like a sewer below the level of our conversation.

The sun had finished another day. With the sudden darkness came chill. Jubal pressed a button, and glass slid round the veranda, enclosing us. Like Venus, I thought; but here you could still smell that spicy, bosomy scent which is the breath of dear Africa herself. On Venus, the smells are imported.

We poured some more wine and talked of family matters. In a short while his wife, Sloe, joined us. I began to feel at home. The feeling was only partly psychological; my glands were now beginning to readjust fully to normal conditions after their long days in space travel.

J-Casta also appeared. Him I was less pleased to see. He was the boss type, the strong-arm man: as Jubal's underling, he pandered wretchedly to him and bullied everyone else on the project. He (and there were many others like him, unfortunately) thought of the Massacre as man's greatest achievement. This evening, in the presence of his superiors, after a preliminary burst of showing off, he was quiet enough.

When they pressed me to, I talked of Venus. As I spoke, back rushed that humbling—but intoxicating—sense of awe to think I had actually lived to stand in full possession of my many faculties on that startling planet. The same feeling had often possessed me on Mars. And (as justifiably) on Earth.

The vision chimed, and an amber light blinked drowsily off and on in Jubal's tank. Even then, no premonition of catastrophe; since then, I can never see that amber heartbeat without anxiety.

Jubal answered it, and a man's face swam up in the tank to greet him. They talked; I could catch no words, but the sudden tension was apparent. Sloe went over and put her arm round Jubal's shoulder.

"Something up," J-Casta commented.

"Yes," I said.

"That's Chief M-Shawn on the vision—from Owenstown, over on Lake Victoria."

Then Jubal flashed off and came slowly back to where we were sitting.

"That was M-Shawn," he said. "The level of Lake Victoria has just dropped three inches." He lit a cheroot with clumsy fingers, his eyes staring in mystification far beyond the flame.

"Dam okay, boss?" J-Casta asked.

"Perfectly. They're going to phone us if they find anything . . ."

"Has this happened before?" I asked, not quite able to understand their worried looks.

"Of course not," my half-brother said scornfully. "Surely you must see the implications of it? Something highly unprecedented has occurred."

"But surely a mere three inches of water . . ."

At that he laughed briefly. Even J-Casta permitted himself a snort.

"Lake Victoria is an inland sea," Jubal said grimly. "It's as big as Tasmania. Three inches all over that area means many thousands of tons of water. Casta, I think we'll get down to Mokulgu; it won't do any harm to alert the first aid services, just in case they're needed. Got your tracer?"

"Yes, boss. I'm coming."

Jubal patted Sloe's arm, nodded to me and left without relaxing his worried look. He and J-Casta shortly appeared outside. They bundled into a float, soared dangerously close to a giant walnut tree and vanished into the night.

Nervously, Sloe put down her cheroot and did not resume it. She fingered a dial and the windows opaqued.

"There's an ominous waiting quality out there I don't like," she said, to explain our sudden privacy.

"Should I be feeling alarmed?" I asked.

She flashed me a smile. "Quite honestly, yes. You don't live in our world, Rog, or you would guess at once what was happening at Lake Victoria. They've just finished raising the level again; for a long time they've been on about more pressure, and the recent heavy rains gave them their chance to build it up. It seems to have been the last straw."

"And what does this three-inch drop mean? Is there a breach in the dam somewhere?"

"No. They'd have found that. I'm afraid it means the bed of the lake has collapsed somewhere. The water's pouring into subterranean reservoirs."

The extreme seriousness of the matter was now obvious even to me. Lake Victoria is the source of the White Nile; if it ceased to feed the river, millions of people in Uganda and the Sudan would die of drought. And not only people: birds, beasts, fish, insects, plants.

We both grew restless. We took a turn outside in the cool night air, and then decided we too would go down to the town.

All the way there a picture filled my head: the image of that great dark lake emptying like a wash-basin. Did it drain in sinister silence, or did it gargle as it went? Men of action forget to tell you vital details like that.

That night was an anticlimax, apart from the sight of the full moon sailing over Mount Kangosi. We joined Jubal and his henchman and hung about uneasily until midnight. As if an unknown god had been propitiated by the sacrifice of an hour's sleep, we then felt easier and retired to bed.

The news was bad next morning. By the time I was dressed Jubal was already back in town; Sloe and I breakfasted alone together. She told me they had been informed that Victoria had now dropped thirteen and a half inches; the rate of fall seemed to be increasing.

I flew into Mokulgu and found Jubal without difficulty. He was just embarking on one of the Dam Authority's survey floats with J-Casta.

"You'd better come, too, Rog," he shouted. "You'll probably enjoy the flight more than we shall."

I did enjoy the flight, despite the circumstances. A disturbance on Lake Tanganyika's eastern fringes had been observed on an earlier survey and we were going to investigate it.

"You're not afraid the bed will collapse here, too, are you?" I asked.

"It's not that," Jubal said. "The two hundred miles between us and Victoria is a faulty region, geologically speaking. I'll show you a map of the strata when we get back. It's more than likely that all that runaway subterranean water may be heading in our direction; that's what I'm afraid of. The possibility has been known for a long while."

"And no precautions taken?"

"What could we do but cross our fingers? The possibility exists that the Moon will spiral to Earth, but we don't all live in shelters because of it."

"Justifying yourself, Jubal?"

"Possibly," he replied, looking away. Again that stupid antagonism.

We flew through a heavy rain shower, which dappled the grey surface of the lake. Then we were over the reported disturbance. A dull brown stain, a blot on a bright new garment, spread over the water, from the steep eastern shore to about half a mile out.

"Put us down, pilot," Jubal ordered.

We sank, and kissed the lake. Several hundred yards away rose the base of Mount Kangosi. I looked with admiration up the slope; great slabs of rock stood out from the verdure; crouching at the bottom of this colossus was a village, part of it forced by the steepness of the incline to stand out on piles into the lake.

"Leave everything to me, boss," J-Casta said, grabbing a hand asdic from the port locker and climbing out on to the float. We followed. It seemed likely that the disturbance was due to a slight subsidence in the side of the lake basin. Such subsidences, Jubal said, were not uncommon, but in this case it might provide a link with Lake Victoria. If they could pinpoint the position of the new fault, frogmen would be sent down to investigate.

"We're going to have company," Jubal remarked to me, waving a hand over the water.

A dozen or so dugouts lay between us and the shore. Each bore two or three shining-skinned fishermen. The two canoes nearest us had swung round and were now being paddled towards our float.

I watched them with more interest than I gave to the asdic sweep. Men like these sturdy fishermen had existed here for countless generations, unchanged: before white men had known of them, before Rome's legions had destroyed the vineyards of Carthage, before—who knows if not before the heady uprush of civilization elsewhere?—such men had fished quietly in this great lake. They seemed not to have advanced at all, so rapidly does the world move; but perhaps when all other races have fallen away, burnt out and exhausted, these steady villagers will come into a kingdom of their own. I would elect to live in that realm.

A man in the leading canoe stood up, raising his hand in greeting. I replied, glancing over his shoulder at the curtain of green behind him. Something caught my eye.

Above some yards of bare rock, a hundred feet up the slope of the mountain, two magnificent Mvules—African teak trees— grew. A china-blue bird dipped suddenly from one of the trees and sped far and fast away over the water, fighting to outpace its reflection. And the tree itself began to cant slowly from the vertical into a horizontal position.

Jubal had binoculars round his neck. My curiosity aroused, I reached to borrow them. Even as I did so, I saw a spring of water start from the base of the Mvules. A rock was dislodged. I saw it hurtle down into the bush below, starting in turn a trail of earth and stones which fell down almost on to the thatched roofs of the village. The spring began to spurt more freely now. It gleamed in the sun: it looked beautiful but I was alarmed.

"Look!" I pointed.

Both Jubal and the fisherman followed the line of my outstretched arm. J-Casta continued to bend over his metal box.

Even as I pointed, the cliff shuddered. The other Mvule went down. Like an envelope being torn, the rock split horizontally and a tongue of water burst from it. The split widened, the water became a wall, pouring out and down.

The sound of the splitting came clear and hard to our startled ears. Then came the roar of the water, bursting down the hill-

side. It washed everything before it. I saw trees, bushes and
boulders hurried down in it. I saw the original fissure lengthen
and lengthen like a cruel smile, cutting through the ground as
fast as fire. Other cracks started, running uphill and across:
every one of them began to spout water.

The fishermen stood up, shouting as their homes were swept
away by the first fury of the flood.

And then the entire lower mountainside began to slip. With a
cumulative roar, mud, water and rock rolled down into the lake.
Where they had been, a solid torrent cascaded out, one mighty
wall of angry water. The escaping flow from Lake Victoria had
found its outlet!

Next moment, our calm surface was a furious sea. Jubal
slipped and fell on to one knee. I grabbed him, and almost went
overboard myself. A series of giant waves plunged outwards
from the shore. The first one rocked us, the second one overturned our flimsy craft completely.

I came to the surface coughing and snorting. J-Casta rose at
my side. We were just in time to see the float slip completely
under: it sank in no time, carrying the pilot with it. I had not
even seen his face, poor fellow.

Jubal came up by the fisherman, who had also overturned.
But dugouts do not sink. We owed our lives to those hollowed
tree trunks. They were righted, and Jubal and his henchman
climbed into one, while I climbed into the other. The waves
were still fierce, but had attained a sort of regularity which
allowed us to cope with them.

The breakthrough was now a quarter of a mile long. Water
poured from it with unabated force, a mighty waterfall where
land had been before. We skirted it painfully, making a landing
as near to it as we dared.

The rest of that day, under its blinding arch of sky, passed in
various stages of confusion and fear.

It was two and a half hours before we were taken off the strip
of shore. We were not idle in that time, although every few
minutes Jubal paused to curse the fact that he was stranded and
powerless. Miraculous as it seems, there were some survivors
from the obliterated village, women mostly; we helped to get
them ashore and built fires for them.

Meanwhile, Dam Authority planes began to circle the area. We managed to attract the attention of one, which landed by our party. Jubal's manner changed at once; now that he had a machine and men who, unlike the villagers, were in his command, he worked with a silent purpose allowing of no question.

Over the vision, he ordered the rest of the floats to attend to the villagers' needs. We sped back to Mokulgu.

On the way, Jubal spoke to Owenstown. They took his news almost without comment. They reported that Victoria was still sinking, although the rate had now steadied. A twenty-four-hour a day airlift was about to go into operation, dropping solid blocks of marble on to the lake bed. There, a fault about three miles square had been located; four frogmen had been lost, drowned.

"It's like tossing pennies into the ocean," Jubal said.

I was thinking of the frogmen, sucked irresistibly down the fault. They would be swept through underground waterways, battered and pulped, to be spat out eventually into our lake.

Vision from Mokulgu, coming on just before we landed there, reported a breach in the lake banks, some twenty miles north of the town. At a word from Jubal, we switched plans and veered north at once to see just how extensive the damage was.

The break was at a tiny cluster of huts, dignified by the name of Ulatuama, growing like a wart on the edge of Lake Tanganyika. Several men, the crew of a Dam Authority patrol boat, were working furiously at a widening gap. The damage had been caused by the very waves which had swamped us, and I learnt that a small, disused lock had stood here, relic of an earlier irrigation scheme; so the weakness had been of man's making. Beyond the lock had been a dried-up channel some twenty yards wide; this was now a swollen, plunging river.

"Is this serious?" I asked Jubal. "Isn't it a good way of getting rid of surplus water?"

He gave me a withering look. "Where are we if we lose control?" he demanded. "If this thing here runs away with us, the combined waters of Victoria and Tanganyika will flood down into the Congo."

Even as he spoke, the bank to the south of the escaping waters crumbled; several yards were swept away, their places instantly taken by the current.

We flew back to Mokulgu. Jubal visioned the mayor and got permission to broadcast to the city. I did not hear him speak; reaction had set in, and I had to go and sit quietly at home with Sloe fussing daintily round me. Although you "know" from a child that Earth is a planet, it is only when you drift towards it from space, seeing it hang round and finite ahead, that you can *realize* the fact. And so, although I had always "known" man was puny, it was the sight of that vast collapsing slab of mountain which had driven the fact into my marrow.

To guess the sort of sentiments Jubal broadcast to the city was easy. He would talk of "rallying round in this our time of crisis". He would speak of the need for "all hands uniting against our ancient enemy, Nature". He would come over big on the tanks; he would be big, his fists clenched, his eyes ablaze. He was in touch with the people. And they would do what he said, for Jubal carried conviction. Perhaps I envied my half-brother.

Labour and supplies began to pour north to mend the damaged bank. Jubal, meanwhile, thought up a typically flamboyant scheme. *Tilly*, one of the lake steamers, was pressed into service and loaded full of rock and clay by steam shovel. With Jubal standing on the bridge, it was manœuvred into the centre of the danger area and scuttled. Half in and half out of the rushing water, it now formed a base from which a new dam could be built to stem the flood. Watched by a cheering crowd, Jubal and crew skimmed to safety in a motor boat.

"We shall conquer if we have to dam the water with our bodies," he cried. A thousand cheering throats told him how much they liked this idea.

The pitch of crisis which had then been engendered was maintained all through the next two days. For most of that time it rained, and men fought to erect their barrier on clinging mud. Jubal's popularity—and consequently his influence—underwent a rapid diminution. The reason for this was two-fold. He quarrelled with J-Casta, whose suggestion to throw open the new dam to relieve pressure elsewhere was refused, and he ran into stiff opposition from Mokulgu Town Council.

This august body, composed of the avariciously successful and the successfully avaricious, was annoyed about *Tilly*. *Tilly* belonged to the local government, and Jubal had, in effect, stolen it. The men from the factories who had downed tools to fight the water were summoned back to work; the Dam Authority must tend its own affairs.

Jubal merely sneered at this dangerous pique and visioned Léopoldville. In the briefest possible time, he had the army helping him.

It was at dawn on the morning of the third day that he visioned me to go down and see him. I said *adieu* to Sloe and took a float over to Ulatuama.

Jubal stood alone by the water's edge. The sun was still swathed in mist, and he looked cold and pinched. Behind him, dimly outlined figures moved to and fro, like allegorical figures on a frieze. He surveyed me curiously before speaking.

"The work's nearly done, Rog," he said. He looked as if he needed sleep, but he added energetically, pointing across the lake: "Then we tackle the main job of plugging that waterfall."

I looked across the silent lake. The far shore was invisible, but out of the layers of mist rose Mount Kangosi. Even at this distance, in the early morning hush, came the faint roar of the new waterfall. And there was another sound, intermittent but persistent: beyond the mountain, they were bombing fault lines. That way they hoped to cause a collapse which would plug Victoria's escape routes. So far, they had had no success, but the bombing went on, making a battlefield of what had once been glorious country.

"Sorry I haven't seen anything of you and Sloe," Jubal said. I disliked his tone. "You've been getting on well together, I suppose?"

"You've been busy. Sloe called you on the vision."

"Oh that. Come on into my hut, Rog."

We walked over to a temporary structure; the grass was overloaded with dew. In Jubal's hut, J-Casta was dressing, smoking a cheroot as he dexterously pulled on a shirt. He gave me a surly greeting, whose antagonism I sensed was directed through me at Jubal.

As soon as the latter closed the door, he said: "Rog, promise me something."

"Tell me what."

"If anything happens to me, I want you to marry Sloe. She's your sort."

Concealing my irritation, I said: "That's hardly a reasonable request."

"You and she get on well together, don't you?"

"Certainly. But you see my outlook on life is . . . well, for one thing I like to stay detached. An observer, you know, observing. I just want to sample the landscapes and the food and the women of the solar system. I don't want to *marry*, just move on at the right time. Sloe's very nice but——"

My ghastly inability to express the pressure of inner feeling was upon me. In women I like flamboyance, wit, and a high spirit, but I tire quickly of them and then have to seek their manifestation elsewhere. Besides, Sloe frankly had had her sensibilities blunted from living with Jubal. He now chose to misunderstand my hesitations.

"Are you standing there trying to tell me that you've already tired of whatever you've been doing behind my back?" he demanded. "You—you——" He called me a dirty name; I forgot to make allowances for the strain he had been undergoing, and lost my temper.

"Oh, calm down," I snapped. "You're overtired and overwrought, and probably over-sexed too. I've not touched your little woman—I like to drink from pure streams. So you can put the entire notion out of your head."

Trouble came to us as suddenly as it had done to the lake, although nobody afterwards could have said there had been no warning.

He rushed at me with his shoulders hunched and fists swinging. It was an embarrassing moment. I am against violence, and believe in the power of words, but I did the only possible thing: spring to one side and catch him a heavy blow over the heart.

Poor Jubal! No doubt, in his frustration against the forces of nature, he was using me only as a safety valve. But with shame, I will now confess what savage pleasure that blow gave me; I was filled with lust to strike him again. I can perceive dimly how atrocities such as the Massacre came about. As Jubal turned on me, I flung myself at him, breaking down his defences, piling blows into his chest. It was, I suppose, a form of self-expression.

J-Casta stopped it, breaking in between us and thrusting his ugly face into mine, his hand like a clamp round my wrist.

"Pack it up," he said. "I'd gladly do the job myself, but this is not the time."

As he spoke, the hut trembled. We were hard pressed to keep our feet, staggering together like drunken men.

"Now what——" Jubal said, and flung open the door. I caught a rectangular view of trees and mist, men running, and the emergency dam sailing away on a smooth black slide of escaping water. The banks were collapsing!

Glimpsing the scene, Jubal instantly attempted to slam the door shut again. The wave struck us, battering the cabin off its flimsy foundations. Jubal cried sharply as he was tossed against a wall. Next moment we were floundering in a hell of flying furniture and water.

Swept along on a giant sluice, the cabin turned over and over like a dice. That I was preserved was the merest accident. Through a maze of foam, I saw a heavy bunk crashing towards me, and managed to flounder aside in time. It missed me by a finger's width and broke through the boarding wall. I was swept helplessly after it.

When I surfaced, the cabin was out of sight and I was being borne along at a great rate; and the ugly scene in the cabin was something fruitless that happened a million years ago. Nearly wrenching my arm off in the process, I seized a tree which was still standing, and clung on. Once I had recovered my breath, I was able to climb out of the water entirely, wedge myself between two branches and regain my breath.

The scene was one of awesome desolation. I had what in less calamitous circumstances might have been called "a good view" of it all.

A lake spread all round me, its surface moving smartly and with apparent purpose. Its forward line, already far away, was marked by a high yellow cascade. In its wake stretched a miscellany of objects, of which only the trees stood out clearly. Most of the trees were eucalyptus: this area had probably been reclaimed marsh.

To the north, the old shore-line of the lake still stood. The ground was higher there and solid rock jutted stolidly into the flood. To the south, the shore-line was being joyously chewed away. Mokulgu had about half an hour left before it was swamped and obliterated. I wondered how the Mokulgu Town Council were coping with the situation.

Overhead, the sun now shining clear, bars of pink, wispy cloud flecked the blue sky. The pink and the blue were of the exact vulgar tints found in two-colour prints of the early twentieth century A.D.—that is, a hundred years before the Massacre. I was almost happy to see this lack of taste in the sky matching the lack of stability elsewhere. I was almost happy: but I was weeping.

"They visioned me that one of the floats had picked you up—and not Jubal. Is there any hope for him, Rog, or is that a foolish question?"

"I can't give you a sensible answer. He was a strong swimmer, don't forget. They may find him yet."

I spoke to Sloe over the heads of a crowd of people. Mokulgu, surely enough, had been washed away. The survivors, homeless and bereaved, crowded on to high ground. Sloe had generously thrown open most of her house as a sort of rest-camp-cum-soup-kitchen. She superintended everything with a cool authority which suitably concealed her personal feelings. For that I was grateful: Sloe's feelings must be no affair of mine.

She smiled at me before turning to address someone behind her. Already the light was taking on the intensity of early evening. Above the babble of voices round me came the deep song of speeding water. It would continue for months yet: Africa was ruptured at her very heart, beyond man's mending.

Instead of flowing northward, fertilizing its old valley, Victoria crashed into our lake, adding its burden to the weight of water rolling west. While twenty-one million people perished of drought in Egypt, as many perished of flood and typhoid in the Congo.

I seemed to know what was coming as I stood in the crowded room, knowing Jubal dead, knowing the nation of Africa to be bleeding to death. We were dying of our own wounds.

The ten years to follow would be as terrible as the ten years of the Massacre, when every member of the white race had been slain.

Now we Negroes, in our turn, stood at the bar of history.

SECOND VARIETY

by *Philip K. Dick*

The Russian soldier made his way nervously up the ragged side of the hill, holding his gun ready. He glanced around him, licking his dry lips, his face set. From time to time he reached up a gloved hand and wiped perspiration from his neck, pushing down his coat collar.

Eric turned to Corporal Leone. "Want him? Or can I have him?" He adjusted the view sight so the Russian's features squarely filled the glass, the lines cutting across his hard, sombre features.

Leone considered. The Russian was close, moving rapidly, almost running. "Don't fire. Wait," Leone tensed. "I don't think we're needed."

The Russian increased his pace, kicking ash and piles of debris out of his way. He reached the top of the hill and stopped, panting, staring around him. The sky was overcast, drifting clouds of grey particles. Bare trunks of trees jutted up occasionally; the ground was level and bare, rubble-strewn, with the ruins of buildings standing out here and there like yellowing skulls.

The Russian was uneasy. He knew something was wrong. He started down the hill. Now he was only a few paces from the bunker. Eric was getting fidgety. He played with his pistol, glancing at Leone.

"Don't worry," Leone said. "He won't get here. They'll take care of him."

"Are you sure? He's got damn far."

"They hang around close to the bunker. He's getting into the bad part. Get set!"

The Russian began to hurry, sliding down the hill, his boots sinking into the heaps of grey ash, trying to keep his gun up. He stopped for a moment, lifting his field-glasses to his face.

"He's looking right at us," Eric said.

The Russian came on. They could see his eyes, like two blue stones. His mouth was open a little. He needed a shave; his chin was stubbled. On one bony cheek was a square of tape, showing blue at the edge. A fungoid spot. His coat was muddy and torn. One glove was missing. As he ran his belt counter bounced up and down against him.

Leone touched Eric's arm. "Here one comes."

Across the ground something small and metallic came, flashing in the dull sunlight of mid-day. A metal sphere. It raced up the hill after the Russian, its treads flying. It was small, one of the baby ones. Its claws were out, two razor projections spinning in a blur of white steel. The Russian heard it. He turned instantly, firing. The sphere dissolved into particles. But already a second had emerged and was following the first. The Russian fired again.

A third sphere leaped up the Russian's leg, clicking and whirring. It jumped to the shoulder. The spinning blades disappeared into the Russian's throat.

Eric relaxed. "Well, that's that. God, those damn things give me the creeps. Sometimes I think we were better off before."

"If we hadn't invented them, they would have." Leone lit a cigarette shakily. "I wonder why a Russian would come all this way alone. I didn't see anyone covering him."

Lieutenant Scott came slipping up the tunnel, into the bunker. "What happened? Something entered the screen."

"An Ivan."

"Just one?"

Eric brought the view screen around. Scott peered into it. Now there were numerous metal spheres crawling over the prostrate body, dull metal globes clicking and whirring, sawing up the Russian into small parts to be carried away.

"What a lot of claws," Scott murmured.

"They come like flies. Not much game for them any more."

Scott pushed the sight away, disgusted. "Like flies. I wonder why he was out there. They know we have claws all around."

A larger robot had joined the smaller spheres. It was directing operations, a long blunt tube with projecting eyepieces. There was not much left of the soldier. What remained was being brought down the hillside by the host of claws.

"Sir," Leone said. "If it's all right, I'd like to go out there and take a look at him."

"Why?"

"Maybe he came with something."

Scott considered. He shrugged. "All right. But be careful."

"I have my tab." Leone patted the metal band at his wrist. "I'll be out of bounds."

He picked up his rifle and stepped carefully up to the mouth of the bunker, making his way between blocks of concrete and steel prongs, twisted and bent. The air was cold at the top. He crossed over the ground towards the remains of the soldier, striding across the soft ash. A wind blew around him, swirling grey particles up in his face. He squinted and pushed on.

The claws retreated as he came close, some of them stiffening into immobility. He touched his tab. The Ivan would have given something for that! Short hard radiation emitted from the tab neutralized the claws, put them out of commission. Even the big robot with its two waving eyestalks retreated respectfully as he approached.

He bent down over the remains of the soldier. The gloved hand was closed tightly. There was something in it. Leone pried the fingers apart. A sealed container, aluminium. Still shiny.

He put it in his pocket and made his way back to the bunker. Behind him the claws came back to life, moving into operation again. The procession resumed, metal spheres moving through the grey ash with their loads. He could hear their treads scrabbling against the ground. He shuddered.

Scott watched intently as he brought the shiny tube out of his pocket. "He had that?"

"In his hand." Leone unscrewed the top. "Maybe you should look at it, sir."

Scott took it. He emptied the contents out in the palm of his hand. A small piece of silk paper, carefully folded. He sat down by the light and unfolded it.

"What's it say, sir?" Eric said. Several officers came up the tunnel. Major Hendricks appeared.

"Major," Scott said. "Look at this."

Hendricks read the slip. "This just come?"

"A single runner. Just now."

"Where is he?" Hendricks asked sharply.

"The claws got him."

Major Hendricks grunted. "Here." He passed it to his companions. "I think this is what we've been waiting for. They certainly took their time about it."

"So they want to talk terms," Scott said. "Are we going along with them?"

"That's not for us to decide." Hendricks sat down. "Where's the communications officer? I want the Moon Base."

Leone pondered as the communications officer raised the outside antenna cautiously, scanning the sky above the bunker for any sign of a watching Russian ship.

"Sir," Scott said to Hendricks. "It's sure strange they suddenly came around. We've been using the claws for almost a year. Now all of a sudden they start to fold."

"Maybe claws have been getting down in their bunkers."

"One of the big ones, the kind with stalks, got into an Ivan bunker last week," Eric said. "It got a whole platoon of them before they got their lid shut."

"How do you know?"

"A buddy told me. The thing came back with—with remains."

"Moon Base, sir," the communications officer said.

On the screen the face of the lunar monitor appeared. His crisp uniform contrasted to the uniforms in the bunker. And he was clean shaven. "Moon Base."

"This is forward command L-Whistle. On Terra. Let me have General Thompson."

The monitor faded. Presently General Thompson's heavy features came into focus. "What is it, Major?"

"Our claws got a single Russian runner with a message. We don't know whether to act on it—there have been tricks like this in the past."

"What's the message?"

"The Russians want us to send a single officer on policy level over to their lines. For a conference. They don't state the nature of the conference. They say that matters of—" He consulted the slip. "—Matters of grave urgency make it advisable that discussion be opened between a representative of the UN forces and themselves."

He held the message up to the screen for the general to scan. Thompson's eyes moved.

"What should we do?" Hendricks asked.

"Send a man out."

"You don't think it's a trap?"

"It might be. But the location they give for their forward command is correct. It's worth a try, at any rate."

"I'll send an officer out. And report the results to you as soon as he returns."

"All right, Major." Thompson broke the connection. The screen died. Up above, the antenna came slowly down.

Hendricks rolled up the paper, deep in thought.

"I'll go," Leone said.

"They want somebody at policy level." Hendricks rubbed his jaw. "Policy level. I haven't been outside in months. Maybe I could use a little air."

"Don't you think it's risky?"

Hendricks lifted the view sight and gazed into it. The remains of the Russian were gone. Only a single claw was in sight. It was folding itself back, disappearing into the ash, like a crab. Like some hideous metal crab . . .

"That's the only thing that bothers me." Hendricks rubbed his wrist. "I know I'm safe as long as I have this on me. But there's something about them. I hate the damn things. I wish we'd never invented them. There's something wrong with them. Relentless little——"

"If we hadn't invented them, the Ivans would have."

Hendricks pushed the sight back. "Anyhow, it seems to be winning the war. I guess that's good."

"Sounds like you're getting the same jitters as the Ivans."

Hendricks examined his wrist watch. "I guess I had better get started, if I want to be there before dark."

He took a deep breath and then stepped out on to the grey, rubbed ground. After a minute he lit a cigarette and stood gazing around him. The landscape was dead. Nothing stirred. He could see for miles, endless ash and slag, ruins of buildings. A few trees without leaves or branches, only the trunks. Above him the eternal rolling clouds of grey, drifting between Terra and the sun.

Major Hendricks went on. Off to the right something scuttled, something round and metallic. A claw, going lickety-split after something. Probably after a small animal, a rat. They got rats, too. As a sort of sideline.

He came to the top of the little hill and lifted his field-glasses. The Russian lines were a few miles ahead of him. They had a forward command post there. The runner had come from it.

A squat robot with undulating arms passed by him, its arms weaving inquiringly. The robot went on its way, disappearing under some debris. Hendricks watched it go. He had never seen that type before. There were getting to be more and more types he had never seen, new varieties and sizes coming up from the underground factories.

Hendricks put out his cigarette and hurried on. It was interesting, the use of artificial forms in warfare. How had they got started? Necessity. The Soviet Union had gained great initial success, usual with the side that got the war going. Most of North America had been blasted off the map. Retaliation was quick in coming, of course. The sky was full of circling disc-bombers long before the war began; they had been up there for years. The discs began sailing down all over Russia within hours after Washington got it.

But that hadn't helped Washington.

The American bloc governments moved to the Moon Base the first year. There was not much else to do. Europe was gone; a slag heap with dark weeds growing from the ashes and bones. Most of North America was useless; nothing could be planted, no one could live. A few million people kept going up in Canada and down in South America. But during the second year Soviet parachutists began to drop, a few at first, then more and more. They wore the first really effective anti-radiation equipment; what was left of American production moved to the moon along with the governments.

All but the troops. The remaining troops stayed behind as best they could, a few thousand here, a platoon there. No one knew exactly where they were; they stayed where they could, moving around at night, hiding in ruins, in sewers, cellars, with the rats and snakes. It looked as if the Soviet Union had the war almost won. Except for a handful of projectiles fired off from the moon daily, there was almost no weapon in use against them.

They came and went as they pleased. The war, for all practical purposes, was over. Nothing effective opposed them.

And then the first claws appeared. And overnight the complexion of the war changed.

The claws were awkward, at first. Slow. The Ivans knocked them off almost as fast as they crawled out of their underground tunnels. But then they got better, faster and more cunning. Factories, all on Terra, turned them out. Factories a long way underground, behind the Soviet lines, factories that had once made atomic projectiles, now almost forgotten.

The claws got faster, and they got bigger. New types appeared, some with feelers, some that flew. There were a few jumping kinds. The best technicians on the moon were working on designs, making them more and more intricate, more flexible. They became uncanny; the Ivans were having a lot of trouble with them. Some of the little claws were learning to hide themselves, burrowing down into the ash, lying in wait.

And then they started getting into the Russian bunkers, slipping down when the lids were raised for air and a look around. One claw inside a bunker, a churning sphere of blades and metal—that was enough. And when one got in others followed. With a weapon like that the war couldn't go on much longer. Maybe it was already over.

Maybe he was going to hear the news. Maybe the Politburo had decided to throw in the sponge. Too bad it had taken so long. Six years. A long time for war like that, the way they had waged it. The automatic retaliation discs, spinning down all over Russia, hundreds of thousands of them. Bacteria crystals. The Soviet guided missiles, whistling through the air. The chain bombs. And now this, the robots, the claws——

The claws weren't like other weapons. They were *alive*, from any practical standpoint, whether the Governments wanted to admit it or not. They were not machines. They were living things, spinning, creeping, shaking themselves up suddenly from the grey ash and darting towards a man, climbing up him, rushing for his throat. And that was what they had been designed to do. Their job.

They did their job well. Especially lately, with the new designs coming up. Now they repaired themselves. They were on their own. Radiation tabs protected the UN troops, but if a man lost his tab he was fair game for the claws, no matter what his uniform. Down below the surface automatic machinery stamped them out. Human beings stayed a long way off. It was too risky; nobody wanted to be around them. They were left to themselves. And they seemed to be doing all right. The new designs were faster, more complex. More efficient.

Apparently they had won the war.

Major Hendricks lit a second cigarette. The landscape depressed him. Nothing but ash and ruins. He seemed to be alone, the only living thing in the whole world. To the right the ruins of a town rose up, a few walls and heaps of debris. He tossed the dead match away, increasing his pace. Suddenly he stopped, jerking up his gun, his body tense. For a minute it looked like—

From behind the shell of a ruined building a figure came, walking slowly towards him, walking hesitantly.

Hendricks blinked. "Stop!"

The boy stopped. Hendricks lowered his gun. The boy stood silently, looking at him. He was small, not very old. Perhaps eight. But it was hard to tell. Most of the kids who remained were stunted. He wore a faded blue sweater, ragged with dirt, and short pants. His hair was long and matted. Brown hair. It hung over his face and around his ears. He held something in his arms.

"What's that you have?" Hendricks said sharply.

The boy held it out. It was a toy, a bear. A teddy bear. The boy's eyes were large, but without expression.

Hendricks relaxed. "I don't want it. Keep it."

The boy hugged the bear again.

"Where do you live?" Hendricks said.

"In there."

"The ruins?"

"Yes."

"Underground?"

"Yes."

"How many are there?"

"How—how many?"

"How many of you. How big's your settlement?"

The boy did not answer.

Hendricks frowned. "You're not all by yourself, are you?"

The boy nodded.

"How do you stay alive?"

"There's food."

"What kind of food?"

"Different."

Hendricks studied him. "How old are you?"

"Thirteen."

It wasn't possible. Or was it? The boy was thin, stunted. And probably sterile. Radiation exposure, years straight. No wonder he was so small. His arms and legs were like pipe-cleaners, knobby and thin. Hendricks touched the boy's arm. His skin was dry and rough; radiation skin. He bent down, looking into the boy's face. There was no expression. Big eyes, big and dark.

"Are you blind?" Hendricks said.

"No. I can see some."

"How do you get away from the claws?"

"The claws?"

"The round things. That run and burrow."

"I don't understand."

Maybe there weren't any claws around. A lot of areas were free. They collected mostly around bunkers, where there were people. The claws had been designed to sense warmth, warmth of living things.

"You're lucky." Hendricks straightened up. "Well? Which way are you going? Back—back there?"

"Can I come with you?"

"With *me*?" Hendricks folded his arms. "I'm going a long way. Miles. I have to hurry." He looked at his watch. "I have to get there by nightfall."

"I want to come."

Hendricks fumbled in his pack. "It isn't worth it. Here." He tossed down the food cans he had with him. "You take these and go back. Okay?"

The boy said nothing.

"I'll be coming back this way. In a day or so. If you're around here when I come back you can come along with me. All right?"

"I want to come along with you now."

"It's a long walk."

"I can walk."

Hendricks shifted uneasily. It made too good a target, two people walking along. And the boy would slow him down. But he might not come back this way. And if the boy were really all alone——

"Okay. Come along."

The boy fell in beside him. Hendricks strode along. The boy walked silently, clutching his teddy bear.

"What's your name?" Hendricks said, after a time.

"David Edward Derring."

"David? What—what happened to your mother and father?"

"They died."

"How?"

"In the blast."

"How long ago?"

"Six years."

Hendricks slowed down. "You've been alone six years?"

"No. There were other people for a while. They went away."

"And you've been alone since?"

"Yes."

Hendricks glanced down. The boy was strange, saying very little. Withdrawn. But that was the way they were, the children who had survived. Quiet. Stoic. A strange kind of fatalism gripped them. Nothing came as a surprise. They accepted anything that came along. There was no longer any *normal*, any natural course of things, moral or physical, for them to expect. Custom, habit, all the determining forces of learning were gone; only brute experience remained.

"Am I walking too fast?" Hendricks said.

"No."

"How did you happen to see me?"

"I was waiting."

"Waiting?" Hendricks was puzzled. "What were you waiting for?"

"To catch things."

"What kind of things?"

"Things to eat."

"Oh." Hendricks set his lips grimly. A thirteen-year-old boy, living on rats and gophers and half-rotten canned food. Down in a hole under the ruins of a town. With radiation pools and claws, and Russian dive-mines up above, coasting around in the sky.

"Where are we going?" David asked.

"To the Russian lines."

"Russian?"

"The enemy. The people who started the war. They dropped the first radiation bombs. They began all this."

The boy nodded. His face showed no expression.

"I'm an American," Hendricks said.

There was no comment. On they went, the two of them, Hendricks walking a little ahead, David trailing behind him, hugging his dirty teddy bear against his chest.

About four in the afternoon they stopped to eat. Hendricks built a fire in a hollow between some slabs of concrete. He cleared the weeds away and heaped up bits of wood. The Russians' lines were not very far ahead. Around him was what had once been a long valley, acres of fruit trees and grapes. Nothing remained now but a few bleak stumps and the mountains that stretched across the horizon at the far end. And the clouds of rolling ash that blew and drifted with the wind, settling over the weeds and remains of buildings, walls here and there, once in a while what had been a road.

Hendricks made coffee and heated up some boiled mutton and bread. "Here." He handed bread and mutton to David. David squatted by the edge of the fire, his knees knobby and white. He examined the food and then passed it back shaking his head.

"No."

"No? Don't you want any?"

"No."

Hendricks shrugged. Maybe the boy was a mutant, used to special food. It didn't matter. When he was hungry he would find something to eat. The boy was strange. But there were many strange changes coming over the world. Life was not the same any more. It would never be the same again. The human race was going to have to realize that.

"Suit yourself," Hendricks said. He ate the bread and mutton by himself, washing it down with coffee. He ate slowly, finding the food hard to digest. When he was done he got to his feet and stamped the fire out.

David rose slowly, watching him with his young-old eyes.

"We're going," Hendricks said.

"All right."

Hendricks walked along, his gun in his arms. They were close; he was tense, ready for anything. The Russians should be expecting a runner, an answer to their own runner, but they were tricky. There was always the possibility of a slip-up. He scanned the landscape around him. Nothing but slag and ash, a few hills, charred trees. Concrete walls. But somewhere ahead was the first bunker of the Russian lines, the forward command. Underground, buried deep, with only a periscope showing, a few gun muzzles. Maybe an antenna.

"Will we be there soon?" David asked.

"Yes. Getting tired?"

"No."

"Why, then?"

David did not answer. He plodded carefully along behind, picking his way over the ash. His legs and shoes were grey with dust. His pinched face was streaked, lines of grey ash in rivulets down the pale white of his skin. There was no colour to his face. Typical of the new children, growing up in cellars and sewers and underground shelters.

Hendricks slowed down. He lifted his field-glasses and studied the ground ahead of him. Were they there, someplace, waiting for him? Watching him, the way his men had watched the Russian runner? A chill went up his back. Maybe they were getting their guns ready, preparing to fire, the way his men had prepared, made ready to kill.

Hendricks stopped, wiping perspiration from his face. "Damn." It made him uneasy. But he should be expected. The situation was different.

He strode over the ash, holding his gun tightly with both hands. Behind him came David. Hendricks peered around, tight-lipped. Any second it might happen. A burst of white light, a blast, carefully aimed from inside a deep concrete bunker.

He raised his arm and waved it around in a circle.

Nothing moved. To the right a long ridge ran, topped with

dead tree trunks. A few wild vines had grown up around the trees, remains of arbours. And the eternal dark weeds. Hendricks studied the ridge. Was anything up there? Perfect place for a lookout. He approached the ridge warily, David coming silently behind. If it were his command he'd have a sentry up there, watching for troops trying to infiltrate into the command area. Of course, if it were his command there would be claws around the area for full protection.

He stopped, feet apart, hands on his hips.

"Are we there?" David said.

"Almost."

"Why have we stopped?"

"I don't want to take any chances." Hendricks advanced slowly. Now the ridge lay directly beside him, along his right. Overlooking him. His uneasy feeling increased. If an Ivan were up there he wouldn't have a chance. He waved his arm again. They should be expecting someone in the UN uniform, in response to the note capsule. Unless the whole thing was a trap.

"Keep up with me." He turned towards David. "Don't drop behind."

"With you?"

"Up beside me! We're close. We can't take any chances. Come on."

"I'll be all right." David remained behind him, in the rear, a few paces away, still clutching his teddy bear.

"Have it your way." Hendricks raised his glasses again, suddenly tense. For a moment—had something moved? He scanned the ridge carefully. Everything was silent. Dead. No life up there, only tree trunks and ash. Maybe a few rats. The big black rats that had survived the claws. Mutants—built their own shelters out of saliva and ash. Some kind of plaster. Adaption. He started forward again.

A tall figure came out on the ridge above him, cloak flapping. Grey-green. A Russian. Behind him a second soldier appeared, Russian. Both lifted their guns, aiming.

Hendricks froze. He opened his mouth. The soldiers were kneeling, sighting down the side of the slope. A third figure had joined them on the ridge top, a smaller figure in grey-green. A woman. She stood behind the other two.

Hendricks found his voice. "Stop!" He waved up at them frantically. "I'm——"

The two Russians fired. Behind Hendricks there ⊙as a faint *pop*. Waves of heat lapped against him, throwing him to the ground. Ash tore at his face, grinding into his eyes and nose. Choking, he pulled himself to his knees. It was all a trap. He was finished. He had come to be killed, like a steer. The soldiers and the woman were coming down the side of the ridge towards him, sliding down through the soft ash. Hendricks was numb. His head throbbed. Awkwardly, he got his rifle up and took aim. It weighed a thousand tons; he could hardly hold it. His nose and cheeks stung. The air was full of the blast smell, a bitter acrid stench.

"Don't fire," the first Russian said, in heavily accented English.

The three of them came up to him, surrounding him. "Put down your rifle, Yank," the other said.

Hendricks was dazed. Everything had happened so fast. He had been caught. And they had blasted the boy. He turned his head. David was gone. What remained of him was strewn across the ground.

The three Russians studied him curiously. Hendricks sat, wiping blood from his nose, picking out bits of ash. He shook his head, trying to clear it. "Why did you do it?" he murmured thickly. "The boy."

"Why?" One of the soldiers helped him roughly to his feet. He turned Hendricks around. "Look."

Hendricks closed his eyes.

"Look!" The two Russians pulled him forward. "See. Hurry up. There isn't much time to spare, Yank!"

Hendricks looked. And gasped.

"See now? Now do you understand?"

From the remains of David a metal wheel rolled. Relays, glinting metal. Parts, wiring. One of the Russians kicked at the heap of remains. Parts popped out, rolling away, wheels and springs and rods. A plastic section fell in, half charred. Hendricks bent shakily down. The front of the head had come off. He could make out the intricate brain, wires and relays, tiny tubes and switches, thousands of minute studs——

"A robot," the soldier holding his arm said. "We watched it tagging you."

"Tagging me?"

"That's their way. They tag along with you. Into the bunker. That's how they get in."

Hendricks blinked, dazed. "But——"

"Come on." They led him towards the ridge, sliding and slipping on the ash. The woman reached the top and stood waiting for them.

"The forward command," Hendricks muttered. "I came to negotiate with the Soviet——"

"There is no more forward command. *They* got in. We'll explain." They reached the top of the ridge. "We're all that's left. The three of us. The rest were down in the bunker."

"This way. Down this way." The woman unscrewed a lid, a grey manhole cover set in the ground. "Get in."

Hendricks lowered himself. The two soldiers and the woman came behind him, following him down the ladder. The woman closed the lid after them, bolting it tightly into place.

"Good thing we saw you," one of the two soldiers grunted. "It had tagged you about as far as it was going to."

"Give me one of your cigarettes," the woman said. "I haven't had an American cigarette for weeks."

Hendricks pushed the pack to her. She took a cigarette and passed the pack to the two soldiers. In the corner of the small room the lamp gleamed fitfully. The room was low-ceilinged, cramped. The four of them sat around a small wood table. A few dirty dishes were stacked to one side. Behind a ragged curtain a second room was partly visible. Hendricks saw the corner of a cot, some blankets, clothes hung on a hook.

"We were here," the soldier beside him said. He took off his helmet, pushing his blond hair back. "I'm Corporal Rudi Maxer. Polish. Impressed in the Soviet Army two years ago." He held out his hand.

Hendricks hesitated and then shook. "Major Joseph Hendricks."

"Klaus Epstein." The other soldier shook with him, a small dark man with thinning hair. Epstein plucked nervously at his ear. "Austrian. Impressed God knows when. I don't remember.

The three of us were here, Rudi and I, with Tasso." He indicated the woman. "That's how we escaped. All the rest were down
in the bunker."

"And—and *they* got in?"

Epstein lit a cigarette. "First just one of them. The kind that
tagged you. Then it let others in."

Hendricks became alert. "The *kind?* Are there more than one
kind?"

"The little boy. David. David holding his teddy bear. That's
Variety Three. The most effective."

"What are the other types?"

Epstein reached into his coat. "Here." He tossed a packet
of photographs on to the table, tied with a string. "Look for
yourself."

Hendricks untied the string.

"You see," Rudi Maxer said, "that was why we wanted to
talk terms. The Russians, I mean. We found out about a week
ago. Found out that your claws were beginning to make up
new designs on their own. New types of their own. Better types.
Down in your underground factories behind our lines. You let
them stamp themselves, repair themselves. Made them more
and more intricate. It's your fault this happened."

Hendricks examined the photos. They had been snapped
hurriedly; they were blurred and indistinct. The first few
showed—David. David walking along a road, by himself. David
and another David. Three Davids. All exactly alike. Each with
a ragged teddy bear.

All pathetic.

"Look at the others," Tasso said.

The next pictures, taken at a great distance, showed a towering wounded soldier sitting by the side of a path, his arm in a
sling, the stump of one leg extended, a crude crutch on his lap.
Then two wounded soldiers, both the same, standing side by
side.

"That's Variety One. The Wounded Soldier." Klaus reached
out and took the pictures. "You see, the claws were designed to
get to human beings. To find them. Each kind was better than
the last. They got farther, closer past most of our defences, into
our lines. But as long as they were merely *machines*, metal

spheres with claws and horns, feelers, they could be picked off like any other object. They could be detected as lethal robots as soon as they were seen. Once we caught sight of them——"

"Variety One subverted our whole north wing," Rudi said. "It was a long time before anyone caught on. Then it was too late. They came in, wounded soldiers, knocking and begging to be let in. So we let them in. And as soon as they were in they took over. We were watching out for machines . . .."

"At that time it was thought there was only the one type," Klaus Epstein said. "No one suspected there were other types. The pictures were flashed to us. When the runner was sent to you, we knew of just one type. Variety One. The big Wounded Soldier. We thought that was all."

"Your line fell to——"

"To Variety Three. David and his bear. That worked even better." Klaus smiled bitterly. "Soldiers are suckers for children. We brought them in and tried to feed them. We found out the hard way what they were after. At least those who were in the bunker."

"The three of us were lucky," Rudi said. "Klaus and I were—were visiting Tasso when it happened. This is her place." He waved a big hand around. "This little cellar. We finished and climbed the ladder to start back. From the ridge we saw. There they were, all around the bunker. Fighting was still going on. David and his bear. Hundreds of them. Klaus took the pictures."

Klaus tied up the photographs again.

"And it's going on all along your line?" Hendricks said.

"Yes."

"How about *our* lines?" Without thinking, he touched the tab on his arm. "Can they——"

"They're not bothered by your radiation tabs. It makes no difference to them, Russian, American, Pole, German. It's all the same. They're doing what they were designed to do. Carrying out the original idea. They track down life, wherever they find it."

"They go by warmth," Klaus said. "That was the way you constructed them from the very start. Of course, those you designed were kept back by the radiation tabs you wear. Now they've got around that. These new varieties are lead-lined."

"What's the other variety?" Hendricks asked. "The David type, The Wounded Soldier—what's the other?"

"We don't know." Klaus pointed up at the wall. On the wall were two metal plates, ragged at the edges. Hendricks got up and studied them. They were bent and dented.

"The one on the left came off a Wounded Soldier," Rudi said. "We got one of them. It was going along towards our old bunker. We got it from the ridge, the same way we got the David tagging you."

The plate was stamped: I-V. Hendricks touched the other plate. "And this came from the David type?"

"Yes." The plate was stamped: III-V.

Klaus took a look at them, leaning over Hendricks' broad shoulder. "You can see what we're up against. There's another type. Maybe it was abandoned. Maybe it didn't work. But there must be a Second Variety. There's One and Three."

"You were lucky," Rudi said. "The David tagged you all the way here and never touched you. Probably thought you'd get it into a bunker, somewhere."

"One gets in and it's all over," Klaus said. "They move fast. One lets all the rest inside. They're inflexible. Machines with one purpose. They were built for only one thing." He rubbed sweat from his lip. "We saw."

They were silent.

"Let me have another cigarette, Yank," Tasso said. "They are good. I almost forgot how they were."

It was night. The sky was black. No stars were visible through the rolling clouds of ash. Klaus lifted the lid cautiously so that Hendricks could look out.

Rudi pointed into the darkness. "Over that way are the bunkers. Where we used to be. Not over half a mile from us. It was just chance Klaus and I were not there when it happened. Weakness. Saved by our lusts."

"All the rest must be dead," Klaus said in a low voice. "It came quickly. This morning the Politburo reached their decision. They notified us—forward command. Our runner was sent out at once. We saw him start towards the direction of your lines. We covered him until he was out of sight."

"Alex Radrivsky. We both knew him. He disappeared about

six o'clock. The sun had just come up. About noon Klaus and
I had an hour relief. We crept off, away from the bunkers. No
one was watching. We came here. There used to be a town here,
a few houses, a street. This cellar was part of a big farmhouse.
We knew Tasso would be here, hiding down in her little place.
We had come here before. Others from the bunkers came here.
Today happened to be our turn."

"So we were saved," Klaus said. "Chance. It might have been
others. We—we finished, and then we came up to the surface
and started back along the ridge. That was when we saw them,
the Davids. We understood right away. We had seen the photos
of the First Variety, the Wounded Soldier. Our Commissar dis-
tributed them to us with an explanation. If we had gone another
step they would have seen us. As it was we had to blast two
Davids before we got back. There were hundreds of them, all
around. Like ants. We took pictures and slipped back here, bolting the lid tight."

"They're not so much when you catch them alone. We moved
faster than they did. But they're inexorable. Not like living
things. They came right at us. And we blasted them."

Major Hendricks rested against the edge of the lid adjusting
his eyes to the darkness. "Is it safe to have the lid up at all?"

"If we're careful. How else can you operate your transmitter?"

Hendricks lifted the small belt transmitter slowly. He pressed
it against his ear. The metal was cold and damp. He blew against
the mike, raising up the short antenna. A faint hum sounded in
his ear. "That's true, I suppose."

But he still hesitated.

"We'll pull you under if anything happens," Klaus said.

"Thanks." Hendricks waited a moment, resting the transmitter against his shoulder. "Interesting, isn't it?"

"What?"

"This, the new types. The new varieties of claws. We're completely at their mercy, aren't we? By now they've probably
gotten into the UN lines, too. It makes me wonder if we're not
seeing the beginning of a new species. The new species. Evolution. The race to come after man."

Rudi grunted. "There is no race after man."

"No? Why not? Maybe we're seeing it now, the end of human beings, the beginning of the new society."

"They're not a race. They're mechanical killers. You made them to destroy. That's all they can do. They're machines with a job."

"So it seems now. But how about later on? After the war is over. Maybe, when there aren't any humans to destroy, their real potentialities will begin to show."

"You talk as if they were alive!"

"Aren't they?"

There was silence. "They're machines," Rudi said. "They look like people, but they're machines."

"Use your transmitter, Major," Klaus said. "We can't stay up here forever."

Holding the transmitter tightly Hendricks called the code of the command bunker. He waited, listening. No response. Only silence. He checked the leads carefully. Everything was in place.

"Scott!" he said into the mike. "Can you hear me?"

Silence. He raised the mast up full and tried again. Only static.

"I don't get anything. They may hear me but they may not want to answer."

"Tell them it's an emergency."

"They'll think I'm being forced to call. Under your direction." He tried again, outlining briefly what he had learned. But still the phone was silent, except for the faint static.

"Radiation pools kill most transmission," Klaus said, after awhile. "Maybe that's it."

Hendricks shut the transmitter up. "No use. No answer. Radiation pools? Maybe. Or they hear me, but won't answer. Frankly, that's what I would do, if a runner tried to call from the Soviet lines. They have no reason to believe such a story. They may hear everything I say——"

"Or maybe it's too late."

Hendricks nodded.

"We better get the lid down," Rudi said nervously. "We don't want to take unnecessary chances."

They climbed slowly back down the tunnel. Klaus bolted the lid carefully into place. They descended into the kitchen. The air was heavy and close around them.

"Could they work that fast?" Hendricks said. "I left the bunker this noon. Ten hours ago. How could they move so quickly?"

"It doesn't take them long. Not after the first one gets in. It goes wild. You know what the little claws can do. Even *one* of these is beyond belief. Razors, each finger. Maniacal."

"All right." Hendricks moved away impatiently. He stood with his back to them.

"What's the matter?" Rudi said.

"The Moon Base. God, if they've gotten there——"

"The Moon Base?"

Hendricks turned around. "They couldn't have got to the Moon Base. How would they get there? It isn't possible. I can't believe it."

"What is this Moon Base? We've heard rumours, but nothing definite. What is the actual situation? You seem concerned."

"We're supplied from the moon. The governments are there, under the lunar surface. All our people and industries. That's what keeps us going. If they should find some way of getting off Terra, on to the moon——"

"It only takes one of them. Once the first one gets in it admits the others. Hundreds of them, all alike. You should have seen them. Identical. Like ants."

"Perfect socialism," Tasso said. "The ideal of the Communist state. All citizens interchangeable."

Klaus grunted angrily. "That's enough. Well? What next?"

Hendricks paced back and forth, around the small room. The air was full of smells of food and perspiration. The others watched him. Presently Tasso pushed through the curtain, into the other room. "I'm going to take a nap."

The curtain closed behind her. Rudi and Klaus sat down at the table, still watching Hendricks. "It's up to you," Klaus said. "We don't know your situation."

Hendricks nodded.

"It's a problem." Rudi drank some coffee, filling his cup from a rusty pot. "We're safe here for a while, but we can't stay here forever. Not enough food or supplies."

"But if we go outside——"

"If we go outside they'll get us. Or probably they'll get us.

We couldn't go very far. How far is your command bunker, Major?"

"What if they're already there?" Klaus said.

Rudi shrugged. "Well, then we come back here."

Hendricks stopped pacing. "What do you think the chances are they're already in the American lines?"

"Hard to say. Fairly good. They're organized. They know exactly what they're doing. Once they start they go like a horde of locusts. They have to keep moving, and fast. It's secrecy and speed they depend on. Surprise. They push their way in before anyone has any idea."

"I see," Hendricks murmured.

From the other room Tasso stirred. "Major?"

Hendricks pushed the curtain back. "What?"

Tasso looked up at him lazily from the cot. "Have you any more American cigarettes left?"

Hendricks went into the room and sat down across from her, on a wood stool. He felt in his pockets. "No. All gone."

"Too bad."

"What nationality are you?" Hendricks asked after a while.

"Russian."

"How did you get here?"

"Here?"

"This used to be France. This was part of Normandy. Did you come with the Soviet army?"

"Why?"

"Just curious." He studied her. She had taken off her coat, tossing it over the end of the cot. She was young, about twenty. Slim. Her long hair stretched out over the pillow. She was staring at him silently, her eyes dark and large.

"What's on your mind?" Tasso said.

"Nothing. How old are you?"

"Eighteen." She continued to watch him, unblinking, her arms behind her head. She had on Russian army pants and shirt. Grey-green. Thick leather belt with counter and cartridges. Medicine kit.

"You're in the Soviet army?"

"No."

"Where did you get the uniform?"

She shrugged. "It was given to me," she told him.

"How—how old were you when you came here?"

"Sixteen."

"That young?"

Her eyes narrowed. "What do you mean?"

Hendricks rubbed his jaw. "Your life would have been a lot different if there had been no war. Sixteen. You came here at sixteen. To live this way."

"I had to survive."

"I'm not moralizing."

"Your life would have been different, too," Tasso murmured. She reached down and unfastened one of her boots. She kicked the boot off, on to the floor. "Major, do you want to go in the other room? I'm sleepy."

"It's going to be a problem, the four of us here. It's going to be hard to live in these quarters. Are there just two rooms?"

"Yes."

"How big was the cellar originally? Was it larger than this? Are there other rooms filled up with debris? We might be able to open one of them."

"Perhaps. I really don't know." Tasso loosened her belt. She made herself comfortable on the cot, unbuttoning her shirt. "You're sure you have no more cigarettes?"

"I had only the one pack."

"Too bad. Maybe if we get back to your bunker we can find some." The other boot fell. Tasso reached up for the light cord. "Good night."

"You're going to sleep?"

"That's right."

The room plunged into darkness. Hendricks got up and made his way past the curtain, into the kitchen.

And stopped, rigid.

Rudi stood against the wall, his face white and gleaming. His mouth opened and closed but no sounds came. Klaus stood in front of him, the muzzle of his pistol in Rudi's stomach. Neither of them moved. Klaus, his hand tight around his gun, his features set. Rudi, pale and silent, spread-eagled against the wall.

"What——" Hendricks muttered, but Klaus cut him off.

"Be quiet, Major. Come over here. Your gun. Get out your gun."

Hendricks drew his pistol. "What is it?"

"Cover him." Klaus motioned him forward. "Beside me. Hurry!"

Rudi moved a little, lowering his arms. He turned to Hendricks, licking his lips. The whites of his eyes shone wildly. Sweat dripped from his forehead, down his cheeks. He fixed his gaze on Hendricks. "Major, he's gone insane. Stop him." Rudi's voice was thin and hoarse, almost inaudible.

"What's going on?" Hendricks demanded.

Without lowering his pistol Klaus answered. "Major, remember our discussion? The Three Varieties? We knew about One and Three. But we didn't know about Two. At least, we didn't know before." Klaus' fingers tightened around the gun butt. "We didn't know before, but we know now."

He pressed the trigger. A burst of white heat rolled out of the gun, licking around Rudi.

"Major, this is the Second Variety."

Tasso swept the curtain aside. "Klaus! What did you do?"

Klaus turned from the charred form, gradually sinking down the wall on to the floor. "The Second Variety, Tasso. Now we know. We have all three types identified. The danger is less. I——"

Tasso stared past him at the remains of Rudi, at the blackened, smouldering fragments and bits of cloth. "You killed him."

"Him? *It*, you mean. I was watching. I had a feeling, but I wasn't sure. At least, I wasn't sure before. But this evening I was certain." Klaus rubbed his pistol butt nervously. "We're lucky. Don't you understand? Another hour and it might——"

"You were *certain*?" Tasso pushed past him and bent down, over the steaming remains on the floor. Her face became hard. "Major, see for yourself. Bones. Flesh."

Hendricks bent down beside her. The remains were human remains. Seared flesh, charred bone fragments, part of a skull. Ligaments, viscera, blood. Blood forming a pool against the wall.

"No wheels," Tasso said calmly. She straightened up. "No

wheels, no parts, no relays. Not a claw. Not the Second Variety."
She folded her arms. "You're going to have to be able to explain
this."

Klaus sat down at the table, all the colour drained suddenly
from his face. He put his head in his hands and rocked back and
forth.

"Snap out of it." Tasso's fingers closed over his shoulder.
"Why did you do it? Why did you kill him?"

"He was frightened," Hendricks said. "All this, the whole
thing, building up around us."

"Maybe."

"What, then? What do you think?"

"I think he may have had a reason for killing Rudi. A good
reason."

"What reason?"

"Maybe Rudi learned something."

Hendricks studied her bleak face. "About what?" he asked.

"About him. About Klaus."

Klaus looked up quickly. "You can see what she's trying to say.
She thinks I'm the Second Variety. Don't you see, Major? Now
she wants you to believe I killed him on purpose. That
I'm——"

"Why did you kill him, then?" Tasso said.

"I told you." Klaus shook his head wearily. "I thought he
was a claw. I thought I knew."

"Why?"

"I had been watching him. I was suspicious."

"Why?"

"I thought I had seen something. Heard something. I thought
I heard him—*whirr.*"

There was silence.

"Do you believe that?" Tasso said to Hendricks.

"Yes. I believe what he says."

"I don't. I think he killed Rudi for a good purpose." Tasso
touched the rifle, resting in the corner of the room. "Major——"

"No." Hendricks shook his head. "Let's stop it right now. One
is enough. We're afraid, the way he was. If we kill him we'll be
doing what he did to Rudi."

Klaus looked gratefully up at him. "Thanks. I was afraid. You understand, don't you? Now she's afraid, the way I was. She wants to kill me."

"No more killing." Hendricks moved towards the end of the ladder. "I'm going above and try the transmitter once more. If I can't get them we're moving back towards my lines tomorrow morning."

Klaus rose quickly. "I'll come up with you and give you a hand."

The night air was cold. The earth was cooling off. Klaus took a deep breath, filling his lungs. He and Hendricks stepped on to the ground, out of the tunnel. Klaus planted his feet wide apart, the rifle up, watching and listening. Hendricks crouched by the tunnel mouth, tuning the small transmitter.

"Any luck?" Klaus asked presently.

"Not yet."

"Keep trying. Tell them what happened."

Hendricks kept trying. Without success. Finally he lowered the antenna. "It's useless. They can't hear me. Or they hear me and won't answer. Or——"

"Or they don't exist."

"I'll try once more." Hendricks raised the antenna. "Scott, can you hear me? Come in!"

He listened. There was only static. Then, still very faintly——

"This is Scott."

His fingers tightened. "Scott! Is it you?"

"This is Scott."

Klaus squatted down. "Is it your command?"

"Scott, listen. Do you understand? About them, the claws. Did you get my message? Did you hear me?"

"Yes." Faintly. Almost inaudible. He could hardly make out the word.

"You got my message? Is everything all right at the bunker? None of them have got in?"

"Everything is all right."

"Have they tried to get in?"

The voice was weaker.

"No."

Hendricks turned to Klaus. "They're all right."

"Have they been attacked?"

"No." Hendricks pressed the phone tighter to his ear. "Scott,

I can hardly hear you. Have you notified the Moon Base? Do they know? Are they alerted?"

No answer.

"Scott! Can you hear me?"

Silence.

Hendricks relaxed, sagging. "Faded out. Must be radiation pools."

Hendricks and Klaus looked at each other. Neither of them said anything. After a time Klaus said, "Did it sound like any of your men? Could you identify the voice?"

"It was too faint."

"You couldn't be certain?"

"No."

"Then it could have been——"

"I don't know. Now I'm not sure. Let's go back down and get the lid closed."

They climbed back down the ladder slowly, into the warm cellar. Klaus bolted the lid behind them. Tasso waited for them, her face expressionless.

"Any luck?" she asked.

Neither of them answered. "Well?" Klaus said at last. "What do you think, Major? Was it your officer, or was it one of *them*?"

"I don't know."

"Then we're just where we were before."

Hendricks stared down at the floor, his jaw set. "We'll have to go. To be sure."

"Anyhow, we have food here for only a few weeks. We'd have to go up after that, in any case."

"Apparently so."

"What's wrong?" Tasso demanded. "Did you get across to your bunker? What's the matter?"

"It may have been one of my men," Hendricks said slowly. "Or it may have been one of *them*. But we'll never know standing here." He examined his watch. "Let's turn in and get some sleep. We want to be up early tomorrow."

"Early?"

"Our best chance to get through the claws should be early in the morning," Hendricks said.

The morning was crisp and clear. Major Hendricks studied the countryside through his field-glasses.

"See anything?" Klaus said.

"No."

"Can you make out our bunkers?"

"Which way?"

"Here." Klaus took the glasses and adjusted them. "I know where to look." He looked a long time, silently.

Tasso came to the top of the tunnel and stepped up on to the ground. "Anything?"

"No." Klaus passed the glasses back to Hendricks. "They're out of sight. Come on. Let's not stay here."

The three of them made their way down the side of the ridge, sliding in the soft ash. Across a flat rock a lizard scuttled. They stopped instantly, rigid.

"What was it?" Klaus muttered.

"A lizard."

The lizard ran on, hurrying through the ash. It was exactly the same colour as the ash.

"Perfect adaptation," Klaus said. "Proves we were right. Lysenko, I mean."

They reached the bottom of the ridge and stopped, standing close together, looking around them.

"Let's go." Hendricks started off. "It's a good long trip, on foot."

Klaus fell in beside him. Tasso walked behind, her pistol held alertly. "Major, I've been meaning to ask you something," Klaus said. "How did you run across the David? The one that was tagging you."

"I met it along the way. In some ruins."

"What did it say?"

"Not much. It said it was alone. By itself."

"You couldn't tell it was a machine? It talked like a living person? You never suspected?"

"It didn't say much. I noticed nothing unusual."

"It's strange, machines so much like people that you can be fooled. Almost alive. I wonder where it'll end."

"They're doing what you Yanks designed them to do," Tasso said. "You designed them to hunt out life and destroy. Human life. Wherever they find it."

Hendricks was watching Klaus intently. "Why did you ask me? What's on your mind?"

"Nothing," Klaus answered.

"Klaus thinks you're the Second Variety," Tasso said calmly, from behind them. "Now he's got his eye on you."

Klaus flushed. "Why not? We sent a runner to the Yank lines and he comes back. Maybe he thought he'd find some good game here."

Hendricks laughed harshly. "I came from the UN bunkers. There were human beings all around me."

"Maybe you saw an opportunity to get into the Soviet lines. Maybe you saw your chance. Maybe you——"

"The Soviet lines had already been taken over. Your lines had been invaded before I left my command bunker. Don't forget that."

Tasso came up beside him. "That proves nothing at all, Major."

"Why not?"

"There appears to be little communication between the varieties. Each is made in a different factory. They don't seem to work together. You might have started for the Soviet lines without knowing anything about the work of the other varieties. Or even what the other varieties were like."

"How do you know so much about the claws?" Hendricks said.

"I've seen them. I've observed them. I observed them take over the Soviet bunkers."

"You know quite a lot," Klaus said. "Actually, you saw very little. Strange that you should have been such an acute observer."

Tasso laughed. "Do you suspect me, now?"

"Forget it," Hendricks said. They walked on in silence.

"Are we going the whole way on foot?" Tasso said, after a while. "I'm not used to walking." She gazed around at the plain of ash, stretching out on all sides of them, as far as they could see. "How dreary."

"It's like this all the way," Klaus said.

"In a way I wish you had been in your bunker when the attack came."

"Somebody else would have been with you, if not me," Klaus muttered.

Tasso laughed, putting her hands in her pockets. "I suppose so."

They walked on, keeping their eyes on the vast plain of silent ash around them.

The sun was setting. Hendricks made his way forward slowly, waving Tasso and Klaus back. Klaus squatted down, resting his gun butt against the ground.

Tasso found a concrete slab and sat down with a sigh. "It's good to rest."

"Be quiet," Klaus said sharply.

Hendricks pushed up to the top of the rise ahead of them. The same rise the Russian runner had come up, the day before. Hendricks dropped down, stretching himself out, peering through his glasses at what lay beyond.

Nothing was visible. Only ash and occasional trees. But there, not more than fifty yards ahead, was the entrance of the forward command bunker. The bunker from which he had come. Hendricks watched silently. No motion. No sign of life. Nothing stirred.

Klaus slithered up beside him. "Where is it?"

"Down there." Hendricks passed him the glasses. Clouds of ash rolled across the evening sky. The world was darkening. They had a couple of hours of light left, at the most. Probably not that much.

"I don't see anything," Klaus said.

"That tree there. The stump. By the pile of bricks. The entrance is to the right of the bricks."

"I'll have to take your word for it."

"You and Tasso cover me from here. You'll be able to sight all the way to the bunker entrance."

"You're going down alone?"

"With my wrist tab I'll be safe. The ground around the bunker is a living field of claws. They collect down in the ash. Like crabs. Without tabs you wouldn't have a chance."

"Maybe you're right."

"I'll walk slowly all the way. As soon as I know for certain——"

"If they're down inside the bunker you won't be able to get back up here. They go fast. You don't realize."

"What do you suggest?"

Klaus considered. "I don't know. Get them to come up to the surface. So you can see."

Hendricks brought his transmitter from his belt, raising the antenna. "Let's get started."

Klaus signalled to Tasso. She crawled expertly up the side of the rise to where they were sitting.

"He's going down alone," Klaus said. "We'll cover him from here. As soon as you see him start back, fire past him at once. They come quick."

"You're not very optimistic," Tasso said.

"No, I'm not."

Hendricks opened the breech of his gun, checking it carefully. "Maybe things are all right."

"You didn't see them. Hundreds of them. All the same. Pouring out like ants."

"I should be able to find out without going down all the way." Hendricks locked his gun, gripping it in one hand, the transmitter in the other. "Well, wish me luck."

Klaus put out his hand. "Don't go down until you're sure. Talk to them from up here. Make them show themselves."

Hendricks stood up. He stepped down the side of the rise.

A moment later he was walking slowly towards the pile of bricks and debris beside the dead tree stump. Towards the entrance of the forward command bunker.

Nothing stirred. He raised the transmitter, clicking it on. "Scott? Can you hear me?"

Silence.

"Scott! This is Hendricks. Can you hear me? I'm standing outside the bunker. You should be able to see me in the view sight."

He listened, the transmitter gripped tightly. No sound. Only static. He walked forward. A claw burrowed out of the ash and raced towards him, studied him intently, and then fell in behind him, dogging respectfully after him, a few paces away. A moment later a second big claw joined it. Silently, the claws trailed him, as he walked slowly towards the bunker.

Hendricks stopped, and behind him, the claws came to a halt. He was close now. Almost to the bunker steps.

"Scott! Can you hear me? I'm standing right above you. Outside. On the surface. Are you picking me up?"

He waited, holding his gun against his side, the transmitter tightly to his ear. Time passed. He strained to hear, but there was only silence, and faint static.

Then, distantly, metallically——

"This is Scott."

The voice was neutral. Cold. He could not identify it. But the earphone was minute.

"Scott, listen. I'm standing right above you. I'm on the surface, looking down into the bunker entrance."

"Yes."

"Can you see me?"

"Yes."

"Through the view sight? You have the sight trained on me?"

"Yes."

Hendricks pondered. A circle of claws waited quietly on all sides of him. "Is everything all right in the bunker? Nothing unusual has happened?"

"Everything is all right."

"Will you come up to the surface? I want to see you for a moment." Hendricks took a deep breath. "Come up here with me. I want to talk to you."

"Come down."

"I'm giving you an order."

Silence.

"Are you coming?" Hendricks listened. There was no response. "I order you to come to the surface."

"Come down."

Hendricks set his jaw. "Let me talk to Leone."

There was a long pause. He listened to the static. Then a voice came, hard, thin, metallic. The same as the other. "This is Leone."

"Hendricks. I'm on the surface. At the bunker entrance. I want one of you to come up here."

"Come down."

"Why come down? I'm giving you an order!"

Silence. Hendricks lowered the transmitter. He looked carefully around him. The entrance was just ahead. Almost at his feet. He lowered the antenna and fastened the transmitter to his belt. Carefully, he gripped his gun with both hands. He moved forward, a step at a time. If they could see him they knew he was starting towards the entrance. He closed his eyes a moment.

Then he put his foot on the first step that led downward.

Two Davids came up at him, their faces identical and expressionless. He blasted them into particles. More came rushing silently up, a whole pack of them. All exactly the same.

Hendricks turned and raced back, away from the bunker, back towards the rise.

At the top of the rise Tasso and Klaus were firing down. The small claws were already streaking up toward them, shining metal spheres going fast, racing frantically through the ash. But he had no time to think about that. He knelt down, aiming at the bunker entrance, gun against his cheek. The Davids were coming out in groups, clutching their teddy bears, their thin knobby legs pumping as they ran up the steps to the surface. Hendricks fired into the main body of them. They burst apart, wheels and springs flying in all directions. He fired again, through the mist of particles.

A giant lumbering figure rose up in the bunker entrance, tall and swaying. Hendricks paused, amazed. A man, a soldier. With one leg, supporting himself with a crutch.

"Major!" Tasso's voice came. More firing. The huge figure moved forward, Davids swarming around it. Hendricks broke out of his freeze. The First Variety. The Wounded Soldier. He aimed and fired. The soldier burst into bits, parts and relays flying. Now many Davids were out on the flat ground, away from the bunker. He fired again and again, moving slowly back, half-crouching and aiming.

From the rise, Klaus fired down. The side of the rise was alive with claws making their way up. Hendricks retreated towards the rise, running and crouching. Tasso had left Klaus and was circling slowly to the right, moving away from the rise.

A David slipped up towards him, its small white face expressionless, brown hair hanging down in its eyes. It bent over suddenly, opening its arms. Its teddy bear hurtled down and leaped across the ground, bounding towards him. Hendricks fired. The bear and the David both dissolved. He grinned, blinking. It was like a dream.

"Up here!" Tasso's voice. Hendricks made his way towards her. She was over by some columns of concrete, walls of a ruined building. She was firing past him, with the hand pistol Klaus had given her.

"Thanks." He joined her, gasping for breath. She pulled him back, behind the concrete, fumbling at her belt.

"Close your eyes!" She unfastened a globe from her waist. Rapidly, she unscrewed the cap, locking it into place. "Close your eyes and get down."

She threw the bomb. It sailed in an arc, an expert, rolling and bouncing to the entrance of the bunker. Two Wounded Soldiers stood uncertainly by the brick pile. More Davids poured from behind them, out on to the plain. One of the Wounded Soldiers moved towards the bomb, stooping awkwardly down to pick it up.

The bomb went off. The concussion whirled Hendricks around, throwing him on his face. A hot wind rolled over him. Dimly he saw Tasso standing behind the columns, firing slowly and methodically at the Davids coming out of the raging clouds of white fire.

Back along the rise Klaus struggled with a ring of claws circling around him. He retreated, blasting at them and moving back, trying to break through the ring.

Hendricks struggled to his feet. His head ached. He could hardly see. Everything was licking at him, raging and whirling. His right arm would not move.

Tasso pulled back toward him. "Come on. Let's go."

"Klaus—He's still up there."

"Come on!" Tasso dragged Hendricks back, away from the columns. Hendricks shook his head, trying to clear it. Tasso led him rapidly away, her eyes intense and bright, watching for claws that had escaped the blast.

One David came out of the rolling clouds of flame. Tasso blasted it. No more appeared.

"But Klaus. What about him?" Hendricks stopped, standing unsteadily. "He——"

"Come on!"

They retreated, moving farther and farther away from the bunker. A few small claws followed them for a little while and then gave up, turning back and going off.

At last Tasso stopped. "We can stop here and get our breaths."

Hendricks sat down on some heaps of debris. He wiped his neck, gasping. "We left Klaus back there."

Tasso said nothing. She opened her gun, sliding a fresh round of blast cartridges into place.

Hendricks stared at her, dazed. "You left him back there on purpose."

Tasso snapped the gun together. She studied the heaps of rubble around them, her face expressionless. As if she were watching for something.

"What is it?" Hendrick demanded. "What are you looking for? Is something coming?" He shook his head, trying to understand. What was she doing? What was she waiting for? He could see nothing. Ash lay all around them, ash and ruins. Occasional stark tree trunks, without leaves or branches. "What——"

Tasso cut him off. "Be still." Her eyes narrowed. Suddenly her gun came up. Hendricks turned, following her gaze.

Back the way they had come a figure appeared. The figure walked unsteadily toward them. Its clothes were torn. It limped as it made its way along, going very slowly and carefully. Stopping now and then, resting and getting its strength. Once it almost fell. It stood for a moment, trying to steady itself. Then it came on.

Klaus.

Hendricks stood up. "Klaus!" He started towards him. "How the hell did you——"

Tasso fired. Hendricks swung back. She fired again, the blast passing him, a searing line of heat. The beam caught Klaus in the chest. He exploded, gears and wheels flying. For a moment he continued to walk. Then he swayed back and forth. He crashed to the ground, his arms flung out. A few more wheels rolled away.

Silence.

Tasso turned to Hendricks. "Now you understand why he killed Rudi."

Hendricks sat down again slowly. He shook his head. He was numb. He could not think.

"Do you see?" Tasso said. "Do you understand?"

Hendricks said nothing. Everything was slipping away from him, faster and faster. Darkness, rolling and plucking at him. He closed his eyes.

Hendricks opened his eyes slowly. His body ached all over. He tried to sit up but needles of pain shot through his arm and shoulder. He gasped.

"Don't try to get up," Tasso said. She bent down, putting her cold hand against his forehead.

It was night. A few stars glinted above, shining through the drifting clouds of ash. Hendricks lay back, his teeth locked. Tasso watched him impassively. She had built a fire with some wood and weeds. The fire licked feebly, hissing at a metal cup suspended over it. Everything was silent. Unmoving darkness, beyond the fire.

"So he was the Second Variety," Hendricks murmured.

"I had always thought so."

"Why didn't you destroy him sooner?" he wanted to know.

"You held me back." Tasso crossed to the fire to look into the metal cup. "Coffee. It'll be ready to drink in a while."

She came back and sat down beside him. Presently she opened her pistol and began to disassemble the firing mechanism, studying it intently.

"This is a beautiful gun," Tasso said, half-aloud. "The construction is superb."

"What about them? The claws."

"The concussion from the bomb put most of them out of action. They're delicate. Highly organized, I suppose."

"The Davids, too?"

"Yes."

"How did you happen to have a bomb like that?"

Tasso shrugged. "We designed it. You shouldn't underestimate our technology, Major. Without such a bomb you and I would no longer exist."

"Very useful."

Tasso stretched out her legs, warming her feet in the heat of the fire. "It surprised me that you did not seem to understand, after he killed Rudi. Why did you think he——"

"I told you. I thought he was afraid."

"Really? You know, Major, for a little while I suspected you. Because you wouldn't let me kill him. I thought you might be protecting him." She laughed.

"Are we safe here?" Hendricks asked presently.

"For a while. Until they get reinforcements from some other area." Tasso began to clean the interior of the gun with a bit of rag. She finished and pushed the mechanism back into place. She closed the gun, running her finger along the barrel.

"We were lucky," Hendricks murmured.

"Yes. Very lucky."

"Thanks for pulling me away."

Tasso did not answer. She glanced up at him, her eyes bright in the fire light. Hendricks examined his arm. He could not move his fingers. His whole side seemed numb. Down inside him was a dull steady ache.

"How do you feel?" Tasso asked.

"My arm is damaged."

"Anything else?"

"Internal injuries."

"You didn't get down when the bomb went off."

Hendricks said nothing. He watched Tasso pour the coffee from the cup into a flat metal pan. She brought it over to him.

"Thanks." He struggled up enough to drink. It was hard to swallow. His insides turned over and he pushed the pan away. "That's all I can drink now."

Tasso drank the rest. Time passed. The clouds of ash moved across the dark sky above them. Hendricks rested, his mind blank. After a while he became aware that Tasso was standing over him, gazing down at him.

"What is it?" he murmured.

"Do you feel any better?"

"Some."

"You know, Major, if I hadn't dragged you away they would have got you. You would be dead. Like Rudi."

"I know."

"Do you want to know why I brought you out? I could have left you. I could have left you there."

"Why did you bring me out?"

"Because we have to get away from here." Tasso stirred the fire with a stick, peering calmly down into it. "No human being can live here. When their reinforcements come we won't have a chance. I've pondered about it while you were unconscious. We have perhaps three hours before they come."

"And you expect me to get us away?"

"That's right. I expect you to get us out of here."

"Why me?"

"Because I don't know any way." Her eyes shone at him in the half-light, bright and steady. "If you can't get us out of here they'll kill us within three hours. I see nothing else ahead. Well, Major? What are you going to do? I've been waiting all night. While you were unconscious I sat here, waiting and listening. It's almost dawn. The night is almost over."

Hendricks considered. "It's curious," he said at last.

"Curious?"

"That you should think I can get us out of here. I wonder what you think I can do."

"Can you get us to the Moon Base?"

"The Moon Base? How?"

"There must be some way."

Hendricks shook his head. "No. There's no way that I know of."

Tasso said nothing. For a moment her steady gaze wavered. She ducked her head, turning abruptly away. She scrambled to her feet. "More coffee?"

"No."

"Suit yourself." Tasso drank silently. He could not see her face. He lay back against the ground, deep in thought, trying to concentrate. It was hard to think. His head still hurt. And the numbing daze still hung over him.

"There might be one way," he said suddenly.

"Oh?"

"How soon is dawn?"

"Two hours. The sun will be coming up shortly."

"There's supposed to be a ship near here. I've never seen it. But I know it exists."

"What kind of a ship?" Her voice was sharp.

"A rocket cruiser."

"Will it take us off? To the Moon Base?"

"It's supposed to. In case of emergency." He rubbed his forehead.

"What's wrong?"

"My head. It's hard to think. I can hardly—hardly concentrate. The bomb."

"Is the ship near here?" Tasso slid over beside him, settling down on her haunches. "How far is it? Where is it?"

"I'm trying to think."

Her fingers dug into his arm. "Nearby?" Her voice was like iron. "Where would it be? Would they store it underground? Hidden underground?"

"Yes. In a storage locker."

"How do we find it? Is it marked? Is there a code marker to identify it?"

Hendricks concentrated. "No. No markings. No code symbol."

"What, then?"

"A sign."

"What sort of sign?"

Hendricks did not answer. In the flickering light his eyes were glazed, two sightless orbs. Tasso's fingers dug into his arm.

"What sort of sign? What is it?"

"I—I can't think. Let me rest."

"All right." She let go and stood up. Hendricks lay back against the ground, his eyes closed. Tasso walked away from him, her hands in her pockets. She kicked a rock out of her way and stood staring up at the sky. The night blackness was already beginning to fade into grey. Morning was coming.

Tasso gripped her pistol and walked around the fire in a circle, back and forth. On the ground Major Hendricks lay, his eyes closed, unmoving. The greyness rose in the sky, higher and higher. The landscape became visible, fields of ash stretching out in all directions. Ash and ruins of buildings, a wall here and there, heaps of concrete, the naked trunk of a tree.

The air was cold and sharp. Somewhere a long way off a bird made a few bleak sounds.

Hendricks stirred. He opened his eyes. "Is it dawn? Already?"

"Yes."

Hendricks sat up a little. "You wanted to know something. You were asking me."

"Do you remember now?"

"Yes."

"What is it?" She tensed. "What?" she repeated sharply.

"A well. A ruined well. It's in a storage locker under a well."

"A well." Tasso relaxed. "Then we'll find a well." She looked at her watch. "We have about an hour, Major. Do you think we can find it in an hour?"

"Give me a hand up," Hendricks said.

Tasso put her pistol away and helped him to his feet. "This is going to be difficult."

"Yes it is." Hendricks set his lips tightly. "I don't think we're going to go very far."

They began to walk. The early sun cast a little warmth down on them. The land was flat and barren, stretching out grey and lifeless as far as they could see. A few birds sailed silently, far above them, circling slowly.

"See anything?" Hendricks said. "Any claws?"

"No. Not yet."

They passed through some ruins, upright concrete and bricks. A cement foundation. Rats scuttled away. Tasso jumped back warily.

"This used to be a town," Hendricks said. "A village. Provincial village. This was all grape country, once. Where we are now."

They came on to a ruined street, weeds and cracks crisscrossing it. Over to the right a stone chimney stuck up.

"Be careful," he warned her.

A pit yawned, an open basement. Ragged ends of pipes jutted up, twisted and bent. They passed part of a house, a bathtub turned on its side. A broken chair. A few spoons and bits of china dishes. In the centre of the street the ground had sunk away. The depression was filled with weeds and debris and bones.

"Over here," Hendricks murmured.

"This way?"

"To the right."

They passed the remains of a heavy duty tank; Hendricks' belt counter clicked ominously. The tank had been radiation blasted. A few feet from the tank a mummified body lay sprawled out, mouth open. Beyond the road was a flat field. Stones and weeds, and bits of broken glass.

"There," Hendricks said.

A stone well jutted up, sagging and broken. A few boards lay across it. Most of the well had sunk into rubble. Hendricks walked unsteadily toward it, Tasso beside him.

"Are you certain about this?" Tasso said. "This doesn't look like anything."

"I'm sure." Hendricks sat down at the edge of the well, his teeth locked. His breath came quickly. He wiped perspiration from his face. "This was arranged so the senior command officer could get away. If anything happened. If the bunker fell."

"That was you?"

"Yes."

"Where is the ship? Is it here?"

"We're standing on it." Hendricks ran his hands over the surface of the well stones. "The eye-lock responds to me, not to anybody else. It's my ship. Or it was supposed to be."

There was a sharp click. Presently they heard a low grating sound from below them.

"Step back," Hendricks said. He and Tasso moved away from the well.

A section of the ground slid back. A metal frame pushed slowly up through the ash, shoving bricks and weeds out of the way. The action ceased, as the ship nosed into view.

"There it is," Hendricks said.

The ship was small. It rested quietly, suspended in its mesh frame, like a blunt needle. A rain of ash sifted down into the dark cavity from which the ship had been raised. Hendricks made his way over to it. He mounted the mesh and unscrewed the hatch, pulling it back. Inside the ship the control banks and the pressure seat were visible.

Tasso came and stood beside him, gazing into the ship. "I'm not accustomed to rocket piloting," she said, after a while.

Hendricks glanced at her. "I'll do the piloting."

"Will you? There's only one seat, Major. I can see it's built to carry only a single person."

Hendricks' breathing changed. He studied the interior of the ship intently. Tasso was right. There was only one seat. The ship was built to carry only one person. "I see," he said slowly. "And the one person is you."

She nodded.

"Of course."

"Why?"

"*You* can't go. You might not live through the trip. You're injured. You probably wouldn't get there."

"An interesting point. But you see, I know where the Moon Base is. And you don't. You might fly around for months and not find it. It's well hidden. Without knowing what to look for——"

"I'll have to take my chances. Maybe I won't find it. Not by myself. But I think you'll give me all the information I need. Your life depends on it."

"How?"

"If I find the Moon Base in time, perhaps I can get them to send a ship back to pick you up. *If* I find the Base in time. If not, then you haven't a chance. I imagine there are supplies on the ship. They will last me long enough——"

Hendricks moved quickly. But his injured arm betrayed him. Tasso ducked, sliding lithely aside. Her hand came up, lightning fast. Hendricks saw the gun butt coming. He tried to ward off the blow, but she was too fast. The metal butt struck against the side of his head, just above his ear. Numbing pain rushed through him. Pain and rolling clouds of blackness. He sank down, sliding to the ground.

Dimly, he was aware that Tasso was standing over him, kicking him with her toe.

"Major! Wake up."

He opened his eyes, groaning.

"Listen to me." She bent down, the gun pointed at his face. "I have to hurry. There isn't much time left. The ship is ready, but you must tell me the information I need before I leave."

Hendricks shook his head, trying to clear it.

"Hurry up! Where is the Moon Base? How do I find it? What do I look for?"

Hendricks said nothing.

"Answer me!"

"Sorry."

"Major, the ship is loaded with provisions. I can coast for weeks. I'll find the Base eventually. And in a half hour you'll be dead. Your only chance of survival——" She broke off.

Along the slope, by some crumbling ruins, something moved. Something in the ash. Tasso turned quickly, aiming. She fired. A puff of flame leaped. Something scuttled away, rolling across the ash. She fired again. The claw burst apart, wheels flying.

"See?" Tasso said. "A scout. It won't be long."

"You'll bring them back here to get me?"

"Yes. As soon as possible."

Hendricks looked up at her. He studied her intently. "You're telling the truth?" A strange expression had come over his face, an avid hunger. "You will come back for me? You'll get me to the Moon Base?"

"I'll get you to the Moon Base. But tell me where it is! There's only a little time left."

"All right." Hendricks picked up a piece of rock, pulling himself to a sitting position. "Watch."

Hendricks began to scratch in the ash. Tasso stood by him, watching the motion of the rock. Hendricks was sketching a crude lunar map.

"This is the Appenine Range. Here is the Crater of Archimedes. The Moon Base is beyond the end of the Appenine, about two hundred miles. I don't know exactly where. No one on Terra knows. But when you're over the Appenine, signal with one red flare and a green flare, followed by two red flares in quick succession. The Base monitor will record your signal. The Base is under the surface, of course. They'll guide you down with magnetic grapples."

"And the controls? Can I operate them?"

"The controls are virtually automatic. All you have to do is give the right signal at the right time."

"I will."

"The seat absorbs most of the take-off shock. Air and temperature are automatically controlled. The ship will leave Terra and pass out into free space. It'll line itself up with the moon, falling into an orbit around it, about a hundred miles above the surface. The orbit will carry you over the Base. When you're in the region of the Appenine, release the signal rockets."

Tasso slid into the ship and lowered herself into the pressure seat. The arm locks folded automatically around her. She fingered the controls. "Too bad you're not going, Major. All this put here for you, and you can't make the trip."

"Leave me the pistol."

Tasso pulled the pistol from her belt. She held it in her hand, weighing it thoughtfully. "Don't go too far from this location. It'll be hard to find you, as it is."

"No. I'll stay here by the well."

Tasso gripped the take-off switch, running her fingers over the smooth metal. "A beautiful ship, Major. Well built. I admire your workmanship. You people have always done good work. You build fine things. Your work, your creations, are your greatest achievement."

"Give me the pistol," Hendricks said impatiently, holding out his hand. He struggled to his feet.

"Good-bye, Major." Tasso tossed the pistol past Hendricks. The pistol clattered and rolled away. Hendricks hurried after it. He bent down, snatching it up.

The hatch of the ship clanged shut. The bolts fell into place. Hendricks made his way back. The inner door was being sealed. He raised the pistol unsteadily.

There was a shattering roar. The ship burst up from its metal cage, fusing the mesh behind it. Hendricks cringed, pulling back. The ship shot up into the rolling clouds of ash, disappearing into the sky.

Hendricks stood watching a long time, until even the streamer had dissipated. Nothing stirred. The morning air was chill and silent. He began to walk aimlessly back the way they had come. Better to keep moving around. It would be a long time before help came—if it came at all.

He searched his pockets until he found a package of cigarettes.

He lit one grimly. They had all wanted cigarettes from him. But cigarettes were scarce.

A lizard slithered by him, through the ash. He halted, rigid. The lizard disappeared. Above, the sun rose higher in the sky. Some flies landed on a flat rock to one side of him. Hendricks kicked at them with his foot.

It was getting hot. Sweat trickled down his face, into his collar. His mouth was dry.

Presently he stopped walking and sat down on some debris. He unfastened his medicine kit and swallowed a few narcotic capsules. He looked around him. Where was he?

Something lay ahead. Stretched out on the ground. Silent and unmoving.

Hendricks drew his gun quickly. It looked like a man. Then he remembered. It was the remains of Klaus. The Second Variety. Where Tasso had blasted him. He could see wheels and relays and metal parts, strewn around on the ash. Glittering and sparkling in the sunlight.

Hendricks got to his feet and walked over. He nudged the inert form with his foot, turning it over a little. He could see the metal hull, the aluminium ribs and struts. More wiring fell out. Like viscera. Heaps of wiring, switches and relays. Endless motors and rods.

He bent down. The brain cage had been smashed by the fall. The artificial brain was visible. He gazed at it. A maze of circuits. Miniature tubes. Wires as fine as hair. He touched the brain cage. It swung aside. The type plate was visible. Hendricks studied the plate.

And blanched.

IV—V.

For a long time he stared at the plate. Fourth Variety. Not the Second. They had been wrong. There were more types. Not just three. Many more, perhaps. At least four. And Klaus wasn't the Second Variety.

But if Klaus wasn't the Second Variety——

Suddenly he tensed. Something was coming, walking through the ash beyond the hill. What was it? He strained to see. Figures. Figures coming slowly along, making their way through the ash.

Coming towards him.

Hendricks crouched quickly, raising his gun. Sweat dripped

down into his eyes. He fought down rising panic, as the figures neared.

The first was a David. The David saw him and increased its pace. The others hurried behind it. A second David. A third. Three Davids, all alike, coming toward him silently, without expression, their thin legs rising and falling. Clutching their teddy bears.

He aimed and fired. The first two Davids dissolved into particles. The third came on. And the figure behind it. Climbing silently towards him across the grey ash. A Wounded Soldier, towering over the David. And——

And behind the Wounded Soldier came two Tassos, walking side by side. Heavy belt, Russian army pants, shirt, long hair. The familiar figure, as he had seen her only a little while before. Sitting in the pressure seat of the ship. Two slim, silent figures, both identical.

They were very near. The David bent down suddenly, dropping its teddy bear. The bear raced across the ground. Automatically, Hendricks' fingers tightened around the trigger. The bear was gone, dissolved into mist. The two Tasso Types moved on, expressionless, walking side by side, through the grey ash.

When they were almost to him, Hendricks raised the pistol waist high and fired.

The two Tassos dissolved. But already a new group was starting up the rise, five or six Tassos, all identical, a line of them coming rapidly towards him.

And he had given her the ship and the signal code. Because of him she was on her way to the moon, to the Moon Base. He had made it possible.

He had been right about the bomb, after all. It had been designed with knowledge of the other types, the David Type and the Wounded Soldier Type. And the Klaus Type. Not designed by human beings. It had been designed by one of the underground factories, apart from all human contact.

The line of Tassos came up to him. Hendricks braced himself, watching them calmly. The familiar face, the belt, the heavy shirt, the bomb carefully in place.

The bomb——

As the Tassos reached for him, a last ironic thought drifted through Hendricks' mind. He felt a little better, thinking about it. The bomb. Made by the Second Variety to destroy the other varieties. Made for that end alone.

They were already beginning to design weapons to use against each other.

THE FEELING OF POWER

by *Isaac Asimov*

JEHAN SHUMAN was used to dealing with the men in authority on long-embattled Earth. He was only a civilian but he originated programming patterns that resulted in self-directing war computers of the highest sort. Generals consequently listened to him. Heads of congressional committees, too.

There was one of each in the special lounge of New Pentagon. General Weider was space-burnt and had a small mouth puckered almost into a cipher. Congressman Brant was smooth-cheeked and clear-eyed. He smoked Denebian tobacco with the air of one whose patriotism was so notorious, he could be allowed such liberties.

Shuman, tall, distinguished, and Programmer-first-class, faced them fearlessly.

He said, "This, gentlemen, is Myron Aub."

"The one with the unusual gift that you discovered quite by accident," said Congressman Brant placidly. "Ah." He inspected the little man with the egg-bald head with amiable curiosity.

The little man, in return, twisted the fingers of his hands anxiously. He had never been near such great men before. He was only an aging low-grade Technician who had long ago failed all tests designed to smoke out the gifted ones among mankind and had settled into the rut of unskilled labour. There was just this hobby of his that the great Programmer had found out about and was now making such a frightening fuss over.

General Weider said, "I find this atmosphere of mystery childish."

"You won't in a moment," said Shuman. "This is not something we can leak to the firstcomer.—Aub!" There was something imperative about his manner of biting off that one-syllable name, but then he was a great Programmer speaking to a mere Technician. "Aub! How much is nine times seven?"

Aub hesitated a moment. His pale eyes glimmered with a feeble anxiety. "Sixty-three," he said.

Congressman Brant lifted his eyebrows. "Is that right?"

"Check it for yourself, Congressman."

The congressman took out his pocket computer, nudged the milled edges twice, looked at its face as it lay there in the palm of his hand, and put it back. He said, "Is this the gift you brought us here to demonstrate? An illusionist?"

"More than that, sir. Aub has memorized a few operations and with them he computes on paper."

"A paper computer?" said the general. He looked pained.

"No, sir," said Shuman patiently. "Not a paper computer. Simply a sheet of paper. General, would you be so kind as to suggest a number?"

"Seventeen," said the general.

"And you, Congressman?"

"Twenty-three."

"Good! Aub, multiply those numbers and please show the gentlemen your manner of doing it."

"Yes, Programmer," said Aub, ducking his head. He fished a small pad out of one shirt pocket and an artist's hairline stylus out of the other. His forehead corrugated as he made painstaking marks on the paper.

General Weider interrupted him sharply. "Let's see that."

Aub passed him the paper, and Weider said, "Well, it looks like the figure seventeen."

Congressman Brant nodded and said, "So it does, but I suppose anyone can copy figures off a computer. I think I could make a passable seventeen myself, even without practice."

"If you will let Aub continue, gentlemen," said Shuman without heat.

Aub continued, his hand trembling a little. Finally he said in a low voice, "The answer is three hundred and ninety-one."

Congressman Brant took out his computer a second time and flicked it. "By Godfrey, so it is. How did he guess?"

"No guess, Congressman," said Shuman. "He computed that result. He did it on this sheet of paper."

"Humbug," said the general impatiently. "A computer is one thing and marks on paper are another."

"Explain, Aub," said Shuman.

"Yes, Programmer.—Well, gentlemen, I write down seven-teen and just underneath it, I write twenty-three. Next I say to myself: seven times three——"

The congressman interrupted smoothly, "Now, Aub, the problem is seventeen times twenty-three."

"Yes, I know," said the little Technician earnestly, "but I *start* by saying seven times three because that's the way it works. Now seven times three is twenty-one."

"And how do you know that?" asked the congressman.

"I just remember it. It's always twenty-one on the computer. I've checked it any number of times."

"That doesn't mean it always will be though, does it?" said the congressman.

"Maybe not," stammered Aub. "I'm not a mathematician. But I always get the right answers, you see."

"Go on."

"Seven times three is twenty-one, so I write down twenty-one. Then one times three is three, so I write down a three under the two of twenty-one."

"Why under the two?" asked Congressman Brant at once.

"Because——" Aub looked helplessly at his superior for sup-port. "It's difficult to explain."

Shuman said, "If you will accept his work for the moment, we can leave the details for the mathematicians."

Brant subsided.

Aub said, "Three plus two makes five, you see, so the twenty-one becomes a fifty-one. Now you let that go for a while and start fresh. You multiply seven and two, that's fourteen, and one and two, that's two. Put them down like this and it adds up to thirty-four. Now if you put the thirty-four under the fifty-one this way and add them, you get three hundred and ninety-one and that's the answer."

There was an instant's silence and then General Weider said, "I don't believe it. He goes through this rigmarole and makes up numbers and multiplies and adds them this way and that, but I don't believe it. It's too complicated to be anything but horn-swoggling."

"Oh no, sir," said Aub in a sweat. "It only *seems* complicated because you're not used to it. Actually, the rules are quite simple and will work for any numbers."

"Any numbers, eh?" said the general. "Come then." He took out his own computer (a severely styled GI model) and struck it at random. Make a five seven three eight on the paper. That's five thousand seven hundred and thirty-eight."

"Yes, sir," said Aub, taking a new sheet of paper.

"Now," (more punching of his computer), "seven two three nine. Seven thousand two hundred and thirty-nine."

"Yes, sir."

"And now multiply those two."

"It will take some time," quavered Aub.

"Take the time," said the general.

"Go ahead, Aub," said Shuman crisply.

Aub set to work, bending low. He took another sheet of paper and another. The general took out his watch finally and stared at it. "Are you through with your magic-making, Technician?"

"I'm almost done, sir.—Here it is, sir. Forty-one million, five hundred and thirty-seven thousand, three hundred and eighty-two." He showed the scrawled figures of the result.

General Weider smiled bitterly. He pushed the multiplication contact on his computer and let the numbers whirl to a halt. And then he stared and said in a surprised squeak, "Great Galaxy, the fella's right."

The President of the Terrestrial Federation had grown haggard in office and, in private, he allowed a look of settled melancholy to appear on his sensitive features. The Denebian war, after its early start of vast movement and great popularity, had trickled down into a sordid matter of manœuvre and countermanœuvre, with discontent rising steadily on Earth. Possibly it was rising on Deneb, too.

And now Congressman Brant, head of the important Committee on Military Appropriations, was cheerfully and smoothly spending his half-hour appointment spouting nonsense.

"Computing without a computer," said the president impatiently, "is a contradiction in terms."

"Computing," said the congressman, "is only a system for handling data. A machine might do it, or the human brain might. Let me give you an example." And, using the new skills he had learned, he worked out sums and products until the president, despite himself, grew interested.

THE FEELING OF POWER

"Does this always work?"

"Every time, Mr. President. It is foolproof."

"Is it hard to learn?"

"It took me a week to get the real hang of it. I think you would do better."

"Well," said the president, considering, "it's an interesting parlour game, but what is the use of it?"

"What is the use of a newborn baby, Mr. President? At the moment there is no use, but don't you see that this points the way towards liberation from the machine. Consider, Mr. President," the congressman rose and his deep voice automatically took on some of the cadences he used in public debate, "that the Denebian war is a war of computer against computer. Their computers forge an impenetrable field of counter-missiles against our missiles, and ours forge one against theirs. If we advance the efficiency of our computers, so do they theirs, and for five years a precarious and profitless balance has existed. .

"Now we have in our hands a method for going beyond the computer, leapfrogging it, passing through it. We will combine the mechanics of computation with human thought; we will have the equivalent of intelligent computers; billions of them. I can't predict what the consequences will be in detail but they will be incalculable. And if Deneb beats us to the punch, they may be unimaginably catastrophic."

The president said, troubled, "What would you have me do?"

"Put the power of the administration behind the establishment of a secret project on human computation. Call it Project Number, if you like. I can vouch for my committee, but I will need the administration behind me."

"But how far can human computation go?"

"There is no limit. According to Programmer Shuman, who first introduced me to this discovery——"

"I've heard of Shuman, of course."

"Yes. Well, Dr. Shuman tells me that in theory there is nothing the computer can do that the human mind cannot do. The computer merely takes a finite amount of data and performs a finite number of operations upon them. The human mind can duplicate the process."

The president considered that. He said, "If Shuman says this,

I am inclined to believe him—in theory. But, in practice, how can anyone know how a computer works?"

Brant laughed genially. "Well, Mr. President, I asked the same question. It seems that at one time computers were designed directly by human beings. Those were simple computers, of course, this being before the time of the rational use of computers to design more advanced computers had been established."

"Yes, yes. Go on."

"Technician Aub apparently had, as his hobby, the reconstruction of some of these ancient devices and in so doing he studied the details of their workings and found he could imitate them. The multiplication I just performed for you is an imitation of the workings of a computer."

"Amazing!"

The congressman coughed gently, "If I may make another point, Mr. President—— The further we can develop this thing, the more we can divert our Federal effort from computer production and computer maintenance. As the human brain takes over, more of our energy can be directed into peacetime pursuits and the impingement of war on the ordinary man will be less. This will be most advantageous for the party in power, of course."

"Ah," said the president, "I see your point. Well, sit down, Congressman, sit down. I want some time to think about this. —But meanwhile, show me that multiplication trick again. Let's see if I can't catch the point of it."

Programmer Shuman did not try to hurry matters. Loesser was conservative, very conservative, and liked to deal with computers as his father and grandfather had. Still, he controlled the West European computer combine, and if he could be persuaded to join Project Number in full enthusiasm, a great deal would be accomplished.

But Loesser was holding back. He said, "I'm not sure I like the idea of relaxing our hold on computers. The human mind is a capricious thing. The computer will give the same answer to the same problem each time. What guarantee have we that the human mind will do the same?"

"The human mind, Computer Loesser, only manipulates

facts. It doesn't matter whether the human mind or a machine does it. They are just tools."

"Yes, yes. I've gone over your ingenious demonstration that the mind can duplicate the computer, but it seems to me a little in the air. I'll grant the theory but what reason have we for thinking that theory can be converted to practice?"

"I think we have reason, sir. After all, computers have not always existed. The cave men with their triremes, stone axes, and railroads had no computers."

"And possibly they did not compute."

"You know better than that. Even the building of a railroad or a ziggurat called for some computing, and that must have been without computers as we know them."

"Do you suggest they computed in the fashion you demonstrate?"

"Probably not. After all, this method—we call it 'graphitics,' by the way, from the old European word 'grapho' meaning 'to write'—is developed from the computers themselves so it cannot have antedated them. Still, the cave men must have had *some* method, eh?"

"Lost arts! If you're going to talk about lost arts——"

"No, no. I'm not a lost art enthusiast, though I don't say there may not be some. After all, man was eating grain before hydroponics, and if the primitives ate grain, they must have grown it in soil. What else could they have done?"

"I don't know, but I'll believe in soil-growing when I see someone grow grain in soil. And I'll believe in making fire by rubbing two pieces of flint together when I see that, too."

Shuman grew placative. "Well, let's stick to graphitics. It's just part of the process of etherealization. Transportation by means of bulky contrivances is giving way to direct mass transference. Communications devices become less massive and more efficient constantly. For that matter, compare your pocket computer with the massive jobs of a thousand years ago. Why not, then, the last step of doing away with computers altogether? Come, sir, Project Number is a going concern; progress is already headlong. But we want your help. If patriotism doesn't move you, consider the intellectual adventure involved."

Loesser said sceptically, "What progress? What can you do

beyond multiplication? Can you integrate a transcendental function?"

"In time, sir. In time. In the last month I have learned to handle division. I can determine, and correctly, integral quotients and decimal quotients."

"Decimal quotients? To how many places?"

Programmer Shuman tried to keep his tone casual. "Any number!"

Loesser's lower jaw dropped. "Without a computer?"

"Set me a problem."

"Divide twenty-seven by thirteen. Take it to six places."

Five minutes later, Shuman said, "Two point oh seven six nine two three."

Loesser checked it. "Well, now, that's amazing. Multiplication didn't impress me too much because it involved integers after all, and I thought trick manipulation might do it. But decimals——"

"And that is not all. There is a new development that is, so far, top secret and which strictly speaking, I ought not to mention. Still—We may have made a breakthrough on the square root front."

"Square roots?"

"It involves some tricky points and we haven't licked the bugs yet, but Technician Aub, the man who invented the science and who has an amazing intuition in connection with it, maintains he has the problem almost solved. And he is only a Technician. A man like yourself, a trained and talented mathematician, ought to have no difficulty."

"Square roots," muttered Loesser, attracted.

"Cube roots, too. Are you with us?"

Loesser's hand thrust out suddenly. "Count me in."

General Weider stumped his way back and forth at the head of the room and addressed his listeners after the fashion of a savage teacher facing a group of recalcitrant students. It made no difference to the general that they were the civilian scientists heading Project Number. The general was the over-all head, and he so considered himself at every waking moment.

He said, "Now square roots are all fine. I can't do them myself and I don't understand the methods, but they're fine. Still, the Project will not be sidetracked into what some of you call the fundamentals. You can play with graphitics any way you want to after the war is over, but right now we have specific and very practical problems to solve."

In a far corner, Technician Aub listened with painful attention. He was no longer a Technician, of course, having been relieved of his duties and assigned to the project, with a fine-sounding title and good pay. But, of course, the social distinction remained and the highly placed scientific leaders could never bring themselves to admit him to their ranks on a footing of equality. Nor, to do Aub justice, did he, himself, wish it. He was as uncomfortable with them as they with him.

The general was saying, "Our goal is a simple one, gentlemen: the replacement of the computer. A ship that can navigate space without a computer on board can be constructed in one fifth the time and at one tenth the expense of a computer-laden ship. We could build fleets five times, ten times, as great as Deneb could if we could but eliminate the computer.

"And I see something even beyond this. It may be fantastic now, a mere dream; but in the future I see the manned missile!"

There was an instant murmur from the audience.

The general drove on. "At the present time, our chief bottleneck is the fact that missiles are limited in intelligence. The computer controlling them can only be so large, and for that reason they can meet the changing nature of anti-missile defences in an unsatisfactory way. Few missiles, if any, accomplish their goal and missile warfare is coming to a dead end; for the enemy, fortunately, as well as for ourselves.

"On the other hand, a missile with a man or two within, controlling flight by graphitics, would be lighter, more mobile, more intelligent. It would give us a lead that might well mean the margin of victory. Besides which, gentlemen, the exigencies of war compel us to remember one thing. A man is much more dispensable than a computer. Manned missiles could be launched in numbers and under circumstances that no good general would care to undertake as far as computer-directed missiles are concerned——"

He said much more but Technician Aub did not wait.

Technician Aub, in the privacy of his quarters, laboured long over the note he was leaving behind. It read finally as follows:

"When I began the study of what is now called graphitics, it was no more than a hobby. I saw no more in it than an interesting amusement, an exercise of mind.

"When Project Number began, I thought that others were wiser than I; that graphitics might be put to practical use as a benefit to mankind, to aid in the production of really practical mass-transference devices perhaps. But now I see it is to be used only for death and destruction.

"I cannot face the responsibility involved in having invented graphitics."

He then deliberately turned the focus of a protein-depolarizer on himself and fell instantly and painlessly dead.

They stood over the grave of the little Technician while tribute was paid to the greatness of his discovery.

Programmer Shuman bowed his head along with the rest of them, but remained unmoved. The Technician had done his share and was no longer needed, after all. He might have started graphitics, but now that it had started, it would carry on by itself overwhelmingly, triumphantly, until manned missiles were possible, with who knew what else.

Nine times seven, thought Shuman with deep satisfaction, is sixty-three, and I don't need a computer to tell me so. The computer is in my own head.

And it was amazing the feeling of power that gave him.

SENSE FROM THOUGHT DIVIDE

by *Mark Clifton*

"Remembrance and reflection, how allied;
What thin partitions sense from thought divide."—POPE

WHEN I opened the door to my secretary's office, I could see
her looking up from her desk at the Swami's face with an expression of fascinated scepticism. The Swami's back was towards me,
and on it hung flowing folds of a black cloak. His turban was
white, except where it had rubbed against the back of his neck.

"A tall, dark, and handsome man will soon come into your
life," he was intoning in that sepulchral voice men habitually
use in their dealings with the absolute.

Sara's green eyes focussed beyond him, on me, and began to
twinkle.

"And there he is right now," she commented dryly. "Mr.
Kennedy, Personnel Director for Computer Research."

The Swami whirled around, his heavy robe following the
movement in a practised swirl. His liquid black eyes looked me
over shrewdly, and he bowed towards me as he vaguely touched
his chest, lips and forehead. I expected him to murmur,
"Effendi," or "Bwana Sahib," or something, but he must have
felt silence was more impressive.

I acknowledged his greeting by pulling down one corner of
my mouth. Then I looked at his companion.

The young lieutenant was standing very straight, very stiff,
and a flush of pink was starting up from his collar and spreading
around his clenched jaws to leave a semicircle of white in front
of his red ears.

"Who are you?" I asked.

"Lieutenant Murphy." He managed to open his teeth a bare
quarter of an inch for the words to come out. "Pentagon!" His
light grey eyes pierced me to see if I were impressed.

I wasn't.

"Division of Matériel and Supply," he continued in staccato, imitating a machine gun.

I waited. It was obvious he wasn't through yet. He hesitated, and I could see his Adam's apple travel up above the knot of his tie and back down again as he swallowed. The pink flush deepened into brilliant red.

"Poltergeist Section," he said defiantly.

"What?" The exclamation was out before I could catch it.

He tried to glare at me, but his eyes were pleading instead.

"General Sanfordwaithe said you'd understand." He intended to make it matter of fact in a sturdy, confident voice, but there was the undertone of a wail. It was time I lent a hand.

"You're West Point, aren't you?" I asked kindly.

He straightened still more. I hadn't believed it possible.

"Yes, sir!" He wanted to keep the gratitude out of his voice, but it was there. And for the first time, he had spoken the habitual term of respect to me.

"Well, what do you have here, Lieutenant Murphy?" I nodded towards the Swami who had been wavering between a proud, free stance and that of a drooping supplicant.

"According to my orders, sir," he said formally, "you have requested the Pentagon furnish you with one half-dozen, six, male-type poltergeists. I am delivering the first of them to you, sir."

Sara's mouth, hanging wide open, reminded me to close my own.

So the Pentagon was calling my bluff. Well, maybe they did have something at that. I'd see.

"Float me over that ash tray there on the desk," I said casually to the Swami.

He looked at me as if I'd insulted him, and I could anticipate some reply to the effect that he was not applying for domestic service. But the humble supplicant rather than the proud and fierce hill man won. He started to pick up the ash tray from Sara's desk.

"No, no!" I exclaimed. "I didn't ask you to hand it to me. I want you to TK it over to me. What's the matter? Can't you even TK a simple ash tray?"

The lieutenant's eyes were getting bigger and bigger.

"Didn't your Poltergeist Section test this guy's aptitudes for telekinesis before you brought him from Washington all the way out here to Los Angeles?" I snapped at him.

The lieutenant's lips thinned to a bloodless line.

"I am certain he must have qualified adequately," he said stiffly, and this time left off the "sir".

"Well, I don't know," I answered doubtfully. "If he hasn't even enough telekinetic ability to float me an ash tray across the room——"

The Swami recovered himself first. He put the tips of his long fingers together in the shape of a swaybacked steeple, and rolled his eyes upward.

"I am an instrument of infinite wisdom," he intoned. "Not a parlour magician."

"You mean that with all your infinite wisdom you can't do it," I accused flatly.

"The vibrations are not favourable——" he rolled the words sonorously.

"All right," I agreed. "We'll go somewhere else, where they're better!"

"The vibrations throughout all this crass, materialistic Western world——" he intoned.

"All right," I interrupted, "we'll go to India, then. Sara, call up and book tickets to Calcutta on the first possible plane!" Sara's mouth had been gradually closing, but it unhinged again.

"Perhaps not even India," the Swami murmured, hastily. "Perhaps Tibet."

"Now you know we can't get admission into Tibet while the Communists control it," I argued seriously. "But how about Nepal? That's a fair compromise. The Maharajadhiraja's friendly now. I'll settle for Nepal."

The Swami couldn't keep the triumphant glitter out of his eyes. He had me.

"I'm afraid it would have to be Tibet," he said positively. "Nowhere else in all this troubled world are the vibrations——"

"Oh go on back to Flatbush!" I interrupted disgustedly. "You know as well as I that you've never been outside New York before in your life. Your accent's as phony as the pear-shaped tones of a midwestern garden club president. Can't even TK a simple ash tray!"

I turned to the amazed lieutenant.

"Will you come into my office?" I asked him.

He looked over at the Swami, in doubt.

"He can wait out here," I said. "He won't run away. There isn't any subway, and he wouldn't know what to do. Anyway, if he did get lost, your Army Intelligence could find him. Give G-2 something to work on. Right through this door, lieutenant."

"Yes, sir," he said meekly, and preceded me into my office.

I closed the door behind us and waved him over to the crying chair. He folded at the knees and hips only, as if there were no hinges at all in the ramrod of his back. He sat up straight, on the edge of his chair, ready to spring into instant charge of battle. I went around back to my desk and sat down.

"Now, lieutenant," I said soothingly, "tell me all about it."

I could have sworn his square chin quivered at the note of sympathy in my voice. I wondered, irrelevantly, if the lads at West Point all slept with their faces confined in wooden frames to get that characteristically rectangular look.

"You knew I was from West Point," he said, and his voice held a note of awe. "And you knew, right away, that Swami was a phony from Flatbush."

"Come now," I said with a shrug. "Nothing to get mystical about. Patterns. Just patterns. Every environment leaves the stamp of its matrix on the individual shaped in it. It's a personnel man's trade to recognize the make of a person, just as you would recognize the make of a rifle."

"Yes, sir. I see, sir," he answered. But of course he didn't. And there wasn't much use to make him try. Most people cling too desperately to the ego-saving formula: Man cannot know man.

"Look, lieutenant," I said, getting down to business, "Have you been checked out on what this is all about?"

"Well, sir," he answered, as if he were answering a question in class, "I was cleared for top security, and told that a few months ago you and your Dr. Auerbach, here at Computer Research, discovered a way to create antigravity. I was told you claimed you had to have a poltergeist in the process. You told General Sanfordwaithe that you needed six of them, males. That's about

all, sir. So the Poltergeist Division discovered the Swami, and I
was assigned to bring him out here to you."

"Well then, Lieutenant Murphy, you go back to the Pentagon
and tell General Sanfordwaithe that——" I could see by the look
on his face that my message would probably not get through
verbatim. "Never mind, I'll write it," I amended disgustedly.
"And you can carry the message."

I punched Sara's button on my intercom.

"After all the exposure out there to the Swami," I said, "if
you're still with us on this crass, materialistic plane, will you
bring your book?"

"My astral self has been hovering over you, guarding you,
every minute," Sara answered dreamily.

"Can it take shorthand?" I asked dryly.

"Maybe I'd better come in," she replied.

When she came through the door the lieutenant gave her one
appreciative glance, then returned to his aloof pedestal of
indifference. Obviously his pattern was to stand in majestic
splendour and allow the girls to fawn somewhere down near his
shoes. These lads with a glamour-boy complex almost always
gravitate towards some occupation which will require them to
wear a uniform. Sara catalogued him as quickly as I did, and
seemed unimpressed. But you never can tell about a woman; the
smartest of them will fall for the most transparent poses.

"General Sanfordwaithe, dear sir," I began, as she sat down
at one corner of my desk and flipped open her book. "It takes
more than a towel wrapped around the head and some mutter-
ings about infinity to get poltergeist effects. So I am returning
your phony Swami to you with my compliments——"

"Beg your pardon, sir," the lieutenant interrupted, and there
was a certain note of suppressed triumph in his voice. "In case
you rejected our applicant for the poltergeist job you have in
mind, I was to hand you this." He undid a lovingly polished
button of his tunic, slipped his hand beneath the cloth and
pulled forth a long, sealed envelope.

I took it from him and noted the three sealing-wax imprints
on the flap. From being carried so close to his heart for so long,
the envelope was slightly less crisp than when he had received
it. I slipped my letter opener in under the side flap, and gently
extracted the letter without, in any way, disturbing the wax

seals which were to have guaranteed its privacy. There wasn't any point in my doing it, of course, except to demonstrate to the lieutenant that I considered the whole deal as a silly piece of cloak and dagger stuff.

After the general formalities, the letter was brief: "Dear Mr. Kennedy: We already know the Swami is a phony, but our people have been convinced that in spite of this there are some unaccountable effects. We have advised your general manager, Mr. Henry Grenoble, that we are in the act of carrying out our part of the agreement, namely, to provide you with six male-type poltergeists, and to both you and him we are respectfully suggesting that you get on with the business of putting the antigravity units into immediate production."

I folded the letter and tucked it into one side of my desk pad. I looked at Sara.

"Never mind the letter to General Sanfordwaithe," I said. "He has successfully cut off my retreat in that direction." I looked over at the lieutenant. "All right," I said resignedly, "I'll apologize to the Swami, and make a try at using him."

I picked up the letter again and pretended to be reading it. But this was just a stall, because I had suddenly been struck by the thought that my extreme haste in scoring off the Swami and trying to get rid of him was because I didn't want to get involved again with poltergeists. Not any, of any nature.

Old Stone Face, our general manager, claimed to follow the philosophy of building men, not machines. To an extent he did. His favourite phrase was, "Don't ask me how. I hired you to tell me." He hired a man to do a job, and I will say for him, he left that man alone as long as the job got done. But when a man flubbed a job, and kept on flubbing it, then Mr. Henry Grenoble stepped in and carried out his own job—general managing.

He had given me the assignment of putting antigrav units into production. He had given me access to all the money I would need for the purpose. He had given me sufficient time, months of it. And, in spite of all this co-operation, he still saw no production lines which spewed out antigrav units at some such rate as seventeen and five twelfths per second.

Apparently he got his communication from the Pentagon about the time I got mine. Apparently it contained some implication that Computer Research, under his management, was not pursuing the cause of manufacturing antigrav units with diligence and dispatch. Apparently he did not like this.

I had no more than apologized to the Swami, and received his martyred forgiveness, and arranged for a hotel suite for him and the lieutenant, when Old Stone Face sent for me. He began to manage with diligence and dispatch.

"Now you look here, Kennedy," he said forcefully, and his use of my last name, rather than my first, was a warning, "I've given you every chance. When you and Auerbach came up with that antigrav unit last fall, I didn't ask a lot of fool questions. I figured you knew what you were doing. But the whole winter has passed, and here it is spring, and you haven't done anything that I can see. I didn't say anything when you told General Sanfordwaithe that you'd have to have poltergeists to carry on the work, but I looked it up. First I thought you'd flipped your lid, then I thought you were sending us all on a wild goose chase so we'd leave you alone, then I didn't know what to think."

I nodded. He wasn't through.

"Now I think you're just pretending the whole thing doesn't exist because you don't want to fool with it."

I couldn't argue with that.

"For the first time, Kennedy, I'm asking you what happened?" he said firmly, but his tone was more telling than asking. So I was to have to discuss frameworks with Old Stone Face, after all.

"Henry," I asked slowly, "have you kept up your reading in theoretical physics?"

He blinked at me. I couldn't tell whether it meant yes or no.

"When we went to school, you and I——" I hoped my putting us both in the same age group would tend to mollify him a little, "physics was all snug, secure, safe, definite. A fact was a fact, and that's all there was to it. But there's been some changes made. There's the co-ordinate systems of Einstein, where the relationships of facts can change from framework to framework. There's the application of multi-valued logic to physics where a fact becomes not a fact any longer. The astronomers talk about the expanding universe—it's a piker compared to man's expanding concepts about that universe."

He waited for more. His face seemed to indicate that I was beating around the bush.

"That all has a bearing on what happened," I assured him. "You have to understand what was behind the facts before you can understand the facts themselves. First, we weren't trying to make an antigrav unit at all. Dr. Auerbach was playing around with a chemical approach to cybernetics. He made up some goop which he thought would store memory impulses, the way the brain stores them. He brought a plastic cylinder of it over to me, so I could discuss it with you. I laid it on my desk while I went on with my personnel management business at hand."

Old Stone Face opened a humidor and took out a cigar. He lit it slowly and deliberately and looked at me sharply as he blew out the first puff of smoke.

"The nursery over in the plant had been having trouble with a little girl, daughter of one of our production women. She'd been throwing things, setting things on fire. The teachers didn't know how she did it, she just did it. They sent her to me. I asked her about it. She threw a tantrum, and when it was all over, Auerbach's plastic cylinder of goop was trying to fall upward, through the ceiling. That's what happened," I said.

He looked at his cigar, and looked at me. He waited for me to tie the facts to the theory. I hesitated, and then tried to reassure myself. After all, we were in the business of manufacturing computers. The general manager ought to be able to understand something beyond primary arithmetic.

"Jennie Malasek was a peculiar child with a peculiar background," I went on. "Her mother was from the old country, a Slav. There's the inheritance of a lot of peculiar notions. Maybe she had passed them on to her daughter. She kept Jennie locked up in their room. The kid never got out with other children. Children, kept alone, never seeing anybody, get peculiar notions all by themselves. Who knows what kind of co-ordinate system she built up, or how it worked? Her mother would come home at night and go about her tasks talking aloud, half to the daughter, half to herself. 'I really burned that foreman up today,' she'd say. Or, 'Oh, boy, was he fired in a hurry!' Or, 'She got herself thrown out of the place,' things like that."

"So what does that mean, Ralph?" he asked. His switch to my first name was encouraging.

"To a child who never knew anything else," I answered, "one who had never learned to distinguish reality from unreality—as we would define it from our agreed framework—a special coordinate system might be built up where 'Everybody was up in the air at work, today,' might be taken literally. Under the old systems of physics that couldn't happen, of course—it says in the textbooks—but since it has been happening all through history, in thousands of instances, in the new systems of multivalued physics we recognize it. Under the old system, we already had all the major answers, we thought. Now that we've got our smug certainties knocked out of us, we're just fumbling along, trying to get some of the answers we thought we had.

"We couldn't make that cylinder activate others. We tried. We're still trying. In ordinary cybernetics you can have one machine punch a tape and it can be fed into another machine, but that means you first have to know how to code and decode a tape mechanically. We don't know how to code or decode a psi effect. We know the Auerbach cylinder will store a psi impulse, but we don't know how. So we have to keep working with psi gifted people, at least until we've established some of the basic laws governing psi."

I couldn't tell by Henry's face whether I was with him or far far away. He told me he wanted to think about it, and made a little motion with his hand that I should leave the room.

I walked through the suite of executive offices and down a sound-rebuffing hallway. The throbbing clatter of manufacture of metallic parts made a welcome sound as I went through the far doorway into the factory. I saw a blueprint spread on a foreman's desk as I walked past. Good old blueprint. So many millimetres from here to there, made of such and such an alloy, a hole punched here with an allowance of five-thousandths plus or minus tolerance. Snug, secure, safe. I wondered if psi could ever be blueprinted. Or suppose you put a hole here, but when you looked away and then looked back it had moved, or wasn't there at all?

Quickly, I got myself into a conversation with a supervisor about the rising rate of employee turnover in his department. That was something also snug, secure, safe. All you had to do was figure out human beings.

I spent the rest of the morning on such pursuits, working with things I understood.

On his first rounds of the afternoon, the interoffice messenger brought me a memorandum from the general manager's office. I opened it with some misgivings.

Mr. Grenoble felt he should work with me more closely on the antigrav project. He understood, from his researches, that the most positive psi effects were experienced during a seance with a medium. Would I kindly arrange for the Swami to hold a seance that evening, after office hours, so that he might analyse the man's methods and procedures to see how they could fit smoothly into Company Operation. This was not to be construed as interference in the workings of my department but in the interest of pursuing the entire matter with diligence and dispatch——

The seance was to be held in my office.

I had had many peculiar conferences in this room—from union leaders stripping off their coats, throwing them on the floor and stamping on them; to uplifters who wanted to ban cosmetics on our women employees so the male employees would not be tempted to think Questionable Thoughts. I could not recall ever having held a seance before.

My desk had been moved out of the way, over into one corner of the large room. A round table was brought over from the salesmen's report writing room (used there more for surreptitious poker playing than for writing reports) and placed in the middle of my office—on the grounds that it had no sharp corners to gouge people in their middles if it got to cavorting about recklessly. In an industrial plant one always has to consider the matter of safety rules and accident insurance rates.

In the middle of the table there rested, with dark fluid gleaming through clear plastic cases, six fresh cylinders which Auerbach had prepared in his laboratory over in the plant.

Auerbach had shown considerable unwillingness to attend the seance; he pleaded being extra busy with experiments just now, but I gave him that look which told him I knew he had just been stalling around the last few months, the same as I had.

If the psi effect had never come out in the first place, there wouldn't have been any mental conflict. He could have gone on with his processes of refining, simplifying and increasing the efficiency ratings of his goop. He would have settled gladly for a chemical compound which could have added two and two upon request; but when that compound can learn and demonstrate that there's no such thing as gravity, teaching it simple arithmetic is like ashes in the mouth.

I said as much to him. I stood there in his laboratory, leaned up against a work bench, and risked burning an acid hole in the sleeve of my jacket just to put over an air of unconcern. He was perched on the edge of an opposite work bench, swinging his feet, and hiding the expression in his eyes behind the window's reflection upon his polished glasses. I said even more.

"You know," I said reflectively, "I'm completely unable to understand the attitude of supposedly unbiased men of science. Now you take all that mass of data about psi effects, the odd and unexplainable happenings, the premonitions, the specific predictions, the accurate descriptions of far away simultaneously happening events. You take that whole mountainous mass of data, evidence, phenomena——"

A slight turn of his head gave me a glimpse of his eyes behind the glasses. He looked as if he wished I'd change the subject. In his dry, undemonstrative way, I think he liked me. Or at least he liked me when I wasn't trying to make him think about things outside his safe and secure little framework. But I wasn't going to stop.

"Before Rhine came along, and brought all this down to the level of laboratory experimentation," I pursued, "how were those things to be explained? Say a fellow had some unusual powers, things that happened around him, things he knew without any explanation for knowing them. I'll tell you. There were two courses open to him. He could express it in the semantics of spiritism, or he could admit to witchcraft and sorcery. Take your pick; those were the only two systems of semantics available to him.

"We've got a third one now—parapsychology. If I had asked you to attend an experiment in parapsychology, you'd have agreed at once. But when I ask you to attend a seance, you balk! Man, what difference does it make what we call it? Isn't it up to us to investigate the evidence wherever we find it? No matter what kind of semantic debris it's hiding in?"

Auerbach shoved himself down off the bench, and pulled out a beat-up package of cigarettes.

"All right, Kennedy," he said resignedly, "I'll attend your seance."

The other invited guests were Sara, Lieutenant Murphy, Old Stone Face, myself, and, of course, the Swami. This was probably not typical of the Swami's usual audience composition.

Six chairs were placed at even intervals around the table. I had found soft white lights overhead to be most suitable for my occasional night work, but the Swami insisted that a blue light, a dim one, was most suitable for his night work.

I made no objection to that condition. One of the elementary basics of science is that laboratory conditions may be varied to meet the necessities of the experiment. If a red-lighted darkness is necessary to an operator's successful development of photographic film, then I could hardly object to a blue-lighted darkness for the development of the Swami's effects.

Neither could I object to the Swami's insistence that he sit with his back to the true North. When he came into the room, accompanied by Lieutenant Murphy, his thoughts seemed turned in upon himself, or wafted somewhere out of this world. He stopped in midstride, struck an attitude of listening, or feeling, perhaps, and slowly shifted his body back and forth.

"Ah," he said at last, in a tone of satisfaction, "there is the North!"

It was, but this was not particularly remarkable. There is no confusing maze of hallways leading to the Personnel Department from the outside. Applicants would be unable to find us if there were. If he had got his bearings out on the street, he could have managed to keep them.

He picked up the nearest chair with his own hands and shifted it so that it would be in tune with the magnetic lines of Earth. I couldn't object. The Chinese had insisted upon such placement of household articles, particularly their beds, long before the Earth's magnetism had been discovered by science. The birds had had their direction-finders attuned to it, long before there was man.

Instead of objecting, the lieutenant and I meekly picked up the table and shifted it to the new position. Sara and Auerbach came in as we were setting the table down. Auerbach gave one quick look at the Swami in his black cloak and nearly white turban, and then looked away.

"Remember semantics," I murmured to him, as I pulled out Sara's chair for her. I seated her to the left of the Swami. I seated Auerbach to the right of him. If the lieutenant was, by chance, in cahoots with the Swami, I would foil them to the extent of not letting them sit side by side at least. I sat down at the opposite side of the table from the Swami. The lieutenant sat down between me and Sara.

The general manager came through the door at that instant, and took charge immediately.

"All right now," Old Stone Face said crisply, in his low, rumbling voice, "no fiddle-faddling around. Let's get down to business."

The Swami closed his eyes.

"Please be seated," he intoned to Old Stone Face. "And now, let us all join hands in an unbroken circle."

Henry shot him a beetlebrowed look as he sat down between Auerbach and me, but at least he was co-operative to the extent that he placed both his hands on top of the table. If Auerbach and I reached for them, we would be permitted to grasp them.

I leaned back and snapped off the overhead light to darken the room in an eerie, blue glow.

We sat there, holding hands, for a full ten minutes. Nothing happened.

It was not difficult to estimate the pattern of Henry's mind. Six persons, ten minutes, equals one man-hour. One man-hour of idle time to be charged into the cost figure of the antigrav unit. He was staring fixedly at the cylinders which lay in random positions in the centre of the table, as if to assess their progress at this processing point. He stirred restlessly in his chair, obviously dissatisfied with the efficiency rating of the manufacturing process.

The Swami seemed to sense the impatience, or it might have been coincidence.

"There is some difficulty," he gasped in a strangulated, high voice. "My guides refuse to come through."

"Harrumph!" exclaimed Old Stone Face. It left no doubt

about what *he* would do if *his* guides did not obey orders on the double.

"Someone in this circle is not a True Believer!" the Swami accused in an incredulous voice.

In the dim blue light I was able to catch a glimpse of Sara's face. She was on the verge of breaking apart. I managed to catch her eye and flash her a stern warning. Later she told me she had interpreted my expression as stark fear, but it served the same purpose. She smothered her laughter in a most unladylike sound somewhere between a snort and a squawk.

The Swami seemed to become aware that somehow he was not holding his audience spellbound.

"Wait!" he commanded urgently; then he announced in awe-stricken tones, "I feel a presence!"

There was a tentative, half-hearted rattle of some castanets—which could have been managed by the Swami wiggling one knee, if he happened to have them concealed there. This was followed by the thin squawk of a bugle—which could have been accomplished by sitting over towards one side and squashing the air out of a rubber bulb attached to a ten-cent party horn taped to his thigh.

Then there was nothing. Apparently his guides had made a tentative appearance and were, understandably, completely intimidated by Old Stone Face. We sat for another five minutes.

"Harrumph!" Henry cleared his throat again, this time louder and more commanding.

"That is all," the Swami said in a faint, exhausted voice. "I have returned to you on your material plane."

The handholding broke up in the way bits of metal, suddenly charged positive and negative, would fly apart. I leaned back again and snapped on the white lights. We all sat there a few seconds, blinking in what seemed a sudden glare.

The Swami sat with his chin dropped down to his chest. Then he raised stricken, liquid eyes.

"Oh, now I remember where I am," he said. "What happened? I never know."

Old Stone Face threw him a look of withering scorn. He picked up one of the cylinders and hefted it in the palm of his hand. It did not fly upward to bang against the ceiling. It weighed about what it ought to weigh. He tossed the cylinder, contemptuously, back into the pile, scattering them over the table. He pushed back his chair, got to his feet, and stalked out of the room without looking at any of us.

The Swami made a determined effort to recapture the spotlight.

"I'm afraid I must have help to walk to the car," he whispered. "I am completely exhausted. Ah, this work takes so much out of me. Why do I go on with it? Why? Why? Why?"

He drooped in his chair, then made a valiantly brave effort to rise under his own power when he felt the lieutenant's hands lifting him up. He was leaning heavily on the lieutenant as they went out the door.

Sara looked at me dubiously.

"Will there be anything else?" she asked. Her tone suggested that since nothing had been accomplished, perhaps we should get some work out before she left.

"No, Sara," I answered. "Good night. See you in the morning."

She nodded and went out the door.

Apparently none of them had seen what I saw. I wondered if Auerbach had. He was a trained observer. He was standing beside the table looking down at the cylinders. He reached over and poked one of them with his fore-finger. He was pushing it back and forth. It gave him no resistance beyond normal inertia. He pushed it a little further out of parallel with true North. It did not try to swing back.

So he had seen it. When I'd laid the cylinders down on the table they were in random positions. During the seance there had been no jarring of the table, not even so much as a rap or quiver which could have been caused by the Swami's lifted knee. When we'd shifted the table, after the Swami had changed his chair, the cylinders hadn't been disturbed. When Old Stone Face had been staring at them during the seance—seance?, hah!—they were lying in inert, random positions.

But when the lights came on, and just before Henry had picked one up and tossed it back to scatter them, every cylinder had been laid in orderly parallel—and with one end pointing to true North!

I stood there beside Auerbach, and we both poked at the

cylinders some more. They gave us no resistance, nor showed that they had any ideas about it one way or the other.

"It's like so many things," I said morosely. "If you do just happen to notice anything out of the ordinary at all, it doesn't seem to mean anything."

"Maybe that's because you're judging it outside of its own framework," Auerbach answered. I couldn't tell whether he was being sarcastic or speculative. "What I don't understand," he went on, "is that once the cylinders having been activated by whatever force there was in action—all right, call it psi—well, why didn't they retain it, the way the other cylinders retained the antigrav force?"

I thought for a moment. Something about the conditional setup seemed to give me an idea.

"You take a photographic plate," I reasoned. "Give it a weak exposure to light, then give it a strong blast of over-exposure. The first exposure is going to be blanked out by the second. Old Stone Face was feeling pretty strongly towards the whole matter."

Auerbach looked at me, unbelieving.

"There isn't any rule about who can have psi talent," I argued. "I'm just wondering if I shouldn't wire General San-fordwaithe and tell him to cut our order for poltergeists to five."

I spent a glum, restless night. I knew, with certainty, that Old Stone Face was going to give me trouble. I didn't need any psi talent for that; it was an inevitable part of his pattern. He had made up his mind to take charge of this antigrav operation, and he wouldn't let one bogus seance stop him more than momentarily.

If it weren't so close to direct interference with my depart-ment, I'd have been delighted to sit on the side lines and watch him try to command psi effects to happen. That would be like commanding some random copper wire and metallic cores to start generating electricity.

For once I could have overlooked the interference with my department if I didn't know, from past experience, that I'd be blamed for the consequent failure. And there was something else, too; I had the feeling that if I were allowed to go along, carefully and experimentally, I just might discover a few of the laws about psi. There was the tantalizing feeling that I was on the verge of knowing at least something.

The Pentagon people had been right. The Swami was an obvious phony of the baldest fakery, yet he had something. He had something, but how was I to get hold of it? Just what kind of turns with what around what did you make to generate a psi force? It took two thousand years for man to move from the concept that amber was a stone with a soul to the concept of static electricity. Was there any chance I could find some short-cuts in reducing the laws governing psi? The one bright spot of my morning was that Auerbach hadn't denied seeing the evidence of the cylinders pointing North.

It turned out to be the only bright spot. I had no more than got to my office and sorted out the routine urgencies from those which had to be handled immediately, when Sara announced the lieutenant and the Swami. I put everything else off, and told her to send them right in.

The Swami was in an incoherent rage. The lieutenant was contracting his eyebrows in a scowl and clenching his fists in frustration. In a voice, soaring into the falsetto, the Swami demanded that he be sent back to Brooklyn where he was appreciated. The lieutenant had orders to stay with the Swami, but he didn't have any orders about returning either to Brooklyn or the Pentagon. I managed, at last, to get the lieutenant seated in a straight chair, but the Swami couldn't stay still long enough. He stalked up and down the room, swirling his slightly odorous black cloak on the turns. Gradually the story came out.

Old Stone Face, a strong advocate of Do It Now, hadn't wasted any time. From his home he had called the Swami at his hotel and commanded him to report to the general manager's office at once. They all got there about the same time, and Henry had waded right in.

Apparently Henry, too, had spent a restless night. He accused the Swami of inefficiency, bungling, fraud, deliberate insubordination, and a few other assorted faults for having made a fool out of us all at the seance. He'd as much as commanded the Swami to cut out all the shilly-shallying and get down to the business of activating antigrav cylinders, or else. He hadn't been specific about what the "or else" would entail.

"Now I'm sure he really didn't mean——" I began to pour oil on the troubled waters. "With your deep insight, Swami—The fate of great martyrs throughout the ages——" Gradually the ego-building phrases calmed him down. He grew willing to listen, if for no more than the anticipation of hearing more of them.

He settled down into the crying chair at last, his valence shifting from outraged anger to a vast and noble forgiveness. This much was not difficult. To get him to co-operate, consciously and enthusiastically, might not be so easy.

Each trade has its own special techniques. The analytical chemist has a series of routines he tries when he wishes to reduce an unknown compound to its constituents. To the chemically uneducated, this may appear to be a fumbling, hit or miss, kind of procedure. The personnel man, too, has his series of techniques, which may appear to be no more than random, pointless conversation.

I first tried the routine process of reasoning. I didn't expect it to work; it seldom does, but it can't be eliminated until it has been tested.

"You must understand," I said slowly, soothingly, "that our intentions are constructive. We are simply trying to apply the scientific method to something which has, heretofore, been wrapped in mysticism."

The shocked freezing of his facial muscles gave me the answer to that.

"Science understands nothing, nothing at all!" he snapped. "Science tries to reduce everything to test tubes and formulae; but I am the instrument of a mystery which man can never know."

"Well, now," I said reasonably. "Let us not be inconsistent. You say this is something man was not meant to know; yet you, yourself, have devoted your life to gaining a greater comprehension of it."

"I seek only to rise above my material self so that I might place myself in harmony with the flowing symphony of Absolute Truth," he lectured me sonorously. The terminology didn't bother me; the jargon of the sciences sometimes grows just as esoteric. Maybe it even meant something.

One thing I was sure it meant. There are two basic approaches to the meaning of life and the universe about us. Man can know: That is the approach of science, its whole meaning. There are mysteries which man was not meant to know: That is the other approach. There is no reconciling of the two on a reasoning basis. I represented the former. I wasn't sure the Swami was a true representative of the latter, but at least he had picked up the valence and the phrases.

I made a mental note that reasoning was an unworkable technique with this compound. Henry, a past master at it, had already tried threats and abuse. That hadn't worked. I next tried one of the oldest forms in the teaching of man, a parable.

I told him of my old Aunt Dimity, who was passionately fond of Rummy, but considered all other card games sinful.

"Ah, how well she proves my point," the Swami countered. "There is an inner voice, a wisdom greater than the mortal mind to guide us——"

"Well now," I asked reasonably, "why would the inner voice say that Rummy was okay, but Casino wasn't?" But it was obvious he liked the point he had made better than he had liked the one I failed to make.

So I tried the next technique. Often an opponent will come over to your side if you just confess, honestly, that he is a better man than you are, and you need his help. What was the road I must take to achieve the same understanding he had? His eyes glittered at that.

"First there is fasting, and breathing, and contemplating self," he murmured mendaciously. "I would be unable to aid you until you gave me full ascendancy over you, so that I might guide your every thought——"

I decided to try inspiration.

"Do you realize, Swami," I asked, "that the one great drawback throughout the ages to a full acceptance of psi is the lack of permanent evidence? It has always been evanescent, perishable. It always rests solely upon the word of witnesses. But if I could show you a film print, then you could not doubt the existence of photography, could you?"

I opened my lower desk drawer and pulled out a couple of the Auerbach cylinders which we had used the night before. I laid them on top of the desk.

"These cylinders," I said, "act like the photographic film.

They will record, in permanent form, the psi effects you command. At last, for all mankind the doubt will be stilled; man will at once know the truth; and you will take your place among the immortals."

I thought it was pretty good. It should have done the trick. But the Swami was staring at the cylinders first in fascination, then fear, then in horror. He jumped to his feet, without bothering to swirl his robe majestically, rushed over to the door, fumbled with the knob as if he were in a burning room, managed to get the door open, and rushed outside. The lieutenant gave me a puzzled look, and went after him.

I drew a deep breath, and exhaled it audibly. My testing procedures hadn't produced the results I'd expected, but the last one had revealed something else—or rather, had confirmed two things we knew already.

One: The Swami believed himself to be a fraud.

Two: He wasn't.

Both cylinders were pointing towards the door. I watched them, at first not quite sure; like the Swami, I'd have preferred not to believe the evidence. But the change in their perspective with the angles of the desk made the motion unmistakable.

Almost as slowly as the minute hand of a watch, they were creeping across the desk towards the door. They, too, were trying to escape from the room.

I nudged them with my fingers. They hustled along a little faster, as if appreciative of the help, even coming from me. I saw they were moving faster, as if they were learning as they tried it. I turned one of them around. Slowly it turned back and headed for the door again. I lifted one of them down to the floor. It had no tendency to float, but it kept heading for the door. The other one fell off the desk while I was fooling with the first one. The jar didn't seem to bother it any. It, too, began to creep across the rug towards the door.

I opened the door for them. Sara looked up. She saw the two cylinders come into view, moving under their own power.

"Here we go again," she said, resignedly.

The two cylinders pushed themselves over the door sill, got clear outside my office. Then they went inert. Both Sara and I tried nudging them, poking them. They just lay there; mission accomplished. I carried them back inside my office and laid them on the floor. Immediately both of them began to head for the door again.

"Simple," Sara said dryly, "they just can't stand to be in the same room with you, that's all."

"You're not just whistling, gal," I answered. "That's the whole point."

"Have I said something clever?" she asked seriously.

I took the cylinders back into my office and put them in a desk drawer. I watched the desk for a while, but it didn't change position. Apparently it was too heavy for the weak force activating the cylinders.

I picked up the phone and called Old Stone Face. I told him about the cylinders.

"There!" he examined with satisfaction. "I knew all that fellow needed was a good old-fashioned talking to. Some day, my boy, you'll realize that you still have a lot to learn about handling men."

"Yes, sir," I answered.

At that, Old Stone Face had a point. If he hadn't got in and riled things up, maybe the Swami would not have been emotionally upset enough to generate the psi force which had activated these new cylinders.

Did that mean that psi was linked with emotional upheaval? Well, maybe. Not necessarily, but Rhine had proved that strength of desire had an effect upon the frequency index of telekinesis.

Was there anything at all we knew about psi, so that we could start cataloguing, sketching in the beginnings of a pattern? Yes, of course there was.

First, it existed. No one could dismiss the mountainous mass of evidence unless he just refused to think about the subject.

Second, we could, in time, know what it was and how it worked. You'd have to give up the entire basis of scientific attitude if you didn't admit that.

Third, it acted like a sense, rather than as something dependent upon the intellectual process of thought. You could, for example—I argued to my imaginary listener—command your nose to smell a rose, and by autosuggestion you might think you were succeeding; that is, until you really did smell a real rose, then you'd know that you'd failed to create it through a thought pattern. The sense would have to be separated from the process of thinking about the sense.

So what was psi? But, at this point, did it matter much? Wasn't the main issue one of learning how to produce it, use it? How long did we work with electricity and get a lot of benefits from it before we formed some theories about what it was? And, for that matter, did we know what it was, even yet? "A flow of electrons" was a pretty meaningless phrase, when you stopped to think about it. I could say psi was a flow of psitrons, and it would mean as much.

I reached over and picked up a cigarette. I started fumbling around in the centre drawer of my desk for a matchbook. I didn't find any. Without thinking, I opened the drawer containing the two cylinders. They were pressing up against the side of the desk drawer, still trying to get out of the room. Single-purposed little beasts, weren't they?

I closed the drawer, and noticed that I was crushing out my cigarette in the ash tray, just as if I'd smoked it. My nerves weren't all they should be this morning.

Which brought up the fourth point, and also took me right back to where I started.

Nerves . . .

Emotional upheavals.

Rhine's correlations between interest, belief, and ability to perform . . .

It seemed very likely that a medium such as the Swami, whose basic belief was There Are Mysteries, would be unable to function in a framework where the obvious intent was to unveil those mysteries!

That brought up a couple more points. I felt pretty sure of them. I felt as if I were really getting somewhere. And I had a situation which was ideal for proving my points.

I flipped the intercom key, and spoke to Sara.

"Will you arrange with her foreman for Annie Malasek to come to my office right now?" I asked. Sara is flippant when things are going along all right, but she knows when to buckle down and do what she's asked. She gave me no personal reactions to this request.

Yes, Annie Malasek would be a good one. If anybody in the

plant believed There Are Mysteries, it would be Annie. Further, she was exaggeratedly loyal to me. She believed I was responsible for turning her little Jennie, the little girl who'd started all this poltergeist trouble, into a Good Little Girl. In this instance, I had no qualms about taking advantage of that loyalty.

While I waited for her I called the lieutenant at his hotel. He was in. Yes, the Swami was also in. They'd just returned. Yes, the Swami was ranting and raving about leaving Los Angeles at once. He had said he absolutely would have nothing more to do with us here at Computer Research. I told Lieutenant Murphy to scare him with tales of the secret underground working of Army Intelligence, to quiet him down. And I scared the lieutenant a little by pointing out that holding a civilian against his will without the proper writ was tantamount to kidnapping. So if the Army didn't want trouble with the Civil Courts, all brought about because the lieutenant didn't know how to handle his man——

The lieutenant became immediately anxious to co-operate with me. So then I soothed him. I told him that, naturally, the Swami was unhappy. He was used to Swami-ing, and out here he had been stifled, frustrated. What he needed was some credulous women to catch their breath at his awe-inspiring insight and gaze with fearful rapture into his eyes. The lieutenant didn't know where he could find any women like that. I told him, dryly, that I would furnish some.

Annie was more than co-operative. Sure, the whole plant was buzzing about that foreign-looking Swami who had been seen coming in and out of my office. Sure, a lot of the Girls believed in seances.

"Why? Don't you, Mr. Kennedy?" she asked curiously.

I said I wasn't sure, and she clucked her tongue in sympathy. It must be terrible not to be sure, so . . . well, it must be just terrible. And I was such a kind man, too . . .

But when I asked her to go to the hotel and persuade the Swami to give her a reading, she was reluctant. I thought my plan was going to be frustrated, but it turned out that her reluctance was only because she did not have a thing to wear, going into a high-toned place like that.

Sara wasn't the right size, but one of the older girls in the

outer office would lend Annie some clothes if I would let her go
see the Swami, too. It developed that her own teacher was a
guest of Los Angeles County for a while, purely on a trumped-
up charge, you understand, Mr. Kennedy. Not that she was a
cop hater or anything like that. She was perfectly aware of
what a fine and splendid job those noble boys in blue did for us
all, but——

In my own office! Well, you never knew.

Yet, what was the difference between her and me? We were
both trying to get hold of and benefit by psi effects, weren't
we?

And the important thing was that we could combine our
efforts to our mutual advantage. My interviewer's teacher had
quite a large following, and now they were all at loose ends. If
the Swami were willing, she could provide a large and ready-
made audience for him. She would be glad to talk to him about
it.

Annie hurriedly said that she would be glad to talk to him
about it, too; that she could get up a large audience, too. So,
even before it got started, I had my rival factions at work. I
egged them both on, and promised that I'd get Army Intelligence to work with the local boys in blue to hold off making any
raids.

Annie told me again what a kind man I was. My interviewer
spoke up quickly and said how glad she was to find an opportunity for expressing how grateful she was for the privilege of
working right in the same department with such an understanding, really intellectually developed adult. She eyed Annie
sidelong, as if to gauge the effects of her attempts to set me up
on a pedestal, out of Annie's reach.

I hoped I wouldn't start believing either one of them. I
hoped I wasn't as inaccurate in my estimates of people as was my
interviewer. I wondered if she were really qualified for the job
she held. Then I realized this was a contest between two women
and I, a mere male, was simply being used as the pawn. Well,
that worked both ways. In a fair bargain both sides receive satisfaction. I felt a little easier about my tactical manœuvres.

But the development of rivalry between factions of the
audience gave me an additional idea. Perhaps that's what the
Swami really needed, a little rivalry. Perhaps he was being a

little too hard to crack because he knew he was the only egg in the basket.

I called Old Stone Face and told him what I planned. He responded that it was up to me. He'd stepped in and got things under way for me, got things going, now it was my job to keep them going. It looked as if he were edging out from under—or maybe he really believed that.

Before I settled into the day's regular routine, I wired General Sanfordwaithe, and told him that if he had any more prospects ready would he please ship me one at once, via air mail, special delivery.

The recital hall, hired for the Swami's Los Angeles debut, was large enough to accommodate all the family friends and relatives of any little Maribel who, having mastered "Daffodils In May," for four fingers, was being given to the World. It had the usual small stage equipped with pull-back curtains to give a dramatic flourish, or to shut off from view the effects of any sudden nervous catastrophe brought about by stage fright.

I got there, purposely a little late, in hopes the house lights would already be dimmed and everything in progress; but about a hundred and fifty people were milling around outside on the walk and in the corridors. Both factions had really been busy.

Most of them were women, but, to my intense relief, there were a few men. Some of these were only husbands, but a few of the men wore a look which said they'd been far away for a long time. Somehow I got the impression that instead of looking into a crystal ball, they would be more inclined to look out of one.

It was a little disconcerting to realize that no one noticed me, or seemed to think I was any different from anybody else. I supposed I should be thankful that I wasn't attracting any attention. I saw my interviewer amid a group of Older Girls. She winked at me roguishly, and patted her heavy handbag significantly. As per instructions, she was carrying a couple of the Auerbach cylinders.

I found myself staring in perplexity for a full minute at another woman, before I realized it was Annie. I had never seen her before, except dressed in factory blue jeans, man's blue

shirt, and a bandanna wrapped around her head. Her companion, probably another of the factory assemblers, nudged her
and pointed, not too subtly, in my direction. Annie saw me
then, and lit up with a big smile. She started towards me, hesitated when I frowned and shook my head, flushed with the
thought that I didn't want to speak to her in public; then got
a flash of better sense than that. She, too, gave me a conspira-
torial wink and patted her handbag.

My confederates were doing nicely.

Almost immediately thereafter a horsefaced, moustached old
gal started rounding people up in a honey-sweet, pear-shaped
voice; and herded them into the auditorium. I chose one of
the wooden folding chairs in the back row.

A heavy-jowled old gal came out in front of the closed curtains
and gave a little introductory talk about how lucky we all were
that the Swami had consented to visit with us. There was the
usual warning to anyone who was not of the esoteric that we
must not expect too much, that sometimes nothing at all happened, that true believers did not attend just to see effects. She
reminded us kittenishly that the guides were capricious, and
that we must all help by merging ourselves in the great flowing
currents of absolute infinity.

She finally faltered, realized she was probably saying all the
things the Swami would want to say—in the manner of people
who introduce speakers everywhere—and with a girlish little
flourish she waved at someone off stage.

The house lights dimmed. The curtains swirled up and back.

The Swami was doing all right for himself. He was seated
behind a small table in the centre of the stage. A pale violet
light diffused through a huge crystal ball on the table, and threw
his dark features into sharp relief. It gave an astonishingly
remote and inscrutable wisdom to his features. In the pale light,
and at this distance, his turban looked quite clean.

He began to speak slowly and sonorously. A hush settled over
the audience, and gradually I felt myself merging with the
mass reaction of the rest. As I listened, I got the feeling that what
he was saying was of tremendous importance, that somehow his
words contained great and revealing wonders—or would contain them if I were only sufficiently advanced to comprehend

their true meanings. The man was good, he knew his trade. All men search for truth at one level or another. I began to realize why such a proportionate few choose the cold and impersonal laboratory. Perhaps if there were a way to put science to music——

The Swami talked on for about twenty minutes, and then I noticed his voice had grown deeper and deeper in tone, and suddenly, without any apparent transition, we all knew it was not really the Swami's voice we were hearing. And then he began to tell members of the audience little intimate things about themselves, things which only they should know.

He was good at this, too. He had mastered the trick of making universals sound like specifics. I could do the same thing. The patterns of people's lives have multiple similarities. To a far greater extent than generally realized the same things happen to everyone. The idea was to take some of the lesser known ones and word them so they seemed to apply to one isolated individual.

For instance, I could tell a fellow about when he was a little boy there was a little girl in a red dress with blonde pigtails who used to scrap with him and tattle things about him to her mother. If he were inclined to be credulous, this was second sight I had. But it is a universal. What average boy didn't, at one time or another, know a little girl with blonde pigtails? What blonde little girl didn't occasionally wear a red dress? What little girl didn't tattle to her mother about the naughty things the boys were doing?

The Swami did that for a while. The audience was leaning forward in a rapture of ecstasy. First the organ tones of his voice soothed and softened. The phrases which should mean something if only you had the comprehension. The universals applied as specifics. He had his audience in the palm of his hand. He didn't need his crystal ball to tell him that.

But he wanted it to be complete. Most of the responses had been from women. He gave them the generalities which didn't sound like generalities. They confirmed with specifics. But most were women. He wanted the men, too. He began to concentrate on the men. He made it easy.

"I have a message," he said. "From . . . now let me get it

right . . . from R. S. It is for a man in this audience. Will the man who knew R. S. acknowledge?"

There was a silence. And that was such an easy one, too. I hadn't planned to participate, but, on impulse, since none of the other men were co-operating, I spoke up.

"Robert Smith!" I exclaimed. "Good old Bob!"

Several of the women sitting near me looked at me and beamed their approval. One of the husbands scowled at me.

"I can tell by your tone," the Swami said, and apparently he hadn't recognized my tone, "that you have forgiven him. That is the message. He wants you to know that he is happy. He is much wiser now. He knows now that he was wrong."

One of the women reached over and patted me on the shoulder.

But the Swami had no more messages for men. He was smart enough to know where to stop. He'd tried one of the simplest come-ons, and there had been too much of a pause. It had almost not come off.

I wondered who good old Bob Smith was? Surely, among the thousands of applicants I'd interviewed, there must have been a number of them. And, being applicants, of course, some of them had been wrong.

The Swami's tones, giving one message after another—faster and faster now, not waiting for acknowledgment or confirmation—began to sink into a whisper. His speech became ragged, heavy. The words became indistinguishable. About his head there began to float a pale, luminescent sphere. There was a subdued gasp from the audience and then complete stillness. As though, unbreathing, in the depths of a tomb, they watched the sphere. It bobbed about, over the Swami's head and around him. At times it seemed as if about to float off stage, but it came back. It swirled out over the audience, but not too far, and never at such an angle that the long, flexible dull black wire supporting it would be silhouetted against the glowing crystal ball.

Then it happened. There was a gasp, a smothered scream. And over at one side of the auditorium a dark object began bobbing about in the air up near the ceiling. It swerved and swooped. The Swami's luminescent sphere jerked to a sudden stop. The Swami sat with open mouth and stared at the dark object which he was not controlling.

The dark object was not confined to any dull black wire. It went where it willed. It went too high and brushed against the ceiling.

There was a sudden shower of coins to the floor. A compact hit the floor with a flat spat. A handkerchief floated down more slowly.

"My purse!" a woman gasped. I recognized my interviewer's voice. Her purse contained two Auerbach cylinders, and they were having themselves a ball.

In alarm, I looked quickly at the stage, hoping the Swami wasn't astute enough to catch on. But he was gone. The audience, watching the bobbing purse, hadn't realized it as yet. And they were delayed in realizing it by a diversion from the other side of the auditorium.

"I can't hold it down any longer, Mr. Kennedy!" a woman gasped out. "It's taking me up into the air!"

"Hold on, Annie!" I shouted back. "I'm coming!"

A chastened and subdued Swami sat in my office the following morning, and this time he was inclined to be co-operative. More, he was looking to me for guidance, understanding, and didn't mind acknowledging my ascendancy. And, with the lieutenant left in the outer office, he didn't have any face to preserve.

Later, last night, he'd learned the truth of what happened after he had run away in a panic. I'd left a call at the hotel for the lieutenant. When the lieutenant had got him calmed down and returned my call, I'd instructed him to tell the Swami about the Auerbach cylinders; to tell the Swami he was not a fake after all.

The Swami had obviously spent a sleepless night. It is a terrible thing to have spent years perfecting the art of fakery, and then to realize you needn't have faked at all. More terrible, he had swallowed some of his own medicine, and all through the night he had shivered in fear of some instant and horrible retaliation. For him it was still a case of There Are Mysteries.

And it was no comfort to his state of mind right now that the four cylinders we had finally captured last night were, at this moment, bobbing about in my office, swooping and swerving around in the upper part of the room, like bats trying to find some opening. I was giving him the full treatment. The first two cylinders, down on the floor, were pressing up against my closed door, like frightened little things trying to escape a room of horror.

The Swami's face was twitching, and his long fingers kept twining themselves into King's X symbols. But he was sitting it out. He was swallowing some of the hair of the dog that bit him. I had to give him A for that.

"I've been trying to build up a concept of the framework wherein psi seems to function," I told him casually, just as if it were all a formularized laboratory procedure. "I had to pull last night's stunt to prove something."

He tore his eyes away from the cylinders which were over exploring one corner of the ceiling, and looked at me.

"Let's go to electricity," I said speculatively. "Not that we know psi and electricity have anything in common, other than some similar analogies, but we don't know they don't. Both of them may be just different manifestations of the same thing. We don't really know why a magnetized core, turning inside a coil of copper wire, generates electricity.

"Oh we've got some phrases," I acknowledged. "We've got a whole structure of phrases, and when you listen to them they sound as if they ought to mean something—like the phrases you were using last night. Everybody assumes they do mean something to the pundits. So, since it is human to want to be a pundit, we repeat these phrases over and over, and call them explanations. Yet we do know what happens, even if we do just theorize about why. We know how to wrap something around something and get electricity.

"Take the induction coil," I said. "We feed a low-voltage current into one end, and we draw off a high-voltage current from the other. But anyone who wants, any time, can disprove the whole principle of the induction coil. All you have to do is wrap your core with a nonconductor, say nylon thread, and presto, nothing comes out. You see, it doesn't work; and anybody who claims it does is a faker and a liar. That's what happens when science tries to investigate psi by the standard methods.

"You surround a psi-gifted individual with nonbelievers and probably nothing will come out of it. Surround him with true believers; and it all seems to act like an induction coil. Things happen. Yet even when things do happen, it is usually impossible to prove it.

"Take yourself, Swami. And this is significant. First we have the North point effect. Then those two little beggars trying to get out the door. Then the ones which are bobbing around up there. Without the cylinders there would have been no way to know that anything had happened at all.

"Now, about this psi framework. It isn't something you can turn on and off, at will. We don't know enough yet for that. Aside from some believers and those individuals who do seem to attract psi forces, we don't know, yet, what to wrap around what. So here's what you're to do: You're to keep a supply of these cylinders near you at all times. If any psi effects happen, they'll record it. Fair enough?

"Now," I said with finality. "I have anticipated that you might refuse. But you're not the only person who has psi ability. I've wired General Sanfordwaithe to send me another fellow; one who will co-operate."

The Swami thought it over. Here he was with a suite in a good hotel; with an army lieutenant to look after his earthly needs; on the payroll of a respectable company; with a ready-made flock of believers; and no fear of the bunco squad. He had never had it so good. The side money, for private readings alone, should be substantial.

Further, and he watched me narrowly, I didn't seem to be afraid of the cylinders.

"I'll co-operate," he said.

For three days there was nothing. The Swami called me a couple times a day and reported that the cylinders just lay around his room. I didn't know what to tell him. I recommended he read biographies of famous mediums. I recommended fasting, and breathing, and contemplating self. He seemed dubious, but said he'd try it.

On the morning of the third day, Sara called me on the intercom and told me there was another Army lieutenant in her office, and another . . . gentleman. I opened my door and went out to Sara's office to greet them.

The new lieutenant was no more than the standard output from the same production line as Lieutenant Murphy, but the wizened little old man he had in tow was from a different and much rarer matrix. As fast as I had moved, I was none too soon. The character reached over and tilted up Sara's chin as I was coming through the door.

"Now you're a healthy young wench," he said with a leer. "What are you doing tonight, baby?" The guy was at least eighty years old.

"Hey, you, pop!" I exclaimed in anger. "Be your age!"

He turned around and looked me up and down.

"I'm younger, that way, than you are, right now!" he snapped.

A disturbance in the outer office kept me from thinking up a retort. There were some subdued screams, some scuffling of heavy shoes, the sounds of some running feet as applicants got away. The outer door to Sara's office was flung open.

Framed in the doorway, breast high, floated the Swami!

He was sitting, cross-legged, on a hotel bathmat. From both front corners, where they had been attached by loops of twine, there peeked Auerbach cylinders. Two more rear cylinders were grasped in Lieutenant Murphy's strong hands. He was propelling the Swami along, mid-air, in Atlantic City Boardwalk style.

The Swami looked down at us with aloof disdain, then his eyes focused on the old man. His glance wavered; he threw a startled and fearful look at the cylinders holding up his bathmat. They did not fall. A vast relief overspread his face, and he drew himself erect with more disdain than ever. The old man was not so aloof.

"Harry Glotz!" he exclaimed. "Why you . . . you faker! What are you doing in that get-up?"

The Swami took a casual turn about the room, leaning to one side on his magic carpet as if banking an aeroplane.

"Peasant!" He spat the word out and motioned grandly towards the door. Lieutenant Murphy pushed him through.

"Why, that no-good bum!" the old man shouted at me. "That no-good from nowhere! I'll fix him! Thinks he's something, does he? I'll show him! Anything he can do I can do better!"

His rage got the better of him. He rushed through the door, shaking both fists above his white head, shouting imprecations, threats, and pleading to be shown how the trick was done, all in the same breath. The new lieutenant cast a stricken look at us and then sped after his charge.

"Looks as if we're finally in production," I said to Sara.

"That's only the second one," she said mournfully. "When you get all six of them, this joint's sure going to be jumping!"

I looked out of her window at the steel and concrete walls of the factory. They were solid, real, secure; they were a symbol of reality, the old reality a man could understand.

"I hope you don't mean that literally, Sara," I answered dubiously.

RESURRECTION

by *A. E. van Vogt*

THE GREAT ship poised a quarter of a mile above one of the cities. Below was a cosmic desolation. As he floated down in his energy bubble, Enash saw that the buildings were crumbling with age.

"No signs of war damage!" The bodiless voice touched his ears momentarily. Enash tuned it out.

On the ground he collapsed his bubble. He found himself in a walled enclosure overgrown with weeds. Several skeletons lay in the tall grass beside the rakish building. They were of long, two-legged, two-armed beings with skulls in each case mounted at the end of a thin spine. The skeletons, all of adults, seemed in excellent preservation, but when he bent down and touched one, a whole section of it crumbled into a fine powder. As he straightened, he saw that Yoal was floating down nearby. Enash waited until the historian had stepped out of his bubble, then he said:

"Do you think we ought to use our method of reviving the long dead?"

Yoal was thoughtful. "I have been asking questions of the various people who have landed, and there is something wrong here. This planet has no surviving life, not even insect life. We'll have to find out what happened before we risk any colonization."

Enash said nothing. A soft wind was blowing. It rustled through a clump of trees nearby. He motioned towards the trees. Yoal nodded and said, "Yes, the plant life has not been harmed, but plants after all are not affected in the same way as the active life forms."

There was an interruption. A voice spoke from Yoal's receiver: "A museum has been found at approximately the centre of the city. A red light has been fixed on the roof."

Enash said, "I'll go with you, Yoal. There might be skeletons of animals and of the intelligent being in various stages of his evolution. You didn't answer my question. Are you going to revive these beings?"

Yoal said slowly, "I intend to discuss the matter with the council, but I think there is no doubt. We must know the cause of this disaster." He waved one sucker vaguely to take in half the compass. He added as an afterthought, "We shall proceed cautiously, of course, beginning with an obviously early development. The absence of the skeletons of children indicates that the race had developed personal immortality."

The council came to look at the exhibits. It was, Enash knew, a formal preliminary only. The decision was made. There would be revivals. It was more than that. They were curious. Space was vast, the journeys through it long and lonely, landing always a stimulating experience, with its prospect of new life forms to be seen and studied.

The museum looked ordinary. High-domed ceilings, vast rooms. Plastic models of strange beasts, many artifacts—too many to see and comprehend in so short a time. The life span of a race was imprisoned here in a progressive array of relics. Enash looked with the others, and was glad when they came to the line of skeletons and preserved bodies. He seated himself behind the energy screen, and watched the biological experts take a preserved body out of a stone sarcophagus. It was wrapped in windings of cloth, many of them. The experts did not bother to unravel the rotted material. Their forceps reached through, pinched a piece of skull—that was the accepted procedure. Any part of the skeleton could be used, but the most perfect revivals, the most complete reconstructions resulted when a certain section of the skull was used.

Hamar, the chief biologist, explained the choice of body. "The chemicals used to preserve this mummy show a sketchy knowledge of chemistry. The carvings on the sarcophagus indicate a crude and unmechanical culture. In such a civilization there would not be much development of the potentialities of the nervous system. Our speech experts have been analysing the recorded voice mechanism which is a part of each exhibit, and though many languages are involved—evidence that the ancient language spoken at the time the body was alive has been reproduced—they found no difficulty in translating the meanings. They have now adapted our universal speech machine, so that anyone who wishes to need only speak into his communicator, and so will have his words translated into the language of the revived person. The reverse, naturally, is also true. Ah, I see we are ready for the first body."

Enash watched intently with the others as the lid was clamped down on the plastic reconstructor, and the growth processes were started. He could feel himself becoming tense. For there was nothing haphazard about what was happening. In a few minutes a full-grown ancient inhabitant of this planet would sit up and stare at them. The science involved was simple and always fully effective.

. . . Out of the shadows of smallness, life grows. The level of beginning and ending, of life and—not life; in that dim region matter oscillates easily between old and new habits. The habit of organic, or the habit of inorganic. Electrons do not have life and un-life values. Atoms know nothing of inanimateness. But when atoms form into molecules, there is a step in the process, one tiny step, that is of life—if life begins at all. One step, and then darkness. Or aliveness.

A stone or a living cell. A grain of gold or a blade of grass, the sands of the sea or the equally numerous animalcules inhabiting the endless fishy waters—the difference is there in the twilight zone of matter. Each living cell has in it the whole form. The crab grows a new leg when the old one is torn from its flesh. Both ends of the planarian worm elongate, and soon there are two worms, two identities, two digestive systems each as greedy as the original, each a whole, unwounded, unharmed by its experience. Each cell can be the whole. Each cell remembers in detail so intricate that no totality of words could ever describe the completeness achieved.

But—paradox—memory is not organic. An ordinary wax record remembers sounds. A wire recorder easily gives up a duplicate of the voice that spoke into it years before. Memory is a physiological impression, a mark on matter, a change in the shape of a molecule, so that when a reaction is desired the *shape* emits the same rhythm of response.

Out of the mummy's skull had come the multi-quadrillion

memory shapes from which a response was now being evoked. As ever, the memory held true.

A man blinked, and opened his eyes.

"It is true, then," he said aloud, and the words were translated into the Ganae tongue as he spoke them. "Death is merely an opening into another life—but where are my attendants?" At the end, his voice took on a complaining tone.

He sat up, and climbed out of the case, which had automatically opened as he came to life. He saw his captors. He froze, but only for a moment. He had a pride and a very special arrogant courage, which served him now. Reluctantly, he sank to his knees and made obeisance, but doubt must have been strong in him. "Am I in the presence of the gods of Egypt?" He climbed to his feet. "What nonsense is this? I do not bow to nameless demons."

Captain Gorsid said, "Kill him!"

The two-legged monster dissolved, writhing in the beam of a ray gun.

The second revived man stood up, pale, and trembled with fear. "My God, I swear I won't touch the stuff again. Talk about pink elephants——"

Yoal was curious. "To what *stuff* do you refer, revived one?"

"The old hooch, the poison in the hip pocket flask, the juice they gave me at that speak ... my lordie!"

Captain Gorsid looked questioningly at Yoal, "Need we linger?"

Yoal hesitated. "I am curious." He addressed the man. "If I were to tell you that we were visitors from another star, what would be your reaction?"

The man stared at him. He was obviously puzzled, but the fear was stronger. "Now, look," he said, "I was driving along, minding my own business. I admit I'd had a shot or two too many, but it's the liquor they serve these days. I swear I didn't see the other car—and if this is some new idea of punishing people who drink and drive, well, you've won. I won't touch another drop as long as I live, so help me."

Yoal said, "He drives a 'car' and thinks nothing of it. Yet we saw no cars. They didn't even bother to preserve them in the museums."

Enash noticed that everyone waited for everyone else to

comment. He stirred as he realized the circle of silence would be complete unless he spoke. He said, "Ask him to describe the car. How does it work?"

"Now, you're talking," said the man. "Bring on your line of chalk, and I'll walk it, and ask any questions you please. I may be so tight that I can't see straight, but I can always drive. How does it work? You just put her in gear, and step on the gas."

"Gas," said engineering officer Veed. "The internal combustion engine. That places him."

Captain Gorsid motioned to the guard with the ray gun.

The third man sat up, and looked at them thoughtfully. "From the stars?" he said finally. "Have you a system, or was it blind chance?"

The Ganae councillors in that domed room stirred uneasily in their curved chairs. Enash caught Yoal's eye on him. The shock in the historian's eye alarmed the meteorologist. He thought: "The two-legged one's adjustment to a new situation, his grasp of realities, was unnormally rapid. No Ganae could have equalled the swiftness of the reaction."

Hamar, the chief biologist, said, "Speed of thought is not necessarily a sign of superiority. The slow, careful thinker has his place in the hierarchy of intellect."

But Enash found himself thinking, it was not the speed; it was the accuracy of the response. He tried to imagine himself being revived from the dead, and understanding instantly the meaning of the presence of aliens from the stars. He couldn't have done it.

He forgot his thought, for the man was out of the case. As Enash watched with the others, he walked briskly over to the window and looked out. One glance, and then he turned back. "Is it all like this?" he asked.

Once again, the speed of his understanding caused a sensation. It was Yoal who finally replied.

"Yes. Desolation. Death. Ruin. Have you any ideas as to what happened?"

The man came back and stood in front of the energy screen that guarded the Ganae. "May I look over the museum? I have to estimate what age I am in. We had certain possibilities of destruction when I was last alive, but which one was realized depends on the time elapsed."

The councillors looked at Captain Gorsid, who hesitated; then, "Watch him," he said to the guard with the ray gun. He faced the man. "We understand your aspirations fully. You would like to seize control of this situation and ensure your own safety. Let me reassure you. Make no false moves, and all will be well."

Whether or not the man believed the lie, he gave no sign. Nor did he show by a glance or a movement that he had seen the scarred floor where the ray gun had burned his two predecessors into nothingness. He walked curiously to the nearest doorway, studied the other guard who waited there for him, and then, gingerly, stepped through. The first guard followed him, then came the mobile energy screen, and finally, trailing one another, the councillors.

Enash was the third to pass through the doorway. The room contained skeletons and plastic models of animals. The room beyond that was what, for want of a better term, Enash called a culture room. It contained the artifacts from a single period of civilization. It looked very advanced. He had examined some of the machines when they first passed through it, and had thought: Atomic energy. He was not alone in his recognition. From behind him, Captain Gorsid said to the man:

"You are forbidden to touch anything. A false move will be the signal for the guards to fire."

The man stood at ease in the centre of the room. In spite of a curious anxiety, Enash had to admire his calmness. He must have known what his fate would be, but he stood there thoughtfully, and said finally, deliberately, "I do not need to go any farther. Perhaps you will be able to judge better than I of the time that has elapsed since I was born and these machines were built. I see over there an instrument which, according to the sign above it, counts atoms when they explode. As soon as the proper number have exploded it shuts off the power automatically, and for just the right length of time to prevent a chain explosion. In my time we had a thousand crude devices for limiting the size of an atomic reaction, but it required two thousand years to develop those devices from the early beginnings of atomic energy. Can you make a comparison?"

The councillors glanced at Veed. The engineering officer hesitated. At last, reluctantly, he said. "Nine thousand years ago we had a thousand methods of limiting atomic explosions." He paused, then even more slowly, "I have never heard of an instrument that counts out atoms for such a purpose."

"And yet," murmured Shuri, the astronomer, breathlessly, "the race was destroyed."

There was silence. It ended as Gorsid said to the nearest guard, "Kill the monster!"

But it was the guard who went down, bursting into flame. Not just one guard, but the guards! Simultaneously down, burning with a blue flame. The flame licked at the screen, recoiled, and licked more furiously, recoiled and burned brighter. Through a haze of fire, Enash saw that the man had retreated to the far door, and that the machine that counted atoms was glowing with a blue intensity.

Captain Gorsid shouted into his communicator, "Guard all exits with ray guns. Spaceships stand by to kill alien with heavy guns."

Somebody said, "Mental control. Some kind of mental control. What have we run into?"

They were retreating. The blue flame was at the ceiling, struggling to break through the screen. Enash had a last glimpse of the machine. It must still be counting atoms, for it was a hellish blue. Enash raced with the others to the room where the man had been resurrected. There, another energy screen crashed to their rescue. Safe now, they retreated into their separate bubbles and whisked through outer doors and up to the ship. As the great ship soared, an atomic bomb hurtled down from it. The mushroom of flame blotted out the museum and the city below.

"But we still don't know why the race died," Yoal whispered into Enash's ear, after the thunder had died from the heavens behind them.

The pale yellow sun crept over the horizon on the third morning after the bomb was dropped, the eighth day since the landing. Enash floated with the others down on a new city. He had come to argue against any further revival.

"As a meteorologist," he said, "I pronounce this planet safe for Ganae colonization. I cannot see the need for taking any risks. This race has discovered the secrets of its nervous system, and we cannot afford——"

He was interrupted. Hamar, the biologist, said dryly, "If they knew so much why didn't they migrate to other star systems and save themselves?"

"I will concede," said Enash, "that very possibly they had not discovered our system of locating stars with planetary families." He looked earnestly around the circle of his friends. "We have agreed that was a unique accidental discovery. We were lucky, not clever."

He saw by the expressions on their faces that they were mentally refuting his arguments. He felt a helpless sense of imminent catastrophe. For he could see that picture of a great race facing death. It must have come swiftly, but not so swiftly that they didn't know about it. There were too many skeletons in the open, lying in the gardens of magnificent homes, as if each man and his wife had come out to wait for the doom of his kind. He tried to picture it for the council, that last day long, long ago, when a race had calmly met its ending. But his visualization failed somehow, for the others shifted impatiently in the seats that had been set up behind the series of energy screens, and Captain Gorsid said, "Exactly what aroused this intense emotional reaction in you, Enash?"

The question gave Enash pause. He hadn't thought of it as emotional. He hadn't realized the nature of his obsession, so subtly had it stolen upon him. Abruptly now, he realized.

"It was the third one," he said, slowly. "I saw him through the haze of energy fire, and he was standing there in the distant doorway watching us curiously, just before we turned to run. His bravery, his calm, the skilful way he had duped us—it all added up."

"Added up to his death!" said Hamar. And everybody laughed.

"Come now, Enash," said Vice-captain Mayad good-humouredly, "you're not going to pretend that this race is braver than our own, or that, with all the precautions we have now taken, we need fear one man?"

Enash was silent, feeling foolish. The discovery that he had had an emotional obsession abashed him. He did not want to appear unreasonable. He made a final protest, "I merely wish to point out," he said doggedly, "that this desire to discover what happened to a dead race does not seem absolutely essential to me."

Captain Gorsid waved at the biologist, "Proceed," he said, "with the revival."

To Enash, he said, "Do we dare return to Gana, and recommend mass migrations—and then admit that we did not actually complete our investigations here? It's impossible, my friend."

It was the old argument, but reluctantly now Enash admitted there was something to be said for that point of view. He forgot that, for the fourth man was stirring.

The man sat up. And vanished.

There was a blank, startled, horrified silence. Then Captain Gorsid said harshly, "He can't get out of there. We know that. He's in there somewhere."

All around Enash, the Ganae were out of their chairs, peering into the energy shell. The guards stood with ray guns held limply in their suckers. Out of the corner of his eye, he saw one of the protective screen technicians beckon to Veed, who went over. He came back grim. He said, "I'm told the needles jumped ten points when he first disappeared. That's on the nucleonic level."

"By ancient Ganae!" Shuri whispered. "We've run into what we've always feared."

Gorsid was shouting into the communicator. "Destroy all the locators on the ship. Destroy them, do you hear!"

He turned with glaring eyes. "Shuri," he bellowed. "They don't seem to understand. Tell those subordinates of yours to act. All locators and reconstructors must be destroyed."

"Hurry, hurry!" said Shuri weakly.

When that was done they breathed more easily. There were grim smiles and a tensed satisfaction. "At least," said Vice-captain Mayad, "he cannot now ever discover Gana. Our great system of locating suns with planets remains our secret. There can be no retaliation for——" He stopped, said slowly, "What am I talking about? We haven't done anything. We're not responsible for the disaster that has befallen the inhabitants of this planet."

But Enash knew what he had meant. The guilt feelings came to the surface at such moments as this—the ghosts of all the races destroyed by the Ganae, the remorseless will that had been in them, when they first landed, to annihilate whatever was here. The dark abyss of voiceless hate and terror that lay behind them; the days on end when they had mercilessly poured poisonous radiation down upon the unsuspecting inhabitants of peaceful planets—all that had been in Mayad's words.

"I still refuse to believe he has escaped." That was Captain Gorsid. "He's in there. He's waiting for us to take down our screens, so he can escape. Well, we won't do it."

There was silence again as they stared expectantly into the emptiness of the energy shell. The reconstructor rested on metal supports, a glittering affair. But there was nothing else. Not a flicker of unnatural light or shade. The yellow rays of the sun bathed the open spaces with a brilliance that left no room for concealment.

"Guards," said Gorsid, "destroy the reconstructor. I thought he might come back to examine it, but we can't take a chance on that."

It burned with a white fury. And Enash, who had hoped somehow that the deadly energy would force the two-legged thing into the open, felt his hopes sag within him.

"But where can he have gone?" Yoal whispered.

Enash turned to discuss the matter. In the act of swinging around, he saw that the monster was standing under a tree a score of feet to one side, watching them. He must have arrived at *that* moment, for there was a collective gasp from the councillors. Everybody drew back. One of the screen technicians, using great presence of mind, jerked up an energy screen between the Ganae and the monster. The creature came forward slowly. He was slim of build, he held his head well back. His eyes shone as from an inner fire.

He stopped as he came to the screen, reached out and touched it with his fingers. It flared, blurred with changing colours. The colours grew brighter, and extended in an intricate pattern all the way from his head to the ground. The blur cleared. The pattern faded into invisibility. The man was through the screen.

He laughed, a soft curious sound; then sobered. "When I first awakened," he said, "I was curious about the situation. The question was, what should I do with you?"

The words had a fateful ring to Enash on the still morning air of that planet of the dead. A voice broke the silence, a voice so strained and unnatural that a moment passed before he recognized it as belonging to Captain Gorsid.

"Kill him!"

When the blasters ceased their effort, the unkillable thing remained standing. He walked slowly forward until he was only a half dozen feet from the nearest Ganae. Enash had a position well to the rear. The man said slowly:

"Two courses suggest themselves, one based on gratitude for reviving me, the other based on reality. I know you for what you are. Yes, *know* you—and that is unfortunate. It is hard to feel merciful. To begin with," he went on, "let us suppose you surrender the secret of the locator. Naturally, now that a system exists, we shall never again be caught as we were."

Enash had been intent, his mind so alive with the potentialities of the disaster that was here that it seemed impossible that he could think of anything else. And yet, a part of his attention was stirred now. "What did happen?" he asked.

The man changed colour. The emotions of that far day thickened his voice. "A nucleonic storm. It swept in from outer space. It brushed this edge of our galaxy. It was about ninety light-years in diameter, beyond the farthest limit of our power. There was no escape from it. We had dispensed with spaceships, and had no time to construct any. Castor, the only star with planets ever discovered by us, was also in the path of the storm." He stopped. "The secret?" he said.

Around Enash, the councillors were breathing easier. The fear of race destruction that had come to them was lifting. Enash saw with pride that the first shock was over, and they were not even afraid for themselves.

"Ah," said Yoal softly, "you don't know the secret. In spite of all your great development, we alone can conquer the galaxy." He looked at the others, smiling confidently. "Gentlemen," he said, "our pride in a great Ganae achievement is justified. I suggest we return to our ship. We have no further business on this planet."

There was a confused moment while their bubbles formed, when Enash wondered if the two-legged one would try to stop their departure. But when he looked back, he saw that the man was walking in a leisurely fashion along a street.

That was the memory Enash carried with him, as the ship began to move. That and the fact that the three atomic bombs they dropped, one after the other, failed to explode.

"We will not," said Captain Gorsid, "give up a planet as easily as that. I propose another interview with the creature."

They were floating down again into the city, Enash and Yoal and Veed and the commander. Captain Gorsid's voice tuned in once more:

". . . As I visualize it"—through the mist Enash could see the transparent glint of the other three bubbles around him—"we jumped to conclusions about this creature, not justified by the evidence. For instance, when he awakened, he vanished. Why? Because he was afraid, of course. He wanted to size up the situation. *He* didn't believe he was omnipotent."

It was sound logic. Enash found himself taking heart from it. Suddenly, he was astonished that he had become panicky so easily. He began to see the danger in a new light. Only one man alive on a new planet. If they were determined enough, colonists could be moved in as if he did not exist. It had been done before, he recalled. On several planets, small groups of the original populations had survived the destroying radiation, and taken refuge in remote areas. In almost every case, the new colonists gradually hunted them down. In two instances, however, that Enash remembered, native races were still holding small sections of their planets. In each case, it had been found impractical to destroy them because it would have endangered the Ganae on the planet. So the survivors were tolerated. One man would not take up very much room.

When they found him, he was busily sweeping out the lower floor of a small bungalow. He put the broom aside and stepped on to the terrace outside. He had put on sandals, and he wore a loose-fitting robe made of very shiny material. He eyed them indolently but he said nothing.

It was Captain Gorsid who made the proposition. Enash had to admire the story he told into the language machine. The commander was very frank. That approach had been decided on. He pointed out that the Ganae could not be expected to revive the dead of this planet. Such altruism would be un-natural considering that the ever-growing Ganae hordes had a continual need for new worlds. Each vast new population incre-ment was a problem that could be solved by one method only. In this instance, the colonists would gladly respect the rights of the sole survivor of this world.

It was at this point that the man interrupted. "But what is the purpose of this endless expansion?" He seemed genuinely curious. "What will happen when you finally occupy every planet in this galaxy?"

Captain Gorsid's puzzled eyes met Yoal's, then flashed to Veed, then Enash. Enash shrugged his torso negatively, and felt pity for the creature. The man didn't understand, possibly never could understand. It was the old story of two different viewpoints, the virile and the decadent, the race that aspired to the stars and the race that declined the call of destiny.

"Why not," urged the man, "control the breeding chambers?"

"And have the government overthrown!" said Yoal.

He spoke tolerantly, and Enash saw that the others were smiling at the man's naiveté. He felt the intellectual gulf between them widening. The creature had no comprehension of the natural life forces that were at work. The man spoke again:

"Well, if you don't control them, we will control them for you."

There was silence.

They began to stiffen. Enash felt it in himself, saw the signs of it in the others. His gaze flicked from face to face, then back to the creature in the doorway. Not for the first time, Enash had the thought that their enemy seemed helpless. "Why," he decided, "I could put my suckers around him and crush him."

He wondered if mental control of nucleonic, nuclear, and gravitonic energies included the ability to defend oneself from a macrocosmic attack. He had an idea it did. The exhibition of power two hours before might have had limitations, but if so, it was not apparent. Strength or weakness could make no difference. The threat of threats had been made: "If you don't control—we will."

The words echoed in Enash's brain, and, as the meaning penetrated deeper, his aloofness faded. He had always regarded himself as a spectator. Even when, earlier, he had argued against the revival, he had been aware of a detached part of himself watching the scene rather than being a part of it. He saw with a sharp clarity that that was why he had finally yielded to the conviction of the others. Going back beyond that to remoter days, he saw that he had never quite considered himself a participant in the seizure of the planets of other races. He was the one who looked on, and thought of reality, and speculated on a life that seemed to have no meaning. It was meaningless no longer. He was caught by a tide of irresistible emotion, and swept along. He felt himself sinking, merging with the Ganae mass being. All the strength and all the will of the race surged up in his veins.

He snarled, "Creature, if you have any hopes of reviving your dead race, abandon them now."

The man looked at him, but said nothing. Enash rushed on, "If you could destroy us, you would have done so already. But the truth is that you operate within limitations. Our ship is so built that no conceivable chain reaction could be started in it. For every plate of potential unstable material in it there is a counteracting plate, which prevents the development of a critical pile. You might be able to set off explosions in our engines, but they, too, would be limited, and would merely start the process for which they are intended—confined in their proper space."

He was aware of Yoal touching his arm. "Careful," warned the historian. "Do not in your just anger give away vital information."

Enash shook off the restraining sucker. "Let us not be unrealistic," he said harshly. "This thing has divined most of our racial secrets, apparently merely by looking at our bodies. We would be acting childishly if we assumed that he has not already realized the possibilities of the situation."

"*Enash!*" Captain Gorsid's voice was imperative.

As swiftly as it had come, Enash's rage subsided. He stepped back. "Yes, commander."

"I think I know what you intended to say," said Captain Gorsid. "I assure you I am in full accord, but I believe also that I, as the top Ganae official, should deliver the ultimatum."

He turned. His horny body towered above the man. "You have made the unforgivable threat. You have told us, in effect, that you will attempt to restrict the vaulting Ganae spirit."

"Not the spirit," said the man.

The commander ignored the interruption. "Accordingly, we have no alternative. We are assuming that, given time to locate the materials and develop the tools, you might be able to build a reconstructor. In our opinion it will be at least two years before you can complete it, *even if you know how.* It is an immensely intricate machine, not easily assembled by the lone survivor of a race that gave up its machines millennia before disaster struck.

"You did not have time to build a spaceship. We won't give you time to build a reconstructor.

"Within a few minutes our ship will start dropping bombs. It is possible you will be able to prevent explosions in your vicinity. We will start, accordingly, on the other side of the planet. If you stop us there, then we will assume we need help. In six months of travelling at top acceleration, we can reach a point where the nearest Ganae planet would hear our messages. They will send a fleet so vast that all your powers of resistance will be overcome. By dropping a hundred or a thousand bombs every minute, we will succeed in devastating every city so that not a grain of dust will remain of the skeletons of your people.

"That is our plan. So it shall be. Now, do your worst to us who are at your mercy."

The man shook his head. "I shall do nothing—now!" he said. He paused, then thoughtfully, "Your reasoning is fairly accurate. Fairly. Naturally, I am not all powerful, but it seems to me you have forgotten one little point. I won't tell you what it is. And now," he said, "good day to you. Get back to your ship, and be on your way. I have much to do."

Enash had been standing quietly, aware of the fury building up in him again. Now, with a hiss, he sprang forward, suckers outstretched. They were almost touching the smooth flesh— when something snatched at him.

He was back on the ship.

He had no memory of movement, no sense of being dazed or harmed. He was aware of Veed and Yoal and Captain Gorsid standing near him as astonished as he himself. Enash remained very still, thinking of what the man had said: *". . . Forgotten one little point."* Forgotten? That meant they knew. What could it be? He was still pondering about it when Yoal said:

"We can be reasonably certain our bombs alone will not work."

They didn't.

Forty light-years out from Earth, Enash was summoned to the council chambers. Yoal greeted him wanly. "The monster is aboard."

The thunder of that poured through Enash, and with it came a sudden comprehension. "That was what he meant we had forgotten," he said finally, aloud and wonderingly. "That he can travel through space at will within a limit—what was the figure he once used—of ninety light-years."

He sighed. He was not surprised that the Ganae, who had to use ships, would not have thought immediately of such a possibility. Slowly, he began to retreat from the reality. Now that the shock had come, he felt old and weary, a sense of his mind withdrawing again to its earlier state of aloofness. It required a few minutes to get the story. A physicist's assistant, on his way to the storeroom, had caught a glimpse of a man in a lower corridor. In such a heavily manned ship, the wonder was that the intruder had escaped earlier observation. Enash had a thought.

"But after all we are not going all the way to one of our planets. How does he expect to make use of us to locate it if we only use the video——" he stopped. That was it, of course. Directional video beams would have to be used, and the man would travel in the right direction the instant contact was made.

Enash saw the decision in the eyes of his companions, the only possible decision under the circumstances. And yet, it seemed to him they were missing some vital point. He walked slowly to the great video plate at one end of the chamber. There was a picture on it, so sharp, so vivid, so majestic that the unaccustomed mind would have reeled as from a stunning blow. Even to him, who knew the scene, there came a constriction, a sense of unthinkable vastness. It was a video view of a section of the milky way. Four hundred *million* stars as seen through telescopes that could pick up the light of a red dwarf at thirty thousand light-years.

The video plate was twenty-five yards in diameter—a scene that had no parallel elsewhere in the plenum. Other galaxies simply did not have that many stars.

Only one in two hundred thousand of those glowing suns had planets.

That was the colossal fact that compelled them now to an irrevocable act. Wearily, Enash looked around him.

"The monster has been very clever," he said quietly. "If we go ahead, he goes with us, obtains a reconstructor, and returns by his method to his planet. If we use the directional beam, he flashes along it, obtains a reconstructor, and again reaches his planet first. In either event, by the time our fleets arrived back here, he would have revived enough of his kind to thwart any attack we could mount."

He shook his torso. The picture was accurate, he felt sure, but it still seemed incomplete. He said slowly, "We have one advantage now. Whatever decision we make, there is no language machine to enable him to learn what it is. We can carry out our plans without his knowing what they will be. He knows that neither he nor we can blow up the ship. That leaves us one real alternative."

It was Captain Gorsid who broke the silence that followed. "Well, gentlemen, I see we know our minds. We will set the engines, blow up the controls, and take him with us."

They looked at each other, race pride in their eyes. Enash touched suckers with each in turn.

An hour later, when the heat was already considerable, Enash had the thought that sent him staggering to the communicator, to call Shuri, the astronomer. "Shuri," he yelled, "when the monster first awakened—remember Captain Gorsid had difficulty getting your subordinates to destroy the locators. We never thought to ask them what the delay was. Ask them . . . ask them———"

There was a pause, then Shuri's voice came weakly over the roar of the static, "They . . . couldn't . . . get . . . into the . . . room. The door was locked."

Enash sagged to the floor. They had missed more than one point, he realized. The man had awakened, realized the situation; and, when he vanished, he had gone to the ship, and there discovered the secret of the locator and possibly the secret of the reconstructor—if he didn't know it previously. By the time he reappeared, he already had from them what he wanted. All the rest must have been designed to lead them to this act of desperation.

In a few moments, now, *he* would be leaving the ship, secure in the knowledge that shortly no alien mind would know his planet existed. Knowing, too, that his race would live again, and this time never die.

Enash staggered to his feet, clawed at the roaring communicator, and shouted his new understanding into it. There was no answer. It clattered with the static of uncontrollable and inconceivable energy. The heat was peeling his armoured hide as he struggled to the matter transmitter. It flashed at him with purple flame. Back to the communicator he ran shouting and screaming.

He was still whimpering into it a few minutes later when the mighty ship plunged into the heart of a blue-white sun.

VINTAGE SEASON

by Henry Kuttner

THREE PEOPLE came up the walk to the old mansion just at dawn on a perfect May morning. Oliver Wilson in his pyjamas watched them from an upper window through a haze of conflicting emotions, resentment predominant. He didn't want them there.

They were foreigners. He knew only that much about them. They had the curious name of Sancisco, and their first names, scrawled in loops on the lease, appeared to be Omerie, Kleph and Klia, though it was impossible as he looked down upon them to sort them out by signature. He hadn't even been sure whether they would be men or women, and he had expected something a little less cosmopolitan.

Oliver's heart sank a little as he watched them follow the taxi driver up the walk. He had hoped for less self-assurance in his unwelcome tenants, because he meant to force them out of the house if he could. It didn't look very promising from here.

The man went first. He was tall and dark, and he wore his clothes and carried his body with that peculiar arrogant assurance that comes from perfect confidence in every phase of one's being. The two women were laughing as they followed him. Their voices were light and sweet, and their faces were beautiful, each in its own exotic way, but the first thing Oliver thought of when he looked at them was, Expensive!

It was not only that patina of perfection that seemed to dwell in every line of their incredibly flawless garments. There are degrees of wealth beyond which wealth itself ceases to have significance. Oliver had seen before, on rare occasions, something like this assurance that the earth turning beneath their well-shod feet turned only to their whim.

It puzzled him a little in this case, because he had the feeling as the three came up the walk that the beautiful clothing they wore so confidently was not clothing they were accustomed to. There was a curious air of condescension in the way they moved. Like women in costume. They minced a little on their delicate high heels, held out an arm to stare at the cut of a sleeve, twisted now and then inside their garments as if the clothing sat strangely on them, as if they were accustomed to something entirely different.

And there was an elegance about the way the garments fitted them which even to Oliver looked strikingly unusual. Only an actress on the screen, who can stop time and the film to adjust every disarrayed fold so that she looks perpetually perfect, might appear thus elegantly clad. But let these women move as they liked, and each fold of their clothing followed perfectly with the movement and fell perfectly into place again. One might almost suspect the garments were not cut of ordinary cloth, or that they were cut according to some unknown, subtle scheme, with many artful hidden seams placed by a tailor incredibly skilled at his trade.

They seemed excited. They talked in high, clear, very sweet voices, looking up at the perfect blue and transparent sky in which dawn was still frankly pink. They looked at the trees on the lawn, the leaves translucently green with an under colour of golden newness, the edges crimped from constriction in the recent bud.

Happily and with excitement in their voices they called to the man, and when he answered his own voice blended so perfectly in cadence with theirs that it sounded like three people singing together. Their voices, like their clothing, seemed to have an elegance far beyond the ordinary, to be under a control such as Oliver Wilson had never dreamed of before this morning.

The taxi driver brought up the luggage, which was of a beautiful pale stuff that did not look quite like leather, and had curves in it so subtle it seemed square until you saw how two or three pieces of it fitted together when carried, into a perfectly balanced block. It was scuffed, as if from much use. And though there was a great deal of it, the taxi man did not seem to find his burden heavy. Oliver saw him look down at it now and then and heft the weight incredulously.

One of the women had very black hair and skin like cream, and the smoke-blue eyes heavy-lidded with the weight of her lashes. It was the other woman Oliver's gaze followed as she came up the walk. Her hair was a clear, pale red, and her face had a softness that he thought would be like velvet to touch. She was tanned to a warm amber darker than her hair.

Just as they reached the porch steps the fair woman lifted her head and looked up. She gazed straight into Oliver's eyes and he saw that hers were very blue, and just a little amused, as if she had known he was there all along. Also they were frankly admiring.

Feeling a bit dizzy, Oliver hurried back to his room to dress.

"We are here on a vacation," the dark man said, accepting the keys. "We will not wish to be disturbed, as I made clear in our correspondence. You have engaged a cook and housemaid for us, I understand? We will expect you to move your own belongings out of the house, then, and——"

"Wait," Oliver said uncomfortably. "Something's come up. I——" He hesitated, not sure just how to present it. These were such increasingly odd people. Even their speech was odd. They spoke so distinctly, not slurring any of the words into contractions. English seemed as familiar to them as a native tongue, but they all spoke as trained singers sing, with perfect breath control and voice placement.

And there was a coldness in the man's voice, as if some gulf lay between him and Oliver, so deep no feeling of human contact could bridge it.

"I wonder," Oliver said, "if I could find you better living quarters somewhere else in town. There's a place across the street that——"

The dark woman said, "Oh, no!" in a lightly horrified voice, and all three of them laughed. It was cool, distant laughter that did not include Oliver.

The dark man said, "We chose this house carefully, Mr. Wilson. We would not be interested in living anywhere else."

Oliver said desperately, "I don't see why. It isn't even a modern house. I have two others in much better condition. Even across the street you'd have a fine view of the city. Here there isn't anything. The other houses cut off the view, and——"

"We engaged rooms here, Mr. Wilson," the man said with

finality. "We expect to use them. Now will you make arrangements to leave as soon as possible."

Oliver said, "No," and looked stubborn. "That isn't in the lease. You can live here until next month, since you paid for it, but you can't put me out. I'm staying."

The man opened his mouth to say something. He looked coldly at Oliver and closed it again. The feeling of aloofness was chill between them. There was a moment's silence. Then the man said, "Very well. Be kind enough to stay out of our way."

It was a little odd that he didn't inquire into Oliver's motives. Oliver was not yet sure enough of the man to explain. He couldn't very well say, "Since the lease was signed, I've been offered three times what the house is worth if I'll sell it before the end of May." He couldn't say, "I want the money, and I'm going to use my own nuisance-value to annoy you until you're willing to move out." After all, there seemed no reason why they shouldn't. After seeing them, there seemed doubly no reason, for it was clear they must be accustomed to surroundings infinitely better than this timeworn old house.

It was very strange, the value this house had so suddenly acquired. There was no reason at all why two groups of semi-anonymous people should be so eager to possess it for the month of May.

In silence Oliver showed his tenants upstairs to the three big bedrooms across the front of the house. He was intensely conscious of the red-haired woman and the way she watched him with a sort of obviously covert interest, quite warmly, and with a curious undertone to her interest that he could not quite place. It was familiar, but elusive. He thought how pleasant it would be to talk to her alone, if only to try to capture that elusive attitude and put a name to it.

Afterwards he went down to the telephone and called his fiancée.

Sue's voice squeaked a little with excitement over the wire.

"Oliver, so early? Why, it's hardly six yet. Did you tell them what I said? Are they going to go?"

"Can't tell yet. I doubt it. After all, Sue, I did take their money, you know."

"Oliver, they've got to go! You've got to do something!"

"I'm trying, Sue. But I don't like it."

"Well, there isn't any reason why they shouldn't stay some-where else. And we're going to need that money. You'll just have to think of something, Oliver."

Oliver met his own worried eyes in the mirror above the tele-phone and scowled at himself. His straw-coloured hair was tangled and there was a shining stubble on his pleasant, tanned face. He was sorry the red-haired woman had first seen him in his untidy condition. Then his conscience smote him at the sound of Sue's determined voice and he said :

"I'll try, darling. I'll try. But I did take their money."

They had, in fact, paid a great deal of money, considerably more than the rooms were worth even in that year of high prices and high wages. The country was just moving into one of those fabulous eras which are later referred to as the Gay Forties or the Golden Sixties—a pleasant period of national euphoria. It was a stimulating time to be alive—while it lasted.

"All right," Oliver said resignedly. "I'll do my best."

But he was conscious, as the next few days went by, that he was not doing his best. There were several reasons for that. From the beginning the idea of making himself a nuisance to his tenants had been Sue's, not Oliver's. And if Oliver had been a little determined the whole project would never have got under way. Reason was on Sue's side, but——

For one thing, the tenants were so fascinating. All they said and did had a queer sort of inversion to it, as if a mirror had been held up to ordinary living and in the reflection showed strange variations from the norm. Their minds worked on a different basic premise, Oliver thought, from his own. They seemed to derive covert amusement from the most unamusing things; they patronized, they were aloof with a quality of cold detachment which did not prevent them from laughing inexplic-ably far too often for Oliver's comfort.

He saw them occasionally, on their way to and from their rooms. They were polite and distant, not, he suspected, from anger at his presence but from sheer indifference.

Most of the day they spent out of the house. The perfect May weather held unbroken and they seemed to give themselves up wholeheartedly to admiration of it, entirely confident that the warm, pale-gold sunshine and the scented air would not be interrupted by rain or cold. They were so sure of it that Oliver felt uneasy.

They took only one meal a day in the house, a late dinner. And their reactions to the meal were unpredictable. Laughter greeted some of the dishes, and a sort of delicate disgust others. No one would touch the salad, for instance. And the fish seemed to cause a wave of queer embarrassment around the table.

They dressed elaborately for each dinner. The man—his name was Omerie—looked extremely handsome in his dinner clothes, but he seemed a little sulky and Oliver twice heard the women laughing because he had to wear black. Oliver entertained a sudden vision, for no reason, of the man in garments as bright and subtly cut as the women's, and it seemed somehow very right for him. He wore even the dark clothing with a certain flamboyance, as if cloth-of-gold would be more normal for him.

When they were in the house at other mealtimes, they ate in their rooms. They must have brought a great deal of food with them, from whatever mysterious place they had come. Oliver wondered with increasing curiosity where it might be. Delicious odours drifted into the hall sometimes, at odd hours, from their closed doors. Oliver could not identify them, but almost always they smelled irresistible. A few times the food smell was rather shockingly unpleasant, almost nauseating. It takes a connoisseur, Oliver reflected, to appreciate the decadent. And these people, most certainly, were connoisseurs.

Why they lived so contentedly in this huge ramshackle old house was a question that disturbed his dreams at night. Or why they refused to move. He caught some fascinating glimpses into their rooms, which appeared to have been changed almost completely by additions he could not have defined very clearly from the brief sights he had of them. The feeling of luxury which his first glance at them had evoked was confirmed by the richness of the hangings they had apparently brought with them, the half-glimpsed ornaments, the pictures on the walls, even the whiffs of exotic perfume that floated from half-open doors.

He saw the women go by him in the halls, moving softly through the brown dimness in their gowns so uncannily perfect in fit, so lushly rich, so glowingly coloured they seemed unreal. That poise born of confidence in the subservience of the world

gave them an imperious aloofness, but more than once Oliver,
meeting the blue gaze of the woman with the red hair and the
soft, tanned skin, thought he saw quickened interest there. She
smiled at him in the dimness and went by in a haze of fragrance
and a halo of incredible richness, and the warmth of the smile
lingered after she had gone.

He knew she did not mean this aloofness to last between them.
From the very first he was sure of that. When the time came she
would make the opportunity to be alone with him. The thought
was confusing and tremendously exciting. There was nothing he
could do but wait, knowing she would see him when it suited
her.

On the third day he lunched with Sue in a little downtown
restaurant overlooking the great sweep of the metropolis across
the river far below. Sue had shining brown curls and brown
eyes, and her chin was a bit more prominent than is strictly
accordant with beauty. From childhood Sue had known what
she wanted and how to get it, and it seemed to Oliver just now
that she had never wanted anything quite so much as the sale of
this house.

"It's such a marvellous offer for the old mausoleum," she said,
breaking into a roll with a gesture of violence. "We'll never
have a chance like that again, and prices are so high we'll need
the money to start housekeeping. Surely you can do *something*,
Oliver!"

"I'm trying," Oliver assured her uncomfortably.

"Have you heard anything more from that madwoman who
wants to buy it?"

Oliver shook his head. "Her attorney phoned again yesterday.
Nothing new. I wonder who she is."

"I don't think even the attorney knows. All this mystery—I
don't like it, Oliver. Even those Sancisco people—— What did
they do today?"

Oliver laughed. "They spent about an hour this morning tele-
phoning movie theatres in the city, checking up on a lot of
third-rate films they want to see parts of."

"Parts of? But why?"

"I don't know. I think . . . oh, nothing. More coffee?"

The trouble was, he thought he did know. It was too unlikely

a guess to tell Sue about, and without familiarity with the Sancisco oddities she would only think Oliver was losing his mind.
But he had from their talk, a definite impression that there was
an actor in bit parts in all these films whose performances they
mentioned with something very near to awe. They referred to
him as Golconda, which didn't appear to be his name, so that
Oliver had no way of guessing which obscure bit-player it was
they admired so deeply. Golconda might have been the name of
a character he had once played—and with superlative skill,
judging by the comments of the Sanciscos—but to Oliver it
meant nothing at all.

"They do funny things," he said, stirring his coffee reflectively.
"Yesterday Omerie—that's the man—came in with a book of
poems published about five years ago, and all of them handled
it like a first edition of Shakespeare. I never even heard of the
author, but he seems to be a tin god in their country, wherever
that is."

"You still don't know? Haven't they even dropped any hints?"

"We don't do much talking," Oliver reminded her with some
irony.

"I know, but—— Oh, well, I guess it doesn't matter. Go on,
what else do they do?"

"Well, this morning they were going to spend studying 'Golconda' and his great art, and this afternoon I think they're
taking a trip up the river to some sort of shrine I never heard of.
It isn't very far, wherever it is, because I know they're coming
back for dinner. Some great man's birthplace, I think—they
promised to take home souvenirs of the place if they could get
any. They're typical tourists, all right—if I could only figure
out what's behind the whole thing. It doesn't make sense."

"Nothing about that house makes sense any more. I do
wish——"

She went on in a petulant voice, but Oliver ceased suddenly
to hear her, because just outside the door, walking with imperial elegance on her high heels, a familiar figure passed. He
did not see her face, but he thought he would know that poise,
that richness of line and motion, anywhere on earth.

"Excuse me a minute," he muttered to Sue, and was out of
his chair before she could speak. He made the door in half a
dozen long strides, and the beautifully elegant passerby was

only a few steps away when he got there. Then, with the words he had meant to speak already half uttered, he fell silent and stood there staring.

It was not the red-haired woman. It was not her dark companion. It was a stranger. He watched, speechless, while the lovely, imperious creature moved on through the crowd and vanished, moving with familiar poise and assurance and an equally familiar strangeness as if the beautiful and exquisitely fitted garments she wore were an exotic costume to her, as they had always seemed to the Sancisco women. Every other woman on the street looked untidy and ill at ease beside her. Walking like a queen, she melted into the crowd and was gone.

She came from *their* country, Oliver told himself dizzily. So someone else nearby had mysterious tenants in this month of perfect May weather. Someone else was puzzling in vain today over the strangeness of the people from the nameless land.

In silence he went back to Sue.

The door stood invitingly ajar in the brown dimness of the upper hall. Oliver's steps slowed as he drew near it, and his heart began to quicken correspondingly. It was the red-haired woman's room, and he thought the door was not open by accident. Her name, he knew now, was Kleph.

The door creaked a little on its hinges and from within a very sweet voice said lazily, "Won't you come in?"

The room looked very different indeed. The big bed had been pushed back against the wall, and a cover thrown over it that brushed the floor all around looked like soft-haired fur except that it was pale blue-green and sparkled as if every hair were tipped with invisible crystals. Three books lay open on the fur, and a very curious-looking magazine with faintly luminous printing and a page of pictures that at first glance appeared three-dimensional. Also a tiny porcelain pipe encrusted with porcelain flowers, and a thin wisp of smoke floating from the bowl.

Above the bed a broad picture hung, framing a square of blue water so real Oliver had to look twice to be sure it was not rippling gently from left to right. From the ceiling swung a crystal globe on a glass cord. It turned gently, the light from the windows making curved rectangles in its sides.

Under the centre window a sort of chaise-longue stood which Oliver had not seen before. He could only assume it was at least partly pneumatic and had been brought in the luggage. There was a very rich-looking quilted cloth covering and hiding it, embossed all over in shining metallic patterns.

Kleph moved slowly from the door and sank upon the chaise-longue with a little sigh of content. The couch accommodated itself to her body with what looked like delightful comfort. Kleph wriggled a little and then smiled up at Oliver.

"Do come on in. Sit over there, where you can see out the window. I love your beautiful spring weather. You know, there never was a May like it in civilized times." She said that quite seriously, her blue eyes on Oliver's, and there was a hint of patronage in her voice, as if the weather had been arranged especially for her.

Oliver started across the room and then paused and looked down in amazement at the floor, which felt unstable. He had not noticed before that the carpet was pure white, unspotted, and sank about an inch under the pressure of the feet. He saw then that Kleph's feet were bare, or almost bare. She wore something like gossamer buskins of filmy net, fitting her feet exactly. The bare soles were pink as if they had been rouged, and the nails had a liquid gleam like tiny mirrors. He moved closer, and was not as surprised as he should have been to see that they really were tiny mirrors, painted with some lacquer that gave them reflecting surfaces.

"Do sit down," Kleph said again, waving a white-sleeved arm towards a chair by the window. She wore a garment that looked like short, soft down, loosely cut but following perfectly every motion she made. And there was something curiously different about her very shape today. When Oliver saw her in street clothes, she had the square-shouldered, slim-flanked figure that all women strove for, but here in her lounging robe she looked— well, different. There was an almost swan-like slope to her shoulders today, a roundness and softness to her body that looked unfamiliar and very appealing.

"Will you have some tea?" Kleph asked, and smiled charmingly.

A low table beside her held a tray and several small covered cups, lovely things with an inner glow like rose quartz, the colour shining deeply as if from within layer upon layer of translucence. She took up one of the cups—there were no saucers—and offered it to Oliver.

It felt fragile and thin as paper in his hand. He could not see the contents because of the cup's cover, which seemed to be one with the cup itself and left only a thin open crescent at the rim. Steam rose from the opening.

Kleph took up a cup of her own and tilted it to her lips, smiling at Oliver over the rim. She was very beautiful. The pale red hair lay in shining loops against her head and the corona of curls like a halo above her forehead might have been pressed down like a wreath. Every hair kept order as perfectly as if it had been painted on, though the breeze from the window stirred now and then among the softly shining strands.

Oliver tried the tea. Its flavour was exquisite, very hot, and the taste that lingered upon his tongue was like the scent of flowers. It was an extremely feminine drink. He sipped again, surprised to find how much he liked it.

The scent of flowers seemed to increase as he drank, swirling through his head like smoke. After the third sip there was a faint buzzing in his ears. The bees among the flowers, perhaps, he thought incoherently—and sipped again.

Kleph watched him, smiling.

"The others will be out all afternoon," she told Oliver comfortably. "I thought it would give us a pleasant time to be acquainted."

Oliver was rather horrified to hear himself saying, "What makes you talk like that?" He had had no idea of asking the question; something seemed to have loosened his control over his own tongue.

Kleph's smile deepened. She tipped the cup to her lips and there was indulgence in her voice when she said, "What do you mean 'like that'?"

He waved his hand vaguely, noting with some surprise that at a glance it seemed to have six or seven fingers as it moved past his face.

"I don't know—precision, I guess. Why don't you say 'don't', for instance?"

"In our country we are trained to speak with precision,"

Kleph explained. "Just as we are trained to move and dress and think with precision. Any slovenliness is trained out of us in childhood. With you, of course——" She was polite. "With you, this does not happen to be a national fetish. With us, we have time for the amenities. We like them."

Her voice had grown sweeter and sweeter as she spoke, until by now it was almost indistinguishable from the sweetness of the flower-scent in Oliver's head, and the delicate flavour of the tea.

"What country do you come from?" he asked, and tilted the cup again to drink, mildly surprised to notice that it seemed inexhaustible.

Kleph's smile was definitely patronizing this time. It didn't irritate him. Nothing could irritate him just now. The whole room swam in a beautiful rosy glow as fragrant as the flowers.

"We must not speak of that, Mr. Wilson."

"But——" Oliver paused. After all, it was, of course, none of his business. "This is a vacation?" he asked vaguely.

"Call it a pilgrimage, perhaps."

"Pilgrimage?" Oliver was so interested that for an instant his mind came back into sharp focus. "To—what?"

"I should not have said that, Mr. Wilson. Please forget it. Do you like the tea?"

"Very much."

"You will have guessed by now that it is not only tea, but an euphoriac."

Oliver stared. "Euphoriac?"

Kleph made a descriptive circle in the air with one graceful hand, and laughed. "You do not feel the effects yet? Surely you do?"

"I feel," Oliver said, "the way I'd feel after four whiskies."

Kleph shuddered delicately. "We get our euphoria less painfully. And without the after-effects your barbarous alcohol used to have." She bit her lip. "Sorry. I must be euphoric myself to speak so freely. Please forgive me. Shall we have some music?"

Kleph leaned backward on the chaise-longue and reached towards the wall beside her. The sleeve, falling away from her round tanned arm, left bare the inside of the wrist, and Oliver was startled to see there a long, rosy streak of fading scar. His inhibitions had dissolved in the fumes of the fragrant tea; he caught his breath and leaned forward to stare.

Kleph shook the sleeve back over the scar with a quick gesture. Colour came into her face beneath the softly tinted tan and she would not meet Oliver's eyes. A queer shame seemed to have fallen upon her.

Oliver said tactlessly, "What is it? What's the matter?"

Still she would not look at him. Much later he understood that shame and knew she had reason for it. Now he listened blankly as she said:

"Nothing . . . nothing at all. A . . . an inoculation. All of us . . . oh, never mind. Listen to the music."

This time she reached out with the other arm. She touched nothing, but when she had held her hand near the wall a sound breathed through the room. It was the sound of water, the sighing of waves receding upon long, sloped beaches. Oliver followed Kleph's gaze towards the picture of the blue water above the bed.

The waves there were moving. More than that, the point of vision moved. Slowly the seascape drifted past, moving with the waves, following them towards shore. Oliver watched, half-hypnotized by a motion that seemed at the time quite acceptable and not in the least surprising.

The waves lifted and broke in creaming foam and ran seething up a sandy beach. Then through the sound of the water music began to breathe, and through the water itself a man's face dawned in the frame, smiling intimately into the room. He held an oddly archaic musical instrument, lute-shaped, its body striped light and dark like a melon and its long neck bent back over his shoulder. He was singing, and Oliver felt mildly astonished at the song. It was very familiar and very odd indeed. He groped through the unfamiliar rhythms and found at last a thread to catch the tune by—it was "Make-Believe" from "Showboat", but certainly a showboat that had never steamed up the Mississippi.

"What's he doing to it?" he demanded after a few moments of outraged listening. "I never heard anything like it!"

Kleph laughed and stretched out her arm again. Enigmatically she said: "We call it kyling. Never mind. How do you like this?"

It was a comedian, a man in semi-clown make-up, his eyes exaggerated so that they seemed to cover half his face. He stood by a broad glass pillar before a dark curtain and sang a gay, staccato song interspersed with patter that sounded impromptu, and all the while his left hand did an intricate, musical tattoo of the nailtips on the glass of the column. He strolled around and around it as he sang. The rhythms of his fingernails blended with the song and swung widely away into patterns of their own, and blended again without a break.

It was confusing to follow. The song made even less sense than the monologue, which had something to do with a lost slipper and was full of allusions which made Kleph smile, but were utterly unintelligible to Oliver. The man had a dry, brittle style that was not very amusing, though Kleph seemed fascinated. Oliver was interested to see in him an extension and a variation of that extreme smooth confidence which marked all three of the Sanciscos. Clearly a racial trait, he thought.

Other performances followed, some of them fragmentary as if lifted out of a completer version. One he knew. The obvious, stirring melody struck his recognition before the figures—marching men against a haze, a great banner rolling backward above them in the smoke, foreground figures striding gigantically and shouting in rhythm, "Forward, forward the lily banners go!"

The music was tinny, the images blurred and poorly coloured, but there was a gusto about the performance that caught at Oliver's imagination. He stared, remembering the old film from long ago. Dennis King and a ragged chorus, singing "The Song of the Vagabonds" from—was it "Vagabond King"?

"A very old one," Kleph said apologetically. "But I like it."

The steam of the intoxicating tea swirled between Oliver and the picture. Music swelled and sank through the room and the fragrant fumes and his own euphoric brain. Nothing seemed strange. He had discovered how to drink the tea. Like nitrous oxide, the effect was not cumulative. When you reached a peak of euphoria, you could not increase the peak. It was best to wait for a slight dip in the effect of the stimulant before taking more.

Otherwise it had most of the effects of alcohol—everything after a while dissolved into a delightful fog through which all he saw was uniformly enchanting and partook of the qualities of a dream. He questioned nothing. Afterwards he was not certain how much of it he really had dreamed.

There was the dancing doll, for instance. He remembered it quite clearly, in sharp focus—a tiny, slender woman with a long-nosed, dark-eyed face and a pointed chin. She moved delicately across the white rug—knee-high, exquisite. Her features were as mobile as her body, and she danced lightly, with resounding strokes of her toes, each echoing like a bell. It was a formalized sort of dance, and she sang breathlessly in accompaniment, making amusing little grimaces. Certainly it was a portrait-doll, animated to mimic the original perfectly in voice and motion. Afterwards, Oliver knew he must have dreamed it.

What else happened he was quite unable to remember later. He knew Kleph had said some curious things, but they all made sense at the time, and afterwards he couldn't remember a word. He knew he had been offered little glittering candies in a transparent dish, and that some of them had been delicious and one or two so bitter his tongue still curled the next day when he recalled them, and one—Kleph sucked luxuriantly on the same kind—of a taste that was actively nauseating.

As for Kleph herself—he was frantically uncertain the next day what had really happened. He thought he could remember the softness of her white-downed arms clasped at the back of his neck, while she laughed up at him and exhaled into his face the flowery fragrance of the tea. But beyond that he was totally unable to recall anything for a while.

There was a brief interlude later, before the oblivion of sleep. He was almost sure he remembered a moment when the other two Sanciscos stood looking down at him, the man scowling, the smoky-eyed woman smiling a derisive smile.

The man said, from a vast distance, "Kleph, you know this is against every rule——" His voice began in a thin hum and soared in fantastic flight beyond the range of hearing. Oliver thought he remembered the dark woman's laughter, thin and distant too, and the hum of her voice like bees in flight.

"Kleph, Kleph, you silly little fool, can we never trust you out of sight?"

Kleph's voice then said something that seemed to make no sense. "What does it matter, *here*?"

The man answered in that buzzing, faraway hum. "The matter of giving your bond before you leave, not to interfere. You know you signed the rules——"

Kleph's voice, nearer and more intelligible: "But here the difference is . . . it does not matter *here*! You both know that. How could it matter?"

Oliver felt the downy brush of her sleeve against his cheek, but he saw nothing except the slow, smoke-like ebb and flow of darkness past his eyes. He heard the voices wrangle musically from far away, and he heard them cease.

When he woke the next morning, alone in his own room, he woke with the memory of Kleph's eyes upon him very sorrowfully, her lovely tanned face looking down on him with the red hair falling fragrantly on each side of it and sadness and compassion in her eyes. He thought he had probably dreamed that. There was no reason why anyone should look at him with such sadness.

Sue telephoned that day.

"Oliver, the people who want to buy the house are here. That madwoman and her husband. Shall I bring them over?"

Oliver's mind all day had been hazy with the vague, bewildering memories of yesterday. Kleph's face kept floating before him, blotting out the room. He said, "What? I . . . oh, well, bring them if you want to. I don't see what good it'll do."

"Oliver, what's wrong with you? We agreed we needed the money, didn't we? I don't see how you can think of passing up such a wonderful bargain without even a struggle. We could get married and buy our own house right away, and you know we'll never get such an offer again for that old trash-heap. Wake up, Oliver!"

Oliver made an effort. "I know, Sue—I know. But——"

"Oliver, you've got to think of something!" Her voice was imperious.

He knew she was right. Kleph or no Kleph, the bargain shouldn't be ignored if there was any way at all of getting the tenants out. He wondered again what made the place so suddenly priceless to so many people. And what the last week in May had to do with the value of the house.

A sudden sharp curiosity pierced even the vagueness of his

mind today. May's last week was so important that the whole sale of the house stood or fell upon occupancy by then. Why? *Why?*

"What's going to happen next week?" he asked rhetorically of the telephone. "Why can't they wait till these people leave? I'd knock a couple of thousand off the price if they'd——"

"You would not, Oliver Wilson! I can buy all our refrigeration units with that extra money. You'll just have to work out some way to give possession by next week, and that's that. You hear me?"

"Keep your shirt on," Oliver said practically. "I'm only human, but I'll try."

"I'm bringing the people over right away," Sue told him. "While the Sanciscos are still out. Now you put your mind to work and think of something, Oliver." She paused, and her voice was reflective when she spoke again. "They're . . . awfully odd people, darling."

"Odd?"

"You'll see."

It was an elderly woman and a very young man who trailed Sue up the walk. Oliver knew immediately what had struck Sue about them. He was somehow not at all surprised to see that both wore their clothing with the familiar air of elegant self-consciousness he had come to know so well. They, too, looked around them at the beautiful, sunny afternoon with conscious enjoyment and an air of faint condescension. He knew before he heard them speak how musical their voices would be and how meticulously they would pronounce each word.

There was no doubt about it. The people of Kleph's mysterious country were arriving here in force—for something. For the last week of May? He shrugged mentally; there was no way of guessing—yet. One thing only was sure: all of them must come from that nameless land where people controlled their voices like singers and their garments like actors who could stop the reel of time itself to adjust every disordered fold.

The elderly woman took full charge of the conversation from the start. They stood together on the rickety, unpainted porch, and Sue had no chance even for introductions.

"Young man, I am Madame Hollia. This is my husband." Her voice had an underrunning current of harshness, which was perhaps age. And her face looked almost corseted, the loose flesh coerced into something like firmness by some invisible method Oliver could not guess at. The make-up was so skilful he could not be certain it was make-up at all, but he had a definite feeling that she was much older than she looked. It would have taken a lifetime of command to put so much authority into the harsh, deep, musically controlled voice.

The young man said nothing. He was very handsome. His type, apparently, was one that does not change much no matter in what culture or country it may occur. He wore beautifully tailored garments and carried in one gloved hand a box of red leather, about the size and shape of a book.

Madame Hollia went on: "I understand your problem about the house. You wish to sell to me, but are legally bound by your lease with Omerie and his friends. Is that right?"

Oliver nodded. "But——"

"Let me finish. If Omerie can be forced to vacate before next week, you will accept our offer. Right? Very well. Hara!" She nodded to the young man beside her. He jumped to instant attention, bowed slightly, said, "Yes, Hollia," and slipped a gloved hand into his coat.

Madame Hollia took the little object offered on his palm, her gesture as she reached for it almost imperial, as if royal robes swept from her outstretched arm.

"Here," she said, "is something that may help us. My dear——" She held it out to Sue—"if you can hide this somewhere about the house, I believe your unwelcome tenants will not trouble you much longer."

Sue took the thing curiously. It looked like a tiny silver box, no more than an inch square, indented at the top and with no line to show it could be opened.

"Wait a minute," Oliver broke in uneasily. "What is it?"

"Nothing that will harm anyone, I assure you."

"Then what——"

Madame Hollia's imperious gesture at one sweep silenced him and commanded Sue forward. "Go on, my dear. Hurry, before Omerie comes back. I can assure you there is no danger to anyone."

Oliver broke in determinedly. "Madame Hollia, I'll have to know what your plans are. I——"

"Oh, Oliver, please!" Sue's fingers closed over the silver cube. "Don't worry about it. I'm sure Madame Hollia knows best. Don't you *want* to get those people out?"

"Of course I do. But I don't want the house blown up or——"

Madame Hollia's deep laughter was indulgent. "Nothing so crude, I promise you, Mr. Wilson. Remember, we want the house! Hurry, my dear."

Sue nodded and slipped hastily past Oliver into the hall. Outnumbered, he subsided uneasily. The young man, Hara, tapped a negligent foot and admired the sunlight as they waited. It was an afternoon as perfect as all of May had been, translucent gold, balmy with an edge of chill lingering in the air to point up a perfect contrast with the summer to come. Hara looked around him confidently, like a man paying just tribute to a stage-set provided wholly for himself. He even glanced up at a drone from above and followed the course of a big transcontinental plane half dissolved in golden haze high in the sun. "Quaint," he murmured in a gratified voice.

Sue came back and slipped her hand through Oliver's arm, squeezing excitedly. "There," she said. "How long will it take, Madame Hollia?"

"That will depend, my dear. Not very long. Now, Mr. Wilson, one word with you. You live here also, I understand? For your own comfort, take my advice and——"

Somewhere within the house a door slammed and a clear high voice rang wordlessly up a rippling scale. Then there was the sound of feet on the stairs, and single line of song, *"Come hider, love, to me——"*

Hara started, almost dropping the red leather box he held. "Kleph!" he said in a whisper. "Or Klia. I know they both just came on from Canterbury. But I thought——"

"Huh." Madame Hollia's features composed themselves into an imperious blank. She breathed triumphantly through her nose, drew back upon herself and turned an imposing façade to the door.

Kleph wore the same softly downy robe Oliver had seen before, except that today it was not white, but a pale, clear blue that gave her tan an apricot flush. She was smiling.

"Why, Hollia!" Her tone was at its most musical. "I thought

I recognized voices from home. How nice to see you. No one knew you were coming to the——" She broke off and glanced at Oliver and then away again. "Hara, too," she said. "What a pleasant surprise."

Sue said flatly, "When did *you* get back?"

Kleph smiled at her. "You must be the little Miss Johnson. Why, I did not go out at all. I was tired of sightseeing. I have been napping in my room."

Sue drew in her breath in something that just escaped being a disbelieving sniff. A look flashed between the two women, and for an instant held—and that instant was timeless. It was an extraordinary pause in which a great deal of wordless interplay took place in the space of a second.

Oliver saw the quality of Kleph's smile at Sue, that same look of quiet confidence he had noticed so often about all of these strange people. He saw Sue's quick inventory of the other woman, and he saw how Sue squared her shoulders and stood up straight, smoothing down her summer frock over her flat hips so that for an instant she stood posed consciously, looking down on Kleph. It was deliberate. Bewildered, he glanced again at Kleph.

Kleph's shoulders sloped softly, her robe was belted to a tiny waist and hung in deep folds over frankly rounded hips. Sue's was the fashionable figure—but Sue was the first to surrender.

Kleph's smile did not falter. But in the silence there was an abrupt reversal of values, based on no more than the measureless quality of Kleph's confidence in herself, the quiet, assured smile. It was suddenly made very clear that fashion is not a constant. Kleph's curious, out-of-mode curves without warning became the norm, and Sue was a queer, angular, half-masculine creature beside her.

Oliver had no idea how it was done. Somehow the authority passed in a breath from one woman to the other. Beauty is almost wholly a matter of fashion; what is beautiful today would have been grotesque a couple of generations ago and will be grotesque a hundred years ahead. It will be worse than grotesque; it will be outmoded and therefore faintly ridiculous.

Sue was that. Kleph had only to exert her authority to make it clear to everyone on the porch. Kleph was a beauty, suddenly and very convincingly, beautiful in the accepted mode, and Sue was amusingly old-fashioned, an anachronism in her lithe, square-shouldered slimness. She did not belong. She was grotesque among these strangely immaculate people.

Sue's collapse was complete. But pride sustained her, and bewilderment. Probably she never did grasp entirely what was wrong. She gave Kleph one glance of burning resentment and when her eyes came back to Oliver there was suspicion in them, and mistrust.

Looking backward later, Oliver thought that in that moment, for the first time clearly, he began to suspect the truth. But he had no time to ponder it, for after the brief instant of enmity the three people from—elsewhere—began to speak all at once, as if in a belated attempt to cover something they did not want noticed.

Kleph said, "This beautiful weather——" and Madame Hollia said, "So fortunate to have this house——" and Hara, holding up the red leather box, said loudest of all, "Cenbe sent you this, Kleph. His latest."

Kleph put out both hands for it eagerly, the eiderdown sleeves falling back from her rounded arms. Oliver had a quick glimpse of that mysterious scar before the sleeve fell back, and it seemed to him that there was the faintest trace of a similar scar vanishing into Hara's cuff as he let his own arm drop.

"Cenbe!" Kleph cried, her voice high and sweet and delighted. "How wonderful! What period?"

"From November 1664," Hara said. "London, of course, though I think there may be some counterpoint from the 1347 November. He hasn't finished—of course." He glanced almost nervously at Oliver and Sue. "A wonderful example," he said quickly. "Marvellous. If you have the taste for it, of course."

Madame Hollia shuddered with ponderous delicacy. "That man!" she said. "Fascinating, of course—a great man. But—so *advanced*!"

"It takes a connoisseur to appreciate Cenbe's work fully," Kleph said in a slightly tart voice. "We all admit that."

"Oh yes, we all bow to Cenbe," Hollia conceded. "I confess the man terrifies me a little, my dear. Do we expect him to join us?"

"I suppose so," Kleph said. "If his—work—is not yet finished, then of course. You know Cenbe's tastes."

Hollia and Hara laughed together. "I know when to look for him, then," Hollia said. She glanced at the staring Oliver and the subdued but angry Sue, and with a commanding effort brought the subject back into line.

"So fortunate, my dear Kleph, to have this house," she declared heavily. "I saw a tridimensional of it—afterwards—and it was still quite perfect. Such a fortunate coincidence. Would you consider parting with your lease, for a consideration? Say, a coronation seat at——"

"Nothing could buy us, Hollia," Kleph told her gaily, clasping the red box to her bosom.

Hollia gave her a cool stare. "You may change your mind, my dear Kleph," she said pontifically. "There is still time. You can always reach us through Mr. Wilson here. We have rooms up the street in the Montgomery House—nothing like yours, of course, but they will do. For us, they will do."

Oliver blinked. The Montgomery House was the most expensive hotel in town. Compared to this collapsing old ruin, it was a palace. There was no understanding these people. Their values seemed to have suffered a complete reversal.

Madame Hollia moved majestically towards the steps.

"Very pleasant to see you, my dear," she said over one well-padded shoulder. "Enjoy your stay. My regards to Omerie and Klia. Mr. Wilson——" she nodded towards the walk. "A word with you."

Oliver followed her down towards the street. Madame Hollia paused half-way there and touched his arm.

"One word of advice," she said huskily. "You say you sleep here? Move out, young man. Move out before tonight."

Oliver was searching in a half-desultory fashion for the hiding place Sue had found for the mysterious silver cube, when the first sounds from above began to drift down the stairwell towards him. Kleph had closed her door, but the house was old, and strange qualities in the noise overhead seemed to seep through the woodwork like an almost visible stain.

It was music, in a way. But much more than music. And it was a terrible sound, the sounds of calamity and of all human reaction to calamity, everything from hysteria to heartbreak, from irrational joy to rationalized acceptance.

The calamity was—single. The music did not attempt to correlate all human sorrows; it focused sharply upon one and followed the ramifications out and out. Oliver recognized these basics to the sounds in a very brief moment. They were essentials, and they seemed to beat into his brain with the first strains of the music which was so much more than music.

But when he lifted his head to listen he lost all grasp upon the meaning of the noise and it was sheer medley and confusion. To think of it was to blur it hopelessly in the mind, and he could not recapture that first instant of unreasoning acceptance.

He went upstairs almost in a daze, hardly knowing what he was doing. He pushed Kleph's door open. He looked inside——

What he saw there he could not afterwards remember except in a blurring as vague as the blurred ideas the music roused in his brain. Half the room had vanished behind a mist, and the mist was a three-dimensional screen upon which were projected—— He had no words for them. He was not even sure if the projections were visual. The mist was spinning with motion and sound, but essentially it was neither sound nor motion that Oliver saw.

This was a work of art. Oliver knew no name for it. It transcended all art-forms he knew, blended them, and out of the blend produced subtleties his mind could not begin to grasp. Basically, this was the attempt of a master composer to correlate every essential aspect of a vast human experience into something that could be conveyed in a few moments to every sense at once.

The shifting visions on the screen were not pictures in themselves, but hints of pictures, subtly selected outlines that plucked at the mind and with one deft touch set whole chords ringing through the memory. Perhaps each beholder reacted differently, since it was in the eye and the mind of the beholder that the truth of the picture lay. No two would be aware of the same symphonic panorama, but each would see essentially the same terrible story unfold.

Every sense was touched by that deft and merciless genius. Colour and shape and motion flickered in the screen, hinting much, evoking unbearable memories deep in the mind; odours floated from the screen and touched the heart of the beholder more poignantly than anything visual could do. The skin scrawled sometimes as if to a tangible cold hand laid upon it. The tongue curled with remembered bitterness and remembered sweet.

It was outrageous. It violated the innermost privacies of a man's mind, called up secret things long ago walled off behind mental scar tissue, forced its terrible message upon the beholder relentlessly though the mind might threaten to crack beneath the stress of it.

And yet, in spite of all this vivid awareness, Oliver did not know what calamity the screen portrayed. That it was real, vast, overwhelmingly dreadful he could not doubt. That it had once happened was unmistakable. He caught flashing glimpses of human faces distorted with grief and disease and death—real faces, faces that had once lived and were seen now in the instant of dying. He saw men and women in rich clothing superimposed in panorama upon reeling thousands of ragged folk, great throngs of them swept past the sight in an instant, and he saw that death made no distinction among them.

He saw lovely women laugh and shake their curls, and the laughter shriek into hysteria and the hysteria into music. He saw one man's face, over and over—a long, dark saturnine face, deeply lined, sorrowful, the face of a powerful man wise in worldliness, urbane—and helpless. That face was for a while a recurring motif, always more tortured, more helpless than before.

The music broke off in the midst of a rising glide. The mist vanished and the room reappeared before him. The anguished dark face for an instant seemed to Oliver printed everywhere he looked, like after-vision on the eyelids. He knew that face. He had seen it before, not often, but he should know its name——

"Oliver, Oliver——" Kleph's sweet voice came out of a fog at him. He was leaning dizzily against the doorpost looking down into her eyes. She, too, had that dazed blankness he must show on his own face. The power of the dreadful symphony still held them both. But even in this confused moment Oliver saw that Kleph had been enjoying the experience.

He felt sickened to the depths of his mind, dizzy with sickness and revulsion because of the superimposing of human miseries he had just beheld. But Kleph—only appreciation showed upon her face. To her it had been magnificence, and magnificence only.

Irrelevantly Oliver remembered the nauseating candies she had enjoyed, the nauseating odours of strange food that drifted sometimes through the hall from her room.

What was it she had said downstairs a little while ago? Connoisseur, that was it. Only a connoisseur could appreciate work as—as *advanced*—as the work of someone called Cenbe.

A whiff of intoxicating sweetness curled past Oliver's face. Something cool and smooth was pressed into his hand.

"Oh, Oliver, I am so sorry," Kleph's voice murmured contritely. "Here, drink the euphoriac and you will feel better. Please drink!"

The familiar fragrance of the hot sweet tea was on his tongue before he knew he had complied. Its relaxing fumes floated up through his brain and in a moment or two the world felt stable around him again. The room was as it had always been. And Kleph——

Her eyes were very bright. Sympathy showed in them for him, but for herself she was still brimmed with the high elation of what she had just been experiencing.

"Come and sit down," she said gently, tugging at his arm. "I am so sorry—I should not have played that over, where you could hear it. I have no excuse, really. It was only that I forgot what the effect might be on one who had never heard Cenbe's symphonies before. I was so impatient to see what he had done with . . . with his new subject. I am so very sorry, Oliver!"

"What was it?" His voice sounded steadier than he had expected. The tea was responsible for that. He sipped again, glad of the consoling euphoria its fragrance brought.

"A . . . a composite interpretation of . . . oh, Oliver, you know I must not answer questions!"

"But——"

"No—drink your tea and forget what it was you saw. Think of other things. Here, we will have music—another kind of music, something gay——"

She reached for the wall beside the window, and as before, Oliver saw the broad framed picture of blue water above the bed ripple and grow pale. Through it another scene began to dawn like shapes rising beneath the surface of the sea.

He had a glimpse of a dark-curtained stage upon which a man in a tight dark tunic and hose moved with a restless, sidelong pace, his hands and face startlingly pale against the black about him. He limped; he had a crooked back and he spoke familiar lines. Oliver had seen John Barrymore once as the crook-backed Richard, and it seemed vaguely outrageous to him that any other actor should essay that difficult part. This one he had never seen before, but the man had a fascinatingly smooth manner and his interpretation of the Plantagenet king was quite new and something Shakespeare probably never dreamed of.

"No," Kleph said, "not this. Nothing gloomy." And she put out her hand again. The nameless new Richard faded and there was a swirl of changing pictures and changing voices, all blurred together, before the scene steadied upon a stageful of dancers in pastel ballet skirts, drifting effortlessly through some complicated pattern of motion. The music that went with it was light and effortless too. The room filled up with the clear, floating melody.

Oliver set down his cup. He felt much surer of himself now, and he thought the euphoriac had done all it could for him. He didn't want to blur again mentally. There were things he meant to learn about. Now. He considered how to begin.

Kleph was watching him. "That Hollia," she said suddenly. "She wants to buy the house?"

Oliver nodded. "She's offering a lot of money. Sue's going to be awfully disappointed if——" He hesitated. Perhaps, after all, Sue would not be disappointed. He remembered the little silver cube with the enigmatic function and he wondered if he should mention it to Kleph. But the euphoriac had not reached that level of his brain, and he remembered his duty to Sue and was silent.

Kleph shook her head, her eyes upon his warm with—was it sympathy?

"Believe me," she said, "you will not find that—important—after all. I promise you, Oliver."

He stared at her. "I wish you'd explain."

Kleph laughed on a note more sorrowful than amused. But it occurred to Oliver suddenly that there was no longer condescension in her voice. Imperceptibly that air of delicate amusement had vanished from her manner towards him. The cool detachment that still marked Omerie's attitude, and Klia's, was not in Kleph's any more. It was a subtlety he did not think she could assume. It had to come spontaneously or not at all. And for no reason he was willing to examine, it became suddenly very important to Oliver that Kleph should not condescend to him, that she should feel towards him as he felt towards her. He would not think of it.

He looked down at his cup, rose-quartz, exhaling a thin plume of steam from its crescent-slit opening. This time, he thought, maybe he could make the tea work for him. For he remembered how it loosened the tongue, and there was a great deal he needed to know. The idea that had come to him on the porch in the instant of silent rivalry between Kleph and Sue seemed not too fantastic to entertain. But some answer there must be.

Kleph herself gave him the opening.

"I must not take too much euphoriac this afternoon," she said, smiling at him over her pink cup. "It will make me drowsy, and we are going out this evening with friends."

"More friends?" Oliver asked. "From your country?"

Kleph nodded. "Very dear friends we have expected all this week."

"I wish you'd tell me," Oliver said bluntly, "where it is you come from. It isn't from here. Your culture is too different from ours—even your names——" He broke off as Kleph shook her head.

"I wish I could tell you. But that is against all the rules. It is even against the rules for me to be here talking to you now."

She made a helpless gesture. "You must not ask me, Oliver." She leaned back on the chaise-longue, which adjusted itself luxuriously to the motion, and smiled very sweetly at him. "We must not talk about things like that. Forget it, listen to the music, enjoy yourself if you can——" She closed her eyes and laid her head back against the cushions. Oliver saw the round tanned throat swell as she began to hum a tune. Eyes still closed, she sang again the words she had sung upon the stairs. *"Come hider, love, to me——"*

A memory clicked over suddenly in Oliver's mind. He had

never heard the queer, lagging tune before, but he thought he knew the words. He remembered what Hollia's husband had said when he heard that line of song, and he leaned forward. She would not answer a direct question, but perhaps——

"Was the weather this warm in Canterbury?" he asked, and held his breath. Kleph hummed another line of the song and shook her head, eyes still closed.

"It was autumn there," she said. "But bright, wonderfully bright. Even their clothing, you know . . . everyone was singing that new song, and I can't get it out of my head." She sang another line, and the words were almost unintelligible—English, yet not an English Oliver could understand.

He stood up. "Wait," he said. "I want to find something. Back in a minute."

She opened her eyes and smiled mistily at him, still humming. He went downstairs as fast as he could—the stairway swayed a little, though his head was nearly clear now—and into the library. The book he wanted was old and battered, interlined with the pencilled notes of his college days. He did not remember very clearly where the passage he wanted was, but he thumbed fast through the columns and by sheer luck found it within a few minutes. Then he went back upstairs, feeling a strange emptiness in his stomach because of what he almost believed now.

"Kleph," he said firmly, "I know that song. I know the year it was new."

Her lids rose slowly; she looked at him through a mist of euphoriac. He was not sure she had understood. For a long moment she held him with her gaze. Then she put out one downy-sleeved arm and spread her tanned fingers towards him. She laughed deep in her throat.

"*Come hider, love, to me,*" she said.

He crossed the room slowly, took her hand. The fingers closed warmly about his. She pulled him down so that he had to kneel beside her. Her other arm lifted. Again she laughed, very softly, and closed her eyes, lifting her face to his.

The kiss was warm and long. He caught something of her own euphoria from the fragrance of the tea breathed into his face. Ana he was startled at the end of the kiss, when the clasp of her arms loosened about his neck, to feel the sudden rush of her breath against his cheek. There were tears on her face, and the sound she made was a sob.

He held her off and looked down in amazement. She sobbed once more, caught a deep breath, and said, "Oh, Oliver, Oliver——" Then she shook her head and pulled free, turning away to hide her face. "I . . . I am sorry," she said unevenly. "Please forgive me. It does not matter . . . I *know* it does not matter . . . but——"

"What's wrong? What doesn't matter?"

"Nothing. Nothing . . . please forget it. Nothing at all." She got a handkerchief from the table and blew her nose, smiling at him with an effect of radiance through the tears.

Suddenly he was very angry. He had heard enough evasions and mystifying half-truths. He said roughly, "Do you think I'm crazy? I know enough now to——"

"Oliver, please!" She held up her own cup, steaming fragrantly. "Please, no more questions. Here, euphoria is what you need, Oliver. Euphoria, not answers."

"What year was it when you heard that song in Canterbury?" he demanded, pushing the cup aside.

She blinked at him, tears bright on her lashes. "Why . . . what year do you think?"

"I know," Oliver told her grimly. "I know the year that song was popular. I know you just came from Canterbury—Hollia's husband said so. It's May now, but it was autumn in Canterbury, and you just came from there, so lately the song you heard is still running through your head. Chaucer's Pardoner sang that song some time around the end of the fourteenth century. Did you see Chaucer, Kleph? What was it like in England that long ago?"

Kleph's eye fixed his for a silent moment. Then her shoulders drooped and her whole body went limp with resignation beneath the soft blue robe. "I am a fool," she said gently. "It must have been easy to trap me. You really believe—what you say?"

Oliver nodded.

She said in a low voice. "Few people do believe it. That is one of our maxims, when we travel. We are safe from much suspicion because people before The Travel began will not believe."

The emptiness in Oliver's stomach suddenly doubled in

volume. For an instant the bottom dropped out of time itself and the universe was unsteady about him. He felt sick. He felt naked and helpless. There was a buzzing in his ears and the room dimmed before him.

He had not really believed—not until this instant. He had expected some rational explanation from her that would tidy all his wild half-thoughts and suspicions into something a man could accept as believable. Not this.

Kleph dabbed at her eyes with the pale-blue handkerchief and smiled tremulously.

"I know," she said. "It must be a terrible thing to accept. To have all your concepts turned upside down—— We know it from childhood, of course, but for you . . . here, Oliver. The euphoriac will make it easier."

He took the cup, the faint stain of her lip rouge still on the crescent opening. He drank, feeling the dizzy sweetness spiral through his head, and his brain turned a little in his skull as the volatile fragrance took effect. With that turning, focus shifted and all his values with it.

He began to feel better. The flesh settled on his bones again, and the warm clothing of temporal assurance settled upon his flesh, and he was no longer naked and in the vortex of unstable time.

"The story is very simple, really," Kleph said. "We—travel. Our own time is not terribly far ahead of yours. No. I must not say how far. But we still remember your songs and poets and some of your great actors. We are a people of much leisure, and we cultivate the art of enjoying ourselves.

"This is a tour we are making—a tour of a year's seasons. Vintage seasons. That autumn in Canterbury was the most magnificent autumn our researchers could discover anywhere. We rode in a pilgrimage to the shrine—it was a wonderful experience, though the clothing was a little hard to manage.

"Now this month of May is almost over—the loveliest May in recorded times. A perfect May in a wonderful period. You have no way of knowing what a good, gay period you live in, Oliver. The very feeling in the air of the cities—that wonderful national confidence and happiness—everything going as smoothly as a dream. There were other Mays with fine weather, but each of them had a war or a famine, or something else wrong." She hesitated, grimaced and went on rapidly. "In a few days we are to meet at a coronation in Rome," she said. "I think the year will be 800—Christmastime. We——"

"But why," Oliver interrupted, "did you insist on this house? Why do the others want to get it away from you?"

Kleph stared at him. He saw the tears rising again in small bright crescents that gathered above her lower lids. He saw the look of obstinacy that came upon her soft, tanned face. She shook her head.

"You must not ask me that." She held out the steaming cup. "Here, drink and forget what I have said. I can tell you no more. No more at all."

When he woke, for a little while he had no idea where he was. He did not remember leaving Kleph or coming to his own room. He didn't care, just then. For he woke to a sense of overwhelming terror.

The dark was full of it. His brain rocked on waves of fear and pain. He lay motionless, too frightened to stir, some atavistic memory warning him to lie quiet until he knew from which direction the danger threatened. Reasonless panic broke over him in a tidal flow; his head ached with its violence and the dark throbbed to the same rhythms.

A knock sounded at the door. Omerie's deep voice said, "Wilson! Wilson, are you awake?"

Oliver tried twice before he had breath to answer. "Y-yes—what is it?"

The knob rattled. Omerie's dim figure groped for the light switch and the room sprang into visibility. Omerie's face was drawn with strain, and he held one hand to his head as if it ached in rhythm with Oliver's.

It was in that moment, before Omerie spoke again, that Oliver remembered Hollia's warning. "Move out, young man—move out before tonight." Wildly he wondered what threatened them all in this dark house that throbbed with the rhythms of pure terror.

Omerie in an angry voice answered the unspoken question. "Someone has planted a subsonic in the house, Wilson. Kleph thinks you may know where it is."

"S-subsonic?"

"Call it a gadget," Omerie interpreted impatiently. "Probably a small metal box that——"

Oliver said, "Oh," in a tone that must have told Omerie everything.

"Where is it?" he demanded. "Quick. Let's get this over."

"I don't know." With an effort Oliver controlled the chattering of his teeth. "Y-you mean all this—all this is just from the little box?"

"Of course. Now tell me how to find it before we all go crazy."

Oliver got shakily out of bed, groping for his robe with nerveless hands. "I s-suppose she hid it somewhere downstairs," he said. "S-she wasn't gone long."

Omerie got the story out of him in a few brief questions. He clicked his teeth in exasperation when Oliver had finished it.

"That stupid Hollia——"

"Omerie!" Kleph's plaintive voice wailed from the hall. "Please hurry, Omerie! This is too much to stand! Oh, Omerie, please!"

Oliver stood up abruptly. Then a redoubled wave of the inexplicable pain seemed to explode in his skull at the motion, and he clutched the bedpost and reeled.

"Go find the thing yourself," he heard himself saying dizzily. "I can't even walk——"

Omerie's own temper was drawn wire-tight by the pressure in the room. He seized Oliver's shoulder and shook him, saying in a tight voice, "You let it in—now help us get it out, or——"

"It's a gadget out of your world, not mine!" Oliver said furiously.

And then it seemed to him there was a sudden coldness and silence in the room. Even the pain and the senseless terror paused for a moment. Omerie's pale, cold eyes fixed upon Oliver a stare so chill he could almost feel the ice in it.

"What do you know about our—world?" Omerie demanded.

Oliver did not speak a word. He did not need to; his face must have betrayed what he knew. He was beyond concealment in the stress of night-time terror he still could not understand.

Omerie bared his white teeth and said three perfectly unintelligible words. Then he stepped to the door and snapped, "Kleph!"

Oliver could see the two women huddled together in the hall, shaking violently with involuntary waves of that strange, synthetic terror. Klia, in a luminous green gown, was rigid with control, but Kleph made no effort whatever at repression. Her downy robe had turned soft gold tonight; she shivered in it and the tears ran down her face unchecked.

"Kleph," Omerie said in a dangerous voice, "you were euphoric again yesterday?"

Kleph darted a scared glance at Oliver and nodded guiltily.

"You talked too much." It was a complete indictment in one sentence. "You know the rules, Kleph. You will not be allowed to travel again if anyone reports this to the authorities."

Kleph's lovely creamy face creased suddenly into impenitent dimples.

"I know it was wrong. I am very sorry—but you will not stop me if Cenbe says no."

Klia flung out her arms in a gesture of helpless anger. Omerie shrugged. "In this case, as it happens, no great harm is done," he said, giving Oliver an unfathomable glance. "But it might have been serious. Next time perhaps it will be. I must have a talk with Cenbe."

"We must find the subsonic first of all," Klia reminded them, shivering. "If Kleph is afraid to help, she can go out for a while. I confess I am very sick of Kleph's company just now."

"We could give up the house!" Kleph cried wildly. "Let Hollia have it! How can you stand this long enough to hunt——"

"Give up the house?" Klia echoed. "You must be mad! With all our invitations out?"

"There will be no need for that," Omerie said. "We can find it if we all hunt. You feel able to help?" He looked at Oliver.

With an effort Oliver controlled his own senseless panic as the waves of it swept through the room. "Yes," he said. "But what about me? What are you going to do?"

"That should be obvious," Omerie said, his pale eyes in the dark face regarding Oliver impassively. "Keep you in the house until we go. We can certainly do no less. You understand that. And there is no reason for us to do more, as it happens. Silence is all we promised when we signed our travel papers."

"But——" Oliver groped for the fallacy in that reasoning. It was no use. He could not think clearly. Panic surged insanely through his mind from the very air around him. "All right," he said. "Let's hunt."

It was dawn before they found the box, tucked inside the ripped seam of a sofa cushion. Omerie took it upstairs without a word. Five minutes later the pressure in the air abruptly dropped and peace fell blissfully upon the house.

"They will try again," Omerie said to Oliver at the door of the back bedroom. "We must watch for that. As for you, I must see that you remain in the house until Friday. For your own comfort, I advise you to let me know if Hollia offers any further tricks. I confess I am not quite sure how to enforce your staying indoors. I could use methods that would make you very uncomfortable. I would prefer to accept your word on it."

Oliver hesitated. The relaxing of pressure upon his brain had left him exhausted and stupid, and he was not at all sure what to say.

Omerie went on after a moment. "It was partly our fault for not ensuring that we had the house to ourselves," he said. "Living here with us, you could scarcely help suspecting. Shall we say that in return for your promise, I reimburse you in part for losing the sale price on this house?"

Oliver thought that over. It would pacify Sue a little. And it meant only two days indoors. Besides, what good would escaping do? What could he say to outsiders that would not lead him straight to a padded cell?

"All right," he said wearily. "I promise."

By Friday morning there was still no sign from Hollia. Sue telephoned at noon. Oliver knew the crackle of her voice over the wire when Kleph took the call. Even the crackle sounded hysterical; Sue saw her bargain slipping hopelessly through her grasping little fingers.

Kleph's voice was soothing. "I am sorry," she said many times, in the intervals when the voice paused. "I am truly sorry. Believe me, you will find it does not matter. I know. I am sorry——."

She turned from the phone at last. "The girl says Hollia has given up," she told the others.

"Not Hollia," Klia said firmly.

Omerie shrugged. "We have very little time left. If she intends anything more, it will be tonight. We must watch for it."

"Oh, not tonight!" Kleph's voice was horrified. "Not even Hollia would do that!"

"Hollia, my dear, in her own way is quite as unscrupulous as you are," Omerie told her with a smile.

"But—would she spoil things for us just because she can't be here?"

"What do you think?" Klia demanded.

Oliver ceased to listen. There was no making sense out of their talk, but he knew that by tonight whatever the secret was must surely come into the open at last. He was willing to wait and see.

For two days excitement had been building up in the house and the three who shared it with him. Even the servants felt it and were nervous and unsure of themselves. Oliver had given up asking questions—it only embarrassed his tenants—and watched.

All the chairs in the house were collected in the three front bedrooms. The furniture was rearranged to make room for them, and dozens of covered cups had been set out on trays. Oliver recognized Kleph's rose-quartz set among the rest. No steam rose from the thin crescent-openings, but the cups were full. Oliver lifted one and felt a heavy liquid move within it, like something half-solid, sluggishly.

Guests were obviously expected, but the regular dinner hour of nine came and went, and no one had yet arrived. Dinner was finished; the servants went home. The Sanciscos went to their rooms to dress, amid a feeling of mounting tension.

Oliver stepped out on the porch after dinner, trying in vain to guess what it was that had wrought such a pitch of expectancy in the house. There was a quarter moon swimming in haze on the horizon, but the stars which had made every night of May thus far a dazzling translucency were very dim tonight. Clouds had begun to gather at sundown, and the undimmed weather of the whole month seemed ready to break at last.

Behind Oliver the door opened a little, and closed. He caught Kleph's fragrance before he turned, and a faint whiff of the fragrance of the euphoriac she was much too fond of drinking. She came to his side and slipped a hand into his, looking up into his face in the darkness.

"Oliver," she said very softly. "Promise me one thing. Promise me not to leave the house tonight."

"I've already promised that," he said a little irritably.

"I know. But tonight—I have a very particular reason for wanting you indoors tonight." She leaned her head against his shoulder for a moment, and despite himself his irritation softened. He had not seen Kleph alone since that last night of her revelations; he supposed he never would be alone with her again for more than a few minutes at a time. But he knew he would not forget those two bewildering evenings. He knew too, now, that she was very weak and foolish—but she was still Kleph and he had held her in his arms, and was not likely ever to forget it.

"You might be—hurt—if you went out tonight," she was saying in a muffled voice. "I know it will not matter, in the end, but—remember you promised, Oliver."

She was gone again, and the door had closed behind her, before he could voice the futile questions in his mind.

The guests began to arrive just before midnight. From the head of the stairs Oliver saw them coming in by twos and threes, and was astonished at how many of these people from the future must have gathered here in the past weeks. He could see quite clearly now how they differed from the norm in his own period. Their physical elegance was what one noticed first—perfect grooming, meticulous manners, meticulously controlled voices. But because they were all idle, all, in a way, sensation-hunters, there was a certain shrillness underlying their voices, especially when heard all together. Petulance and self-indulgence showed beneath the good manners. And tonight, an all-pervasive excitement.

By one o'clock everyone had gathered in the front rooms. The teacups had begun to steam, apparently of themselves, around midnight, and the house was full of the faint, thin fragrance that induced a sort of euphoria all through the rooms, breathed in with the perfume of the tea.

It made Oliver feel light and drowsy. He was determined to sit up as long as the others did, but he must have dozed off in his own room, by the window, an unopened book in his lap.

For when it happened he was not sure for a few minutes whether or not it was a dream.

The vast, incredible crash was louder than sound. He felt the whole house shake under him, felt rather than heard the timbers grind upon one another like broken bones, while he was still in the borderland of sleep. When he woke fully he was on the floor among the shattered fragments of the window.

How long or short a time he had lain there he did not know. The world was still stunned with that tremendous noise, or his ears still deaf from it, for there was no sound anywhere.

He was half-way down the hall towards the front rooms when sound began to return from outside. It was a low, indescribable rumble at first, prickled with countless tiny distant screams. Oliver's eardrums ached from the terrible impact of the vast unheard noise, but the numbness was wearing off and he heard before he saw it the first voices of the stricken city.

The door to Kleph's room resisted him for a moment. The house had settled a little from the violence of the—the explosion?—and the frame was out of line. When he got the door open he could only stand blinking stupidly into the darkness within. All the lights were out, but there was a breathless sort of whispering going on in many voices.

The chairs were drawn around the broad front windows so that everyone could see out; the air swam with the fragrance of euphoria. There was light enough here from outside for Oliver to see that a few onlookers still had their hands to their ears, but all were craning eagerly forward to see.

Through a dream-like haze Oliver saw the city spread out with impossible distinctness below the window. He knew quite well that a row of houses across the street blocked the view—yet he was looking over the city now, and he could see it in a limitless panorama from here to the horizon. The houses between had vanished.

On the far skyline fire was already a solid mass, painting the low clouds crimson. That sulphurous light reflecting back from the sky upon the city made clear the rows upon rows of flattened houses with flame beginning to lick up among them, and farther out the formless rubble of what had been houses a few minutes ago and was now nothing at all.

The city had begun to be vocal. The noise of the flames rose loudest, but you could hear a rumble of human voices like the beat of surf a long way off, and staccato noises of screaming made a sort of pattern that came and went continuously through the web of sound. Threading it in undulating waves the shrieks of sirens knit the web together into a terrible symphony that had, in its way, a strange, inhuman beauty.

Briefly through Oliver's stunned incredulity went the memory of that other symphony Kleph had played here one day, another catastrophe retold in terms of music and moving shapes.

He said hoarsely: "Kleph——"

The tableau by the window broke. Every head turned, and Oliver saw the faces of strangers staring at him, some few in embarrassment avoiding his eyes, but most seeking them out with that avid, inhuman curiosity which is common to a type in all crowds at accident scenes. But these people were here by design, audience at a vast disaster timed almost for their coming.

Kleph got up unsteadily, her velvet dinner gown tripping her as she rose. She set down a cup and swayed a little as she came towards the door, saying, "Oliver . . . Oliver——" in a sweet, uncertain voice. She was drunk, he saw, and wrought up by the catastrophe to a pitch of stimulation in which she was not very sure what she was doing.

Oliver heard himself saying in a thin voice not his own, "W-what was it, Kleph? What happened? What——" But *happened* seemed so inadequate a word for the incredible panorama below that he had to choke back hysterical laughter upon the struggling questions, and broke off entirely, trying to control the shaking that had seized his body.

Kleph made an unsteady stoop and seized a steaming cup. She came to him, swaying, holding it out—her panacea for all ills.

"Here, drink it, Oliver—we are all quite safe here, quite safe." She thrust the cup to his lips and he gulped automatically, grateful for the fumes that began their slow, coiling surcease in his brain with the first swallow.

"It was a meteor," Kleph was saying. "Quite a small meteor, really. We are perfectly safe here. This house was never touched."

Out of some cell of the unconscious Oliver heard himself saying incoherently, "Sue? Is Sue——" he could not finish.

Kleph thrust the cup at him again. "I think she may be safe —for a while. Please, Oliver—forget about all that and drink."

"But you *knew*!" Realization of that came belatedly to his stunned brain. "You could have given warning, or——"

"How could we change the past?" Kleph asked. "We knew—

but could we stop the meteor? Or warn the city? Before we come we must give our word never to interfere——"

Their voices had risen imperceptibly to be audible above the rising volume of sound from below. The city was roaring now, with flames and cries and the crash of falling buildings. Light in the room turned lurid and pulsed upon the walls and ceiling in red light and redder dark.

Downstairs a door slammed. Someone laughed. It was high, hoarse, angry laughter. Then from the crowd in the room some-one gasped and there was a chorus of dismayed cries. Oliver tried to focus upon the window and the terrible panorama beyond, and found he could not.

It took several seconds of determined blinking to prove that more than his own vision was at fault. Kleph whimpered softly and moved against him. His arms closed about her automatic-ally, and he was grateful for the warm, solid flesh against him. This much at least he could touch and be sure of, though every-thing else that was happening might be a dream. Her perfume and the heady perfume of the tea rose together in his head, and for an instant, holding her in this embrace that must certainly be the last time he ever held her, he did not care that something had gone terribly wrong with the very air of the room.

It was blindness—not continuous, but a series of swift, widen-ing ripples between which he could catch glimpses of the other faces in the room, strained and astonished in the flickering light from the city.

The ripples came faster. There was only a blink of sight be-tween them now, and the blinks grew briefer and briefer, the intervals of darkness more broad.

From downstairs the laughter rose again up the stairwell. Oliver thought he knew the voice. He opened his mouth to speak, but a door nearby slammed open before he could find his tongue, and Omerie shouted down the stairs.

"Hollia?" he roared above the roaring of the city. "Hollia, is that you?"

She laughed again, triumphantly. "I warned you!" her hoarse, harsh voice called. "Now come out in the street with the rest of us if you want to see any more!"

"Hollia!" Omerie shouted desperately. "Stop this or——"

The laughter was derisive. "What will you do, Omerie? This time I hid it too well—come down in the street if you want to watch the rest."

There was angry silence in the house. Oliver could feel Kleph's quick, excited breathing light upon his cheek, feel the soft motions of her body in his arms. He tried consciously to make the moment last, stretch it out to infinity. Everything had happened too swiftly to impress very clearly on his mind anything except what he could touch and hold. He held her in an embrace made consciously light, though he wanted to clasp her in a tight, despairing grip, because he was sure this was the last embrace they would ever share.

The eye-straining blinks of light and blindness went on. From far away below the roar of the burning city rolled on, threaded together by the long, looped cadences of the sirens that linked all sounds into one.

Then in the bewildering dark another voice sounded from the hall downstairs. A man's voice, very deep, very melodious, saying:

"What is this? What are you doing here? Hollia—is that you?"

Oliver felt Kleph stiffen in his arms. She caught her breath, but she said nothing in the instant while heavy feet began to mount the stairs, coming up with a solid, confident tread that shook the old house to each step.

Then Kleph thrust herself hard out of Oliver's arms. He heard her high, sweet, excited voice crying, "Cenbe! Cenbe!" and she ran to meet the newcomer through the waves of dark and light that swept the shaken house.

Oliver staggered a little and felt a chair seat catching the back of his legs. He sank into it and lifted to his lips the cup he still held. Its steam was warm and moist in his face, though he could scarcely make out the shape of the rim.

He lifted it with both hands and drank.

When he opened his eyes it was quite dark in the room. Also it was silent except for a thin, melodious humming almost below the threshold of sound. Oliver struggled with the memory of a monstrous nightmare. He put it resolutely out of his mind and sat up, feeling an unfamiliar bed creak and sway under him.

This was Kleph's room. But no—Kleph's no longer. Her shining hangings were gone from the walls, her white resilient rug, her pictures. The room looked as it had looked before she came, except for one thing.

In the far corner was a table—a block of translucent stuff—out of which light poured softly. A man sat on a low stool before it, leaning forward, his heavy shoulders outlined against the glow. He wore earphones and he was making quick, erratic notes upon a pad on his knee, swaying a little as if to the tune of unheard music.

The curtains were drawn, but from beyond them came a distant, muffled roaring that Oliver remembered from his nightmare. He put a hand to his face, aware of a feverish warmth and a dipping of the room before his eyes. His head ached, and there was a deep malaise in every limb and nerve.

As the bed creaked, the man in the corner turned, sliding the earphones down like a collar. He had a strong, sensitive face above a dark beard, trimmed short. Oliver had never seen him before, but he had that air Oliver knew so well by now, of remoteness which was the knowledge of time itself lying like a gulf between them.

When he spoke his deep voice was impersonally kind.

"You had too much euphoriac, Wilson," he said, aloofly sympathetic. "You slept a long while."

"How long?" Oliver's throat felt sticky when he spoke.

The man did not answer. Oliver shook his head experimentally. He said, "I thought Kleph said you don't get hangovers from——" Then another thought interrupted the first, and he said quickly, "Where is Kleph?" He looked confusedly towards the door.

"They should be in Rome by now. Watching Charlemagne's coronation at St. Peter's on Christmas Day a thousand years from here."

That was not a thought Oliver could grasp clearly. His aching brain sheered away from it; he found thinking at all was strangely difficult. Staring at the man, he traced an idea painfully to its conclusion.

"So they've gone on—but you stayed behind? Why? You . . . you're Cenbe? I heard your—symphonia, Kleph called it."

"You heard part of it. I have not finished yet. I needed—

this." Cenbe inclined his head towards the curtains beyond which the subdued roaring still went on.

"You needed—the meteor?" The knowledge worked painfully through his dulled brain until it seemed to strike some area still untouched by the aching, an area still alive to implication. "The *meteor*? But——"

There was a power implicit in Cenbe's raised hand that seemed to push Oliver down upon the bed again. Cenbe said patiently, "The worst of it is past now, for a while. Forget if you can. That was days ago. I said you were asleep for some time. I let you rest. I knew this house would be safe—from the fire at least."

"Then—something more's to come?" Oliver only mumbled his question. He was not sure he wanted an answer. He had been curious so long, and now that knowledge lay almost within reach, something about his brain seemed to refuse to listen. Perhaps this weariness, this feverish, dizzy feeling would pass as the effect of the euphoriac wore off.

Cenbe's voice ran on smoothly, soothingly, almost as if Cenbe too did not want him to think. It was easiest to lie here and listen.

"I am a composer," Cenbe was saying. "I happen to be interested in interpreting certain forms of disaster into my own terms. That is why I stayed on. The others were dilettantes. They came for the May weather and the spectacle. The aftermath—well why should they wait for that? As for myself—I suppose I am a connoisseur. I find the aftermath rather fascinating. And I need it. I need to study it at first hand, for my own purposes."

His eyes dwelt upon Oliver for an instant very keenly, like a physician's eyes, impersonal and observing. Absently he reached for his stylus and the note pad. And as he moved, Oliver saw a familiar mark on the underside of the thick, tanned wrist.

"Kleph had that scar, too," he heard himself whisper. "And the others."

Cenbe nodded. "Inoculation. It was necessary, under the circumstances. We did not want disease to spread in our own time-world."

"Disease?"

Cenbe shrugged. "You would not recognize the name."

"But, if you can inoculate against disease——" Oliver thrust himself up on an aching arm. He had a half-grasp upon a thought now which he did not want to let go. Effort seemed to make the ideas come more clearly through his mounting confusion. With enormous effort he went on.

"I'm getting it now," he said. "Wait. I've been trying to work this out. You can change history? You can! I know you can. Kleph said she had to promise not to interfere. You all had to promise. Does that mean you really could change your own past—our time?"

Cenbe laid down his pad again. He looked at Oliver thoughtfully, a dark, intent look under heavy brows. "Yes," he said. "Yes, the past can be changed, but not easily. And it changes the future, too, necessarily. The lines of probability are switched into new patterns—but it is extremely difficult, and it has never been allowed. The physio-temporal course tends to slide back to its norm, always. That is why it is so hard to force any alteration." He shrugged. "A theoretical science. We do not change history, Wilson. If we changed our past, our present would be altered, too. And our time-world is entirely to our liking. There may be a few malcontents there, but they are not allowed the privilege of temporal travel."

Oliver spoke louder against the roaring from beyond the windows. "But you've got the power! You could alter history, if you wanted to—wipe out all the pain and suffering and tragedy——"

"All of that passed away long ago," Cenbe said.

"Not—*now*! Not—*this*!"

Cenbe looked at him enigmatically for a while. Then—"This, too," he said.

And suddenly Oliver realized from across what distances Cenbe was watching him. A vast distance, as time is measured. Cenbe was a composer and a genius, and necessarily strongly empathic, but his psychic locus was very far away in time. The dying city outside, the whole world of *now* was not quite real to Cenbe, falling short of reality because of that basic variance in time. It was merely one of the building blocks that had gone to support the edifice on which Cenbe's culture stood in a misty, unknown, terrible future.

It seemed terrible to Oliver now. Even Kleph—all of them

had been touched with a pettiness, the faculty that had enabled
Hollia to concentrate on her malicious, small schemes to acquire
a ringside seat while the meteor thundered in towards Earth's
atmosphere. They were all dilettantes, Kleph and Omerie and
the others. They toured time, but only as onlookers. Were they
bored—sated—with their normal existence?

Not sated enough to wish change, basically. Their own time-
world was a fulfilled womb, a perfection made manifest for their
needs. They dared not change the past—they could not risk
flawing their own present.

Revulsion shook him. Remembering the touch of Kleph's
lips, he felt a sour sickness on his tongue. Alluring she had
been: he knew that too well. But the aftermath——

There was something about this race from the future. He had
felt it dimly at first, before Kleph's nearness had drowned
caution and buffered his sensibilities. Time travelling purely as
an escape mechanism seemed almost blasphemous. A race with
such power——

Kleph—leaving him for the barbaric, splendid coronation at
Rome a thousand years ago—*how had she seen him?* Not as a
living, breathing man. He knew that, very certainly Kleph's
race were spectators.

But he read more than casual interest in Cenbe's eyes now.
There was an avidity there, a bright, fascinated probing. The
man had replaced his earphones—he was different from the
others. He was a connoisseur. After the vintage season came the
aftermath—and Cenbe.

Cenbe watched and waited, light flickering softly in the translucent block before him, his fingers poised over the note pad.
The ultimate connoisseur waited to savour the rarities that no
non-gourmet could appreciate.

Those thin, distant rhythms of sound that was almost music
began to be audible again above the noises of the distant fire.
Listening, remembering. Oliver could very nearly catch the
pattern of the symphonia as he had heard it, all intermingled
with the flash of changing faces and the rank upon rank of the
dying——

He lay back on the bed letting the room swirl away into the
darkness behind his closed and aching lids. The ache was implicit in every cell of his body, almost a second ego taking

possession and driving him out of himself, a strong, sure ego taking over as he himself let go.

Why, he wondered dully, should Kleph have lied? She had said there was no aftermath to the drink she had given him. No aftermath—and yet this painful possession was strong enough to edge him out of his own body.

Kleph had not lied. It was no aftermath to drink. He knew that—but the knowledge no longer touched his brain or his body. He lay still, giving them up to the power of the illness which was aftermath to something far stronger than the strongest drink. The illness that had no name—yet.

Cenbe's new symphonia was a crowning triumph. It had its première from Antares Hall, and the applause was an ovation. History itself, of course, was the artist—opening with the meteor that forecast the great plagues of the fourteenth century and closing with the climax Cenbe had caught on the threshold of modern times. But only Cenbe could have interpreted it with such subtle power.

Critics spoke of the masterly way in which he had chosen the face of the Stuart king as a recurrent motif against the montage of emotion and sound and movement. But there were other faces, fading through the great sweep of the composition, which helped to build up to the tremendous climax. One face in particular, one moment that the audience absorbed greedily. A moment in which one man's face loomed huge in the screen, every feature clear. Cenbe had never caught an emotional crisis so effectively, the critics agreed. You could almost read the man's eyes.

After Cenbe had left, he lay motionless for a long while. He was thinking feverishly——

I've got to find some way to tell people. If I'd known in advance, maybe something could have been done. We'd have forced them to tell us how to change the probabilities. We could have evacuated the city.

If I could leave a message——

Maybe not for today's people. But later. They visit all through time. If they could be recognized and caught somewhere, some time, and made to change destiny——

It wasn't easy to stand up. The room kept tilting. But he managed it. He found pencil and paper and through the swaying of the shadows he wrote down what he could. Enough. Enough to warn, enough to save.

He put the sheets on the table, in plain sight, and weighted them down before he stumbled back to bed through closing darkness.

The house was dynamited six days later, part of the futile attempt to halt the relentless spread of the Blue Death.